THE SONG OF
KWASIN

THE KHOKARSA SERIES

Hadon of Ancient Opar
*Flight to Opar**
*The Song of Kwasin**
*Hadon, King of Opar**
*Blood of Ancient Opar**

KHOKARSA SERIES PREQUELS

Time's Last Gift
*Exiles of Kho**

* Available or forthcoming from Meteor House.

THE SONG OF KWASIN

Philip José Farmer &
Christopher Paul Carey

Meteor House

THE SONG OF KWASIN

by Philip José Farmer and Christopher Paul Carey

Meteor House
ISBN 978-0-9905673-6-3
First Trade Edition

TABLE OF CONTENTS

Introduction 11
Preface to the Meteor House Edition 17
The Story So Far 27
Maps 35
The Song of Kwasin 43
Kwasin and the Bear God 331

Addendum 1: The World of Khokarsa

The Khokarsan Calendar 389
The Plants of Khokarsa 391
A Guide to Khokarsa 397

Addendum 2: Philip José Farmer's Notes and Correspondence

Notes on the Khokarsa Series 423
Philip José Farmer's Original Outline 439
Philip José Farmer's Alternate Outline 451
Correspondence on the Khokarsa Series 457

Acknowledgments 463
About the Authors 465

Dedicated to the immortal spirit and works of
EDGAR RICE BURROUGHS and H. RIDER HAGGARD.

INTRODUCTION

PAUL DI FILIPPO

The genre of fantastika—to employ critic John Clute's handy omnibus term that stretches to cover everything from science fiction to fantasy, horror to surrealism, slipstream to New Weird—has many unique features. The aspect I would like to look at now, in preparation for discussing the remarkable novel you hold in your hands, is the intimacy and devotion which the literature inspires between fans and writers, acolytes and mentors.

No other genre—the mystery novel, the thriller, the western, the spy novel, romances—displays this same fraternal and sororal bond between creator and readers, and between older writers and younger ones. The devotion of fantastika readers to their literary heroes, exemplified by the hosting of conventions, the writing of scholarly articles and pastiches, the creating of cosplay, is extraordinary and unparalleled. Perhaps outside of fantastika, fans of Sherlock Holmes come closest to this passionate response to their sleuth (who, given some of his more outlandish adventures, might well be subsumed into fantastika anyhow).

But what might be even more remarkable is the lineage-honoring efforts by younger writers to uphold and promulgate the work of those who came before them, as well as the generosity of older writers who mentor younger ones. In the field of fantastika, the infamous egocentricity of the typical author gets shelved all the time, in order to celebrate work by peers or grand masters or new-comers. Consider the famous labors by August Derleth and Donald Wandrei, who kept the Lovecraftian flame alive with Arkham House. Or look today at the creative dedication of Stephen Haffner of Haffner Press, who is holding aloft the torch for Jack Williamson, Leigh Brackett, Henry Kuttner, and Edmond Hamilton. When's the last time you heard of, oh, Philip Roth, ushering a debut novel by someone else into print? Or maybe you've seen the latest flavor-of-the-month *New Yorker* whiz kid taking time out from self-promotion to help get a forgotten classic back into print? About the only person who actually does this kind of selfless service is Jonathan Lethem, and he's not-so-secretly One of Us.

But in our field, this kind of thing happens all the time. It's just considered to be proper pay-it-forward, honor-our-ancestors behavior.

Which brings us to the actual topic of this little essay, the appearance of Philip José Farmer and Christopher Paul Carey's 2012 novel *The Song of Kwasin* in this handsome and much-welcome new edition.

Carey has been a scholar of the canon of Philip José Farmer for over twenty years now, and was a personal friend of the Grand Master as well, until Farmer's death in 2009. Outside these pages, you can—and should—take the time to read in the preface of this book and various online interviews how Carey came to connect with Farmer, and how this novel came into being to brighten the declining years of the Wizard of Peoria. The story is a historical account that is unashamedly pathos-producing in its sentimental nobility and mutual human affection—incidents of which can seem all too sparse in this current, hopefully anomalous, semi-debased day and age when we seem to hear more often of internecine bickering and feuding among authors, of hatred and jealousy and revenge, an absolute overturning of these old standards which I am praising. We should celebrate all the counterexamples we can find, as a guide to the restoration of the old ways. The story of how Carey found the aborted manuscript of the third Khokarsa novel, along with supporting notes, then consulted at length with Farmer to produce the capstone to the trilogy, is certainly one of the standout anecdotes of recent fannish memory.

But all this good will and fellow-feeling and lineage-honoring would mean naught, if the resulting work was not up to snuff, carrying forward the vision and high standards of the originals. And that's where I can step forward to reassure potential purchasers and readers of this book that Carey has accomplished a minor miracle of inspired extension and fidelity.

But before the third volume could appear, of course, we had to have the Farmer originals.

Hadon of Ancient Opar was published as a DAW Books original back in 1974, when Farmer was arguably at his best. Our venue is the dim mists of prehistory, when the city of Opar—well known to Tarzan—was at its height. But Opar is merely one urban enclave in a rich matrix of cities and cultures, all centered around two nowadays-vanished inland seas of Africa. Our hero is Hadon, an exemplar of brains and physical prowess. The thickness of the cultural invention recalls a Jack Vance or Le Guin tale.

Readers had to wait two years for *Flight to Opar*, which picks up precisely where the cliffhanger ending of the first book left us, and in as fine a style. Hadon and his pals are now rebels and outlaws, harried up and down the countryside. Hadon's indomitable prowess and superhuman exertions pile higher and higher, in bold fashion. Engaging new characters emerge, as well as heretofore unvisited venues. By the end, Hadon is a father twice over. Appearing on the final page, his daughter by wife Lalila, La, whose namesake still rules in Tarzan's distant era, ties us back to ERB's mythos.

But notably missing from the second book was Hadon's gigantic cousin Kwasin, a man-mountain of unrestrained appetites and passions and ambitions. We do learn that the fellow has set himself up as the king of a city, but he never appears onstage. Here's where Carey arrives, with *The Song of Kwasin*, a truly bardic odyssey.

The great opening sentence—"The strongest man in the world came puffing over the top of a hill and met a god"—kicks off this novel with the mythic, adventurous, highly colored richness that it will exhibit throughout. Very deftly and swiftly, the authors acquaint us with Kwasin's formidable physical aspect (Conan has nothing on Kwasin!), his backstory, and his temperament. A stunning, unpredictable, adroitly staged battle scene follows—just the first of numerous such stirring and pulse-pounding martial encounters, small-scale and large-scale—and then a bleeding and bruised but indomitable Kwasin is back on the road to his exotic destiny.

I cannot—and should not—here disclose the plethora of incidents awaiting Kwasin and the reader in these pages. Suffice it to say that our gigantic hero, a man of immense appetites and passions, will fight for and inherit a throne, lose it, fall to the depths of captivity, then win back his pride amidst a bloody vengeance-taking, all while encountering evil priests, gorgeous women, spooky supernatural oracles, fellow soldiers high and low, and the Mad Emperor Minruth. The shade of Robert E. Howard, as well as that of Burroughs, hovers benignly over this enterprise.

The characters whom Farmer and Carey created (I'm particularly thinking of the great women in Kwasin's path, as well as the absurdly comic yet somehow noble figure of the minstrel Bhako) are as big and engaging as life itself. But no portrait is more complex than that of our hero, Kwasin. His troubled "dual souls"—"One that rages and is possessed by death's spirit and produces only sorrow and destruction. The other that rejoices with great humor and love of adventure."—are limned with remarkable psychological astuteness that never gets in the way of the action.

As is the case with Farmer's own writing, Carey's prose is poetic and practical by shifts. This pleasing combination of modes causes the pages to practically turn themselves. But aside from sheer solid sentence construction, Carey also exhibits a valuable story-telling trait that Farmer himself possessed in abundance. I call this skill "stagecraft." This knack adds immensely to the storytelling verisimilitude and reader involvement, but it is not the common pure capability of plotting. Rather, it is the ability to delineate action in the most clarified, visual manner possible, varying one's prose across similar moments throughout the narrative in a way so as not to bore the reader, while also providing a wealth of satisfying practical details: what is eaten, worn, carried; how characters move about; where characters stand in relation to each other; etc., etc. Maybe we should call this talent something like "substantive experiential transcription." Whatever you name it, Carey exhibits it in full.

At points, particularly in Kwasin's descent of the exterior of a ziggurat, the narrative passes from simple naturalism into mythic, symbolical realms. The ending especially is like some passage out of Joseph Campbell's *The Hero with a Thousand Faces*, befitting Farmer's own insistence on a numinous aspect to the most mundane actions. Given the subliminal readerly recognition that these events have all been drowned in the well of prehistory, the book's affect—once the excitement has been absorbed—is one of a timeless, almost Biblical melancholy. We battle and rage, but all for naught, as our exploits go down into the dust.

Unless, that is, we are lucky enough to have our lives chronicled by imperishable word-mages like Farmer and Carey.

PREFACE TO THE METEOR HOUSE EDITION

CHRISTOPHER PAUL CAREY

For a period of almost thirty years, it became increasingly unlikely the novel you now hold in your hands would ever be written, let alone published. Even after the manuscript fragment and outline were discovered in Philip José Farmer's filing cabinet in July 2005, the odds were stacked against the third volume of the Khokarsa series ever being completed and seeing print. Farmer had retired from writing after the publication of *The Dark Heart of Time: A Tarzan Novel* in 1999 and was in declining health, so who would complete the manuscript? And then there was the even more daunting challenge: who would be willing to publish a new installment in a heroic historical fantasy series whose last chapter had been published in 1976, and that had been out of print in the author's native country for nearly twenty-five years?

The first volume of the Khokarsa series, *Hadon of Ancient Opar*, first landed on the bookstore shelves in April 1974. Its sequel, *Flight to Opar*, followed in June 1976. When a third "Ancient Opar" novel (a misnomer, as soon will become apparent) was announced in May 1975 in *Science Fiction Review* #13, it appeared as if the Khokarsa books were well on their way to becoming one of Farmer's major series.

Farmer discussed the forthcoming novel in a letter dated November 26, 1976 that was published in *Science Fiction Review* #20 (February 1977), stating that he was "busy with the 330,000-word draft of the third Riverworld novel," though he was in the meantime trying to come up with a suitable title for the third "Opar" novel. But there was a problem, as Farmer went on to explain in the letter:

> Don Wollheim insists that "Opar" be in the title of every one of the series. What do you do when the action takes place nowhere near that fabled city? Or if Hadon isn't in the tale? I'm planning on devoting the third book to the mighty Kwasin, and all events take place on the island of Khokarsa. How about *Far from Opar*?

Science Fiction Review editor Richard E. Geis wrote back to Farmer suggesting the title *Kwasin of Opar*, to which Farmer replied in a letter dated December 3, 1976:

> Actually, Kwasin was born in the city of Dythbeth, but he is a cousin of Hadon's, and he did spend almost all his early life in the Opar area. So, *Kwasin of Opar* is a title stretching the truth only a little bit . . .
>
> I look forward to writing *Nowhere Near Opar* some day. Let Don Wollheim chew on that.

Over the next few years, projects that were both higher profile and higher paying kept Farmer from writing the third novel of the Khokarsa series. These included the aforementioned third Riverworld novel, *The Dark Design* (1977), as well as *Dark Is the Sun* (1979), *Jesus on Mars* (1979), and *The Magic Labyrinth* (1980). During this same period Farmer also wrote two drafts of the ecological disaster novel *Up from the Bottomless Pit*, which went unpublished until its serialized appearance in *Farmerphile:*

The Magazine of Philip José Farmer (issues #1–10, July 2007–October 2007), a fanzine dedicated to bringing into print the author's rare and unpublished work.

But the busy schedule did not mean Farmer had lost interest in the sequel to *Flight to Opar*, and he in fact outlined the novel and began writing the manuscript; this was likely around late 1975, when the novel was contracted with DAW Books. In 1978, the novel's contract was renewed, showing clearly that Farmer still had plans to continue the series. Disagreements with the publisher, however, led to a parting of ways, and rights to the Khokarsa series reverted to Farmer in October 1983, leaving the third book without a publisher. Meanwhile, Farmer continued working on his more popular properties, wrapping up the Riverworld and World of Tiers series, and launching a new major series with the Dayworld trilogy.

Even so, Farmer continued to express interest in completing the Khokarsa series over the years, such as in this excerpt from an interview conducted by Michael Croteau and Craig Kimber in September 1997 for *The Unofficial Philip José Farmer Home Page*:

> I have thought about finishing [the Khokarsa series]. But instead of the proposed five or seven books, I'd just try to finish it in one book. I knew the final cataclysmic ending right from the beginning. A huge earthquake wrecks the civilizations and opens the inland sea to flow into the Congo. The dry spells were just starting then, before the Sahara became a desert. 12,000 years ago there was a lot of water there; it was the end of the Ice Age.

As late as January 1999, Farmer was still tossing around the idea of writing the third book, as illustrated in the following passage from a letter to Alan Hanson that appeared in *Heritage of the Flaming God: Ancient Mysteries of La and Savage Opar* (eds. Alan Hanson and Michael Winger, Waziri Press, 1999), a collection that at long last saw the publication of the monumental study on Opar and its motherland civilization that inspired the Khokarsa series:

> If I were to write the final book now, and this is important, where would I find a publisher? The old days are gone. Nowadays, all the major publishers are part of a conglomerate, and the driving motive is in big money. BIG. Not a modest profit. BIG profits. The first two books would have to be reprinted so that the reader could get reacquainted with the Opar books. Wouldn't work. No publisher would want to reprint them and then print a new one.
>
> Yet, on skimming through these Opar novels, *Hadon* and *Flight*, I'm tempted. Could I find a small publisher to invest in the novels? Would it be worth my time? I'm aged eighty-one, and I have left writing science fiction for the crime novel. Well, we'll see.

Despite such teasing statements to his readers, Farmer never returned to the series before his retirement, leaving *Hadon of Ancient Opar* and *Flight to Opar* appearing as if they would join the ranks of hundreds of other yellow-spined DAW original paperbacks from the 1970s in literary oblivion. And yet the "Ancient Opar" novels continued to be reprinted and popular among Farmer's fans the world over. *The Philip José Farmer International Bibliography*, a website that catalogs every known appearance of Farmer's work in print, records that *Hadon of Ancient Opar* saw at least eight printings by DAW Books in the years spanning 1974 to 1983, as well as eight foreign editions published outside of the United States. The exhaustive bibliography also lists five printings of *Flight to Opar* published by DAW Books from 1976 to 1983, and seven foreign editions. Clearly, there *was* an audience for the series, but with only two novels published in the cycle, the great Khokarsan revival seemed at best unlikely, and at worst doomed to obscurity.

But fortunately, good ideas never die; they only lie fallow for a season waiting to be cultivated.

So it was that in July 2005, Michael Croteau—now Farmer's official webmaster and the publisher of *Farmerphile*—was given permission by Phil Farmer and his wife Bette to go on a treasure-hunting excursion through the author's files looking for material to use in the fanzine. This was the same trip during which Mike and our good friend Win Scott Eckert uncovered several other unpublished gems written by Farmer, including the outline and partial manuscript of *The Evil in Pemberley House*. At the time, I was serving, along with my colleague Paul Spiteri, as *Farmerphile's* coeditor. Upon his return from Peoria, Mike emailed me with the discoveries in order to discuss which pieces we might want to run in *Farmerphile*, casually listing the following item among the other finds: "*Kwasin of Opar*. Not sure what to do with this. Need to read it and see if it is compelling enough to either put in *Farmerphile* or sell photocopies [on behalf of Phil on his official website]."

To say that I was stunned by this last discovery would be an understatement. I instantly fired off an email to Mike requesting photocopies, which he promptly mailed to me. I received them a few days later just as I was heading out to an author reading at the Science Fiction Museum in Seattle. I brought the photocopies along with me to the reading and, having arrived at the museum early, read the novel's entire outline while I sat in the theater. That evening I barely listened to a word of the speaker, who was quite well renowned, and to whom, under other circumstances, I would have paid attention quite intently. But I was off in another world of "gold, and silver, ivory, and apes, and peacocks." The outline galloped along at the pace of a charging Cape buffalo, and Farmer's enthusiasm leaped from every line. Here at last was the story of what happened on the island of Khokarsa after Hadon flew with Lalila and their companions to distant Opar—the long and bloody war with King Minruth in its entirety!

I knew then and there that the story had to be told. That same month I drafted a proposal for how I would complete the novel, and sent it off to Phil Farmer. I had first corresponded with Phil in 1997 and met him in person the following year, later visiting with him and his lovely wife Bette at their home in Peoria. I had written over the years a number of articles on his work, which (much to my astonishment) Phil had told me and others were among his favorites. Like Phil, I also had a background in anthropology, which was the field of my undergraduate study, and a longtime love of all things Edgar Rice Burroughs and H. Rider Haggard, the two main inspirations for the Khokarsa series. To round it all out, I was currently working on a master's degree in Writing Popular Fiction. Phil knew all of this. Still, I had no expectation of a positive response.

Phil's reply, however, was warm, enthusiastic, and encouraging—and to my great surprise, he said yes to my proposal, closing out his email with the morale-boosting imperative of "forward it is." I think my letter had rekindled Phil's excitement to see his epic saga of Khokarsa through to its completion—if that happened by his hand or another's mattered less at this point in his life than whether the story would be told at all.

As soon as my proposal was accepted, I drafted a new outline in accordance to Phil's express wishes and comments, now that the novel was to be repositioned as the climax of a trilogy. Then, at Phil and Bette's recommendation, I stopped work on the novel and continued my master's program, which I completed in January 2007.

The delay turned out to be fortunate. While I was working on my degree, I was able to visit Phil at his home in Peoria and examine his extensive notes on the Khokarsa series. I had discovered a partial Khokarsan syllabary in his files that made the names I needed to coin for the new novel that much more authentic. I also reread *Hadon of Ancient Opar* and *Flight to Opar* more times than I can remember, as well as a number of Burroughs and Haggard novels for inspiration. Further, I created a glossary of names and terms from the books that I was able to fill in and expand with the help of Phil's original Khokarsa notes.

In early 2008, I completed the first draft of the novel, which was accepted by Phil's agent and began to make the rounds with prospective publishers. Now that Phil did not have to bow to Wollheim's demand to use "Opar" in the title, we decided to retitle the novel *The Song of Kwasin*. Opar simply did not figure into the plot, and Kwasin was not, in fact, from Opar. *The Song of Kwasin* made a fitting title for a number of reasons. First, it indicated that the novel was a departure from the first two books in that it concentrated on Kwasin's epic struggle against Minruth rather than Hadon of Opar's adventures. Second, the title evoked the great ballads of the Khokarsan bards. In the Khokarsan language, the title would be rendered *Pwamwotkwasin*, or "The Song of the Hero Kwasin." And finally, the title was a play on "The Song of Hiawatha," the poem that inspired Phil to create the character of Kwasin in the first place. In Longfellow's poem, the character Kwasind is Hiawatha's giant strongman friend. For all of these reasons, we knew we had the right title.

By this time, Phil's health had worsened, but Bette Farmer read the novel aloud to him, and told me how Phil lit up at hearing of Kwasin's adventures. I will always regard the moment I learned this as a touchstone in my career as a writer.

Then, in January 2009, while visiting Phil on the occasion of his ninety-first birthday, I unexpectedly uncovered another trove of Khokarsa materials in the files. These newly found papers included the complete Khokarsan syllabary and several drafts of an article on Khokarsan linguistics, as well as other addenda and, perhaps most interestingly, an aborted alternate outline fragment to "*Kwasin of Opar*." The best sense I can give you of Phil's world building is to say that it's truly Tolkienesque in scope and detail. Or perhaps Farmerian is a better term for it, as it is wholly unique in its anthropological and metafictional approach. In any event, the new papers were a lucky find, and I was able to use the complete syllabary to revise a number of names and terms in the novel to fully line up with the linguistic rules of the Khokarsan language.

As fate would have it, Phil passed away only a month after I discovered the new materials. Though he did not live to see the novel published, I take some solace in the fact that he was able to see it completed in manuscript form and put on the market to publishers. I will never be able to thank Philip José Farmer enough for the opportunity he gave me as a younger writer trying to break into the field. I'm both a better writer and a better person for having known him.

In October 2009, I signed the contracts for *Gods of Opar: Tales of Lost Khokarsa*, an omnibus to be published by Subterranean Press that would collect *Hadon of Ancient Opar*, *Flight to Opar*, and *The Song of Kwasin*. However, due to the vagaries of publishing, *The Song of Kwasin* ended up waiting in the wings for another two and a half years while a different Farmer collection made it through the publisher's pipeline. As Philip José Farmer had passed in February 2009, this later led to the mistaken belief by many that *The Song of Kwasin* was completed by me after Phil's death. *The Song of Kwasin*—the plot, the characters, the mythic structure—is ultimately Philip José Farmer's tale; I just helped get the words on paper.

While I waited for *The Song of Kwasin* to be published, I studied Phil's alternate outline fragment for the novel. It became apparent almost instantly that the outline, while unusable in terms of the novel for a host of continuity reasons, told a lost adventure of Kwasin that fit seamlessly between the first and second chapters of *The Song of Kwasin*. Mike Croteau, now the publisher at Meteor House, urged me to do something with the idea, and so, using the outline, as well as some text from Phil's notes, I proceeded to write a 20,000-word novella titled "Kwasin and the Bear God."

I wrestled with the notion of incorporating the tale into the body of the novel. However, Phil had already put his stamp of approval on *The Song of Kwasin*, and was now no longer with us. Further, I worried that inserting the novella would create an imbalance in the dramatic unfolding of the novel's opening. For those reasons, I ultimately decided the novella should stand on its own. "Kwasin and the Bear God" first saw print in *The Worlds of*

Philip José Farmer 2: Of Dust and Soul (Meteor House, 2011), almost a full year before *The Song of Kwasin* was published in *Gods of Opar* in June 2012. "Kwasin and the Bear God" has been included in this new definitive edition of *The Song of Kwasin*. Readers may now decide for themselves whether they wish to read the first chapter of *The Song of Kwasin*, flip to the back of the book to read "Kwasin and the Bear God," and then turn back to the second chapter of the novel to resume Kwasin's adventures in chronological order—or whether they instead wish to read *The Song of Kwasin* in its entirety before returning back in time to read an earlier adventure of Kwasin.

When *Gods of Opar* was published in 2012, I felt vindicated in the face of all the naysayers who had believed a thirty-year-old series inspired by a hundred-year-old series could never be revived. The book was a resounding success, received high praise from critics, and sold out almost immediately upon publication. But that success and the quick sellout also left *The Song of Kwasin* out of print for a number of years, a deficiency I am pleased Meteor House has been able to rectify with this handsome new edition.

So now that the third novel of the series is again in print, where does that leave Khokarsa and its far-flung queendom of Opar? While *The Song of Kwasin* closes out one chapter of ancient history, Farmer left a large part of the tale untold. After all, he once said he meant for the series to encompass anywhere from five to twelve volumes. Therefore, I am using Farmer's notes, as well as translations of ancient inscriptions by the late great linguist Sir Beowulf William Clayton, to continue the saga in a new cycle about Hadon and his son Kohr and daughter La, in addition to writing an earlier cycle that records the history of Opar's founder, the priestess-heroine Lupoeth.

Where will the grand adventure of Khokarsa end? Who can say? Perhaps like any good story, it won't, so long as there's someone around to tell the tale and someone to listen to it.

THE STORY SO FAR

CHRISTOPHER PAUL CAREY

The Song of Kwasin *is the third volume in Philip José Farmer's* Khokarsa *series. Readers who wish to refresh their memories about the events that transpired in the first two volumes of the series—*Hadon of Ancient Opar *and* Flight to Opar—*should read the following summary.*

It is twelve thousand years ago at the close of the last ice age, and the mighty empire of Khokarsa thrives along the fertile shores of ancient Africa's two great inland seas. The empire comprises thirty shining queendoms, all under the rule of the priestesses of the Great Mother Goddess Kho and the empress who presides over them. Though the emperor of Khokarsa controls the military, he does so only at the mercy of the empress, but this has not tempered his ambitions, nor those of the priests of the sungod Resu who follow him. The current emperor, King Minruth, has managed to hold on to power by marrying his dead wife's cousin. But when his new wife dies unexpectedly, it is time to hold the Great Games that will at last determine Minruth's successor.

Having won the Lesser Games in his home city of Opar, nineteen-year-old Hadon departs in a galley with a group of other competitors, traveling across the landlocked seas to the capital of the empire on the distant island of Khokarsa. Here he competes in the Great Games against the best athletes and warriors of the land, performing daring feats of physical skill and endurance and entering into bloody combat in the arena against both man and beast—all for the chance to wed Awineth, the empress of Khokarsa, for only he who survives the games and wins the golden crown of victory will rule at her side as emperor of the known world.

In his final bout in the arena, Hadon strikes down his last and fiercest opponent: his childhood nemesis, the ill-tempered Hewako. With his dying breaths, Hewako proclaims he has had a vision that Hadon will never rule as the king of kings, that instead his life will be troubled and he will travel to a distant land where he is fated to die before his time. Shaken by Hewako's prophecy, Hadon rises and accepts the gold crown of the champion.

But it seems Hewako's grim prediction is destined to take hold all too soon. Though Hadon has emerged victorious from the bloodthirsty games, he is summoned to an audience with Queen Awineth and her father, King Minruth. Here Hadon hears a strange tale from a scribe named Hinokly, the only survivor of an expedition sent to explore the Wild Lands beyond the empire. Far to the north on the shores of the Ringing Sea, the travelers encountered a deity in the flesh—Sahhindar, the Gray-Eyed Archer God! Accompanying Sahhindar—who is said to have traveled back in time from the distant future—were his three companions: a beautiful golden-haired, violet-eyed woman named Lalila; her young daughter, Abeth; and a one-eyed manling named Paga, who bore a huge iron ax said to be fashioned from a fallen star. The god told the explorers that all three were under his protection, and must be escorted back to the capital of Khokarsa, where they were to be received as honored guests. But after the expedition took custody of the Archer God's companions, disaster struck when a band of barbarians attacked, slaying all of the Khokarsans in the party except for Hinokly and leaving the fate of the three outlanders unknown. After Hinokly managed to make his way back to the capital, Awineth and Minruth visited the oracle in her cave high atop Khowot, the great volcano overlooking the city. There the oracle decreed that the greatest hero of the land must set out immediately to look for Lalila, Abeth, Paga, and the manling's extraordinary ax. Now Minruth declares that Hadon—who, having won the Great Games, is clearly Khokarsa's greatest hero—cannot become king of kings until he leads an expedition into the Wild Lands and recovers the missing foreigners under Sahhindar's protection. Hadon fumes, but there is nothing he can do but obey.

Accompanied by Hinokly, the bard Kebiwabes, and a misfit contingent of soldiers and half-neanderthal Klemqaba, Hadon leads his expedition into the Wild Lands, where he runs across his mad giant of a cousin, Kwasin, who was exiled from Khokarsa for ravishing a priestess of Kho. Reluctantly, Hadon allows Kwasin to join the expedition, for when the giant was exiled, the oracle had decreed that he would one day be permitted to return to the empire.

After arriving at the Ringing Sea far to the north of Khokarsa, Hadon speaks with the chief of a village and gains information that leads him to Lalila, Abeth, and Paga. Soon Hadon falls in love with Lalila, but she shows no interest in him, being committed to the memory of her lover, the hero Wi, who died so that she, her daughter, and Paga might live. Hadon also learns the history of what Paga calls the Ax of Victory, which he had forged for Wi from the iron of a fallen star. But Paga says the great ax is cursed, and so gives it to Kwasin, who is little bothered by the manling's superstitions.

Following many adventures, the expedition makes its way to a fort near the northern Khokarsan city of Mukha. After a brief stay at the fort, the travelers depart, only to be arrested by a force of soldiers loyal to King Minruth. Although Kwasin makes a violent escape, the others are captured and brought back to the capital, where they learn that Minruth has overthrown his daughter, the queen, and proclaimed himself the sole ruler of Khokarsa.

Minruth declares Hadon and his companions to be traitors and imprisons them in the dungeon beneath the palace. Here they find Kwasin, who was captured and taken to the dungeon not long after his escape from the soldiers. With Kwasin's help, the party escapes through an air shaft high in the prison cell just as

Khowot erupts and an earthquake strikes the city. In the confusion of the tremor, Hadon and his companions rescue Queen Awineth and flee toward the mountains beyond the city. Kwasin takes off on his own, and is last seen by Hadon standing in a boat on the Gulf of Gahete, bellowing of his great love for Lalila and swinging his mighty Ax of Victory against an overwhelming force of Minruth's soldiers.

Hadon leads his companions into the mountains. Lalila injures her ankle and cannot go on. Awineth, bitter that Hadon has spurned her love, orders him to leave the woman behind. Hadon refuses, saying he will remain with Lalila in the narrow, highly defensible pass, sacrificing his life so that the others might escape. Awineth tries to stab Lalila with her dagger, but Hadon stops her and orders Paga, Hinokly, and Kebiwabes to take the queen and Abeth through the pass. Lalila at last declares her love for Hadon, but they know their joy is to be short-lived. Hadon leans on his sword and waits for the soldiers to come.

Hadon caches Lalila in a tree so she will be safe while he takes on the soldiers. Through a combination of agility, skill, and intelligence, he manages to survive the onslaught and fend off the soldiers and their vicious tracehounds. While the soldiers wait for reinforcements, Hadon and Lalila flee. Hadon again leaves Lalila while he reconnoiters, and discovers Awineth is being harbored by a village sympathetic to her cause. Hadon trespasses on the sacred Isle of Karneth, forbidden to all males, and rescues Awineth during an orgiastic ceremony conducted by the priestesses of Kho just as a group of soldiers loyal to Minruth converge upon them. Hadon and Awineth flee to the village, where Kebiwabes, Hinokly, and Abeth await them. Against Awineth's wishes, Hadon sets out to retrieve Lalila, but finds her a captive of a group of outlaws. The outlaws managed to capture Awineth, too, and plan to take both women back to the capital and ransom them to the king. Hadon besieges the camp and rescues the two captives.

The adventurers retreat to the valley of Kloepeth, where Awineth establishes the headquarters of her resistance effort. Here

Hadon learns not only that Kwasin escaped the capital and fled to his native queendom of Dythbeth, but that he married its queen and has been declared that city's king! While Awineth consults with her military advisors about her next step in the civil war against her father, Lalila visits the local temple and discovers she is pregnant, and that the oracle—who is hiding out in Kloepeth—wishes to see both her and Hadon. They obey, and the oracle declares that if the daughter Lalila carries is born in Hadon's home city of Opar, she will be the savior of a city and the founder of a dynasty that will rule for twelve thousand years. But if the child is not born in Opar, she will have a short and terrible life. The oracle dies suddenly after making the prophecy. Awineth, who was also present at the divination, orders Hadon to remain at her side until Minruth is defeated and forbids him from going to Opar. The chief priestess of the local temple tells Lalila that the oracle's prophecy decreed that Hadon himself must accompany his lover to the faraway city of gold, so Hadon and his friends sneak off into the night on the long road to Opar.

The party meets up with a young sailor named Ruseth, who has invented a new type of sail—the fore-and-aft—that is much more efficient than the traditional square sail. He takes them in his vessel, the *Wind-Spirit*, across the northern sea to the pile city of Rebha, where they are to meet with allies who will aid them on the dangerous journey to Opar. But disaster strikes and the city burns down to its piles just after they arrive. As the flames consume Rebha and a storm rages on the sea, the party transfers to a trireme, and Hinokly falls from the ship and disappears into the black waters. Soon the trireme begins to sink as well, but before it does, its front half collides with a colossal floating raft of the K'ud"em'o people. Hadon and the others board the great raft and are taken to the city of Wethna, where Ruseth parts company with the group, intent on returning to the island of Khokarsa to help the priestesses in the fight against Minruth.

Hadon and his friends remain in Wethna long enough to earn enough money to buy a boat, which they outfit with Ruseth's new type of sail. They pass through the Strait of Keth into the southern sea, and sail past the coast where once rose the city of Mibessem, whose inhabitants were said to have been lured away and driven mad by a flute-playing demon. Just as Hadon finishes telling the tale of the haunted, ruined city, the sound of a flute comes to them from the shore, and they flee the area as quickly as the wind will take them.

At long last, the travelers reach Nangukar, the port of Opar, which has been burned to the ground in a recent attack by pirates from Mikawuru. A priestess named Klyhy, with whom Hadon spent an intimate evening just before he left Opar for the Great Games, meets him at the port. She tells him King Gamori has brought Minruth's revolt to Opar and seeks to overthrow the city's queen, Phebha. While they are talking, a boy of about four years of age runs up to Klyhy. The priestess introduces the boy to a shocked Hadon as their son, Kohr.

Klyhy takes Hadon and Lalila to the Temple of Kho in Opar. Lalila goes into labor and is rushed off to the Chamber of the Moon to prepare for the birth. Klyhy brings Hadon to Queen Phebha. Speaking with Hadon, the queen alludes vaguely to a prophecy about Lalila, of which no male has known until this moment. Phebha says she is sick and will soon die, so she will appoint Lalila as her successor and make Hadon Opar's king. But first they must defeat her husband, King Gamori.

During an assault on the temple by the king's forces, Hadon's father, Kumin, and his brother, Methsuh, are slain. Hadon and Klyhy descend into the labyrinth of tunnels beneath the city, intent on accessing Gamori's chambers via a secret route and assassinating him. They encounter soldiers in the tunnels who collapse a bridge out from under Hadon and Klyhy, hurling them into a subterranean river infested with carnivorous fish. Klyhy dies from her wounds, and Hadon goes on alone. He comes upon a vault deep in the tunnels where gold ingots are stored, and then continues down a long corridor that ends in stairs leading up to the top of the massive boulder. He realizes he is standing upon the sacred Isle of Lupoeth in the river to the east of Opar.

Though males are forbidden to set foot on the islet, its three resident priestesses aid Hadon in his plan to defeat the king and his men, who are converging on the boulder to kill Queen Phebha's newly chosen successor. Hadon disguises himself in the robes of a priestess while the chief acolyte stands in the shadows and coaxes Gamori to come closer. Suddenly, Hadon looms large in his disguise and hurls the golden spear of the demigoddess Lupoeth, impaling Gamori and killing him.

Hadon hurries back to the Temple of Kho, where Lalila has just given birth. As he takes his newborn baby into his arms, Queen Phebha cries out, "Hadon, behold your daughter! La of Opar!"

Map 1: Ancient Africa circa 10,000 B.C.

Key: 1. Mukha; 2. Miklemres; 3. Qethruth; 4. Siwudawa; 5. Wethna;
6. Kethna; 7. Wentisuh; 8. Sakawuru; 9. Mikawuru; 10. Bawaku;
11. Towina; 12. Rebha; A. Klemqaba country

Map 2: Island of Khokarsa

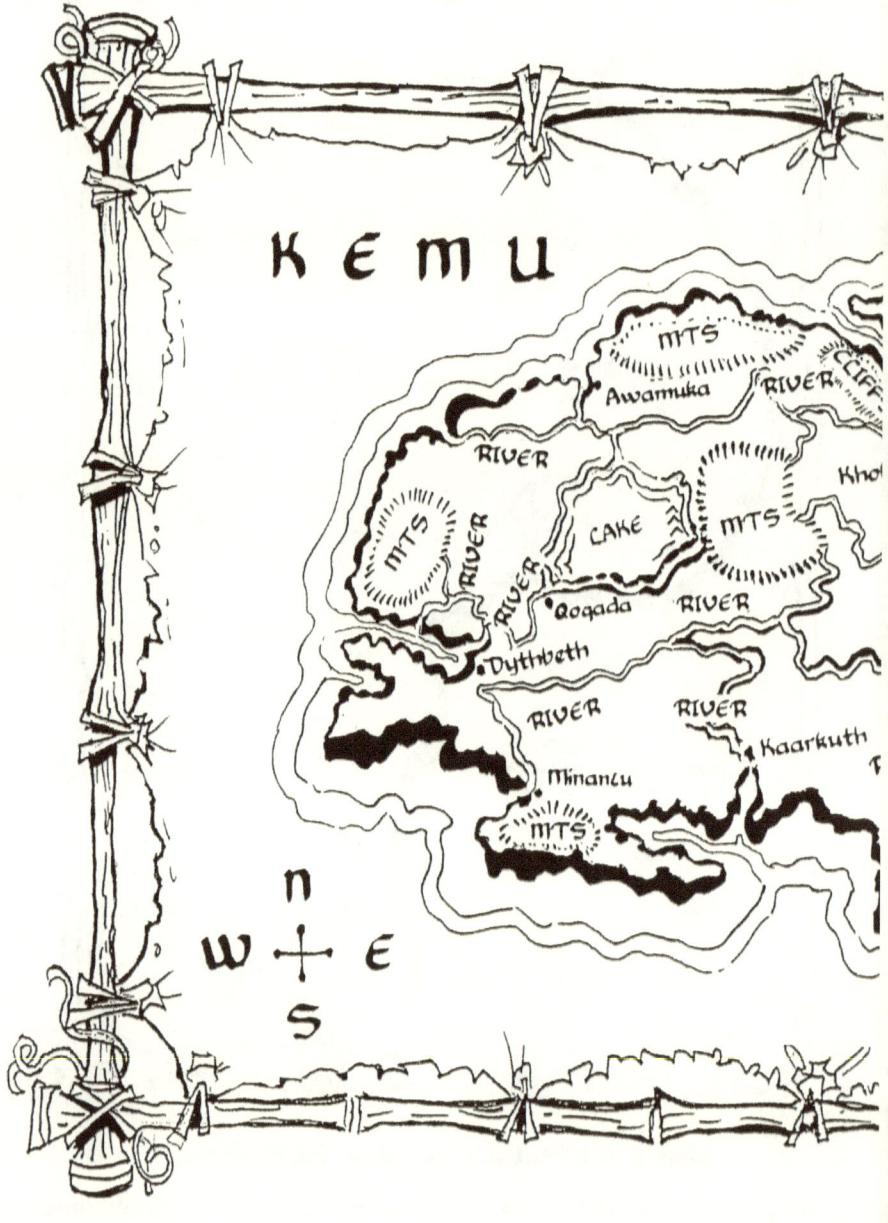

ISLAND OF KHOKARSA

(150 MILES LONG. ONLY MAJOR CITIES SHOWN)

MTS

Khowot
Volcano

MTS

RIVER

MTS

Mimego

RIVER

Saqaba

RIVER

RIVER

Asema

Kunesu

Oinva

KEMU

Map 3: Central Section of City of Khokarsa

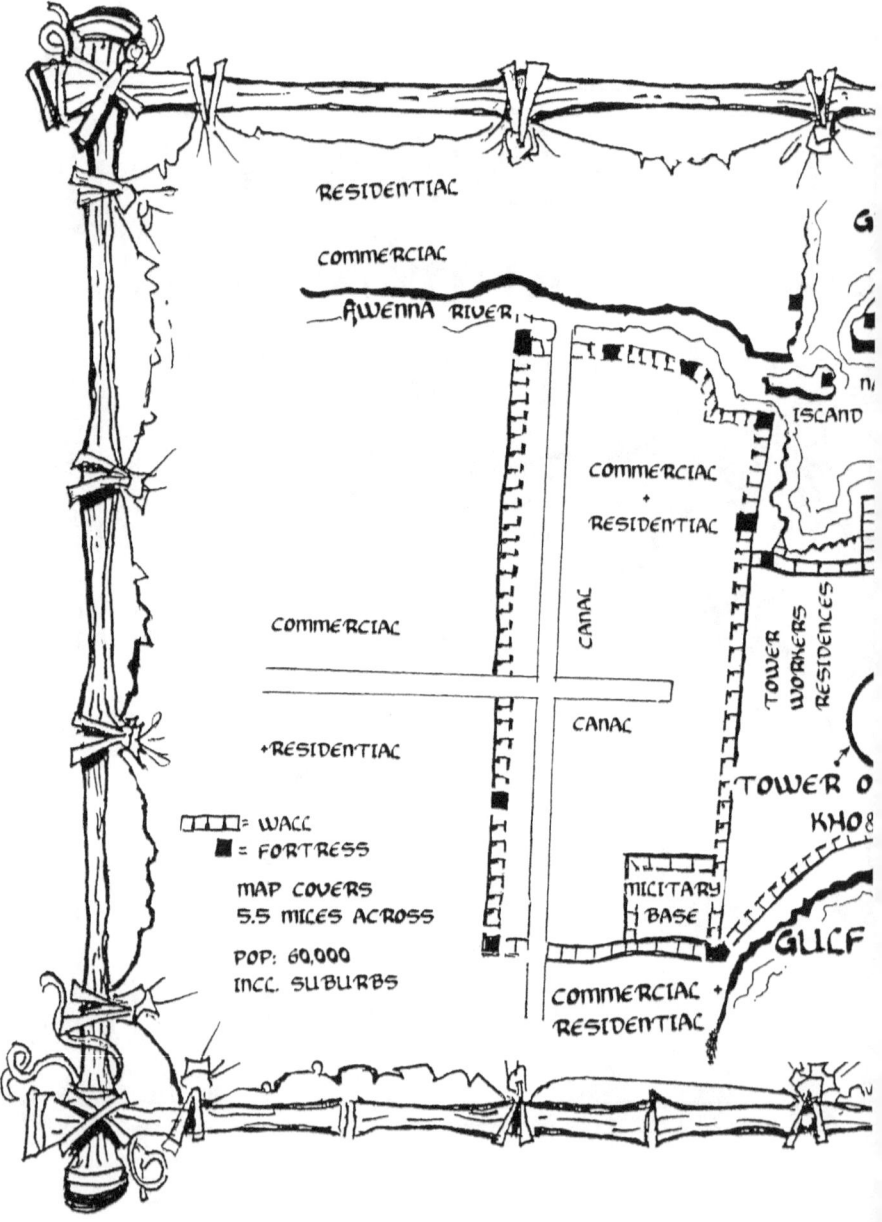

RESIDENTIAL

COMMERCIAL

AWENNA RIVER

G

ISLAND

COMMERCIAL
+
RESIDENTIAL

COMMERCIAL

CANAL

CANAL

TOWER WORKERS RESIDENCES

TOWER O

KHO&

+RESIDENTIAL

🔲🔲🔲 = WALL
⬛ = FORTRESS

MAP COVERS
5.5 MILES ACROSS

POP: 60,000
INCL. SUBURBS

MILITARY
BASE

GULF

COMMERCIAL +
RESIDENTIAL

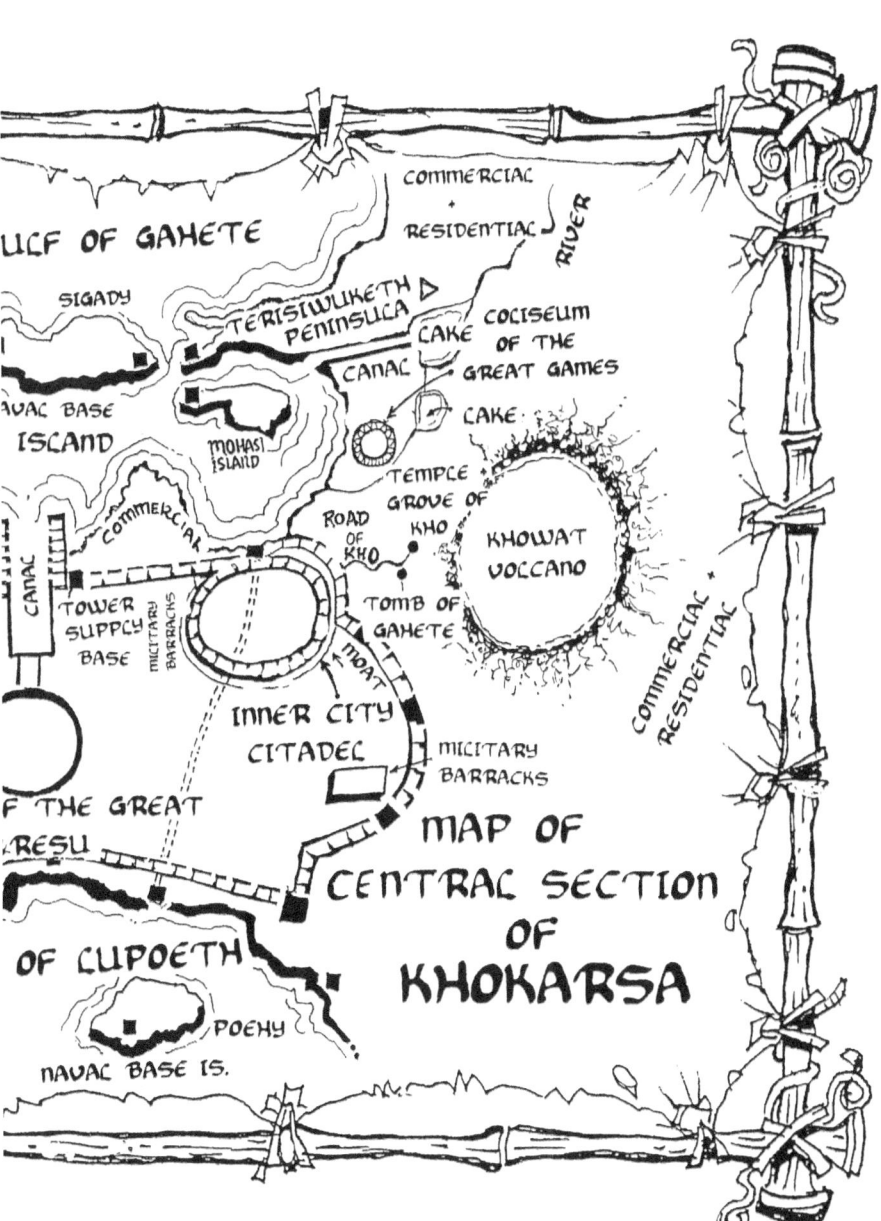

MAP OF CENTRAL SECTION OF KHOKARSA

Map 4: Dythbeth and Surrounding Region

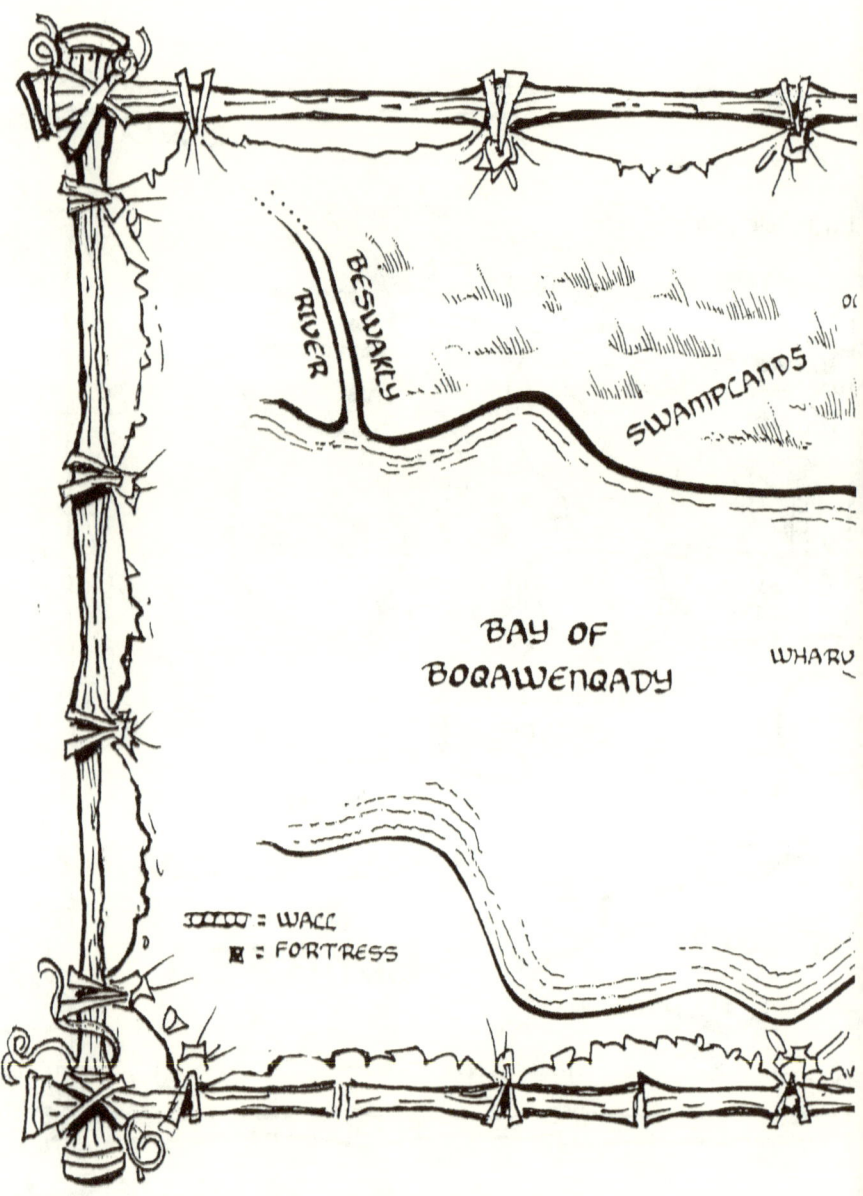

RIVER

BESWAKLY

SWAMPLANDS

OC

BAY OF
BOQAWENQADY

WHARV

⚏⚏⚏ = WALL
🏰 = FORTRESS

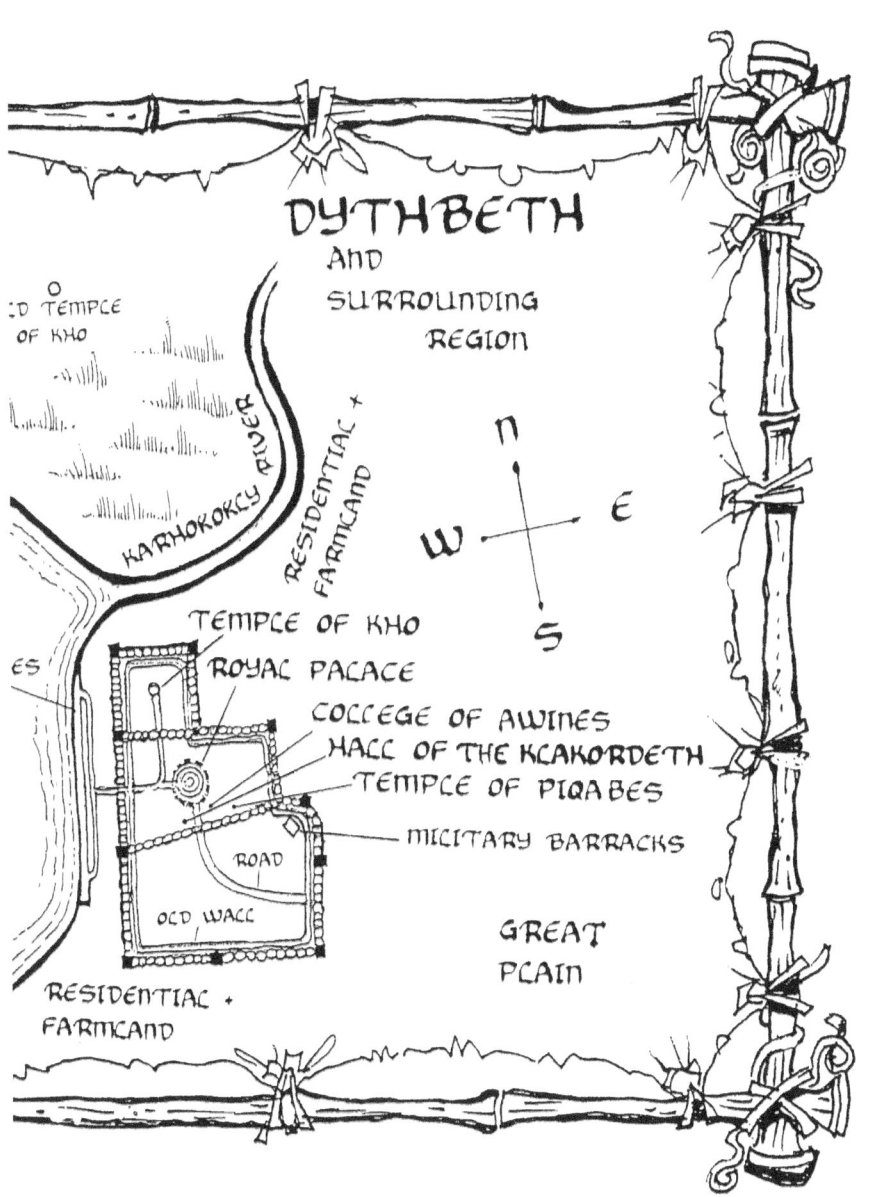

DYTHBETH

AND SURROUNDING REGION

KARHOKORCY RIVER

O
:D TEMPLE
OF KHO

RESIDENTIAC + FARMLAND

N
W   E
S

TEMPLE OF KHO

ROYAL PALACE

COLLEGE OF AWINES

HALL OF THE KLAKORDETH

TEMPLE OF PIQABES

MILITARY BARRACKS

ES

ROAD

OLD WALL

GREAT PLAIN

RESIDENTIAL + FARMLAND

ONE

The strongest man in the world came puffing over the top of the hill and met a god.

The being whom he saw leaning against an oak tree never claimed to be a god. Nor did Kwasin know that he was one when he first saw him.

Later, he thought that a third person, an observer objective because he'd never before seen either of them, might have guessed that it was Kwasin, not the other, who had the strongest claim to divinity.

There was Kwasin, seven feet tall and muscled like a bull, like an elephant, like a gorilla, like the long-dead heroes of old. A dragon of a man, his bones thick and with mighty muscles attached. Like no other man living and like few men of past ages. He had a thick growth of curly black hair and a long curly black beard which did not hide the extreme handsomeness of his face. Sweat made his body shine, that body which was the envy of men and the desire of women. He wore only a lionskin kilt, and he carried only a huge ax. It was one which no ordinary man could wield and few extraordinary.

The man leaning against the oak was fully a head shorter than Kwasin. Though well-muscled and thick-boned, the stranger was built more after the fashion of Kwasin's cousin Hadon, with corded thews, narrow hips, and long arms and legs. Like Hadon, the man might be quite an athlete, but he would make no match for Kwasin, who outweighed him by a hundred pounds of bone and muscle.

Despite death being close at his heels, Kwasin stopped in his tracks and regarded the stranger. The man's arms were folded across his chest and his ruggedly handsome face—beardless, in opposition to the tradition imposed by King Minruth's followers—was smirking. Almost, it seemed to Kwasin, as if the fellow had been waiting for him.

By Wenqath's ass! Kwasin cast a cautious look down the valley behind him. He had no time for delay; a group of Minruth's soldiers followed right behind him. They had spotted him three miles back as he crossed a stream and dashed across a field for a thickly wooded forest. Normally, Kwasin's great stride would have allowed him to easily outpace his pursuers, but he was winded from his swim across the Gulf of Gahete, not to mention his escape from Minruth's prison and his battle on the water as Hadon and his companions fled. If Kwasin had been rested, he might not have run to begin with but rather turned and charged, his great Ax of Victory swinging. He had seen twelve men. In his adventures in the Wild Lands he had faced many more single-handedly and lived to brag about it. But these men were not ill-equipped primitives; they were armed with slings and accompanied by three wardogs. He had hoped to elude them in the forested hills outside the city of Khokarsa, but so far he had been unable to find a tributary of the stream he had passed and thus get the dogs off his scent. He could hear their barking coming from over the next hill.

"That ax of yours. Where did you get it?"

Kwasin looked at the stranger, who still lolled casually against the tree. Something about the man woke bees in Kwasin's stomach. Moments later he understood why he felt this way.

"I'd like nothing more than to discuss the virtues of this most faithful of women," Kwasin said, panting, and he swung his ax in a mighty arc sure to give any mortal enemy pause. "But the hounds are at bay, and if you don't get out of my way, my loving bride may yet turn fickle and leap out of my hands at you."

The stranger seemed unfazed by Kwasin's bravado. He no longer even looked at Kwasin, but now seemed intent on studying an insect crawling up a long grass stem at his feet.

Kwasin started up the hill toward the stranger, but when the man spoke again, surprise froze him.

"If I find that harm has come to Lalila, her child, or the manling Pag," the stranger said, "I will hunt you down and kill you." Then the man threw back his head and, shaking a black mane of hair, sniffed the air like a lion scenting its prey. "Though the wind tells me you may already be doomed," he added, his keen eyes again returning to Kwasin.

"How do you . . . ?" Then the cloud of befuddlement cleared as if Resu, the Flaming God, shone forth his brilliant glory inside Kwasin's skull.

So this, then, must be the man said by many to be Sahhindar, the Gray-Eyed Archer God! The Son of Kho in the flesh! Or so the scribe Hinokly had claimed when he told the story of how his expedition encountered Kho's exiled son in the hinterlands beyond the empire. Sahhindar, protector of the golden-haired, violet-eyed beauty Lalila, the *moon of change*, and her daughter Abeth, and the dwarf Paga, who had given Kwasin his mighty ax and whose name the god pronounced strangely. If not for them, Kwasin would never have ended his exile and returned to Khokarsa, at least not yet.

No, Kwasin thought, he would not now be standing upon this hill outside the capital if his cousin Hadon had not won the Great Games of Klakor, and if the oracle had not then sent him off on a fool's quest to the Wild Lands to bring back the woman, her daughter, and the manling, who were said to be under Sahhindar's guardianship. But the oracle of Khokarsa had decreed that only upon accomplishing this task would Hadon be granted the king's crown that should have been his right as victor of the Great Games. And it was during his fated expedition to the Wild Lands that Hadon had run into Kwasin, serving out the sentence of exile that had been imposed upon him for ravishing a priestess of Kho. Kwasin had counted himself blessed by the Goddess and sworn an oath to obey his cousin until they got back to civilization, hoping that Hadon, with his expedition's goal achieved, would then assume the throne and pardon his exile.

That had not happened. Instead the journeyers returned from their adventures to find that King Minruth and his priests had revolted and overthrown the natural ascendancy of the Goddess and the rule of Her priestesses. War and chaos reigned in Khokarsa.

Now that Kwasin was here, at the empire's hub, he was released from his irksome contract with Hadon. Free, he thought, if not for the soldiers at his heels, the priestesses who wanted him exiled, and the god who stood mockingly before him.

"Sahhindar!" Kwasin bellowed. "If indeed you are the Son of Kho, then we are brothers! Both exiled by the Great Mother to spend our days wandering the Wild Lands. But an exile's dishonor need not be our fate. Let us turn and seek Kho's forgiveness by slaughtering Her enemies!" Kwasin waved his ax back toward the adjoining hill. The dogs' barking was much louder now and at any moment the soldiers might charge over the hill's crest.

Cool gray eyes regarded Kwasin. "Not my fight," the god said; then he turned and scrambled up the oak tree like a monkey. "If you run into Lalila or Pag," Sahhindar shouted down at Kwasin through the leaves, "tell them to head south, far south, as quickly as the wind will take them. There is not much time left." The leafy foliage swished in the god's wake and Sahhindar was gone.

Kwasin turned around just in time to see the first soldier sprint over the nearby hilltop. The soldier fought to hold the reins of a monstrous dog, its mane thick and bristling, and fangs so large Kwasin could see them even at a distance of two hundred yards. Several more soldiers followed over the lip of the hill, two of them also led by the large, hyena-like dogs. But Kwasin did not take long to look at them. Quickly he slipped behind the same oaken trunk against which Sahhindar had leaned.

He waited. No longer would he run. He was not like his cousin Hadon, who had turned and fled as he, Kwasin, leaped into the nearest boat of Minruth's soldiers and stood alone against those who would have killed Hadon and his friends. No, Kwasin had stayed behind then, like any red-blooded man would have, to give the beauteous Lalila a chance at survival. As he had done then, Kwasin promised himself that one day, if the woman lived, he would look into those violet eyes again and that in them he would see Lalila's burning desire for him. He grinned at the thought. Then he corded the leather thong of his ax around his wrist and hand, stepped from behind the tree, and charged.

Down the hill he went, roaring like a mad lion, his mighty ax swinging above his head.

The three wardogs at the front of the group of soldiers strained against their handlers' reins. The men and dogs had already passed the bottom of the adjoining hill and were halfway up the hill down which Kwasin madly ran. He was too close now for the soldiers to use their sling-stones effectively.

The plumed iron helmet of a captain in the Sixth Army of Khokarsa appeared behind the dogs. The handlers, amid much snapping of their charges, managed to steer the dogs off to the sides. The officer raced forward. Though Kwasin could not hear the man's words over the dogs' hellacious barking, he could see the officer cursing at the handlers as he passed them and moved into the lead. The man pulled a square-ended iron sword from its scabbard as he pumped furiously with his legs. A *numatenu*. Though Kwasin did not belong to the order of the *tenu*, the fool officer undoubtedly saw it as a matter of honor to confront the giant before his soldiers did. To kill Kwasin, exiled ravisher of Kho's priestess, would certainly bring the fellow much fame. The man was so sure of himself he did not even carry a round wooden shield like his fellows.

Now the war dogs and handlers closed in on his left and right. No doubt they meant to flank Kwasin while the officer took him on. Kwasin had just enough time to take this in. Then they were upon him. Or he upon them.

Kwasin's ax crashed against the officer's swinging blade, ripped it from the man's grasp. The man did not even have time to look surprised before Kwasin, bellowing with laughter, kicked him in the face with the thickly callused sole of his bare foot. Blood spurted from the man's crushed nose and teeth and he fell backward down the hill. They did not make *numatenu* like they used to.

Kwasin whirled, expecting the dogs to be upon him. Then he saw why they were not. The handlers had backed off and two men with plumed helmets now stood to either side of him on the sloping hill, their long, slightly curving iron swords drawn. Minruth had sent not one, but three *numatenu* after him. Kwasin's reputation had grown large indeed.

In the time it took for him to observe this, Kwasin did not pause. Already his ax whistled at the man to his right. At the same time as the ax smashed a hole in the soldier's wooden shield, Kwasin spun toward the man on his left and with his bare foot kicked off against the advancing man's raised shield. The *numatenu* stumbled backward but did not lose his feet.

Kwasin turned back to the man with the damaged shield. He clung to the useless thing for a moment, but seeing the giant before him raise his enormous ax, the man cast the shield at Kwasin's face and retreated several steps. Kwasin raised his free arm to block the hurtled shield, which upon impact pivoted on his forearm and whacked hard against the bridge of his nose. Warm blood gushed from his nostrils onto his lips and bearded chin. Kwasin howled out his rage and whirled about with his ax.

The massive head of the weapon caught against the edge of the other man's shield and tore it from him. Under the momentum of the blow, the officer fell back and to the side, pummeling into one of the dogs behind him. This was too much for the blood-frenzied descendant of the wild dog of the plains. Barking and snarling, the dog leaped ahead and pulled its handler helplessly forward. Then the beast was on the fallen *numatenu*, its large, clawed feet scraping furiously at the man's lacquered breastplate as it tore open his throat with its teeth.

Even over the yelping and growling of the dogs Kwasin heard the heavy footsteps coming from behind. He had no time to again raise and swing his heavy ax, so he jumped forward, landing on his stomach close to, but not touching, the dog that had just dethroated the other *numatenu*. Then he rolled to one side and hurled himself downhill through the gap between two of the surrounding soldiers. By the time he got back to his feet, he was grinning. The *numatenu* who had charged him had come too near the ravenous wardog, which—infuriated because it had not caught Kwasin before he rolled away—had locked its monstrous jaws upon the soldier's leather-kilted upper thigh. The man was down on both knees. Then a moment later, facedown, dead.

Kwasin's delight evaporated quickly. Now situated downslope from the soldiers, he was at a severe disadvantage. In addition to the fact that the high ground now made it much easier for his opponents to attack him, the soldiers could unleash their sling-stones on him. And though pleased to have eliminated three *numatenu* so easily, he had hoped to take down at least five or six men and one of the dogs while he still held the high ground.

No. He had not incapacitated all of the *numatenu*. The first man he had engaged in his charge down the hill was up again, shouting orders at his men. Blood spewed from the gap in the man's front teeth, but he did not seem to notice. Perhaps here was a real *numatenu* after all.

Under the officer's orders, the two handlers on Kwasin's upper-right flank sicced their dogs on him, uncoiling the dogs' long leashes. Why the man did not order his slingers to take down their enemy, Kwasin did not know. Perhaps the idiot officer hoped for the beasts to bring down Kwasin so the man could then deliver the fatal blow to the legendary exile personally.

That did not matter now. His current situation was bad enough. The leopard-sized beasts bolted down the hill, and at less than half a dozen yards away the lead dog launched itself into the air at Kwasin.

Kwasin dropped to his knees and simultaneously heaved up his ax before him in a quick underhand swing that only he could have been powerful enough to accomplish. It hit the canine squarely beneath its jaw, cleaving in two the beast's head. Kwasin did not see what happened to the dog's corpse after that, as its two companions hurtled onto him from above.

He toppled back beneath the blow of their bodies, his ax arm carried backward over his head. One dog's jaws clamped his right thigh, and his left shoulder seared with pain under the other's teeth. While this happened he was sliding headfirst on his back down the wet, grassy hill, all the while trying to maintain a hold on his massive weapon, which preceded him down the slope. The slick, resin-covered shaft that made it possible for Kwasin to wield the ax with lightning speed now almost made it slip from his fingers. He sought to get a grip on the knobby protuberance at the bottom of the haft, but a sharp rock on the hillside struck his hand. The ax flew out of his grasp, though the leather thong attached to it yanked hard against his wrist.

But the pain in his wrist was nothing compared to the fire in his leg and shoulder. As he writhed under his attackers, a thick doggy odor sought to smother him and he gagged. For a moment he thought he saw Sisisken's dread face, but then the visage of the goddess of the underworld vanished in the dark well of his anger. He was a hero—more of one than his spoiled cousin Hadon—and he refused to die under the fangs of the hyena's cousins.

When Kwasin and the mass of canine fangs and fur hit a shallow gulley in the hill, their wild slide stopped. Kwasin roared. He twisted his hips toward the dog biting his thigh and crossed his free leg over the beast's torso, sliding down along its body as he squirmed uphill, so that the dog's fangs could not emasculate him. But if the beast wriggled free, it would. Still, he had to do something, and as he clamped the dog with his legs, he reached for the other beast—its teeth sunk deeply into his shoulder's flesh—and grabbed it by the throat beneath its powerful jaw. He squeezed both dogs, the one with his hand, the other with his legs.

The dog between his legs squealed. Kwasin heard ribs breaking beneath the corded thews of his thighs, but he was forced to let the canine go when the other dog arched its neck and snapped out a fleshy chunk of his forearm.

With his free arm, Kwasin yanked and swung upward with all

his strength against the ax's leather thong. He had not known if could do it, but he managed to tug the thong hard enough to send the bony ball on the end of the ax haft into his fingertips. He jerked the ball toward him, released it, and grasped the haft firmly.

A crimson haze swathed his vision, whether of blood or anger he did not know or care. In the haze, he saw the ax gleam as if lightning incarnate—or was it just the strong Khokarsan sunlight glinting off the weapon's metallic head? Whatever the case, it seemed as if the Ax of Victory moved of its own accord, arcing first in one direction, and then another. Using the impetus of the ax's swing to aid him, he jumped to his feet and found both dogs dead—laid low by his wild and brutal outburst. One of the canines' heads was rent in two, the other's chest gaping open, its vital organs spilling onto the ground in a deluge of blood.

Still Kwasin's anger raged. He charged up the hill, the turf tearing out from beneath his feet. A sling-stone whirred past his right temple, and then a second ricocheted off the iron head of his ax, which he had just raised to face-level as he ran. Though fury still held him, he grinned fiercely, recalling Paga's claim that the ax was cursed. Perhaps it had cursed the ugly manling, but right now Kwasin would not have traded it for all the women he had ever bedded.

He made for the five soldiers clustered around the surviving *numatenu*. Four other men stood several paces uphill to Kwasin's right. Whistling slings swirled at their sides, but he didn't believe the men would let loose their missiles for fear of hitting their fellows, whom Kwasin now engaged head-on.

Three soldiers' heads exploded under one terrific swoop of Kwasin's ax. A violent arc of blood, hair, brains, and skull fragments flew through the air and sprayed across the grassy incline. The remaining officer, who had recovered his *tenu*, swung his blade at Kwasin. Vulnerable because his own swing had carried the tremendous weight of the iron ax to the end of its arc, Kwasin stepped downhill, forcing the *numatenu* to advance. The man sliced his blade at him but Kwasin was out of reach, his ax already swaying back like a murderous pendulum.

Kwasin jumped forward with the ax's momentum. He landed on his knees, which burned as they slid across the wild grasses. He came to a stop with his ax buried deep in the swordsman's side.

Out of the corner of an eye Kwasin saw the dull sheen of metal reflecting sunlight. He rolled in the opposite direction, and a short sword cut the air within an inch of his neck. Now on his side, Kwasin kicked out at his opponent's leg and hit the soldier squarely on the kneecap. The man buckled forward with a throaty yell. Kwasin raised his ax and smashed it through his fallen foe's helmet as if it were but an eggshell.

Then Kwasin was up, heaving the dead soldier's body before him as a shield and barreling toward the slingers. Hot blood coursed through him in the frenzy of battle and he barely took note of the ax's tremendous weight as it dangled from the antelope-hide thong around his wrist. The corpse he held up in front of him—or was the man yet alive?—jarred as sling-stones impacted it. One of the projectiles tore through the flesh of the man's underarm and grazed Kwasin's shoulder where the dog had bitten him. He growled like an enraged lion through his clenched teeth.

Two of the slingers broke before Kwasin could reach them. Though he could not see them over his human shield, the two remaining slingers had to be directly in front of him. Then one of the men appeared over the corpse just before Kwasin rammed him.

Upon collision, Kwasin dropped the dead man and drove his uninjured shoulder into the slinger's chin. He fell with his full weight on the man. Wind whoofed from Kwasin's lungs. He rolled away from the slinger and onto his feet, gasping for air. The man on the ground did not move, but another man was running away. Kwasin slipped his ax's thong from around his wrist and, pivoting on one foot, swirled his whole body with the ax extended at arm's length. Just before he completed his circle, he released the ax. It arced shallowly upward, then down. The fleeing soldier fell beneath it.

The two remaining soldiers dashed for the hill's tree-covered top. One soldier lagged behind the other, appearing encumbered by his armor and the heavy iron *tenu* he had lifted from the corpse of one of the officers. The fleeing man must have been truly frightened. And stupid. If the other soldier witnessed his action and reported it to his superiors, the man, if apprehended, would be executed for thieving from a member of the noble swordsman class.

Grinning darkly, Kwasin picked up a sling and missile from the dead soldier at his feet and placed the stone in the leather pocket of the sling. Swiftly but calmly, he wrapped one end of the sling's strap around a finger and slipped the other knotted end between his thumb and forefinger. Then he held the sling to his side and with a motion of his wrist and forearm began whirling it parallel to his body. He released the free end of the sling on the fifth whirl. The stone missile shot off in a shallow arc.

When the man fell, Kwasin threw back his head and whooped with laughter.

Then he saw the remaining soldier disappear into the tree line as if fleeing the ugly face of Kopoethken herself. His voice still shaking with laughter, Kwasin shouted, "Go! Spread far and wide the name of Kwasin of Dythbeth, who has returned from his exile to slay the feeble *numatenu* of Minruth the Mad and turn the innards of his soldiers to soup!"

But with the words dying on his lips, Kwasin looked about at the dead that lay scattered across the hillside. As he surveyed the aftermath of his fury, a sudden emptiness replaced the joy he had experienced but a moment before, and he considered how easily he might have been one of the corpses. He had seen much death in his lonely wanderings in the Wild Lands. No living being could hold off personal oblivion, the ultimate writing off of self. Even the priestesses of Kho, with all their prayers, blessings, and ancient wisdom, could not avoid it or prevent it for another. Nor could the great Kwasin, who possessed more stamina and strength than any other, ever hope to vanquish the terrifying void of *nothingness* that even now lay in wait for him in dread Sisisken's hollow dominion.

Kwasin left behind the hillside's bloody testament and

climbed the next rise, yet the pall of his gloomy soliloquy hung over him. He thought of the oracle who had pronounced his exile, and of the priestess who had caused it.

Suddenly, as if Great Kho had granted him a vision, he knew where his wanderings would take him next. Though maybe, he mused, his soul had secretly known where it had intended to carry him all along. Why else had he not traveled northward to learn the fate of Hadon and his companions and instead had swum westward across the Gulf of Gahete and set off over the hills in the direction of his native Dythbeth?

The thought—whether a gift from the Goddess or a quirk of his weary soul—raised up the dark veil that had hung over him, and his spirits lifted. He would return home, after eight long years of adventures and sufferings in the Wild Lands. Home, where he would somehow find a way to exonerate himself from the crimes of his past. Once again, he would be a free man.

Of course, he expected the priestess there would have something to say about that.

Two

Two weeks later, having endured a journey over land, sea, and river that included as many adventures as it did hardships, Kwasin stared down from his mountain perch at the cyclopean queendom of Dythbeth. The harbor city's gilt-trimmed, white granite domes gleamed brightly in the distance beneath the strong noonday sun of the island of Khokarsa. A sparkling river, the Karhokokly, stretched beneath him, its two tributaries snaking down to the marshlands that surrounded the old temple of Kho and emptying into the long and narrow Bay of Boqawenqady. He breathed in deeply the minty fragrance of the thick fir and pine forest that edged the rocky overhang on which he stood. For a moment, he smiled.

The sweet smell of the trees triggered memories of his happy youth exploring the mountains outlying his birth city while under the supervision of his godfather. The husband of his mother's best friend, Pwamkhu had acted more like an older brother to Kwasin than a dutiful grownup. Together the two had engaged in much good-natured deviltry, often finding creative ways to bait Kwasin's peers into fights with the already large, athletic boy or taking joy in enraging shop owners with clandestine visits in the dead of night to egg their market stalls.

Those happy times had been in the years before Kwasin's mother, Wimake, had died. After that sorrowful event, the ten-year-old

Kwasin had left Pwamkhu behind, having been sent off to the eastern shores of the southern sea to live with his uncle Phimeth in the dark caves of his cliff-side home. Though at first eager to experience an exotic new land and thrilled to learn the way of the *tenu* from a legendary swordmaster, Kwasin found his optimism quickly evaporating under his uncle's disapproving glare, and soon longing for his native Dythbeth gnawed at the boy's heart.

Phimeth turned out to be a strict and joyless man, at least as far as his ill-behaved nephew was concerned. The young Kwasin was a temple child. His mother, having failed to become pregnant at the time of her marriage to Toekha, a prominent merchant, had conceived Kwasin while serving as a divine prostitute in the temple of a god. Thus Kwasin's father was, religiously speaking, Khukhaken, the Leopard God, divine consort of Khukhaqo, the patron goddess of Dythbeth. Since Toekha had died in a skirmish with bandits before Wimake gave birth to her only son, Kwasin had known no earthly father figure besides the boisterous Pwamkhu.

Phimeth, a bachelor, did not like children, and the innately wild and rebellious Kwasin—made more unruly in the absence of his mother—did not make his newfound task of childrearing any easier. Phimeth had tried to instill discipline in his adolescent charge, but Kwasin resisted and was often disobedient, though he dared not step too far out of line for fear of his uncle's harsh punishments. Still, Kwasin attempted to bridge the gap between them and begged to be trained as a *numatenu*. Phimeth stubbornly refused and told Kwasin he was not mature enough. Though Kwasin fumed, he could do nothing. The will of the old *numatenu* was as iron as his square-ended weapon of trade. When, a few years later, Kwasin's cousin Hadon came to stay with them in the caves, the relationship between Kwasin and his uncle had only worsened. Phimeth suddenly announced that it was time to begin training with the *tenu*, and it was immediately clear to Kwasin that his uncle favored Hadon, the spry, long-armed son of Kumin. Kwasin's anger and resentment had blackened.

Kwasin heaved a deep sigh. Even Sahhindar, the god of Time, could not travel to the past now that Kho had banished him for his insolence, so why should he, Kwasin, be bothered by times gone by? The trivialities of the past could not touch him, especially now that Phimeth was dead, and probably Hadon as well. And were not events at last turning in Kwasin's favor? The oracular priestess at Dythbeth had condemned Kwasin to wander the Wild Lands beyond the empire, but she had also declared that one day, when Kho decreed it, he would be permitted to return. Had that time not come at last? Had he not paid his debt to the past, even stood up against the enemies of Kho by smiting down the insolent soldiers of Minruth? The Goddess and Her priestesses would surely forgive him his past transgressions.

His plan was to traverse the passes through the mountains and follow the river southeast. Then he would slip unnoticed into the city and, under cloak of night, enter the chambers of Weth, now high priestess and queen of Dythbeth—the very woman who had accused him of ravishing her. Well, perhaps in his drunkenness he would have liked to have ravished her, but even he would never dare violate a priestess. But he had not hesitated when she had beckoned him to her bedchamber. Who was he to disobey a priestess of Kho? Besides, the dalliance had ended when Weth had become frightened upon seeing his naked manhood, or perhaps it was the furious fire of lust burning in his eyes that had unsettled her. Whatever the case, she had screamed and her guards had entered and set upon him before ascertaining the situation. Kwasin had only killed them in self-defense. He knew the woman carried in her heart the truth of what had occurred that night, and now that the Voice of Kho at Khokarsa was in hiding from Minruth's forces, Weth remained his best hope to clear his name. The endless wanderings of his exile wore at him, and if he had to endure even one more day in the Goddess-forsaken Wild Lands, he would go mad—madder than he already was, he thought, grinning.

The distant sound of men shouting, accompanied by a dull thudding that might have been weapons clashing, awoke Kwasin from his reverie. He stepped back from the rocky overhang, cupped a hand to an ear, and listened.

When passing south of Awamuka's farmlands, Kwasin had spied a large, well-organized assemblage marching out of the north. He had sneaked close enough to determine the group was a contingent of Minruth's Sixth Army, numbering perhaps five thousand strong. To avoid them, Kwasin had detoured far to the west and entered the landward region of the tall coastal mountain range about forty miles due northwest of Dythbeth, only to run headlong into a group of soldiers occupying a small mountain village of bear worshipers to the north. This had resulted in one of Kwasin's stranger adventures, in which, with some help from the local priestess and a sloth of trained bears, he had assailed the village and managed to rally its residents to rise up against their oppressors.[1] But Kwasin had been lucky. If he had not succeeded in fully routing the soldiers and they had been able to quickly summon reinforcements, things would have ended up much differently. Now, in the southern reaches of the Saasamaro, Kwasin feared the shouting from beyond the ridge might be evidence of a much larger contingent of Minruth's troops moving through the region.

Then again, it might be nothing more than bandits attacking a trader's party. Years of experience in the Wild Lands, however, had convinced Kwasin that it was better to know one's surroundings than to be surprised by the unknown. Lack of curiosity squashed the dung beetle.

He jogged up the forested incline, angling toward the source of the disturbance. Upon nearing the ridge, he slowed and advanced with caution. Crouching, he peered over the summit and down at the scene below.

Outside of a wooden-walled fort at the base of the pass, a group of soldiers flying the leopard standard of the Fifth Army at Dythbeth had taken a defensive position against a much larger body of soldiers. Or two larger bodies. The attackers streamed into the pass from both the main road and an adjoining pass to

---

[1] For a full recounting of this adventure, see the novella "Kwasin and the Bear God" by Philip José Farmer and Christopher Paul Carey on page 335.

the southeast. These soldiers carried the rising sun standard of Khokarsa's Sixth Army.

Minruth's mad ambitions had at last reached faraway Dythbeth.

The sight made Kwasin livid. Though Dythbeth had forsaken him and its oracle had condemned him to exile, the thought of Minruth and his power-hungry priests overturning the rightful rule of the Goddess outraged him. For all of his bravado, Kwasin could not escape the bowel-aching fear of Kho that had been instilled in him during his youth. The Great Mother, in Her anger at Minruth's blasphemy, would be sure to send pestilence and famine across the land, or worse, destroy the land altogether. Had not the sacred volcano, Khowot, the Voice of Kho, belched its black smoke and fiery lava in the days following Minruth's revolt? Even a week ago, as Kwasin had passed south of Awamuka, the anger of the Goddess had rumbled the earth and a great cleft had appeared in the grassy plain before his astonished eyes.

Kwasin ducked behind the ridge and jogged eastward along it. When he felt he had gone far enough ahead of the soldiers in the pass, he again peered over the ridge. Since he saw no soldiers in the pass or forest below, he bounded downward, weaving through the trees. When he got to the pass, he continued on across it and up the next ridge. The rise here was rock strewn and less thickly wooded, and Kwasin made his way to the mountain's opposite side, fearing the Sixth Army might have positioned scouts to follow along its rear.

He now headed west, back toward the fighting. The battle cries and wailings of the wounded grew louder. Kwasin stopped when he reached the southeastern cross-pass down which one arm of the Sixth Army had marched. Minruth's soldiers no longer occupied the area, though Kwasin could see the rearguard moving down the main pass.

Though he risked a scout seeing him, Kwasin ran down into the cross-pass and up its opposite side, so that he now darted behind boulders and the occasional tree on the steep and uneven mountainside above the clash of the two armies. The larger mass of Minruth's army had pinned the soldiers from Dythbeth up against the walls of their fort. Still the Dythbethans fought on, refusing to retreat into the fort, though the enemy seemed an unending river before them. Despite Kwasin's status as an exile, no small amount of pride swelled in his breast at the heroic display, though the plight of the Dythbethans seemed all but futile. By sheer numbers, Minruth's legions held the upper hand and Kho only knew the short span of time before they would crush the Fifth Army and take the fort.

But Kwasin cared little for odds when the mad fury of battle seized him. He spied his target and said a brief prayer to Khu-khaken, whose spirit was still said to inhabit these mountains over fifteen hundred years after the hero Dythbeth had cleared the area of the Leopard God's four-footed children. Then Kwasin pumped his mighty legs and ran farther up the mountainside.

Midway into his ascent, he heard a shout. He looked up. A man's silhouette loomed above on the craggy summit. Then Kwasin saw three bronze-helmeted men with spears emerge from behind a boulder about two hundred yards to his right. Though he had thought he could run no faster, Kwasin leaned forward and increased his speed, using his hands to help propel himself up the steep incline. He reached his target ahead of the spearmen who now ran at breakneck speed toward him.

Kwasin stood before an immense boulder resting on a shallow projection of dirt and stone. The giant rock might have been pitched there during one of Kho's recent upheavals of the land.

The spearmen had closed only half the distance between Kwasin and their original position. Kwasin glanced up at the summit. The man, having come only partway down the mountainside, hovered half a dozen yards above Kwasin, his short sword drawn. Fortunately, he did not bear a spear. He made furtive glances toward the men on Kwasin's right. The fellow, shieldless like the spearmen, wore a conical helmet sprouting the black raven feather of a *rekokha*, or sergeant. He was apparently waiting for his men to close on their target before advancing on Kwasin himself. By now Minruth would have sent word out to his troops to be on the lookout for the ax-bearing giant who had escaped his prison and killed dozens of the faithful soldiers of Resu. The *rekokha* must have known that he faced the legendary Kwasin of Dythbeth, returned from his exile in the Wild Lands.

Kwasin grinned. Khukhaken must have heard his prayer. The officer's cowardice gave Kwasin just enough time to execute his plan.

He dropped his ax onto the shallow ledge and, groaning like a dying demon, leaned into the huge boulder and pushed off against the slope with his feet. The rock did not move. One of the men, now on his left as he faced the pass below, slipped on the treacherous incline and slid on his belly some ways down the mountainside. His companion did not pause to help his fallen comrade and was now almost within a spear's throw of Kwasin.

Kwasin looked back at the officer above him. The man had closed the distance between them, apparently bolstered by his proximity to the other soldier.

Roaring, Kwasin heaved again. His spine crackled under the force of his action. Then, at last, the great boulder gave out before him and he pitched forward in the rock's sudden absence. Something sharp grazed his back as he landed chest-first on the grit of the ledge and his torso slid halfway off the shelf. A spear. Below he saw the boulder rolling violently down the mountainside, following a trajectory that would land it in the midst of the Sixth Army's rearguard.

Without waiting to see if the boulder would hit its target, Kwasin swung around on the narrow ledge and pulled himself up just as the man with the short sword jumped from above, his blade stabbing downward. Kwasin canted hard to his left and kicked at the sword's flat side near its hilt. The blade dropped from the soldier's hand, and Kwasin, now on his side, kicked again, this time at the man's ankle. The soldier crumpled.

Kwasin got to his feet. The man who had launched the spear that grazed Kwasin's back booted recklessly along the sharp mountainside only paces away, his short sword drawn. Kwasin reached down and, groaning, lifted up the body of the stunned *rekokha*, who shouted in surprise and probably also pain from his injured ankle. The other soldier, seeing his superior raised high above the head of the giant, skidded to a halt. The man's face stretched long with fear just before Kwasin hurled the body of the officer at him. Both soldiers went tumbling down the sheer mountainside, a tangle of arms and legs. Kwasin smiled broadly when he saw the soldier who had earlier slid partway down the rocky incline turn tail and head down the mountain.

Chaos reigned below, at least for Minruth's troops. The boulder now lay at rest in the center of the pass, having left behind a trail of corpses in its wake. The giant rock had hit the rearguard squarely, creating havoc among the slingers and spearmen. Those missed by the boulder ceased launching their deadly rain of missiles over the heads of their fellows in the mad rush to get out of the way. The men immediately in front of the rearguard, panicking, ran forward, creating a stampede that left many soldiers fallen and crushed beneath a human tide.

This would have also spelled disaster for the Dythbethans, who easily could have been crushed against the wall of their fortress, if not for the quick thinking of their leader. Kwasin could see the man now, his *tenu* drawn, his king's crown gleaming golden in the sunlight, leading one flank of his men northward along the wall of the fortress. The other flank, apparently under the king's rapid orders, headed south along the wall. Meanwhile, the Khokarsan soldiers, attempting to escape the stampede that surged behind them, continued to charge forward.

Kwasin shouted his approval when the Dythbethan king signaled for his men to reverse course and converge on both sides of the Khokarsan phalanx. Now bottled between two flanks of their enemy, the panic-frenzied soldiers of Minruth fell before the swords and spears of the Dythbethan king's men.

Weth had chosen her husband well. Though, of course, the king's fortune had depended solely on Kwasin's actions. And, Kwasin thought, I would have made her a better lover.

"But then," he said aloud, laughing, "what mortal man, king or otherwise, can compare to me?"

Kwasin recovered his ax and headed down toward the battle.

THREE

By the time Kwasin stepped into the pass, the bulk of the Sixth Army was in retreat, the members of its advance guard dead or dying. The Dythbethans shouted taunts and insults at the fleeing soldiers while the victorious king got to the business of reining in his men to scavenge the bodies of the fallen for precious armor and weaponry. The accoutrements of war, always valuable commodities, would become even more crucial to the Dythbethans now that trade was cut off from the capital and the other cities over which Minruth held his sway. The latter would be many, at least according to the rumors Kwasin had heard while imprisoned in Minruth's dungeons. Still, other whisperings among his former guards told of thousands of Kho's worshipers who had formed a resistance in the mountains across the island. Of all the cities on Khokarsa, only proud Dythbeth stood any chance of holding out against Minruth's blasphemous new order.

When Kwasin approached, many of the soldiers stood up from their task of foraging among the dead. The jaws of the men gaped wide at the giant warrior, who might have been a hero stepping out of an epic of ancient times. Kwasin watched with amusement as the soldiers dropped their spoils and backed slowly away as he passed. Murmurs of "Defiler of the Great Mother!" and "Traitor to Kho!" shot between the men. They must not have seen his exploits on the mountainside above and how he had saved them from certain defeat. Or if they had, they did not care. To them he was a blasphemer, excommunicated by the oracle for his sacrilege against she who was now the high priestess of Dythbeth. Only a pronouncement from the city's oracle, endorsed by Queen Weth, would change their minds.

One man, however, did not step out of Kwasin's way but instead navigated through the carnage, making straight for the giant. Ankle-length priestly robes—yellow, scarlet-slashed, and tasseled—hung from the gaunt frame of the long-faced man. A stiff roach of greased hair, running from the nape of the neck to the forehead, stuck up on his otherwise shaven head. In disobedience to Minruth's decree that all priests grow beards, the man sported a clean-shaven face, though on his forehead he had painted in yellow ochre an inverted arrow on a horizontal line, the character in the syllabary that represented Resu, the sungod. He stopped about twenty paces from Kwasin and made the sign of Kho, touching his forehead with his three longest fingers, then circling the fingers out and over his loins before returning them to his forehead.

"Are you all cowards?" The man shouted his question at the soldiers. "In the names of Kho and Resu, take custody of this man! He is the criminal Kwasin, exiled from the land by the oracle!"

At the priest's words, the soldiers stopped backing away and yet did not advance. The face of the priest reddened and his fist shook at the men.

"Where are the valiant warriors of Dythbeth? Detain this man or I'll have your hides skinned and used as drapes in the temple of Resu!"

Kwasin, hefting his ax onto a shoulder, narrowed his eyes and stopped within arm's reach of the priest.

"Priest of Resu," Kwasin rumbled, "you speak of Kho from one side of your mouth but from the other cry forth the name of Resu. Can you blame the men of Dythbeth for hesitating to carry out your orders in this Time of Troubles, when an outlaw has saved them from Minruth's treacherous army and the words of the priests are as mutable as the face of the Shapeless Shaper?"

The priest's lips pruned as if he had just taken a bite of rotten pomegranate. "You? *You* saved them?"

"Lo!" Kwasin swept a mightily thewed arm to indicate the great boulder lying in the midst of the dead on the field of battle. "You think this rock fell from the sky? The oracle who banished me from the empire said one day I would return, and so I have, in the hour of my people's greatest need."

Slowly, and with caution written clearly on their faces, a number of soldiers crept closer until they crowded round Kwasin and the priest. The soldiers' attitude, Kwasin noted, was not threatening, and though some of the men carried the swords, spears, and slings they had looted from the dead, none of them presented the weapons menacingly. Instead, the eyes of the fighting men of Dythbeth seemed to sparkle with growing awe and admiration.

The priest's hands shook and his already reddened face grew darker. "Though a priest of Resu," he said, "I, Taphiru, have not forsaken Kho as many of my brethren have so foolishly done." As the man spoke, he looked up into the eyes of the giant before him, but his words projected loudly so that Kwasin knew the real audience was the group of soldiers about them.

"Yes, I remember you well, Kwasin the Troublemaker, from the days of your rabblerousing youth. Always causing grief, ever the bully. And always in the company of that . . . what was that lout's name? Ah, yes, that good-for-nothing ass, Pwamkhu. He bragged he was such a great warrior until one day that tiny little daughter of Besbesbes buzzed his way and stung him in the ass." Taphiru pealed with laughter. "Why, he just puffed up like a toad and died!"

All too keenly did Kwasin recall the story of Pwamkhu's death, and indeed, what a shameful end it had been for the hero of his childhood. After leaving Dythbeth to live in the caves with his uncle, Kwasin had never seen his godfather again. Years later, when Kwasin returned to his native city, he had visited the site of Pwamkhu's burial, with its pitiful marker consisting of a mere brick instead of a grand pylon and a hero's tomb. And on that sorry grave Kwasin had sworn never to let live any creature that dishonored the memory of the one man who had befriended him in his youth.

For a moment it seemed to Kwasin that the fury inside him would erupt like wrathful Khowot. Then he did explode, though in laughter, not rage.

"I will not fall into your trap, priest!" Kwasin's cavernous voice boomed. "Though it is easy enough to see how the fork-tongued followers of Resu convinced so many to join their wicked cause . . . and how they yet seek to divide the allies of the Goddess." Kwasin's eyes narrowed slightly. "By the way, where is the army's priestess? Surely the king has not gone into battle with only a priest to guide him?"

"The priestess Waneth has taken ill," Taphiru said, and Kwasin thought he saw a slight curl of satisfaction upon the man's lips. "Her attendants nurse her inside the fort."

Kwasin wondered if the man had poisoned Waneth so that he could broaden his sway over the army, but he said nothing of his suspicions. Instead, he put a hand to his forehead and staggered about the men, feigning a swoon. "I too feel ill," he moaned. "Summon the doctor! Now! Lest the plague vapors carried on this priest's putrid breath lay the whole army to waste!"

The soldiers standing about hooted at Kwasin's buffoonery and the priest's red-faced outrage. Taphiru seemed about to launch himself on Kwasin despite the disparity of their sizes when a measured voice rang out from behind the man.

"What goes on here?"

The group of soldiers parted and a stocky, long-bearded man of about fifty, wearing battle-worn armor and a golden crown in the place of an iron helmet, stepped forward. Kwasin had never met King Roteka in person, though he had seen the old soldier about Dythbeth in the years before the man's marriage to Weth and his subsequent sovereignty. In his youth, Roteka had earned a generalship under Minruth when he turned back a much larger force of barbarians that had crossed the Saasares and threatened the coastal city of Mukha. The man seemed to wear his armor more comfortably than his crown, and Kwasin took an immediate liking to him.

When Taphiru, his voice quavering with outrage, explained that the infamous exile—and undoubtedly a spy for Minruth—stood before them, and that the king's soldiers had better do their duty and arrest Kwasin, King Roteka pulled at his graying beard and nodded.

"No," he said, "this man has opened the way for victory. Did you not see him, Taphiru, high on the mountain fighting our enemy? Like a thunder god he hurled this great stone from the mountain and made Minruth's pawns scatter so that we might rout them. And a messenger has just arrived this morning from Q"okwoqo to the north, bringing news of how Kwasin freed the village from the sun worshipers' tyranny."

"But this is the man who defiled the high priestess, your wife!" Taphiru exclaimed in disbelief.

Roteka regarded the priest, and Kwasin thought the king's eyes carried a look of shrewd suspicion. Then the king took hold of Taphiru's arm and whispered something in the priest's ear. Taphiru did not speak after that, though his temples pulsed with suppressed rage.

"I know well who this man is," the king said, "and the heinous crimes for which he has been sentenced." Roteka stared fiercely up at Kwasin, then looked away. "But I remember too that the oracle didn't order him killed outright for his transgressions. I can only trust in the Goddess that the Voice of Kho knew what she was doing when she spared him castration and death. For that reason, and for the good of the people, I must put my personal feelings aside, as well as those of the queen . . . at least for the moment. Another Time of Troubles is upon us, and Dythbeth is in dire need of its own troublemaker. I won't so hastily dispose of a man who, by his recent actions, has demonstrated his capacity to leave our enemy reeling."

Then King Roteka, clearly uncomfortable and not hiding his disgust, lifted his gaze to meet Kwasin's. "Will you not join the men of Dythbeth in the struggle against the blasphemers? I could use your brawn almost as much as your reputation. In payment for your conscription, when we return within the city gates I shall petition the queen to consult the oracle on your behalf. It has been many years since you departed in exile and old Wasemquth may have changed her mind. But if she has not, you must agree to obey the oracle's pronouncement, whether that order be your immediate execution or the proclamation of your freedom."

Kwasin did not need any convincing. Even if he hadn't desired the old king's help in clearing his name, he knew accepting Roteka's offer still benefited him. Minruth had put a price on his head. Unless Kwasin gave up and returned to the Wild Lands, he would not be able to rest until someone defeated Minruth and returned suzerainty to Kho and her priestesses. He had to take the risk that the oracle would revoke his sentence. And besides, Kwasin thought, who better to break Minruth's neck than himself?

And so he who was loath to bow before any man dropped to a knee and, laying his great ax on the ground before him, swore his allegiance to the king of Dythbeth. For now, he thought, at least while Minruth yet lived.

When Kwasin arose, the surrounding troops broke out in a throaty cheer, apparently overjoyed to have the frightful, ax-wielding colossus fighting on their side and not against them. Kwasin, his spirits lifting, hefted up his ax and stood grim and terrible before them.

"Enough!" Roteka said before the cheer had yet quieted. "The enemy is in retreat and we must rout them out while the piss still wets their kilts. You, Kwasin, will fight by my side where I can keep an eye on you." The king turned to the priest. "And you, Taphiru, will return to the fort where your slick words won't confound the decisions of war."

The priest hesitated a moment, his brow creased with fury; then, still fuming, he obeyed his king and left for the fort while Kwasin set off with Roteka, a thousand strong surging behind them as they marched up the pass.

At the cross-pass they again engaged Minruth's troops, and throughout the day many men fell beneath the giant Kwasin's ax and the long *tenu* of King Roteka. At times it seemed as if the Dythbethans would inflict enough damage to again send the Khokarsans running. Then, late in the day, a courier arrived.

The man brought intelligence that a large enemy contingent moved along the vast plain to the south of Qoqada. The soldiers garrisoned at Dythbeth numbered too few to repel the new wave of invaders, and if Roteka and his men remained holed up in the mountains, the city would be taken.

King Roteka ordered an immediate pullback, ceding the mountain fort and the surrounding terrain to the enemy. The twenty-mile march back to Dythbeth would take two and a half days for the large contingent, and as they moved through the passes to the grasslands, they would be vulnerable to attack. Fortunately, as Roteka's troops pulled out, the Sixth Army made no move to pursue them. The fatigued and severely battered enemy seemed content to occupy the fort and lick their wounds.

On the trip out of the mountains, Kwasin spoke with the king and learned the reason for the presence of the Dythbethan troops in the high passes. "I received a plea of help," Roteka said, "from a group of guerrillas fighting in the mountains. Refugees from Awamuka whose allegiance stands with Kho. Some of them are still up here, though when we arrived we found many mutilated corpses strung up by the enemy. My intelligence had brought me word that Qoqada and Minanlu were in revolt. I thought that would buy me time, and so I left my best general, Hahinqo, in charge at Dythbeth and took half of my troops to the mountains to reclaim some of my old glory. I wanted to bloody the nose of Minruth the Mad, but I've been a fool—I should have stayed in Dythbeth!"

When, two days later, the Fifth Army bridged the ford of the Karhokokly, Kwasin could already see a dark mass moving across the great plain toward the city. The king ordered his men to cut a beeline across the plain and intercept the invaders. Soon, however, it became evident that if Roteka did not take his men directly to the city, the enemy would reach it first. Roteka had his lieutenants issue orders for the drivers to abandon their oxen and wagons and to hike it as fast as they could on foot. They arrived none too soon. As the bloody red eye of Resu cast its sickly light upon the city's proud towers and high granite walls, the two armies clashed on the great plain before Dythbeth.

The warring did not go well for King Roteka's already combat-weary forces. The battle consisted of a series of advances and retreats, and after each lull the Dythbethans found themselves pushed farther back. By early evening they were forced to retreat across the plain to the city. There they entered the eastern gate and took up position atop the city's fortified walls, launching spears and sling-stones and catapulting vessels of flaming oil down upon the invaders.

On fought Kwasin, bolstering the exhausted troops of Dyth-beth with his crude taunts at the enemy and his unending vigor. When the Sixth Army's supply train brought hastily constructed wooden ladders across the plain and propped them up against the walls, Kwasin was the first among the defenders to jump upon one, scale down it, and meet the ascending soldiers halfway, his blood-covered ax swinging.

The soldiers below began to climb back toward the ground. Apparently they recognized the man on the ladder as the terrible giant who had single-handedly slain so many of them during the battle on the plain. Kwasin, seeing the men descend, clambered upward as quickly as he could. By the time he reached the ladder's top, the men below had already begun to swing the ladder back from the wall.

The gap between Kwasin and the wall widened to almost two yards. He hurled his ax to the battlement. Now three yards from the wall, the ladder stood almost vertical. Without using his hands, he footed his way to the top rung and, just as the ladder was about to swing out from under his feet, launched himself into the air.

Kwasin hit the wall hard, narrowly managing to wrap his arms over the wall's upper edge. His legs flailed in the air, and for a moment he thought his prodigious strength would fail him. Then a hand reached out of the void of night. Kwasin grasped it, heaved himself onto the wall, and looked into the grimly smiling face of King Roteka.

"Like a hero of old!" he said to Kwasin. "I had my doubts about you, but no more. The day has darkened with men's blood, but because of you I still hold out hope."

Kwasin grasped arms with the old king and grinned. "Don't worry, O King! In the morning Resu will once again look down upon a free and gallant Dythbeth!"

The king seemed about to speak, but suddenly his body jolted and fell forward into Kwasin's arms. Blood spurted from Roteka's mouth and down his regal beard, and a long spear stuck out from his back.

Kwasin lowered the king's body to the wall, looking for a sign of life, but the man was already dead.

He cursed. Squinting into the darkness, Kwasin scanned for any evidence that an enemy soldier might have somehow surmounted the wall unnoticed. Right now the defenders of Dythbeth had moved along the wall to the south, battling more of the ladder-climbing enemy. No other soldiers remained in the vicinity.

Then Kwasin saw something: a dark form moving among the shadows of the inner wall.

A burning bottle of oil hurled out of the night and exploded in flames along the wall top. For just a second, the fiery blaze illuminated the fleer, the only person who could have held a position to cast the spear into King Roteka's back—Taphiru, the high priest of Resu.

FOUR

K wasin had no time to pursue the treacherous priest. The enemy, climbing off the ladders, swarmed en mass onto the wall.

He rose from the king's lifeless form. Then, raising his ax before him, Kwasin charged in among the men of Dythbeth in their attempt to beat back the attackers.

The Dythbethans rallied around Kwasin, and the first wave of Minruth's troops to come over the wall fell beneath their fury. When Kwasin smote down four men with a single swoop of his ax and then heaved two of the enemy ladders—heavily laden with climbers—to the ground, the men looked to the giant as if a god stood among them in the flesh. At least for the moment, the attack on the walls had been repelled.

Then a shout of despair rang out in the night.

"Kho help us! The king is dead!"

A member of the king's guard had found Roteka's body. Kwasin wondered why Roteka's men had been absent when their king had needed them most. Of course, the guards might have been separated from him in the confusion of the Khokarsan assault, or else the king had ordered them to assist in repelling the attackers. But another thought made Kwasin's blood turn as frigid as the ice floes north of the Ringing Sea: the guard might have abandoned Roteka on purpose and been involved in a conspiracy to assassinate him.

The soldiers stood dumbstruck at the news—even Hahinqo, Roteka's general—and muted cries of anguish spread along the wall. Kwasin, fearing the men's discipline was on the verge of snapping, stepped forward and stood among the soldiers.

"Men of Dythbeth!" he shouted. "They have slain our king, whose dying wish was to protect the city and put an end to the foul stench that is Minruth's reign! Don't tarry over the king's broken and empty shell, but leave it where it lies and let the Goddess take care of his spirit! Now follow me and, Kho willing, together we shall wipe the followers of Resu from the land in the name of King Roteka!"

As if the men were a tuning fork and Kwasin's words the hammer that struck them, the Dythbethan troops bellowed forth a harsh cheer and surged about him. Ignoring General Hahinqo—who, red-faced, shouted at his men to come to order—Kwasin ran along the wall and then down the stairway that led between Dythbeth's inner and outer walls.

Already cries of "Kwasin! Kwasin!" filled the night as the soldiers charged behind him. When he had reached the bottom of the stairs, he found the city gate groaning open upon its enormous wooden hinges. Whoever was in charge of the gate had calculated that, rather than following the proper chain of command, it was better to let the giant and the men who followed him through. Either that or the commander in charge recognized that Kwasin and his mad band of followers might be the city's last hope and had ordered the gate to be opened.

In the end it did not matter. Whoever had let Kwasin and his men through had made the correct decision. Taken by surprise at the force and ferocity of the Dythbethan tide pouring from the gate, Minruth's troops fell into disarray. The fighting continued with its wearying cycle of advances and retreats well into the early hours of the morning, when at last the men of Khokarsa found they could no longer hold their ground against the fury-driven Dythbethans, who, enraged at the death of their king, fought with all the fierce spirit of Khukhaqo, the Leopard Goddess. The soldiers of the Sixth Army retreated across the plain, their losses heavy.

The army of Dythbeth, though victorious, had also lost many men. Those among the living who were not too exhausted to walk scoured the plain along the city's eastern wall, putting to death the lame and seriously wounded. Many women would be weeping for their lost lovers with the next coming of Resu over the great plain.

Kwasin, bone-tired and covered in sweat, grime, and blood, much of the latter his own, dragged himself from the field of battle. He had not forgotten Taphiru's treachery, but rather than report the man's crime to the army commander, he wanted to deal with the priest himself. Besides, if he reported the crime to the authorities, there would be an official inquiry, and in the meantime he feared mob justice might rob him of the personal vengeance he desired.

He approached the towering city gate, its bronze exterior streaked with flickerings of orange from the burning torches of the men outside. A sentry, looking nervous, stood before the huge doors, which had been cracked open to allow soldiers to reenter the city with their wounded and scavenged war loot. When Kwasin arrived at the gate, the sentry blocked his way and asked him to identify himself, though the man's face looked ashen with uncertainty.

In no mood to be challenged by the soldier after the grueling day and night of combat, Kwasin said, "If you don't know who I am, then you have no business guarding the gate." As he spoke, he grabbed the man's spear, yanked it roughly from his hands, and tossed it to the ground.

Suddenly a group of twelve men—looking too fresh to have engaged in the recent battle—ran out of the gate and surrounded Kwasin. Their polished bronze helmets gleamed under the torches, and they pointed cleanly oiled spearpoints at him. A wiry, tough-looking man of about forty led the group.

"Kwasin!" he said. "Exile of the empire, and violator of the holy Temple of Kho! By order of the queen of Dythbeth, I place you under arrest!"

Kwasin groaned. Then, wearily, he shook his head. "Fortunately for you I am too exhausted to argue," he said. "I will go with you peacefully. But I have urgent news for Queen Weth concerning the death of her husband. Before you imprison the man who led the charge that saved your worthless hides, grant me an audience with the queen."

He expected his request to be ignored, but the commander of the guard sighed in apparent relief and said, "You will see her now, but not because of any leniency on my part. The queen has ordered that you be brought to the palace immediately. Surrender your weapon and come with us."

Reluctantly, Kwasin complied. He groaned again, however, when he handed over the ax to one of the guardsmen, who seemed awed to hold the weapon, with its enormous head of exceptionally heavy iron. Or perhaps it was the legendary giant who awed the man. Right now Kwasin did not care.

When another guardsman moved forward to place chains on his wrists, Kwasin said, "You may try, little man, but I will wring your neck first, and then that of your commander, before anyone can stop me." Kwasin glowered at the blanching man, and the commander of the queen's guard pressed his lips tightly together as if weighing the words of the giant before him.

Then Kwasin shook with laughter. "Don't look so sickly, commander. I swear to you on my honor as a Bear man that I won't harm the queen and will do as she bids. We are all allies against Minruth, are we not?"

The commander, from whose belt dangled a bone-carven fetish of the Bear Totem, stood silent. Then, somewhat to Kwasin's surprise, he ordered his man to stand down. Totemic glue had proven stronger than royal decree.

Kwasin and his escort passed through the giant doorways of the outer wall, and a moment later through the gate of the older inner wall. The latter rose not quite as tall as its companion, white plaster covering its granite foundation. While the stone of the outer fortification was barefaced, sculpted effigies of various animals and deities decorated the tops of its turrets. These included leopards, serpents, trumpeting elephants, Lahhindar pulling back her divine bow, and Kho as the Goat-Headed

Mother, Her horns aimed menacingly at approachers to the city. Even though Dythbeth had for many hundreds of years sworn allegiance to the empire, the fierce and intimidating sculptures looming upon the city's walls bore witness to its long history of stubborn independence.

They followed the wide, stone-block road that curved round the massive military barracks on one side and a commercial and residential district on the other. The latter was made up of white plastered adobe buildings that stood two to four stories high, divided by a crisscross of narrow streets and back alleys, many of which hosted bazaars and markets in the daylight hours. Torches and oil lamps burned in both sections of the city; the army still had much post-battle work to do and the concerned citizens undoubtedly could not sleep through the night's excitement. Overall, three main double-fortified enclosures, each decreasing in size with its relative age, outlined Dythbeth. The section through which Kwasin and his guards passed, the newest and largest, was built to provide support for the Fifth Army, with homes and shops densely distributed throughout the enclosed area.

Soon they came to the towering bronze gate that led to the city's center. At seeing the queen's guard, the sentries ordered the great doors swung open, and Kwasin and the guardsmen passed inside. This sector housed the royal palace and governmental buildings, and was also home to the many temples dedicated to various goddesses and gods. On their right, the temple of Piqabes, the green-eyed daughter of Kho and goddess of the sea—one of the most important deities in this port city—jutted proudly into the sky, taller than any other building except the royal palace and the Temple of Kho. They passed the College of Awines, the native genius of Dythbeth who a thousand years before invented the syllabary that was used across the empire, as well as conceived for the first time algebra, the science of linguistics, knowledge of the circulation of blood, the invention of the catapult, wooden blocks for printing, the water clock, the magnifying glass, and a solar calendar, among many other inventions, theories, and formulations.

And there was the temple of Khukhaken, where Kwasin's mother, Wimake, had conceived him while serving as a divine prostitute. Beside a great marble-hewn statue of the Leopard God, a priestess stood counting the jewels of her rosary, offering prayers of thanks to the returning soldiers who passed wearily by. Kwasin leered at her. He had not had a woman since the priestess at Q"okwoqo, and though he had thought himself utterly fatigued, lust stirred in his loins. Upon seeing Kwasin, the woman stopped fingering her rosary and, glaring at him, muttered something beneath her breath. Recalling the reason for his long exile, Kwasin grimaced and looked away.

Kwasin's stomach growled as the aroma of stewed buffalo meat wafted his way from the hall of the Klakordeth, or Thunder Bear Totem. He had not eaten since early last morning, and that had been only a paltry meal of millet bread and *mowometh* berries, accompanied by one small spoonful of honey cultivated by the bee farmers of Qoqada, dished out to him by a stingy army cook. Hunger tempted him to ask the head of the guard if they could stop to eat an early breakfast with their totem brothers, but again Kwasin pushed desire from his mind and remained silent.

Leaving behind the temples, totem halls, colleges, taverns, and shops, they walked over the drawbridge that crossed the moat and led within the palace citadel. The dome-shaped palatial hall was ancient. Its original foundation was said to have been laid in the days when the hero Dythbeth settled the region. The building itself, however, had been built much later, when the science of architecture had advanced enough to allow for the lofty arches and the massive columns that supported the cavernous rotunda of the palace.

They climbed the palace's shallow marble steps, numbering one hundred and seventeen to honor the syllabary of Awines, and passed beyond the tall golden doorways and into a side room. Here buckets of warm, perfumed water were thrown over Kwasin to purify him and wash away the muck of sweat and battle. The palatial attendants allowed him to drink briefly from a tall cask of cool water, and though they offered him no food, he was provided with a new loincloth and a kilt of fine lion skin. From there his guards escorted him into an antechamber outside the grand rotunda, where he was forced to stand at attention in front of the royal doors for half an hour while waiting for the queen to beckon him. When, after that period, Kwasin asked that he be allowed to relieve his bladder, the attendant in charge refused. He changed his mind, however, when Kwasin threatened to empty himself on the queen's doors. Accompanied by six guardsmen, Kwasin was permitted to enter an adjoining room, a spacious and elaborately decorated lavatory meant for visiting dignitaries. He returned to the antechamber under the chief attendant's scornful eye just as the brass gong rang out to announce that the queen was ready to condescend to his presence.

The tall doors opened and a herald cried out, "Behold, priestess of Kho and of Her daughter, the moon, Queen Weth of the queendom of Dythbeth! Behold, Kwasin the Exiled!"

Kwasin smirked somewhat pridefully at his epithet and sauntered into the hall. Six guardsmen carrying bronze-tipped spears followed him on either side, their weapons angled toward him.

In his boyhood years in Dythbeth, and after his subsequent return as an adult following his almost eight-year stay with Phimeth, Kwasin rarely had occasion to visit the royal palace, and he had never been within the throne room's jewel-encrusted and gold-lined walls. Though not one to be impressed by such grand displays of opulence, the seven-foot-tall Kwasin found himself feeling diminutive beneath the chamber's immense, high-vaulted dome, whose colorful mosaic artwork illustrated exotic scenes of the Khokarsan and local pantheon.

If the great rotunda and lavish affluence of the palace did not quite take away Kwasin's breath, the sight of Queen Weth on her throne did. Indeed, he thought, the high priestess of Dythbeth shone with more dazzling brilliance than all of the diamonds, rubies, and emeralds embedded in the walls of her throne room. And again, though he had thought himself too tired, Kwasin grew hot with lust. Then the queen locked a frozen gaze upon him and he felt as if Kho Herself saw through to his soul.

Still, he could not help but take in Weth's shapely hips wrapped in their leopardess-skin kilt, the smooth bronze skin above a narrow girdle of jewel-encrusted golden rings, the full and large-nippled breasts, and her long, glossy black hair tied up in a Psyche knot. Though dark half-moons of fatigue hung beneath her bloodshot eyes, the woman seemed not to have aged at all in the intervening nine years since he had last seen her. In fact, she looked more beautiful than he remembered.

He stopped before the throne. General Hahinqo stood to the queen's left, eyeing Kwasin coolly; on the queen's right stood a stooping, prune-faced priestess. The king's chair, its platform slightly lower than the queen's and its decorations not quite as elaborate, remained empty.

Kwasin bowed his head and examined the mosaic-tiled floor, not out of respect for the queen, but so that she might not see the desire in his eyes. Normally he cared little how anyone, be it royalty or savage heathen, might perceive him, but he could not risk offending the priestess this time. Besides, her husband had just been killed, and even if Kwasin were fortunate enough to discover that time had softened Weth's ire at him, the queen's mood was certain to be black.

He was not wrong.

The queen rose from her throne, her eyes cold flames, and said, "How comes it that Kwasin, desecrator of Kho's temple, exiled by the oracular priestess to the hinterlands beyond the empire, dares to show his face in the queendom of Dythbeth and expects to live?"

Kwasin looked up and spoke in a rumbling voice made even more cavernous under the throne room's great dome.

"My wanderings in the Wild Lands have taken me to many wondrous and astonishing places," he said with his usual bombast, "and I have stood upon the shores of the Ringing Sea and witnessed the very edge of the world. But never have I seen a more welcoming sight than the proud homeland of my birth." He looked askance at the spearpoints aimed at him and smiled wryly. Then he bent to one knee before the queen and spread his arms wide as if in supplication. "Nor have I ever looked upon a woman as fair and virtuous as Kho's priestess at Dythbeth!"

"Rise, you honey-tongued fool!" Weth cried.

Kwasin felt cold bronze spear tips press against his shoulders. He got to his feet.

"You are a giant like out of myth," Weth said in a shrill voice. "But your mind is very small if you think your fawning compliments will erase your crimes against the Goddess. Do you think the queen does not watch over her city and know all the evil that you do here?" Then she looked to the herald and cried, "Bring in the priest!"

As the royal guards escorted Taphiru, high priest of Resu, into the chamber, Kwasin stood as still as one of the cold granite pillars that circled the hall. When Taphiru stood beside the queen, facing Kwasin with his narrowed, snake-gray eyes, Weth said, "Tell us what you have witnessed, vicar."

Taphiru played his part well. As he spoke, his face grew red and his hands shook with feigned outrage. "I saw the exile, the defiler of Kho's temple, slinking in the shadows along the outer wall. While the king fought gloriously against our enemy, this traitorous monster Kwasin crept up from behind, and before I could shout a warning, cast a spear into the back of King Roteka! He is the king's murderer!"

Gasps and murmurs came from the courtiers, and the queen's eyes flashed with fury.

"How do you speak now, Kwasin?" the queen asked. "With words dripping of sweetness?"

Silence settled across the hall. Then Kwasin's booming laughter shook the chamber.

"Yes, O Priestess, the king's murderer does stand before you," he said. "Indeed, while many brave men died defending Dythbeth against Minruth's blasphemous followers, this fork-tongued priest slithered into the shadows like a frightened snake." He looked to Hahinqo. "Any of the men who fought with me on the walls will testify to that. They cannot all have been bought with the coins of the priests."

Hahinqo's expression remained stony.

"Just what are you insinuating?" Weth asked, and Kwasin saw doubt cross her face.

"Why should I kill King Roteka, who promised to have you consult the oracle on my behalf?"

Weth looked to Hahinqo.

"It is true," the general said. "The king made such a promise."

"Kwasin is a necromancer!" the priest cried. "He has learned the dark ways of the outlanders during his exile. His enchanted words twisted the mind of the king!"

"And yet they do not twist mine," Weth said. A shrewd look came over her, and she addressed Kwasin.

"How would Taphiru benefit from the murder of my husband?"

"Perhaps he sees himself as king once Dythbeth's priests revolt, as the priests of the capital did under Minruth." Then he added, "Though I would certainly make a better king for her highness than this gutless priest."

Again the room filled with gasps, and Weth's long nails dug into the flesh of her palms. Then her hands relaxed and she summoned Hahinqo to ascend the royal platform, where the two whispered for close to a minute. When Hahinqo had resumed his position at the foot of the dais, the queen said, "After your terrible crimes, the oracle spared you, Kwasin, from the death you so rightly deserved, and instead she condemned you to exile. But even as she cast you from the empire, the oracle decreed that one day you would return, whether to be executed or forgiven she did not say. General Hahinqo tells me that the city would have fallen without your mad charge, and so, until I have time to consult with the oracular priestess, I am forced to interpret the oracle's words as meaning that the Goddess, in Her unending generosity, has forgiven your transgressions against Her . . . and against me. The oracle foresaw that Dythbeth would one day need your great strength—no matter the severity of your past crimes or the unbounded stupidity of your loutish behavior."

"This is not Kho's justice!" Taphiru howled. "I saw him murder the king!"

"Silence, priest! Do not interrupt me!"

Two of the queen's guard moved away from Kwasin and stood beside Taphiru. Kwasin could not hold back his amusement and he haw-hawed loudly.

"Restrain yourself, Kwasin," the queen said, "or I may change my mind about how to interpret the oracle's words." Weth stepped down from her throne to the empty chair of King Roteka and placed her hand upon its arm. Wetness filled her reddened eyes; then her face hardened.

"You speak of the just Kho, Taphiru, even while across the land your fellow priests betray the Goddess and conspire to place Resu above Her. Yes, Kho is certainly just . . . and so She will replace one exile with another."

The queen motioned to her guard. Taphiru shouted in protest as the men took him by either arm and dragged him across the chamber toward the great doors.

"I am a faithful servant of Kho!" the priest yelled as he fought to free himself from the grip of the men. "The wrath of Resu will be on your head if you do this!"

"Did I not tell you he was fork-tongued?" Kwasin said.

"Throw the priest outside the walls," Weth ordered her guards, "and let Minruth's troops do with him as they will." She turned to Hahinqo. "General, I've kept you long enough."

Hahinqo followed the men. The golden doors swung open and then closed. Taphiru's muted cries grew distant.

Weth ordered the men on either side of Kwasin to leave the chamber, then stepped down from King Roteka's chair and spoke low so that only Kwasin could hear.

"Years ago you almost cost me the queenship! But we were young, only eighteen, and we both know the truth of that night. Your mad lust frightened me! I should have known better than to let you into my chambers—I'd had my intelligence check you out, so I knew about your fits. But in the folly of youth, I thought you'd be different with me! So, yes, Kho is fair, as is Her priestess." Weth's eyes narrowed. "You, Kwasin, ravisher of priestesses, scourge of women everywhere, are about to be tamed."

Before Kwasin could speak, Weth turned from him and addressed the old woman who stood by the throne.

"Gather the priestesses and tell them to prepare for a wedding in the morning. And clean up this rank-smelling giant of the wilderness! We are at war and the people will need to respect their new king!"

Then the queen strode from the throne room with the old priestess shuffling behind, leaving Kwasin to stand alone in the hall, for once in his life utterly speechless.

FIVE

Preparations for the marriage of Kwasin and Queen Weth proceeded rapidly. Royal attendants ushered Kwasin to a luxurious sleeping quarters within the palace, with a large mahogany-framed bed piled high with soft, thick furs and fine linens. Kwasin felt he had just closed his eyes when a bronze gong sounded and three attendants lined up in the doorway to assist their soon-to-be king with his morning toilet.

Still exhausted from his long exertions and hurting from his many small wounds of battle, Kwasin threw off his coverings and raged against the men, who skittered off down the royal passageway, their faces pale and fear stricken. Though he returned to his bed and tried again to woo sleep, it would not come. His mind whirled with the events of the past few weeks, conjuring up visions of his escape from Minruth's prison, his confrontation with the treacherous priest, the murder of the king, and the astounding pardon of his crimes by the beautiful Weth. The faces of the men he had killed in battle also flittered before his mind's eye, as if their ghosts sought to avenge themselves upon him by depriving him of sleep. When he opened his eyes and once again saw the frightened attendants lining up in the doorway, Kwasin cursed and got out of bed, stretching with a yawning moan that almost sent his royal attendants fleeing for a second time.

The men led him through a series of passageways and down a

short flight of steps before they arrived at a spacious room with bright mosaics tiling the floor, walls, and ceiling, and a great pool of steaming water inlaid in its center. Kwasin took off his kilt and loincloth—which in his fatigue he had slept in—and climbed into the perfumed, salted, and almost scalding water. He hadn't taken a hot bath since the years before his exile, and the heat and minerals soothed his throbbing aches and sores. If this were a king's life, he thought, the annoyance of having royal attendants might be worth it after all.

His bliss did not last long. The chief attendant, bearing the determined yet hopeless look of a man committing suicide, strode up to the edge of the bath holding a large wooden bucket. "I do this by order of the queen!" he cried. Then he poured the bucket of ice-cold water over Kwasin's head, turned on his heel, and ran from the chamber. Again, Kwasin raged. He jumped out of the bath and ran after the man, but his feet, made slick from the bathwater, slipped out from under him and he landed hard on his rear. He roared with fury, but by the time he got to his feet, his anger had turned into howling laughter at the thought of the fleeing attendant's sick-faced expression. A moment later the man poked his head through the doorway, a hopeful half-smile on his face at the transformation of his lord's anger, then emerged fully and signaled the other two attendants to come dry off Kwasin with soft linen towels. Kwasin grabbed a towel from one of the men and brusquely ordered them away. Soon a fourth man appeared bearing a bowl of hot water and an iron razor. When the chief attendant dipped the razor into the water and made to shave off his lord's long, thick, and still-dripping beard, Kwasin grabbed the man's wrist.

"It must be done, your majesty-to-be," the man said. "It is the queen's decree. Her new king cannot look like a follower of Resu."

"King Roteka wore a beard," Kwasin said, "and yet the queen did not shear off his manhood."

"With all due respect, O King-in-Waiting, but you are not King Roteka, and . . ." The man hesitated, either too embarrassed or too frightened to go on.

Kwasin squeezed the man's wrist until he continued. ". . . and there are those within the palace and in the army who question your loyalties. You have been in exile for many years, and in that time your reputation has spread across the empire. Though your sentence has been suspended, the guilt of your crime still stands. The oracle is never wrong."

Kwasin cursed and let go the man's wrist. The doubt among the troops might be due to his sullied reputation. Then again, it could be that Taphiru's priests had spread lies about Kwasin to foster sedition among the ranks.

"Shave off my beard," Kwasin said finally, "but if you so much as nick me I'll cut out your tongue with that razor!"

Once the remains of his beard lay in wet clumps on the tiled floor, the men led him into another room where he found a doctor waiting who proceeded to rub healing ointments into his wounds and bandage them. Then the attendants fitted Kwasin with a loincloth, a kilt of fine lion skin, and calf-high antelope-skin moccasins, after which they escorted him to another room with a table on which sat a cask of water, a plate of sautéed termites mixed with assorted greens, and three large baskets filled with pomegranates, sweet *mowometh* berries, millet bread, and hard-boiled duck eggs. Kwasin devoured almost all of the food before yet another gong rang out. An attendant brought him some minty leaves to chew on and freshen his breath and then Kwasin was led down several more passageways and up a flight of steps.

They entered a waiting chamber outside the throne room. Here the attendants made him remove his clothing and three priestesses entered to chant prayers of ablution and to brush consecrated papyrus reeds against his naked skin. Two more priestesses entered, bearing earthenware pots containing ochre paint. With a stiff reed brush, one of the women painted the stylized symbol of the Thunder Bear Totem in yellow upon his chest, while the other decorated him in red with assorted geometrical designs. When they were done, another priestess instructed him that, unless prompted, he was not to speak during either the procession to the Temple of Kho or the wedding ceremony. Then she made him memorize his vows, which he did not understand because they were in the secret ritual language of the priestesses. When Kwasin asked what the words meant, he was told, "It is the vow all men must take who assume the queendom's highest station: 'I serve at the disposition of Kho. Death comes to all, even the greatest of kings.'" The woman ended Kwasin's instruction by showing him the particular manner in which he should kneel when ordered, on one knee with his forehead touching the ground and his arms extended palms upward.

A herald cried out to announce that Kwasin should enter the throne room. The doors swung open and Kwasin strode into the great high-domed chamber, where he stood waiting with his back to the empty throne. A moment later the herald called out again, this time to announce the queen's arrival. Weth entered from her private waiting room and stood beside Kwasin. She was naked except for a jewel-studded, golden-sheathed dagger belted around her waist by many interlocking gold rings, and a circlet of gold with a single large emerald in its center crowning her head and holding back her long and sleek dark hair. Black and green painted spirals of various sizes decorated her face and body, representing her sisterhood among the priestesses of Kho. Kwasin thought her stunning and smiled widely at her, but Weth met him with a stony expression and looked away.

With the blaring of bronze trumpets and the throoming of bull-roarers, the procession began. Followed by a long line of priestesses, priests, heralds, courtiers, and musicians—and surrounded on all sides by the queen's guard—they passed from the throne room into the spacious foyer, with its murals of the kings of Dythbeth acting out their many great deeds of heroism. Someday, Kwasin thought, he would be there among them. Then he recalled the ritual words the priestess had made him memorize, and his pride at being king faded. When it came time for his image to be painted upon the palace walls, he would most likely be dead, extinguished, a specter living his hollow afterlife in dread Sisisken's dark house. Once a year, if he were lucky, the people of Dythbeth would sacrifice a bull to him, as well as to the other fallen kings of the queendom, so that his spirit might quench its thirst on the beast's blood.

All the more reason to take from this life what one could, he thought, and as a king, he could take plenty. Beginning with Minruth's head.

They walked down the many shallow marble steps that led from the palace and turned north onto the temple road. Before long they passed through the looming bronze gates into the oldest, smallest, and holiest section of the city.

Spectators thronged along either side of the stone-block road. Some cheered their queen, but a general confusion seemed to mark the crowd. By now, the citizens of Dythbeth would be waking up to the news of King Roteka's death and of the exiled Kwasin's return. He heard a scattering of men throughout the crowd cheer out his name. These must have been soldiers who had accompanied him on his mad charge onto the great plain. No insults were volleyed at the infamous outcast—probably out of respect for the queen, and perhaps for fear of her heavily armed guard—but Kwasin could see many dark and doubtful looks cast his way as he passed.

They approached the Temple of Kho—the very building where Kwasin, drunk and full of lust, had wooed Weth and then killed the temple guards who had come upon hearing her scream. A well-tended and carefully landscaped garden of sculpted trees and shrubbery stretched along the slight rise that led to the temple's entrance. Here the road ended and a narrow stone path snaked ahead, flanked at its outset by two towering oaks. The building itself was round, dome-shaped, and constructed of great blocks of white, red-veined marble. The temple had been built close to fifteen hundred years ago in response to a rapid growth in population that had made it inconvenient for the multitude of worshipers to travel from the city to the original temple of Kho, which now languished in disrepair in the marshlands between the forks of the Karhokokly.

Kwasin and Weth entered the temple's nine-sided entrance, accompanied by the priestesses and the queen's guard, with the remainder of the procession expected to wait patiently outside until the newly married couple exited the temple. They passed through three rooms with alternating high and low ceilings before passing into the vast, oval-shaped, and most sacred temple chamber. Many colorful mosaic tiles were set into the floor of the large room, forming in their entirety a great spiral representing the chain of time since the creation of the world by Kho. Kwasin had seen such artwork upon the floors in other temples dedicated to the Great Mother, and as with those, a single tile remained unpainted where the spiral reached out to touch a great marble statue of Kho, looming with terrifying beauty in the chamber's center. What the blank tile meant, no one but the priestesses knew, but it disturbed Kwasin. Was Time itself destined to meet the same fate as every creature that had ever lived? Now he lamented that he had not asked Sahhindar, the god of Time, at their chance meeting.

A priestess, whose shapely figure and shining blonde hair made up for a nose that was a trifle too long and narrow, presided over the ceremony. Even as he prepared to say his vows to Weth, Kwasin knew he would not be able to resist this priestess were she to ask him to bed her. He also knew, however, that he must be careful. Though kings were permitted to take lovers, they did so at the grace of the queen. If Weth's cold look meant anything, she would extend little grace to her future husband.

The ceremony itself was simple. Kwasin and Weth stood before the presiding priestess, who announced herself as Nelahnes, chief keeper of the temple for the queen. While Nelahnes began uttering a long incantation in the ritual language of Kho's holy order, twelve other priestesses circled about them in a slow gait, carrying small bowls of burning incense. The priestesses stopped walking when Nelahnes bade Kwasin to kneel. He did as the priestess in the temple had instructed him earlier, touching his head to the floor with his arms extended before him, palms facing upward.

Then he heard the unmistakable sound of a knife drawn from its sheath, and a moment later felt the cold, sharp point of a blade press into the soft flesh on the nape of his neck. Kwasin tensed. Was the wedding but a ploy to lure him to this vulnerable position, so that Weth herself might have the pleasure of killing him? What if Weth had been lying when she said the oracle had yet to be consulted regarding his fate? The old and wizened Voice of Kho might have decreed that Kwasin, his exile ended, should be executed by the very woman whom he had wronged.

A long silence followed, with the blade's icy point still digging into the back of Kwasin's neck. Then he remembered the words he had been told to memorize—that death came to even the greatest of kings—and he spoke aloud the strange vow, acknowledging his subservience to Kho and the mortality of kings. Nelahnes spoke again in the ritual language and the knife lifted from his neck. The woman stepped forward and placed a golden crown upon his head. Cautiously, he rose.

Nelahnes uttered a final pronouncement, again in words he could not understand, and the ceremony was over. The priestesses escorted Kwasin and Weth to the temple's entrance, where a herald cried out, "Behold, priestess of Kho and of Her daughter, the moon, Queen Weth of Dythbeth! Behold, brother of the Klakordeth, son of Khukhaken, the Leopard God, King Kwasin of Dythbeth!"

The crowd waiting at the end of the temple path cheered and whistled, and again trumpets blared and bullroarers throomed. The dark faces he had seen earlier seemed to have disappeared.

The queen and her new king reveled before the crowd's adulations for only a moment before Weth took Kwasin by the hand and led him back into the temple.

At first he thought she might bring him into one of the many rooms off the entry chamber so they could consummate their marriage. Weth, however, pulled him aside and said, "I have not married you for love, Kwasin, but because the queendom needs you. King Roteka was much adored by all of our people but especially by the men in his military. His death has dealt a severe, possibly fatal, blow to their morale. But your deeds last night have brought hope to many, and the priestesses have already begun to spread rumors that your reappearance in our time of need has been foretold by Kho." Weth laughed darkly. "Your murderous reputation is being played up as well. The priestesses are spreading the story that you have vowed to make amends for your past crimes by defeating Minruth's armies. The people see you as a giant and unstoppable man-killer, and in a time of war, that is exactly the type of king they want to lead them. As do I."

"Is it true?" Kwasin asked. "Did the oracle foretell my coming at this time? And where is the oracular priestess? I did not see her during the ceremonies."

"For her own mysterious reasons, Wasemquth has taken up vigil in the old temple of Kho, and truth be told, not all of her prescience with regard to your doings is known even to me. But the story has its own truth. You have indeed appeared at a time fortuitous for Dythbeth and for yourself. Still, you must visit the oracle and receive her blessing if you are to remain king. General Hahinqo has already been informed that he must provide you safe passage."

Weth eyed Kwasin sharply for a moment, then continued. "But before beseeching the oracle, you must review the troops and assert your authority as their commander. Though you are a mighty warrior, your insubordinate action last night could just as well have failed, and I don't expect you know anything about how to lead men. But don't worry. Hahinqo is really the one in charge, and unless I command otherwise, you must from now on obey him in all things. Even now he waits for you at the barracks."

Kwasin's face grew hot with anger as the queen turned her back on him and made to leave. Then she stopped and again faced him.

"I will watch you closely, Kwasin," she said, "and if I see that reason has finally entered your apish mind, I may grant you small favors. But if you don't control your failings, know that there are consequences, even for kings. Remember well the blade I set upon your neck this day."

SIX

K wasin felt like tearing the temple apart, but instead he quelled his anger, accepted the adornments brought to him by a priestess—a leather kilt, a lacquered cuirass, and a bronze helmet trimmed with gold to replace his golden crown—and put them on. He found his own personal guard waiting for him outside the temple, but his black mood left him feeling only bothered by their presence. He longed to be alone, stalking the Wild Lands with no one to bother him—hunting on his own, fighting on his own, thinking on his own. And most importantly, free from the humiliating manipulations of his new wife and queen.

He shouted at the stunned guardsmen as he strode down the path from the temple. "Follow at my heels like yapping dogs for all I care, but keep out of my way! Remember what I did to the guards at this temple nine years ago!" He didn't look back, but he could hear the clap and scuffle of the guardsmen's feet on the stone path as they tried to keep up with his great strides.

Soon a tall, pale-faced man of about twenty-five appeared at Kwasin's side, his bright green eyes twinkling in the morning sun from beneath thick brows and mop of black hair. The gangly fellow wore a long white robe and carried under his arm a seven-stringed boxwood lyre. At six feet tall, the newcomer managed to keep pace with his giant king, though his pale face was quickly gaining color. Kwasin looked blackly at the man, who grinned back as if to taunt his king.

"Either you're a fool who wishes an early end to his life," Kwasin said, "or you're a drunken bard who will get the same."

"The latter," the man said in a singsong voice. "Though I'm not drunk. Hung over, maybe. And I mean to live a long life. The name's Bhako, and I've been assigned to you as royal bard."

Kwasin growled. "At least your name isn't Kebiwabes."

"You mean Hadon's bard? Of course, you do! You came back from the Wild Lands as a member of the same expedition."

"How do you know that?"

"It's my job," Bhako said. "You know, to ask around, learn of your noble deeds so that I might put them to verse. Is it true that in your adventures you encountered a tribe of barbarians, where you lingered long enough to know you had made all of its women heavy with child? And that this tribe, with the exception of some justifiably resentful husbands, worshiped you as a god?"

Despite his dark mood, Kwasin laughed. "Yes," he said, not altogether lying. "With women more fair than any in Khokarsa. I bedded them all. Their heathen priests said they would train my sons by their women to become great warriors, who will one day storm out of the west and lay waste to the empire in honor of their great father." Maybe someday his travels would indeed give birth to legends among the savages about the giant foreigner who came among them with his brassbound club, wooing their women and entertaining their men with tall tales of his divinity—but he wondered if any sons that might seek him out would want to kill him, not honor him.

"You don't seem intimidated, bard, to inconvenience your new king with your hot wind."

"Again, it's my job." Bhako was panting now. "And after hearing so many puffed-up songs of glory during my apprentice-ship in the bards' guild, I no longer believe in being intimidated. All men, even great ones, have flaws, and the greater the flaw, the more poignant the ballad I can write." When Kwasin looked at him through narrowed eyes and with nostrils flaring, Bhako added, "But I do respect your authority, O King."

Kwasin came to the end of the temple path, but just before he passed onto the wide, stone-block palace road, Bhako leaped ahead into the throngs who stood waiting for a glimpse of their new sovereign. "Make way!" he shouted. "King Kwasin comes!"

The sea of onlookers, oohing and aahing, scrambled to get out of the way, though many reached out so they might be blessed by the touch of their king. Kwasin pushed them away with the back of his hand like so many bothersome insects.

"Keep back from the king!" Bhako exclaimed. "He has matters of war on his mind and cannot be disturbed." Many in the swarming multitude, however, ignored the bard's words. Kwasin quickly became irritated, though he had an idea. In the meantime he ironed his will and shouldered his way through the fawning touchers.

Kwasin headed for the palace rather than following the road around the moat that would eventually lead to the military barracks. A few minutes later, after entering the palace and yelling at the guards there, he once again possessed his great ax. He left via the south palace road and made his way toward the barracks. This time, however, Bhako did not need to part the crowds; Kwasin did that by himself by rolling the imposing ax before him in wide arcs. The onlookers quickly got out of the way, though Kwasin heard several men shout his name in encouraging tones. As during the morning's procession, the cheers must have come from soldiers who had fought alongside him on the previous night.

With the king's guard still trailing behind like obedient dogs, Kwasin made his way to the southern section of the city. He proceeded east down a street that paralleled the wall until he arrived at the barracks to find General Hahinqo waiting outside.

The short, ruddy-faced man saluted his new king. Then he scowled and said, "As your chief of command, O King, I must recommend that your guardsmen be allowed to do their duty and protect you. The king's guard is the army's elite. If the troops see that their superiors are not respected, dissention will surely follow in the ranks."

"And I am your superior, General!" Kwasin said. "Do not forget that!" He had had enough of Weth controlling him and was not about to let this man do so as well.

Again Hahinqo saluted, his lips pressed together into two whitish lines.

"The queen controls the city's bureaucrats," Kwasin said, "but the king its military. And if you had the proper respect for your king, you'd know his guard is not the general's guard. Now report!"

General Hahinqo's face reddened, though his voice maintained a quiet dignity. "May we speak where the men cannot hear us?" he asked. Kwasin nodded for his guard to move off, then followed Hahinqo from the barracks and across the courtyard, where they walked along the city's inner wall. The bard followed behind at a discreet distance.

"The army is in a poor state," Hahinqo said. "Already we're faced with severe supply shortages—food, drink, weapons, good armor. In stemming off last night's siege, we lost many spears, javelins, and lead missiles. And the farmers from the countryside have come within the city walls for fear of Minruth's army, so we are sustaining ourselves on our stores. Perhaps equally important, many of the men are, despite your inspiring presence, severely distressed at King Roteka's death. And frankly, if I may say so— and I must, because if I didn't I'd make you a poor general— many in the army are distrustful of you as their king. According to my feelers, rumors have already begun to circulate that you are a worshiper of Resu. They say you intend to overthrow the queen and place Resu over Kho."

"I have always worshiped the Goddess! Did the men not see me mock the priest Taphiru?" Kwasin let out a deep sigh of frustration. He had no patience for politics. "What do you recommend, General?" he asked at last.

"I have already sent spies into the ranks to root out the rumor-mongers, who will then discreetly disappear. Further, Bhako here has spent the morning balladeering among the men about what you have told him of your amazing feats of heroism in the Western Lands."

"But I have told him nothing!" Kwasin stopped walking along the wall and turned to glare at the bard.

"We of the sacred order can tell much from a hero's mere presence," Bhako said, grinning. "You might say we read the syllabary of silence. Truth is for the Goddess and dread Sisisken to decide! The bard merely uses his skills to interpret for us mortals. But the blood of gods runs deep in your veins, O King, and your giant presence conveys that you are a man of great deeds! Were you not fathered in the temple of Khukhaken? And indeed, it is said you can trace your lineage back to Sahhindar himself!"

"Do not remind the men of the king's relation to the Archer God," Hahinqo said. "The priests of Resu have spread word that even now Sahhindar returns from his exile to ally himself with his brother, the sungod. Then he will chain up Kho until She acknowledges Resu as Her master." Hahinqo shuddered, as did the bard.

"Sahhindar has already returned," Kwasin said. "I saw him in the foothills near Khokarsa."

"What?" said Hahinqo.

"Though he did not carry his bow, and he seemed more monkey than god."

"Then how did you know it was Sahhindar?" the bard asked.

"He knew of the woman Lalila, the *moon of change*, and her companions, the same people who claimed to be under his protection. And of my ax as well."

Hahinqo's face became even graver than before. "Have you informed the priestesses? They must know immediately about this matter."

"I have been king for only minutes and just arrived in Dythbeth last night. It hardly seemed important, what with the fighting on the walls and King Roteka's death. Now on with your report!"

Hahinqo looked like he wanted to question Kwasin further about the matter, but the man took a deep breath and continued as they resumed their walk along the wall. "The Sixth Army is holding position two miles east on the great plain. They have set up camp there, though I don't expect them to hunker down for long. Word has come that Minruth's troops have abandoned the fort in the Saasamaro and are moving down the foothills. And though the armies of Minanlu still fight the Khokarsans, my intelligence reports that the situation there is worsening. If Minanlu falls, or if Minruth decides to pull his troops from there to reinforce those from Qoqada, we shall have a battle here at Dythbeth such as no one—goddess, god, or mortal—has ever heard tell."

"Let them come!" Kwasin cried. "That is a battle worth fighting!"

Hahinqo sighed wearily. "And that's not all. Two-thirds of Dythbeth's navy, along with the combined fleet of Asema, Minanlu, and Kaarquth, have been sunk in two pitched battles off the western coast of the island. The survivors of our fleet only escaped the second engagement by hightailing it into the bay, where our ships remain blockaded. Already rumors are spreading across the island that our entire fleet has been sunk. Admiral Poedy, who leads Minruth's navy, is said to be diverting more ships to the western coast, where he undoubtedly hopes to finish off our fleet. Admiral Nemusaketh wants to run the blockade, but he's doubtful of success. The last battle on the water expended much of the *s"okendon*[2] his navy needs to make its fire bombs and missiles."

Kwasin growled. "The men who fought at my side last night seemed high-spirited enough. Perhaps it is not the men who have a morale problem, but their general. Do you have any good news?"

"Intelligence from the other side of the island is spotty at best. By last report, the southeastern cities are in revolt. Minruth has stretched his forces thin. His obsession with building the Great Tower continues despite the war, and much treasure and manpower is yet being devoted to its completion. It is said that in the bowels of the tower he houses a great and terrifying serpent, a creature brought in from the hinterlands at such enormous expense

---

[2] The Khokarsan equivalent of Greek fire, invented by the native Dythbethan genius Awines by the year 11,118 B.C. (482 A.T.). Probably a liquid hydrocarbon used in conjunction with grease, oil, sulfur, and natural saltpeter. The breakdown of the Khokarsan word is -*s"o*- (referring to liquids, jellies, or gases in containers), -*ken*- (meaning *death*), and -*don*- (meaning *red*); in other words, "red death water."

it nearly caused one of the king's generals to turn against him. But Minruth is ruthless. He executed the general after accusing him of being a spy for the priestesses and replaced him with an ambitious underling. But even more cruel is Phoeken, Minruth's supreme general, though the man is a genius. In the initial revolt, Phoeken rounded up all of Saqaba's farmers and drove them before his troops toward the city. Though the number of Phoeken's troops was small, he managed to fool the Saqabans into thinking he had a great horde at his command and the city surrendered. Then, when Phoeken led the attack on Oliwa, he cunningly gathered together a number of monkeys, and after dousing them with—"

Kwasin stopped walking and looked threateningly at Hahinqo. "I said good news!"

The general, clearly uncomfortable at being berated by his king, combed back invisible hair from his bald pate. "Truthfully, there is not much, your highness." Then the man's expression of discomfort lessened, though not by much. "But a rumor—and I emphasize, this is only a rumor, it's not coming from my couriers— has recently arrived from the east that Queen Awineth, Kho's high vicar, is alive and fostering the resistance in the valley at Kloepeth, in the mountains north of Khowot. This would be good news indeed, but I have not been able to confirm it. Just in case it's true, however, I've sent a courier to Kloepeth with word of our situation here."

If the rumor was true, then Hadon had probably succeeded in escaping Minruth's soldiers and both he and the fair Lalila might still be alive. Kwasin cared little about Hadon's fate, but he smiled as he recalled the woman's exotically violet eyes and the attractive curve of her lithe form. What a consort she would make him! Then his exuberance faded as the implication of Hahinqo's words sank in. If Awineth's resistance managed to overthrow Minruth, Hadon—if he still lived—would be named king of kings. Kwasin, as king of Dythbeth, would be obligated to bow down to and serve his cousin. And that, he resolved, would never happen, even if he had to declare Dythbeth an independent city-state at odds with the empire.

Still glaring at Hahinqo, Kwasin said, "If this is the best you can offer me, General, then I will take it and do with it what you apparently cannot! Summon together the men, and separate from the ranks those who accompanied me on last night's charge. The latter men will be given ranking above all the others, including the officers, and the best among them will serve as my personal terror guard."

Hahinqo gasped. "But my king! That can't be done! The commissioned officers will be outraged, and who knows, they could desert and join the enemy. And besides, most of the lot that followed your charge was made up of the lowest of the low. They know nothing about how to lead men!"

"You will assemble the army, General," Kwasin growled.

Upon seeing Kwasin's face darken, Hahinqo said no more.

Within an hour, Kwasin, in the full regalia of war, stood outside the city's eastern gate before the assembled fighting men of Dythbeth. Numbering more than twenty thousand, row upon row of soldiers—spearmen, javelin throwers, slingers, and infantry—stretched thickly before the wall. The war drums boomed deep and heavy beneath Kho's blue bowl. Kwasin, standing fully a head above the tallest warrior, strode back and forth before the ranks, his great ax resting on his shoulder. The soldiers who had made up the previous night's mad charge to save the city stood front and center. Kwasin grinned terribly at them as he paced, and they in turn cried out the name of King Kwasin until almost all of the soldiers in the great horde before him joined in the fury-fevered chant.

"I am not like any king you have ever served!" Kwasin said to Hahinqo, who stood at attention before the ranks. "I shall be like the giant leopard that in ancient times ravaged this land and terrorized the people! And these men, the proud soldiers of Dythbeth, will be my death-bringing children!"

General Hahinqo said nothing, but he did not look pleased. Neither did the commissioned officers who now stood at a lower station behind the king's new elite. The officers looked confused and angry, but even more they looked frightened by the frenzied shouts of the men around them. Kwasin, by his mere presence, had stoked the wild flame of Dythbethan independence and set afire the men's fury. Kwasin doubted even the lies of Taphiru's priests would be enough to dampen the men's hearts. For a moment he feared that even he might be unable to control the raging mass of flesh before him.

As the drums boomed and the men thundered, Kwasin looked high upon Dythbeth's wall and saw something sparkle golden with the sun's reflected light. Even without being able to discern in the distance the identity of the person looking down at him, he instinctively knew it must be Queen Weth.

Kwasin lifted his ax on high, causing the men to thunder even louder. Then he lowered his weapon and again addressed Hahinqo.

"I have given the queen what she wants," Kwasin said over the tumult. "An army that will follow me to the ends of the earth. Now tell her to stay out of matters of war, or I will hand her your faithful head on a platter. You work for me now."

SEVEN

On the night before he was to visit the oracle, Kwasin dreamed of his dead mother. Wimake appeared floating before him in the black void, her face moon-pale, as it had been when she had given the ten-year-old Kwasin her last tear-filled smile. In her dying moments, Wimake had meant to reassure her son, to fix him with that loving gaze that only a mother can give, so that he should feel no guilt at his unintentional role in her death. In the dream vision, however, the eyes of Kwasin's ghost mother did not beam at him reassuringly, but rather penetrated his soul with a white-hot intensity that woke him from his sleep and left his heart galloping out of control. Kwasin sat up in his sweat-drenched bed coverings, gasping for breath that would not come.

Though the daylight hours remained distant, he rang the brass bell that summoned his chief attendant, who scurried in a few moments later, rubbing sleep from his swollen lids and reddened eyes. Kwasin had the man bring him a hare, a dagger, and a bowl. There, on the cold stone floor before his bed, he sacrificed the animal to his mother and drained its blood into the clay vessel. After the attendant had cleaned up the animal's remains and promised to have the bowl and its contents set upon the altar in the Temple of Kho, Kwasin returned to his bed of soft furs and linens. There he lay awake until Resu's red-orange glare regarded him through the tall and narrow arch of the room's window. Finally he fell asleep, only to be awakened an hour later by his chief attendant, who informed him that General Hahinqo waited outside with the men who were to escort the king to the old temple of Kho.

This time Kwasin did not mind being awakened. He tired of the dream visions that had haunted him since his return from the Wild Lands. Perhaps the oracle would tell him to what deity he needed to sacrifice and then the nocturnal apparitions would at last leave him in peace.

After a quick breakfast, Kwasin met Hahinqo at the foot of the palace steps. The escort—consisting of twelve of the king's terror guard, handpicked by Kwasin—stood at attention around a royal cart along with eight brawny bearers.

Kwasin swore and said, "I'm not a toothless old woman! I don't need my food chewed by another before I can swallow it, and I certainly won't be carried about as if I'm too feeble to walk!" He ordered the bearers to take away the cart and never to let it or them come within the king's sight again.

A moment later Bhako came scampering along the palace road. "Good morning, O King!" he exclaimed. "Your faithful servant is here with good cheer and song for your journey."

"I don't need a bard cluttering my thoughts before I see the oracle," Kwasin said.

"I am sorry, O King," said Bhako, "but I have orders to accompany you. I am to deliver the oracular priestess a message from Queen Weth herself."

"Why doesn't she send a priestess?"

"I don't know, my king, but you may ask the queen if you like. However, if you do, we'll have to wait until this afternoon to depart, as her highness is currently conducting special rites in the Temple of Kho that may not be interrupted."

Bhako looked smugly at his king, and Hahinqo bounced on his heels, clearly amused.

"So be it!" Kwasin said at last. "But the swamps around the temple are deep, and the chirping of the frogs and insects so loud that I'll hardly notice if my expedition's bard happens to sink into the mud and drown." Then, after one last glare at Hahinqo, Kwasin strode off with the bard and his terror guard down the royal road and toward the city's western gate.

The towering bronze doors swung open before them and they passed through the gate, turning north along the wharves, which—though bustling at this time of morning—seemed less busy than Kwasin could ever remember them having been. The strained, wearied expressions of the fishermen hauling their feeble catches along the road confirmed the report he had received from Hahinqo: the bay was being fished out. Now that the Sixth Army's expeditions had successfully raided the silos of the local farmers, the only new foodstuffs entering the city came out of the bay. The food shortage was only one of the many problems Kwasin needed to deal with immediately upon his return from visiting the oracle. If need be, he would garrison each farmhouse and its silos, though that would not replace the grains that had already been stolen or destroyed by the enemy.

Farther out in the bay he saw floating on the still waters the pitiful remnants of what had once been Dythbeth's shining navy. In the center of the bay rose Admiral Nemusaketh's tall galley, the last surviving trireme in the fleet. Around it some forty-five biremes, uniremes, and an assortment of smaller craft lay at anchor. Their sails were furled and their oars drawn up, waiting for their king to once again send them out into battle against King Minruth's much vaster and better supplied fleet. That fleet now choked the mouth of the bay, cutting off Dythbeth and her increasingly hungry citizens from any supplies that might be bartered or begged from the rebelling cities of the mainland coast. Admiral Nemusaketh desperately wanted to break the blockade, not out of any expectation that his ships could destroy Minruth's fleet but instead hoping to get a vessel through to Mukha, the mainland city whose fleet was rumored to have sunk the triremes of two of Minruth's best admirals. Like General Hahinqo, Nemusaketh badly wanted to foster an alliance with Mukha's King Qanaketh.

Before long, Kwasin and his escort came to the end of the

wharf road. Here he cursed and covered his nose at the stench carried to him from the barrels of excrement that lay in immense piles just north of the city wall. The barrels normally would have been transported out to the farms to be used as fertilizer, but even at this distance Kwasin could see the fields were empty of their workers.

Kwasin led his men up the dirt road that passed through the once-thriving residential farming district to the north. They walked by many white plastered adobe buildings, all of them deserted, until the silence began to wear on his nerves. After eight years of exile and excruciating loneliness, he had thought himself used to the absence of his kind. Now the forlorn desolation of the farmlands seemed to echo the hollowness that so often plagued him now, and his thoughts grew darker as they walked on.

Just as he began to think he could take the ghost houses no longer, the farmlands fell behind the party and the banks of the Karhokokly stretched before them. Here Kwasin smiled wickedly as he spied what the others did not: a dark form hiding in the shade of a large rock about half a mile upstream on the opposite bank. Kwasin ordered his men to lie low in the grasses while he took off his armor and helmet and set his ax behind the bole of a sprawling khaya tree. Then, alone, he crawled down the bank and slipped into the frigid ice-melt of the Saasamaro Mountains. The water here ran rough and fast, and swimming against the current was a difficult task even for Kwasin's powerful muscles. But Suhkwaneth, goddess of the scales, must have been with him, for the bad in this instance was equally weighed with the good. The rush of the water babbling over the river's many outcroppings served to cover the splashings caused by his efforts, so that the man on the bank remained oblivious when a heavily thewed arm reached out of the water to throttle him.

Before the man could scream, Kwasin clapped a giant hand over his victim's mouth and dragged him ashore. Then he shook the man like a dog does a caught rat.

"Are there any more of you? Answer me!" Kwasin removed his hand and the man shrieked in terror.

"Be quiet if you want to live!" Kwasin rapped his knuckles hard against his captive's brow. The man's eyes crossed for a moment and grew dull. Then Kwasin again shook his captive, until the man's eyes again widened with fright.

"I'm not your enemy!" the man pleaded between choked sobs. "Please leave me be!"

Kwasin scowled. "Your trappings reveal you're a sergeant in the Sixth Army."

"I'm a deserter! My name is Mimseth. I've had enough of war and wish to go back home to Wentisuh to see my wife and family. May Siwudawa poke out my eyes and eat my tongue if I am lying!"

Kwasin regarded the man's shield, which lay on the ground in the shadow of the great rock. It looked as if the man had used his knife to whittle away at the insignia on the face of the shield, perhaps in an effort to disguise the army division to which he was assigned. The man's voice did betray Siwudawan inflections and his reverence for the parrot-headed god seemed genuine.

Kwasin growled, and once again he shook the man. "You will go to Wentisuh!" he said. "But if I find out you have lied to me, I will kill you and then seek out your entire family. Go!" He lifted Mimseth to his feet and gave him a kick in the buttocks to set him on his way. The man ran off toward the northeast like a terrified hare.

Kwasin shook his head. He did not know why he had let the man go, and felt angry at himself that he had. For all he knew the fellow was a liar, a spy sent to reconnoiter the area, and he would return to the enemy to report the whereabouts of the king of Dythbeth. Though he did not really believe the man had lied, in war it was best to trust no one.

He signaled his men to retrieve his belongings and wade across the river. When the soldiers joined Kwasin on the other side, they asked him about the man and he told them it was but a frightened farmer. A squat, muscular sergeant named Rowaku looked at Kwasin askance but did not otherwise outwardly question his assertion. Still, Kwasin resolved to keep his eye on the man. He could not risk Rowaku spreading doubts among the men about the king's allegiances.

The sweltering sun dried Kwasin and his company as they marched northward through a region tangled with thick, prickly undergrowth. Soon, however, the ground grew soggy as they entered the marshlands that stretched between the forks of the Karhokokly. The clear and relatively clean water through which they waded quickly transformed into a thick, dark soup that carried the rank stench of stagnant water and rotting vegetation. Though the water was in many places only ankle- or knee-deep, the soft quaggy ground beneath the surface often fell off without warning and submerged the men to their necks in the foul-smelling morass.

As a youth, Kwasin had heard tales of Konabasi, a demon rumored to inhabit the area, who lurked beneath the waters waiting for a stray boar or foolish human to wander into the marshes and become lost. It was said the swamp demon would wrap his long and powerful tongue around the ankle of his prey and pull the man or beast down into the dark mud. There, beneath the lurching slime, he devoured the spirit of his victim, afterward leaving the living but soulless body to rise up and float for all eternity in the swampy waters. The men of the king's escort appeared to have heard the stories as well, but Kwasin mocked their fearful faces and jittery whisperings.

"Are the men of Dythbeth such cowards?" he asked. "I have visited hundreds of villages in my long exile and heard many spectacular folktales, none of them true on the surface. Your soul-eating swamp beast is merely an old wives' tale, concocted to keep children from becoming lost in the marshes."

The whisperings of the men ceased after Kwasin's chiding, but their faces remained fearful.

As they trudged on, Kwasin regretted he had not permitted the bearers to accompany the expedition so that he might rest in the dry comfort of the royal box while his men carried him through cold and stinking slop. In many places, however, the depth of the water made thoughts of such transport a mere fantasy. How the ancient, stoop-shouldered oracular priestess had traversed the marshlands that lay between Dythbeth and the old temple, Kwasin could not imagine. The interweaving trees and vegetation, and the long stretches where the water receded to slurping, ankle-deep mud, would have also made travel by boat impossible.

By midafternoon, the blue sky that had peeked between the gnarled branches of the dark trees disappeared behind a veil of gray clouds, causing the spirits of Kwasin and his men to fall even further into gloom. Suddenly a man cried out, splashing in panic as he attempted to make his way as quickly as possible through the waist-deep water and back the way they had come.

Kwasin grabbed the man as he passed.

"Speak, Komwi! What have you seen?"

"The living dead, my lord! Floating in the waters, just as the stories tell!" Komwi's voice quivered on the brink of hysteria. The other men, even the normally cheerful and fearless Bhako, also seemed ready to break for home.

"Run away, all of you!" Kwasin yelled. "But by nightfall you still will be only halfway home and will have to spend the night in the ghost-haunted swamp!"

He released Komwi. The man did not flee, though his face looked as ashen as the clouds above.

The men remained a good distance behind as Kwasin waded through the slimy waters to check out what had so unnerved the soldier. He returned to them a few moments later and said, "You have seen nothing but a waterlogged stump, Komwi, floating like a bloated fish below the surface."

Komwi sighed with relief but still looked somewhat uncertain.

Moving ahead, Kwasin made sure to steer clear of the area where Komwi had cried out, shouting scornfully that he would not have the other men imagining the rotting stump to be a monster or demon. Silently, however, Kwasin prayed to the Goddess that She might see them safely through the marsh and to the temple before nightfall. What he could not tell the men was that Komwi had seen no log in the depths. Indeed, it had looked like a man, floating beneath the surface, its ghastly face pruned and lifeless but with blackened skin that bore no sign of decay. Kwasin shivered as the clammy waters suddenly seemed even more frigid, and he tried to quicken his pace through the waters.

Just as daylight began to fade and Kwasin began to fear that he and his men would indeed have to spend the night in the seemingly endless swamp, a narrow and winding platform of compacted dirt and stone rose up out of the muck. With exclamations of relief, the men climbed to the top of the platform, which seemed to be a road, ancient and long abandoned. Perhaps once it had run all the way from the old temple and across the river to Dythbeth, when the great city had been nothing more than a fledgling village. Now the road's southern stretch had collapsed and been sucked into the swamp's dreary sludge, though the northern way wound through the trees and into the distance. Kwasin could not imagine why the ancients had placed the temple of Kho in the inhospitable wetlands, though he intended to ask the priestess when he arrived.

For more than a mile they followed the old road, which snaked its dizzying way through the marshes and maintained an even height about fifteen feet above the surface of the swamp. The sky dimmed and Kwasin could see little of the road ahead, though the land on either side looked drier and the trees not quite as dense. Then, almost immediately, the land angled sharply upward. Here the road ended and the trees disappeared completely. At the top of an immense hill, a temple appeared before them, its white marble dome glowing faintly in the moonlight that shone through the soft blanket of clouds.

The soldiers, cold and exhausted, ran up the hillside in an undisciplined mass, overwhelmed with joy to find at last Kho's welcoming sanctuary. With his rumbling voice, Kwasin yelled at the men to stop and form a line behind him. When they turned around and saw Kwasin's giant form standing in the moonlight, his ax raised threateningly above his head, the men quickly complied. Grumbling that he should have listened to Hahinqo and chosen other men for his guard, Kwasin climbed the hill. When he reached the top, he found a priestess standing in the temple's doorway.

"Priestess!" Kwasin said, and he laid down his ax and knelt before the woman to allay any fears she might have at his unexpected appearance. "I have traveled far to consult the oracle and ask her if—"

"The oracle already knows your questions, Kwasin of Dythbeth," the priestess said sharply, "and she is not pleased you have failed to heed your mother's ghost."

Kwasin's skin prickled like gooseflesh.

EIGHT

The priestess led Kwasin and his men into the temple. In a side room off the entry chamber blazed a great hearth before which the journeyers took off their foul-smelling and soaked clothing. A very young and strikingly beautiful priestess brought each of the men a linen towel. She stayed a safe distance away from Kwasin and set down his towel on a stool instead of handing it to him as she had done with the others. Though Kwasin smiled at her as she passed to exit the room, the woman shrank back from him, her dark eyes wide with horror. Kwasin shrugged. It seemed that everywhere he went, his reputation preceded him.

The chief priestess of the temple, whose name was Qenwath, returned bearing a large basket of fruit, which Kwasin and his companions ravenously devoured. A short while later the young woman whom Kwasin had frightened entered lugging a great pot of steaming stew. Though the contents of the pot smelled only of garlic and wild turnips and did not appear to contain any meat, Kwasin's mouth watered and his stomach growled loudly. As the young woman dished out the stew to him in a bowl much too shallow for his liking, Kwasin questioned the chief priestess about how she had managed to obtain such food in the inhospitable swamp.

Qenwath said that she and her young initiate, Awamethna, were the only inhabitants of the old temple besides the oracular priestess. Together they tended a small garden and fruit orchard in a clearing just north of the temple, which proved sufficient for their needs. They would not, however, be able to feed Kwasin and his men for any lengthy period, and the two women had only gathered such a large amount of fruit because the oracular priestess had warned them of Kwasin's coming.

Again Kwasin's skin crawled, as it had when upon his arrival the priestess had mentioned the oracle's awareness of his dream visions. Though old Wasemquth had spared Kwasin by exiling him when his crimes deemed that he should have been castrated and his body flung to the hogs, he still felt no love for her. While it was conceivable, though extremely improbable, that the oracle had received word of his coming from the network of priestesses, no earthy means existed for her knowledge of his mother's recent appearances in his dreams. The thought of the old crone, who knew things that no mortal should, unnerved him. The only thing that frightened him more was terrible Kho Herself.

Though famished, Kwasin suddenly realized he had allowed his bowl of stew to go cold. Dismissing his thoughts of the oracle, he downed the bowl's contents with his usual gusto and went back for seconds, thirds, and fourths. Still his enormous appetite left him hungering and he asked Awamethna for some more fruit. When she told him no more remained, he nearly threw his bowl against the wall. However, he stopped himself. He knew he must behave in the temple or the oracle might decide to renew his exile or commit him to an even worse fate. Forcing a smile, he proclaimed loudly that what he had eaten would do for now but that in the morning he would hunt down a deer, or at the very least a hare, and devour it raw—bones, hair, and all.

Qenwath regarded Kwasin coldly and sent the wide-eyed Awamethna away on some errand. Then the temple's priestess led him into a room that held a basin of hot water with which he could wash himself. When he was done, Qenwath came with his still damp but now clean kilt and told him to wait with the other men until the oracle summoned him.

Kwasin returned to the chamber, where he found his companions slumbering in their towels around the warmth of the great hearth. He kicked the bard, who had been sleeping with his arms wrapped around his instrument, the lyre having survived the wetness of the swamp within a waxed and airtight leather satchel Bhako had devised for their journey. Grumbling, the bard slid over to afford his king some room, and Kwasin, his back propped against the fire-warmed stone wall, quickly found himself nodding in sleep.

When the priestess awoke him, the fire had burned nearly to its embers. Groggily, he arose and reached for his ax.

"Leave your weapon behind," Qenwath said.

Kwasin nodded to indicate the Khokarsan denial. "Where I go, the ax goes," he said. "And besides, the voice of the Voice of Kho at Khokarsa commanded Queen Awineth herself to find the greatest hero in the land to retrieve the ax from the Wild Lands. I am that hero, and surely Dythbeth's oracular priestess will want to see my ax."

Qenwath frowned. "The Queen chose the hero Hadon, the winner of the Great Games, to bring back the ax, along with the three said to be under the protection of Sahhindar. The network of the priestesses tells me that it was Hadon who found the weapon you now hold."

"But it was I who brought back the ax," Kwasin said in a rumbling voice that roused the men sleeping at his feet. "My weakling cousin would never have succeeded in his quest if not for me, and I would be foolish to tell lies in the temple of the oracle, who sees and knows all."

Qenwath glared at him and said, "There is a reason, O King of Dythbeth, that you are known throughout the land as the ill-fated Kwasin. Now come. The oracle waits."

He followed the woman through two prayer rooms and into a vast, oval-shaped chamber with torches guttered high along the walls. Like its counterpart in the temple at Dythbeth, the same mosaic collage representing the chain of time since the creation of the world by Kho spiraled from the center of the chamber's floor.

Kneeling on the brightly tiled floor before an imposing marble-and-ivory statue of the Great Mother crouched a white-shrouded figure. The being before Kwasin seemed to be painting the single blank tile at the end of one of the mosaic's spiral arms.

Kwasin shivered. Though the figure's back was to him, it must be Wasemquth, the oracular priestess, and with a brush and paint she was completing the artwork on the tile that many said would one day illustrate the last great event in Khokarsan history. What could it mean? The tile had remained blank for centuries.

He tried to peer over and around the oracle, but could not quite manage to see the image she painted. Qenwath nudged him and whispered that they should take off their clothes. He did so, but he could not keep his eyes off the oracular priestess and her foreboding task.

"Priestess, we have come," Qenwath announced.

The old woman before them said nothing but continued on with her painting. About a minute later she rose and hobbled, stoop-shouldered, behind the base of the towering statue of Kho. Kwasin looked at the tile, and though it remained only half painted, he could see on it the image of what looked like the Great Tower of Kho and Resu at Khokarsa. He stepped forward for a better look, but Qenwath held out an arm and pushed him back. The oracle returned carrying a three-legged oaken stool, which she positioned in front of the area where previously she had knelt, thus again obscuring the newly painted tile from view.

"Leave us, Qenwath," the old woman said. "Warrior, leave your ax against the wall and come forward."

Qenwath looked as if she wanted to object, but after making sure that Kwasin had propped his ax against the wall, she left the chamber.

Kwasin stepped forward until he towered above the oracle on her stool.

"Kneel, warrior, so that I may look into your eyes."

Kwasin obeyed, and upon doing so noticed a narrow crevice in the tiled floor before the oracle's chair. From this hole rose thin wisps of bluish smoke, the aroma of which was heavy and sweet. The only time he had previously smelled its like was in the Temple of Kho at Dythbeth when old Wasemquth had sentenced him to exile.

The oracle smiled, revealing dark-stained teeth and several

gaps where those which had rotted had obviously been pulled. "The Voice of Kho would much rather reside in the temple at Dythbeth," the woman said, "but the quaking and shifting of the earth has extinguished the holy vapors there. Here the fires of Kho yet smolder, at least for now."

Kwasin said nothing, but it unsettled him that the oracle had answered the question he had been pondering. Wasemquth leaned forward and inhaled deeply the rising fumes. Her mysterious smile also unnerved him.

"Why, O Oracle, have I been permitted to speak with you directly?" Kwasin asked finally, for it was customary to have a priestess translate the oracle's holy utterances. Out of respect, Kwasin tried to speak in low tones but found that his deep voice resounded like rolling thunder within the cavernous chamber. A dizziness had seized him, however, so he was not sure—perhaps he only thundered in his own mind. His eyes had begun to tear from the smoke, and he felt queasy as the room seemed to contract to the size of a needle's eye and then expand into infinity.

When Wasemquth laughed it was with the sound of a gargantuan web being plucked by the legs of some monstrous and hideously insane spider. "You have long wondered," she said, "why Great Kho spared you from a sentence of death and instead sent you off into exile. I say to you, sometimes those who must accomplish great deeds need be forged in the fires of trial and denial. What have you denied yourself, warrior?" Again the woman made her hair-raising cackle, and Kwasin had no idea how to respond. Then the oracle continued.

"It is said by some that you are cursed with two souls. One that rages and is possessed by death's spirit and produces only sorrow and destruction. The other that rejoices with great humor and love of adventure."

Indeed, Hadon had volleyed such a taunt at him on more than one occasion, and Kwasin had always retorted by saying it was better to possess two souls than the half-soul with which Hadon had been born. His cousin's gibe, however, now took on an air of truth, coming as it did from the lips of the oracle. Had Hadon somehow actually caught a glimpse of his soul? Or souls?

"Is it true?" Kwasin whispered, fighting off a tremor of fear that sought to shake through his great frame. Cold sweat dripped from his forehead and onto his cheeks.

"Two souls may be forged together by fire," the oracle said, and now her eyes glazed as if the sacred trance had at last fully seized her. "Look up and know how a soul is divided!"

Kwasin lifted his gaze to the statue of Kho, whose blank marble eyes seemed to look down on him in judgment. Then something long and thick and dark moved beneath the crook of Kho's arm. He gasped and his heart raced as two tiny eyes glimmered redly in the torchlight. With a slow, malevolent grace, a cowled and thick-bodied serpent slithered from behind the statue and down its front.

"Do not move!" The oracle's shrill voice stopped Kwasin as he rose to back away from the snake. "Kneel or Kho will strike you dead! But do so slowly if you wish to live."

He almost found it impossible to obey. Though he held no fear of snakes beyond the usual caution, this serpent was different, for he had seen it many years before. But no, he thought, his eyes must deceive him—it could not be the same snake, but instead must be one of its kin. Still, fear constricted his throat and his heart hammered a chaotic rhythm against his ribs.

The oracle peered up at him with her watery, red-veined eyes as the snake glided along the floor and caressed her ankles. Kwasin resumed his kneeling position but readied himself to jump up at the slightest indication of the snake's interest in him.

"Ask yourself, O Black-Hearted One, why you have allowed this one to divide your soul." The old woman bent forward. The snake coiled itself around one of Wasemquth's spindly arms and slid into her lap like an obedient pet.

Kwasin found himself unable to speak. He had never told anyone the story of how one day, when ten years old, he had brought home a long, black serpent such as the one the oracle now held before him in her lap. On that long-gone day, the young Kwasin's plaything had shot into a hole in the wall of his mother's house, and almost as quickly as it had gone from sight, the snake had vanished from the boy's mind. Kwasin had left home to spend the remainder of the day stealing fruit from the local shopkeepers, and when he had returned, it was to inhale the delightful aroma of his mother's cooking drifting from the kitchen. A few moments later Kwasin's mother had screamed, and his blood had run cold as he recalled his escaped pet. He had run into the kitchen to find his mother prone on the floor, the snake coiled and ready to strike. He had grabbed a heavy mallet used to soften meat and with a single blow had crushed the serpent's head, immediately killing the creature, for even at that young age Kwasin's muscles had been immensely strong. But looking at his mother's face, he had seen he was too late. Already a paleness had seized her, and she had cradled her arm where the snake had struck. With a kitchen knife he had cut open her wound and sucked the venom from it as Pwamkhu had once taught him, but still his mother moaned softly and shivered, saying nothing. Kwasin, tears streaming down his cheeks, had confessed to his mother how he had let the snake into the house and that it was his fault the creature had struck her. Wimake had shushed her son and, too weak to speak, had looked at him with her kind, forgiving eyes and then passed quietly into dread Sisisken's shadowy domain.

Wasemquth grinned malevolently at Kwasin, stroking a hand along the snake's sleek, black body. As if drunk on Kho's sacred breath, the woman bobbed her head back and forth, and spittle ran down her chin in periodic gushes. Kwasin began to think the woman would never come out of her mind-numbing trance when, after a long period of silence, she looked to the far wall against which Kwasin's ax lay propped and said, "The serpent and the ax will be your undoing or your succor, and so shall it be for all the land."

The woman slid off her stool, and the snake that had been in her lap slithered down her leg and onto the floor. Old Wasemquth followed her familiar as it glided across the tiles. Then both woman and snake disappeared behind the base of the great statue.

Kwasin was about to rise and leave the chamber, which now seemed to spin dizzyingly, when the oracle returned bearing a large double-handled amphora made of fine black clay. The front side bore in somewhat crude bas-relief an image of what appeared to be Sahhindar, his bow pulled wide, launching a forbidden arrow into the side of a fleeing antelope. Wasemquth crawled onto her three-legged stool and passed the vase to Kwasin from her shaky grip.

"Drink, warrior!" Wasemquth hissed.

Kwasin lifted the vase to his lips and swallowed a mouthful of what tasted like mead or extremely sweet millet beer. When he pruned his face at the bitter, faintly charcoal aftertaste, the oracle motioned for him to down more of the liquid. After three additional mouthfuls he felt sick to his stomach and passed the amphora back to the woman.

Kwasin looked at her questioningly.

"I grow tired," she said, rising. "One day another may yet initiate you into these mysteries, but if that day comes and you dare forsake the Goddess, you will endure much suffering and pass even more to your descendants. Go now!" Then Wasemquth turned away from Kwasin and hobbled past the statue of Kho and into the darkness.

"Oracle!" Kwasin cried after her. "Our business is not complete! I must at least know if I am free to lead Dythbeth against her enemies. Has my exile indeed been ended?"

Wasemquth stopped in the shadows and turned. The light from the torches caught her eyes, which glared back at him demon-like.

"You are free to lead the city of Khukhaqo," she said, "but never shall your guilt be lifted. Never."

The oracle turned and disappeared around the base of the statue. A moment later Qenwath appeared at Kwasin's side. After Kwasin had risen and retrieved his clothing and ax, she led him from the chamber and asked him what he had learned of his fate.

"All is well!" Kwasin boomed with all the inflated ego he could feign. "I have been forgiven!"

Qenwath looked at him sidewise, but said nothing.

Beneath his stony exterior, Kwasin felt his two souls tremble.

NINE

For three days Kwasin lay ill in the old temple of Kho while Qenwath and her apprentice administered to him. No matter the great pile of blankets with which they covered him nor the roaring hearth that burned in the chamber where he slept, Kwasin shivered with a coldness that ached to the marrow. He told himself he must have picked up the sickness from the journey through the fetid swamp, but deep in his heart he feared the oracle's words had struck him down. Either that or the illness came from the queer liquid she had made him drink, which burned in his stomach long after he had consumed it.

One night Kwasin awoke and in his delirium thought he saw the oracle's terrible black serpent slithering along the chamber's high ceiling. He cried out for the temple priestess, but when she did not come, Kwasin swallowed his pride and summoned the bard to sit at his side and strum his lyre to drive away the nightmares. Bhako, happy to at last be of service to his habitually ungrateful king, took out his instrument and hummed a soft and tuneful ballad about the courtship of the priestess-heroine Lupoeth. Within minutes, Kwasin fell into a dreamless sleep.

That evening, Kwasin awoke to a terrible thirst and found himself hot and sweating out his fever. He finished off two great bowls of water and again fell asleep, only to awaken in the morning with a ravenous hunger and feeling surprisingly rejuvenated.

He devoured the food brought to him and announced that it was time for him and his party to return to Dythbeth.

At first Qenwath objected and said he should remain at the temple to rest for another day. Then she said, "Perhaps it is just as well. While you slept, your men have eaten so much fruit from our small orchard that I fear we won't be able to survive the season with what is left to us."

And so Kwasin, the bard, and the king's guard left behind the temple and its oracle—both of which Kwasin wanted very much to forget—and entered the dreary swamp on their way back to the city. This time, however, they proceeded with instructions from Qenwath to follow a secret path that wound through the wetlands to the north and thus avoid the swamp's deepest and most treacherous regions. When he learned of the route, Kwasin swore. He wondered if Queen Weth had known of the path all along but had withheld the information so that he and his men would be forced to wade almost directionless through the wretched and nearly impassible quagmire. It would be like the woman to torture him so, he thought.

In any case, his spirits lifted when he and his company managed to pass through the swamp without incident. By mid-afternoon, they emerged on eastern edge of the marshlands just south of the confluence of the Karhokokly and Beswakly rivers, thankful to see the dry and open plain before them. Here they waded across the Karhokokly and marched south along its eastern bank, stopping only to kill and feast upon an antelope that had been watering at the river.

Not long after they had again set out, a great cloud of black smoke arose from behind the river's curve. Fearing the worst, Kwasin ordered his men to quicken their pace while he jogged ahead.

Soon it became clear that Dythbeth's walls indeed lay under siege. He could see fiery spheres—tiny from this distance, though he knew the missiles to be the size of small boulders—fly up from behind the city walls, only to land on the great plain, where black and gray smoke billowed skyward. Since he saw no missiles catapulted in the direction of the city, he surmised that Dythbeth still held out.

Kwasin ran ahead of the others until he could at last make out the field of battle. He stopped for a moment and tried to take it in. A dark mass of soldiers swarmed across the great plain, surrounding the city's northern and eastern walls, and perhaps the southern as well, though he could not see it from his position. In the midst of the troops, harnessed oxen drew forward many large-wheeled catapults. Hahinqo had positioned his own troops in a great mass along the city walls, though their ranks looked feebly thin compared to the vast hordes of the Sixth Army. Indeed, Kwasin had never before seen such a staggeringly large gathering of men.

Bhako, panting heavily, jogged up to Kwasin's side. "Minruth's troops have been reinforced," he said. "Either Minanlu has been taken or our mad emperor has abandoned his efforts there and come after a prize more sweet. That is, your head."

"I must get through to the men," Kwasin said, gazing out at a vast phalanx of perhaps ten thousand enemy soldiers that stood between him and Hahinqo's troops.

"You are an imposing presence, O King," Bhako said, "but to rush madly into that fray would be suicide. It would be better if the king lived to fight another day. Queen Awineth is said to be leading a resistance in the eastern mountains. Perhaps if we joined with—"

"Flee if you wish, bard!" Kwasin growled. "I need no cowards at my side!"

And then Kwasin was off, running as fast as his long legs would carry him along the banks of the Karhokokly. If he could not cross the plain to rejoin his troops, then he would find another way.

When he neared the shallows where he and his men had forded the river on their journey to the old temple, he climbed a low rise and saw in the distance the rearguard of the Sixth Army's northern flank moving along the plain. Quickly, he ran back to the river and slid down its bank into the cold waters. He waded through the shallows for about a quarter mile before he noticed an old fisherman's boat abandoned on the bank. He pulled the craft into the river and boarded it. Soon the river deepened and he paddled with the strong current for half a mile until the river widened as it neared the opening of the Bay of Boqawenqady.

He fought against the strong urge to continue on into the bay to meet up with Dythbeth's navy. He did not know, however, if the fleet still lay at anchor in the bay or if Admiral Poedy, the commander of Minruth's navy, had staged an attack against the fleet to coincide with the Sixth Army's land assault. He might enter the bay only to find it occupied by Poedy's vessels.

He guided his craft toward the eastern bank, a steep ridge that traced the waterline and made it impossible for him to know what lay beyond it. In his previous scouting he had witnessed a flank of enemy troops not far from the area. He had no idea how he would pass through this thick contingent of Minruth's soldiers and enter the city, but from what he had seen, the enemy here was spread thinner than to the east. Perhaps chance would open a way—and if not chance, then his ax.

After fighting the river's current, which sought to carry him toward the mouth of the bay, he ran the boat up against the steeply angled eastern bank. Since no footing existed on which he could draw up the boat and anchor it, he hurled himself from the craft and dug his fingers deep into the weeds that grew on the nearly vertical incline. The weeds, however, were neither deep nor strong enough to support his great weight and that of the ax strapped on his back. Almost immediately, the roots ripped out of the soft dirt and Kwasin plunged into the river. Sputtering and cursing, he scrambled on hands and knees up the sloping and sludge-covered river bottom, which continued to slip out from under him the more he struggled. When he finally made it out of the water and managed to prop himself up in a semi-standing position hugging the bank, he saw out of the corner of an eye his boat drifting sluggishly downstream. He hoped it would not alert the Sixth Army to his presence.

He looked up. The top of the bank ended about a foot higher

than he could extend his hands. Carefully, so that he would not lose his balance and fall back into the river, he reached back and unbuckled the strap which fastened the ax to his back. As the ax slid free, he caught its haft, though the weapon's great weight nearly caused him to lose his footing. Slowly, he lifted the ax alongside his body and above his head. Then he tried to lodge the heel of the ax into the ridge above. Several times the ax cut through the soft dirt, which rained down in Kwasin's face. Blinded by the dirt, he continued to gouge the ridge to the left and right until at last the heel caught on a rock. He pulled down on the ax's bone haft to make sure the rock would not come free. Hoping it would hold his weight and that of the heavy weapon, Kwasin released the hand that he had dug into the weeds along the bank and, gripping with both hands, hung suspended from the haft. Trying not to groan too loudly, he used his mighty biceps to pull himself up. He hooked one elbow, then another, over the riverbank's rim, swung a leg up over the edge, and rolled onto solid and level ground.

As Kwasin stood up, something whizzed by his head and thudded in the grass ahead. He turned quickly and saw on the opposite side of the river five soldiers emerging from the swamp's wooded edge. Each man was whirling a sling parallel to his body in synchronized motion with his fellows.

The object that nearly hit him in the face had been a sling-stone.

Kwasin felt the blood drain from his limbs. Behind him stretched a broad field that offered no protection from the deadly projectiles, and the weeds along the riverbank were too thin to hide in. For a moment he considered setting off across the field to get as much distance as he could between himself and the slingers. Then he noticed something strange. More men, how many he could not say because of the denseness of the trees and overgrowth, hid in the forest behind the five visible slingers. He knew from his previous scouting upriver that the Sixth Army amassed openly in great numbers nearby. Why would these soldiers be hiding in the woods unless . . . unless they were not members of Minruth's army.

Kwasin dropped his ax to the ground and raised both hands over his head. The five men continued to whirl their slings. Kwasin began to fear he would be cut down without mercy when a plume-helmeted officer appeared on the forest's edge. The slingers put down their weapons and now gestured violently with their arms. Apparently they wanted Kwasin to get out of sight so he would not reveal their position to any enemy scouts that might be in the vicinity.

The only thing Kwasin could do to comply besides jumping into the river was to crouch low to the ground. He did this, but when the soldiers indicated he should cross the river to them, he nodded deeply to indicate "no." Again, the slingers began whirling their leather thongs.

Growling, Kwasin gestured profanely to the men, then began removing his heavy leather-and-bronze cuirass.

The slingers stopped their whirling and shouted to him to lay down his weapons.

Kwasin grimaced but did as they ordered. It pained him to leave behind the ax but there was nothing he could do. If he held onto it, the soldiers would use their slings on him. He stripped down to his loincloth, but at the last moment he decided to take his chances and leave on the antelope-hide belt that supported his short sword and its leather scabbard. Then he leaped into the cold waters of the Karhokokly.

When he pulled himself up on the opposite bank—thankfully of shallower slope than its companion—he found the soldiers had retreated back into the forest. Kwasin joined them there and stood before the fuming officer, surrounded by many soldiers in the shadows of the thick woods. Though the officer dressed in a common soldier's cuirass, the many feathers that fanned from his helmet indicated the rank of a high commander in the army. Like the other soldiers, he looked ragged and filthy.

"I am King Kwasin of Dythbeth. Who are you and do you bring aid to the servants of the Goddess?"

The officer scowled. "Kwasin? The madman who defiled a holy temple of Kho?"

"The same," Kwasin said. "And now king of Dythbeth."

The officer looked incredulous. "What of King Roteka?"

"He died fighting on the walls. Queen Weth is now my wife and I command the Fifth Army."

The man's eyes narrowed. "What brings the king of Dythbeth alone to the swamplands?"

Kwasin explained his journey to the oracle and that his companions were but a short distance to the east along the Karhokokly.

"Even if you truly are king," the officer replied after hearing Kwasin's story, "you're a fool. If the enemy has seen you, he's now on the alert. Were you stupid enough to think you could attack the enemy alone?"

Kwasin remained silent but his mood blackened.

"You haven't yet explained who you are," Kwasin said finally, "though by your ill-kept appearance I'd guess you might be from Mukha. All the women I encountered from there while on my way to the Western Lands were as ugly and foul-smelling as the Klemqaba."

A number of soldiers stepped forward out of the shadows, hands on the hilts of their swords. The officer, however, reined in his men with an irritated look.

"I am Wahesa of Mukha," the officer said, "high general of King Qanaketh's army. But I suspect you know that. You're not as thick-headed as your reputation allows, though you're certainly as boorish. But I have no time to waste on your hot air. My army has landed on the western shore of the island, just south of the Saasamaro. From there we marched overland to the Beswakly River and crossed into the swamplands, traveling east along the bay. At a much slower rate than I had hoped, I might add. My scouts have informed me about the present attack on Dythbeth. Have you any news on that front?"

Kwasin told Wahesa what he had seen of the enemy positions and the defensive catapult volley by the citizens of Dythbeth. "I don't believe the walls have been breached," he said. "And though the Dythbethan line is weak compared to the numbers opposing it, each of my men is worth at least two or three of these Khokarsan amateurs."

The general wiped a hand across his dirty forehead, looking tired. "Then perhaps we aren't needed here," he said, "and I should turn my troops around."

Kwasin was about to reply when the soldiers standing on his right stirred. They parted and a number of Mukhan soldiers came from the rear, herding ahead of them Bhako and the rest of the expedition that had escorted Kwasin to the old temple of Kho. Bhako smiled widely when he saw his king, but the smile did not last. He held up the leather satchel which held his instrument and exclaimed, "The heavy-handed louts broke my lyre! Now how am I to chronicle the great doings of my king?"

Ignoring the bard and turning back to Wahesa, Kwasin said, "What's your plan, General? We may have begun our acquaintance on the bad foot of Suhkwaneth, but let me assure you I welcome your help against the enemies of Kho."

While Kwasin spoke, a woman came out of the trees and stood next to Wahesa. She resembled in dress and physical type the tribespeople Kwasin had encountered in the Western Lands. About her neck, arms, and ankles she wore many circlets of gold and ivory. A long and richly colored sash wrapped around her waist and upper torso in place of the kilt customarily worn by Khokarsan women, but her black hair was drawn in a Psyche knot like that of a priestess of Kho. She was the tallest woman Kwasin had ever seen. Taller, in fact, than Wahesa, who himself was only an inch shorter than Hadon, one of the tallest men in the empire, Kwasin himself being the tallest. The woman's chestnut eyes held fast on Kwasin as she whispered something in Wahesa's ear. Wahesa in turn whispered back to her.

Kwasin felt lust stir up inside him as he drank in the woman's exotic beauty, but he forced himself to look away. She and Wahesa were obviously lovers. Not that this would have stopped Kwasin from making advances on the woman under normal circumstances. But he needed Wahesa's help, if not his respect, in opposing Minruth's vastly larger forces. He could not let his longings put the delicate alliance between Mukha and Dythbeth in jeopardy.

"While you whisper sweet words to your lover," Kwasin said, yawning, "I am going to fetch my ax." But when he made to leave, the soldiers closed in around him.

Kwasin reached for his short sword and had already drawn it halfway from its sheath when the woman said in a heavy accent, "You may be Dythbeth's king as you claim, but you will obey my husband for now if you want his help."

Grimacing, Kwasin slid his sword back into its bronze scabbard. The general motioned his soldiers to stand down and ordered a private to retrieve Kwasin's ax from the opposite side of the river.

"Daka is also the expedition's priestess," Wahesa said. "While you travel with us, you would do well to obey her orders as well as mine."

Kwasin raised an eyebrow but said nothing. It was not uncommon for a commander to become involved with his priestess. Still, while a priestess outranked her male counterparts in every area of government except those that dealt with the army, the navy, and engineering matters, she had no place giving orders in a military context. He wondered what unusual pull Daka had upon her husband.

Suddenly a courier, puffing, his face drenched with sweat, elbowed his way forward through the soldiers surrounding them. He saluted his general, then stood aside. When Wahesa told him to report, the man said, "Captain Gawethmi asks that you come at once. A large contingent of Phoeken's troops is on the march just south of the river."

Wahesa grinned, then cast a measured look at Kwasin. "Time to see if the legends about you are true."

TEN

As the Mukhan army resumed its march along the edge of the swamp, Kwasin questioned General Wahesa further about the strategy of his campaign. What he learned both encouraged and disgusted him.

Wahesa told him that just before war broke out across the empire, Minruth had harbored a large contingent of troops at the port of Mukha. When Minruth launched his revolution in Khokarsa, his forces at Mukha struck like lightning and seized the royal palace. King Qanaketh and all his family found themselves under house arrest before they could even mount a resistance.

Unwilling to see his family slaughtered, Qanaketh announced his allegiance to Minruth and offered his assistance in the revolt. Secretly, however, Qanaketh sent word to General Wahesa, who had been abroad negotiating a treaty with tribes in the west. Afraid a direct attack on Mukha would precipitate the execution of the royal family, the king ordered Wahesa to announce he had gone renegade while Qanaketh himself feigned outrage. Instead of bringing his troops to Mukha, Wahesa was to take them to Towina, which still remained faithful to the Goddess.

Or at least it did at the time, Wahesa said. Now he was unsure. His last report informed him that the priests of Towina had begun to challenge the high priestess there with accusations of scandal, which was surely a precursor to all-out rebellion. Such outbreaks were flaring up in all the queendoms of the empire.

In any case, following King Qanaketh's secret orders, Wahesa was to regroup his forces in Towina and launch an attack on the island of Khokarsa herself. News had arrived of King Roteka's valiant fight against Minruth and that Dythbeth was being eyed as a possible last stand for the forces loyal to the Goddess on the island. Wahesa and his men were to go there and aid Dythbeth in its fight to extinguish the ambitions of the priests.

Like any good soldier, Wahesa had obeyed, though he admitted his shame at his king's seemingly two-faced actions. Still, Wahesa was a realist. He knew politics guided all wars and his king had acted only for the good of his people.

"And his own self-serving head," Kwasin said with disgust. "Kho will not forgive his blasphemy."

Wahesa looked at Kwasin keenly and said, "The snake who speaks ill of another risks knotting his own forked tongue."

Kwasin felt hot blood rush to his face. He would not suffer any more of the man's insults, alliances be damned! With murderous thoughts on his mind, Kwasin moved toward Wahesa, but suddenly he found himself tripping over Bhako, who had been fiddling with his damaged instrument as the group trudged through the swamp.

"Get out of my way, bard!" Kwasin shouted, and with a shove he sent Bhako flying. Then Kwasin stopped and watched the bard pull himself up from the stinking sludgewater.

"Forgive me, O King," Bhako said, picking up his now thoroughly soaked lyre. "I didn't see you, so absorbed was I in my own troubles."

Kwasin considered knocking down the bard again, but then it dawned on him that Bhako's clumsiness had seemed all too calculated. Perhaps the bard was not the fool he appeared. In any case, though still somewhat rankled, Kwasin found his welling anger had subsided. The general for his part seemed to act as if nothing had transpired between them. Kwasin breathed a prayer of thanks to Kho. He had come within a hair's breadth of attacking the commander of Dythbeth's only ally. He would have to be more careful in the future.

When the travelers came to a place where the river narrowed, the general ordered his troops to halt. He whispered instructions to his lieutenant, a man named Kaminsuh, who took off into the swamp. A short while later, men came forward out of the woods carrying many wide, flat-bottomed boats. Using heavy ropes, the men connected the boats together sidewise on the rocky riverbank and, drawing the craft into the river, tied them to some trees growing near the water's edge. Meanwhile, other men waded out into the cold waters and climbed onto the opposite bank, where they secured the other end of the chain of boats to a pair of sturdy oaks. Next, the men went back into the forest and emerged lugging long and narrow cedar beams, which were placed lengthwise across the river and then bound together with rope. In this way Wahesa's men had in a very short time constructed a crude but nonetheless effective pontoon bridge. Within minutes, soldiers were crossing the river and assembling in formation on the opposite side.

"Now you know why it took us so long to cross the swamp," Wahesa said, standing before the rapidly growing contingent on the southern bank of the Karhokokly.

Recalling his own difficult journey through the swamp to the oracle, Kwasin said nothing, but quietly he marveled at both the stamina and organizational efficiency of Wahesa's army. The Mukhans would make great allies indeed.

The stream of soldiers, appearing to have no end, continued to march out of the boggy wood and across the pontoon. When a substantial grouping had assembled on the riverbank, Lieutenant Kaminsuh ordered his men forward in battle formation while the new arrivals took up position behind. At the moment a grouping of low hills prevented a direct view of the plain, thus obscuring the actions of the Mukhan army from Phoeken's hordes. Still, Kwasin wondered if enemy scouts along the river might have already reported to their commanders the location and actions of the Mukhan troops. He did not relish the thought that Phoeken would be waiting for them.

Captain Gawethmi, however, arrived to report that Phoeken's

troops seemed, at least for the moment, oblivious to the Mukhans' presence. Though Wahesa had not yet heard from the courier he had sent to Dythbeth to coordinate a joint attack, the news prompted him to act quickly. He ordered Kwasin to take charge of an advance battalion that would strike Phoeken's regiment head-on from the north. Meanwhile, Wahesa and Kaminsuh were to circle ahead with their own men and attack Phoeken's eastern and western flanks. "I can't rely on the hope that my courier got through to General Hahinqo," Wahesa told Kwasin. "I need you to cause as much hell as possible so that Phoeken will be unable to organize his men against the flank attacks. Do you understand?"

Kwasin unslung the ax from the harness on his back and grinned widely. "You don't need to worry, General." He caressed the ax's handle. "Causing hell is my specialty."

At Wahesa's command, Kwasin went to his men. Here he found Gawethmi waiting. The man was to serve as Kwasin's second-in-command.

The captain issued instructions to his troops while Kwasin donned his war gear. This consisted of a conical bronze helmet with neck and nose guards and a heavy leather apron to protect his genitals and upper legs. Kwasin almost refused the leather leggings brought to him by a sergeant, as he did not wish to be encumbered in battle by the hot and stiff coverings, but in the end he relented. He had seen too many one-legged soldiers begging in the streets of Dythbeth. Kwasin already wore a leather cuirass affixed with a bronze breastplate molded roughly into the shape of a leopard's head, and a leather kilt to further shield his groin and legs. In addition to the ax he carried in his hands, a short, though heavy, iron sword and an iron dagger hung in scabbards attached to a thick belt that circled his waist. A round brassbound wooden shield completed his armament.

Now fully clad for battle, Kwasin took the lead as Gawethmi sent the wedge-shaped formation marching forward up the wide hill that stretched along the river. When they neared the top, Gawethmi ordered the men to stand just below the hilltop and remain quiet. Together, Kwasin and Gawethmi lay on their bellies at the top of the hill and looked out across the plain. About a mile to the south an enormous dark mass was moving westward. Kwasin nearly cried out in surprise as a large group of men emerged from behind a knoll and passed directly before them less than fifty feet away at the bottom of the hill.

In long rows of twenty men abreast, the soldiers marched west along the uneven hills that skirted the Karhokokly. Near the front of the marchers, the party's commanding officers filed ahead. One man stood out from the rest, though the warriors who walked on either side of him were extraordinary in their own right. The man was obviously the commander of the group. While his leather cuirass and kilt looked battle worn, a fine gold-hilted *tenu* hung from his belt, and a fan of fish-eagle feathers sprouted from the top of the man's bronze, gold-inlaid helmet, which gleamed brilliantly in the harsh glare of the Khokarsan sun. Though Kwasin had never before seen the man, he knew it must be General Phoeken himself.

Kwasin also recognized two of the large men who strode alongside the general, though he had not seen them before either. Still, their faces gave them away, as they were identical except for a gouged cheek that marred the features of one of the men. It could only be the hero-twins Bhaqeth and Klaqeth. Klaqeth would be the one with the disfigured face, a token from his most renowned exploit.

At the time of Kwasin's exile, the fame of the twins was spreading throughout the empire like a wildfire across the savannas. The two claimed to have entered a valley to the east of Sakawuru where they had battled and slain a creature they called a *ko'bok'ul"ikadeth*, a giant three-horned, armor-cowled rhinoceros with skin as thick as iron and a temper as black as a starless and moonless night. Though the brothers brought back with them three enormous tusks to prove their claim, an expedition sent back to the valley by Minruth had found no trace of the daunting creature. Many began to question the brothers' account, but popular belief still held up their reputation as heroic monster-killers.

Kwasin did not doubt the twins' story. Stranger beasts stalked the shadowy jungles around the two great inland seas. After all, he himself had once heard the terrifying cry of the *r"ok'og'a* while camping with his uncle along the shores of the southern sea—a hair-raising shriek that haunted him to this day. And if the dragon of the Kemus was real, why not an oversized, armor-plated, three-horned rhinoceros?

He eyed the hero-twins and the three other hulking warriors who surrounded Phoeken. Surely the tattooed one with the earring and the hook-ended broadsword was the hero Miwanes of Sakawuru. And the large, dark-skinned brute with the claw-raked face must be Toesem, the lion fighter of Towina. The third would be Kadyth the Silent, recognizable by the bright red scar across his larynx where a barbarian king had cut him before dying under Kadyth's ax. Minruth's greatest warriors—heroes all. And though none met Kwasin in terms of brawn or towering height, any one of them would have made a fearsome opponent; together, they might best a small army.

A bronze helmet, a cuirass affixed with a bronze breastplate, and a heavy leather kilt and leggings adorned each of the heroes. Each man except Kadyth, armed only with his ax, wore a *tenu*. Kwasin wondered if the warriors truly belonged to the brotherhood of swordsmen or if Minruth, following his mad reformations, had so adorned his champions in defiance of tradition.

"My scouts did not reveal this party, O King," Gawethmi whispered. "They must have been hiding in the hills when—"

But Kwasin did not want to hear the man's excuses, nor did he want to let the valuable target slip by while Gawethmi took the time to signal his men. Further, he feared that the Mukhans would make too much noise as they charged up and over the hill, thus alerting the enemy and allowing Phoeken to escape. He would just have to trust that the Mukhans would follow his lead. If they did not, what he did next would be an act of suicide.

Kwasin left the still-speaking Gawethmi and barreled down the hill alone toward General Phoeken.

At the bottom of the hill, Kwasin leaped among the spearmen

who marched along the party's flank. He let loose his wild energy, which had been pent up since his recovery from the illness that afflicted him in the temple. His ax swung out and cleaved clean through the bronze helmets of two marchers. The men fell, their skulls gashed open, before they even knew an enemy was upon them.

Kwasin surged through the men toward his goal, his swinging ax clearing an opening before him as the startled soldiers retreated from his fury. Behind him, he heard a mighty uproar. The Mukhans had not abandoned him. They were charging as one down the hillside.

The tall form of the hero-twin Klaqeth appeared out of the confusion of men. Kwasin swung at him but the man parried with a spear he had grabbed out of the hands of a soldier. The spear shaft splintered like a dried twig. Klaqeth hurled himself backward, landing hard on his buttocks but unharmed by Kwasin's ax.

Not for long. Kwasin raised his weapon above the man, who unsuccessfully tried to dig his heels in the soft and yielding dirt in a frantic attempt to stand up. Then Kwasin lost his own balance as the force of many bodies hurled into him from behind. The weight of the falling ax carried him forward and he landed chest-first on the ground, air heaving from his great lungs. He had somehow missed Klaqeth, who had mysteriously disappeared.

Feeling both helpless and foolish—like a mighty but doomed elephant he once saw downed by barbarians during his exile—Kwasin rolled onto his side as many feet trampled or jumped over him. Then, noticing he had still somehow managed to hold on to the ax, he yelled at the stampeding men to get out of his way and cut his weapon at their legs. They were his own men, but their trampling would kill him if he did not act.

The charging men made clear. Kwasin got to his feet, groaning at the pain in his ribs from injuries yet unhealed from his previous battles. Before him, not fifteen feet away, stood Captain Gawethmi. His shield and helmet lay next to him on the ground and the man cradled the bloody stump of his right arm beneath an armpit.

Towering behind Gawethmi, whose face shone as pale as the moon's, stood the hero-twin Klaqeth.

Kwasin shouted and ran forward, but too late. Klaqeth drove his sword through the back of Gawethmi's neck, withdrew the blade, then leaped over the collapsing body and advanced on Kwasin.

By the grace of the Goddess, Kwasin looked over his shoulder in time to see Bhaqeth running at him from the rear. Kwasin crouched low and swung his ax at the advancing man, who fell back to escape the blow that would have cut him down at the knees. Kwasin allowed the weight of the ax to spin him back around at Klaqeth. Klaqeth jumped back. Kwasin, completing his rotation, found himself again confronting the other brother. The men were like hyenas, Kwasin thought, one retreating while the other advanced in a cowardly but deadly cycle. Doubtless they had slain the fearsome *ko'bok'ul"ikadeth* in the same manner.

A terrible din assaulted Kwasin's ears and all about him a tangle of soldiers surged forward. Then he was being pushed along by his own troops. Klaqeth and Bhaqeth were forced to run with him to escape from being trampled to death by the advancing Mukhan line. He no longer saw Miwanes, Toesem, or Kadyth. Perhaps they had retreated to protect Phoeken.

A cacophonous mix of shrill and throaty screams, accompanied by a heavy thudding and the sharp cracking and splintering of wood, filled Kwasin's ears. Soldiers ahead of Kwasin slammed into one another, thrusting spears and hacking swords against their enemies' shields. The splintering sound was that of many spears breaking, and doubtless many bones. The odor of blood, urine, and excrement caught on the hot wind.

The forward momentum stopped. He heard a whistling and looked up to see a blur of lead missiles crisscrossing overhead. Both forces had unleashed their slingers, though the predominant number belonged to the Mukhans. So far Phoeken's men had been unsuccessful in their attempt to regroup after the initial assault. Now they would have a harder time as the Mukhan javelin throwers momentarily darkened the bright sky with their weapons.

Kwasin had little time to take it in. Now that the troops' forward motion had stopped, Bhaqeth was fighting through the men toward Kwasin. He turned and saw Klaqeth doing the same.

Shoving his own soldiers out of the way, Kwasin ran forward and took on Klaqeth. Kwasin slid the ax's thong from around his wrist and, with a mighty heave, launched the ax at the man. Letting go of the ax in the midst of battle carried much risk, as he might never recover it. But he could not hope to defeat the brothers by playing it safe.

The ax smacked hard against Klaqeth's shield and tore it from the man's grasp. Kwasin drew a dagger from his belt, swung it back behind an ear, and flung it at Klaqeth. The man raised his *tenu* and threw himself to one side in a reflexive attempt to escape Kwasin's throw.

Too late. The dagger plunged through Klaqeth's scarred cheek and impaled itself between his jaws. Klaqeth fell backward, dead.

Just behind Kwasin, a man howled. Kwasin whirled and drew his short sword barely in time to deflect Bhaqeth's descending *tenu*. The blade hit with such force that even Kwasin's mighty muscles could not prevent him from being forced to a knee. A demon rage seemed to possess the surviving twin now that his brother had been slain. Kwasin parried blow after blow, regaining his feet but falling back as Bhaqeth lunged with his longer, square-ended sword.

Stepping back, Kwasin nearly tripped over Klaqeth's corpse. Still blocking Bhaqeth's repeated blows, he bent down, gripped a giant hand around Klaqeth's limp neck, and drew up the dead man before him as a shield. Bhaqeth's blade, which had been swinging out toward Kwasin, pulled back to avoid slashing his brother's corpse. Kwasin grinned devilishly. Taking advantage of Bhaqeth's hesitation, he hurled himself forward and slammed a foot against the surviving twin's shield. Again, a risky move. If Bhaqeth had not been so unnerved by the unconventional use of his brother's corpse, he would have been able to chop off Kwasin's leg at the knee. Instead, stepping backward from the momentum of Kwasin's kick, Bhaqeth lost his footing and fell to the ground.

Kwasin stood over Bhaqeth. Then, with all his weight, he pressed a foot down on the shield that rested on the man's chest. Bhaqeth groaned under the great pressure, his eyes bulging with terror as the end of Kwasin's short sword stabbed down at his head. The man turned away and the blade tore through his cheek and impaled his skull. It reminded Kwasin of the way he had skewered the other brother with his dagger. He smiled at the epic symmetry, and at the fact he had finished what the legendary three-horned rhino could not.

Now the soldiers about Kwasin surged backward as the enemy reversed the gains made by the Mukhans' initial charge. Kwasin shouted hoarsely and shouldered his way forward against the tide. He needed to recover his ax before he lost his bearings in the mad rush of men.

Then he saw the ax on the ground before him, just as a large hand reached out of the chaos and wrapped itself around the weapon's haft. Kwasin looked into the face of Kadyth the Silent and swore. Kadyth must have lost his own ax in the melee. The man, greed twinkling in his eyes, took aim at Kwasin and swung back the ax.

Out of sheer reflex, Kwasin grabbed a man running by him and heaved the fellow at Kadyth. Fortunately the man was a Khokarsan soldier, though Kwasin had not checked beforehand—it could just as well have been an ally. Kadyth's ax sliced through the man's leather armor. With a cry, the man collapsed. Before Kadyth could recover from his swing, Kwasin lunged forward and chopped with his sword. Kadyth screamed as the blade cut through the heavy leather kilt covering his thigh, but he did not fall or let go of the ax. Instead, unable to swing the massive weapon back without again giving Kwasin the opportunity to attack with his sword, he thrust forward the ax. The blunt eye of the ax's head drove into Kwasin's chest, and though he wore a cuirass, the terrific blow heaved the breath from his lungs. His breastbone and ribs seared with pain as he fell backward and to the ground. His vision filled with sparkling stars, through which he saw his own giant ax descending upon him. He willed his muscles to respond, to no avail. At last, the hollow oblivion of death had come.

Suddenly his vision cleared. Kwasin saw the ax that had been falling toward him drop from Kadyth's hand and land harmlessly on the ground. Kwasin dropped the sword he had forgotten he still held and grabbed the ax, rolling out of the way just in time to prevent Kadyth's body from falling on top of him.

Kwasin vaulted to his feet to find himself looking into the dark and ugly face of Miwanes of Sakawuru. Blood rivered down the pirate warrior's hook-ended broadsword and onto the downtrodden grass, a testament to the gruesome work he had just finished on Kadyth.

"Why kill him?" Kwasin shouted, advancing toward Miwanes. "Are you an ally of Kho?"

Miwanes' laugh croaked like the caw of a dry-throated raven. "Haven't you heard?" he said. "Minruth has promised the kingship of Dythbeth to the man who brings him your head!"

Miwanes' sword whistled through the air at Kwasin, who deflected the blow with his ax. Somehow Miwanes managed to hold on to his blade, though his scarred face winced with pain at Kwasin's blow. Seizing on the man's discomfort and the opening caused by the lowering of his sword, Kwasin slammed frontally into his opponent, grabbing Miwanes' bronze nose guard and roughly heaving off his helmet. The two men fell backward into the grass.

Miwanes dropped his sword, which was useless at this proximity, then drew a dagger from a sheath on his belt and tried to stab it into Kwasin's throat. Kwasin grabbed Miwanes' wrist before the man could complete his motion and thrust the ax at the man's unhelmeted temple. Though Kwasin had little room to swing his ax at such close quarters, the heavy iron head still carried enough force to crush Miwanes' skull.

Kwasin rose from the body of his dead opponent and scanned the chaos of battle around him. Somewhere amid the fighting, Toesem, the lion fighter of Towina, would be looking for him. But then, on the ground beyond the fallen body of Kadyth the

Silent, he saw the bloodied corpse of the man he sought. Miwanes, in his greed for the king's reward, had already done Kwasin's work for him.

"So much for Minruth's great heroes," Kwasin muttered, and then turned to rejoin the fighting.

ELEVEN

By morning the tides began to turn in favor of the Dythbethans and their new allies. Phoeken's troops already stood demoralized by their losses in the face of General Wahesa's reinforcements. Then, shortly after dawn, yet another army appeared on the southern horizon. Kwasin immediately sought out General Wahesa in his tent, where he had been planning his next moves.

When Kwasin entered the tent he found a tall tribesman standing before Wahesa, his wife, and a captain of the army. The general, his eyes beaming as with satisfaction, looked up at Kwasin and said, "Just as your city entreated Mukha for support, I too have fostered an alliance." Wahesa eyed his wife as if pleased with her. "The army that approaches is under Mukhan command," he said at Kwasin's questioning look, "though Wan"so tribesmen make up nearly a third of the force."

Kwasin's eyes grew wide. He had never heard of anyone making an alliance with the west-coast or northern tribes.

"Times are changing," Wahesa said, "but so obsessed are we with this Time of Troubles, we fail to take notice. You may have heard reports lately that some of the more distant outposts have been engaged in skirmishes with the pygmies. As the seasons grow warmer, their tribes are growing in number. And as they hunger for new and fertile lands, they, along with the natives hitherto restricted to isolated regions in the west and northwest, have begun to encroach on the outskirts of the empire."

Kwasin had not heard these reports, but then he had returned to the island only months ago. He had encountered several tribes during his travels through the Western Lands, but he had found most of the territory he passed through stark and uninhabited. That Wahesa could gather together enough of the tribesmen to organize a working army surprised him.

General Wahesa went on to explain that the tribes from which he had recruited were under the suzerainty of Daka's father, King Mahedana of the Wan"so. Suddenly Kwasin understood the great sway Daka held over Wahesa and why the general had accepted an outlander as his army's priestess. Their marriage had been political. Wahesa would gain reinforcements for his invasion of Khokarsa, while Daka achieved for her father's confederation the lucrative support of the mighty Khokarsan Empire—that is, should Wahesa be victorious in his campaign against Minruth. Not to mention the fact that Daka was now a revered initiate of the Temple of Kho, a position rarely granted to foreigners.

Kwasin regarded Wahesa. The man was a keen politician, perhaps too keen. He would have to watch out for him. Kwasin's own marriage had been one of convenience and he knew Weth held little love for him. The queen of Dythbeth was as shrewd as Wahesa. When the time came for the two to meet, they might conspire, and then things would go very badly for Kwasin.

The next few days passed by in a whirlwind of activity. Phoeken and his troops retreated to the west of the great plain, but Wahesa and General Hahinqo didn't want to give the enemy a chance to rest and regroup. The second Mukhan contingent was ordered to swing to the west and cut off Phoeken's retreat. Then the combined forces of the Dythbethan and Mukhan armies were to draw the enemy to the north, in the hope of forcing the Khokarsans up against the banks of the Karhokokly.

But things did not go exactly as planned. Some of the Wan"so warriors accompanying the Mukhans could not understand the ancient ban on the bow and arrow enforced throughout the empire. Consequently, several of the Wan"so smuggled the Goddess-forbidden weapons aboard the galleys that had landed their people on the southern shores of the Kemsilemu, or Great Claw Peninsula. Somehow the Wan"so had concealed their bows and arrows from their Mukhan commanders on the trip overland to Dythbeth. Now that the Wan"so had encountered the enemy, they hungered to use the prohibited weapons.

A great argument ensued between the Mukhan commanders and the Wan"so, the result of which was that a handful of the more forceful agitators were executed. When it seemed that an all-out insurrection was brewing, the Wan"so officers serving as liaisons between the tribesmen and their Mukhan commanders turned to someone their men would listen to. This was Daka, who proclaimed to the assembled tribesmen that anyone who disobeyed the prohibition would be cursed by his own gods and goddesses, as well as the Great Mother goddess of the Khokarsan people. Further, all descendants of the disobedient would also be cursed.

Almost immediately, the prohibited bows and arrows were turned over. The Wan"so regarded their King Mahedana as a god, and therefore Daka, his daughter, as a goddess. They believed every word she uttered, or at least believed in the reality of her threat, for often the deities had their own hidden reasons to mislead mortals. Thus the Wan"so's fear of divine wrath settled an argument that had begun over the Khokarsans' fear of their own Goddess' prohibition. Kwasin believed in Kho's wrath himself, but he did see the irony in the outcome.

In the time it took for the situation to be resolved, Phoeken brought his men north and, after successfully breaking through the forces stationed on the southern bank of the Karhokokly, crossed the river. He undoubtedly hoped to regroup and relaunch his campaign from the northern hills. But General Hahinqo, as supreme commander of the forces of the Goddess at Dythbeth, still wanted to take the battle to Phoeken. Thus he ordered Wahesa to take his men and draw the Khokarsans up into the mountains. Hahinqo arranged for several of his own officers to accompany General Wahesa and his troops, believing that the Dythbethans, being familiar with the terrain, would be able to help the

Mukhans bring devastating losses to the enemy. Kwasin was to join the mountain campaign, as Hahinqo also believed the fearsome presence of Dythbeth's giant king would inspire the Mukhans and dishearten their adversaries.

Meanwhile, Hahinqo would try to bring order out of the chaos that was Dythbeth. Though many fields had been torched by the enemy, perhaps somewhere among the abandoned farmsteads a few crops had survived that could be scavenged to help feed the city's increasingly famished inhabitants. And the opening caused by diverting the enemy would allow Queen Weth to send out more couriers seeking help from the mainland cities. Not that she expected them to send assistance. The war between Kho and Resu had enveloped the whole empire, leaving the mainland forces loyal to the Goddess with enough problems of their own.

The fighting in the mountain passes stretched on for weeks as Kwasin and the men under his command picked off Phoeken's soldiers one by one. The rugged slopes and the deep ravines of the Saasamaro made for good guerrilla warfare, and Kwasin felt invigorated by the clean, fragrant mountain air of his boyhood haunts.

Often Kwasin took off on his own, taking pleasure in finding devious ways to torment and otherwise lower the morale of the enemy. One of these occasions went so far as to make the Khokarsan commanders scream in high dudgeon for the head of Dythbeth's king, while many soldiers undoubtedly lay awake at night sweating in fear of the mad giant.

Kwasin had set out one morning to scout a large enemy encampment that had recently been set up only two miles northeast of the Dythbethan fort situated at the opening of the main pass—much too close for Kwasin's comfort. Attempting to avoid detection, Kwasin skirted the wall of a treacherous gorge as he made his way toward the encampment.

As he proceeded along the gorge, the morning sun peeked over the lower lip of a crevasse and cast its blood-red glare in his eyes. He looked away for a moment, but when he looked up again a sight met him that might have been a vision from angry Resu himself. Or perhaps, he thought a moment later, the vision came from the Goddess, and She had only brought Kwasin to this precise spot so that he could see the weakness of the Flaming God that had been revealed in his arrogant gaze. Surely Kho, in Her recent upheavals of the land, had created the peculiar formation of rock and dirt that stood silhouetted against the rising sun's blinding radiance. Whatever the case, it gave Kwasin an idea.

He surveyed the distance he would have to traverse up the steep side of the gorge for his plan to work. For a moment he considered returning to the fort to get help. But he knew the situation could very well change by the time he returned with soldiers. Besides, accomplishing the task on his own would only aggrandize his already legendary status.

Cautiously, he ascended the mountainside and passed along its summit so that he could look down on the rock formation from above. Yes, that would do, he thought. Even more cautiously than he had climbed up, he descended into the saddle between the two great mountains and headed for the enemy encampment.

When he reached the northern mouth of the gorge, he was forced to scale a sharp rise of terrain littered with fir and pine trees. Some of the trees had been uprooted by the recent quakes, while others were only half uprooted and crisscrossed one another, angling out of the reddish soil in chaotic patterns. Kwasin looked for the easiest route through the labyrinth but did not find one. The entire slope was a treacherous tangle of Great Kho's wrath.

He shrugged. If the way would be difficult for him, it would be even harder for dozens of armored soldiers.

Finally, another valley appeared over the rim. A small lake rested on the valley's northern edge, and a great military encampment, consisting of half a dozen large tents and many smaller ones, lay upon the lake's nearer shore. The soldiers were already up, drilling under the supervision of a *rekokha* on the flat terrain in front of the tents.

Kwasin's timing could not have been better. He took a shallow drink from a sea-otter-skin flask slung over his shoulder, then paused for a moment to recover his breath from the climb up the tree-knotted slope.

While he was resting, Kwasin heard a rustling in the trees behind him and to his left. A man burst out of a copse of half-fallen firs and bolted for the pass into the adjoining valley. Kwasin took off after the man.

By the time the soldier—obviously a scout sent to monitor the valley pass—reached the crest of the slope, Kwasin was already upon him. The man died under a single mighty blow from Kwasin's ax.

Shouts now arose from below. The camp's inhabitants had witnessed the murder of their comrade. Kwasin lifted up the body of the slain soldier and held it high so that the men in the camp could see it. Then he cast the corpse down the slope before him.

A captain, holding his feathered helmet in his hands, came out of one of the tents and followed the collective gaze of the soldiers.

Kwasin stood on the top of the slope and held up his ax. He wanted the officer below to know that it was the giant king of Dythbeth who taunted him.

The captain raised an arm in Kwasin's direction. The *rekokha* who had been drilling his men turned toward the captain as if listening to orders. Then the sergeant turned back to his men and gestured rapidly for them to move out.

Still Kwasin waited. The longer he stood there, the more likely the officer in charge of the camp would send additional men to the ridge. The captain wouldn't believe a lone man would be foolish enough to take on his whole contingent and would think an entire army must lie in wait over the ridge in the bordering valley.

Kwasin grinned as his hopes were realized and what must have been more than a hundred soldiers peeled from the larger body of men and headed toward the pass. Something whirred by Kwasin's head and his smile faded. He had gauged the soldiers too far away for their sling-stones to reach him, but now he saw one man below so skilled with the sling he could have competed in the Great Games of Klakor. The fellow was reloading his sling. Kwasin dropped below the ridge and as fast as he could began making his way through the interwoven mass of trees.

When he reached the bottom of the tangled slope, he stopped and took out his own sling. The barking of dogs, muted somewhat by the thick foliage, carried through the trees. The soldiers were already descending upon him.

He began whirling his sling. A patch of moving color appeared between two trunks. He estimated the speed and direction of the pursuer, and a brief moment later the soldier appeared again. Already Kwasin had released his sling-stone. He failed to see the soldier fall because the man passed behind the trees, but he heard a soft cry and the thud of a body hitting the ground.

Once more he downed a soldier in this way, but that was all he had time for. He wanted to raise the men's bloodlust so they would follow him, but he hoped he had not waited too long. As he bolted into the gorge, Kwasin turned to see several soldiers nearing the bottom of the slope, pulled along by the tethers of their yapping and slathering canines. The many fallen tree trunks caused the men to proceed slowly, though not slow enough for Kwasin.

His great lungs heaved like a bellows as he pumped his legs across the basin of the rock-strewn gorge. Again he looked behind. The larger body of the soldiers pursuing him had left the forest and now charged across the mostly flat ground between the two immense mountains. Kwasin veered to his left and skirted a shelf of rock that soared almost vertically for several hundred feet. Suddenly the shelf forked to the left and he turned with it, crossing behind the mountainside and out of view of the soldiers.

Kwasin looked up. An enormous projection of rock cantilevered from the mountainside and blocked out the sky above him. Above it, he knew, another similar though slightly larger projection jutted out of the mountain. Though the soldiers were quickly closing on him, he slowed his pace. The great mass of stone and earth above unnerved him. He didn't want his pounding footfalls to cause his plan to end in disaster—at least not for him.

At last the sky's blue vault again appeared overhead and Kwasin thanked the Goddess. Here a wedge-shaped channel creased the steep mountainside. Kwasin crawled across the gravelly debris that led into the channel and began ascending the natural trail.

The dogs' barking and the gritty crunch of men's feet as they ran across the canyon floor echoed oddly from the overhanging stone. As he passed above the second and higher projection of rock on his left, Kwasin felt a hard blow to his back that almost caused him to lose his footing. He looked below and saw a man reloading his sling. It was the same fellow who'd made the long throw when Kwasin had stood upon the ridge over the camp. The soldier had hit his target true, but the massive iron head of the ax slung across Kwasin's back had deflected the deadly projectile.

Kwasin stopped his ascent and picked up a large rock. Leaning with his back against the inclined channel, he thrust forward the rock and watched it swing out into the air, plummeting in its arc toward the slinger. Though the rock did not hit him, the man retreated from the mountainside toward the center of the gorge. As he did so, he looked up and to his left. Then the man began shouting and waving his arms, not at Kwasin, but in the direction of the immense overhang of rock.

Kwasin cursed. The slinger's new perspective had alerted him to Kwasin's intent and the man was now attempting to warn his fellows to stay clear of the trap. Kwasin had hoped to ascend another seventy-five feet and then traverse a narrow ledge to his destination. Now he would be forced to go another way.

He climbed out of the channel. He would have to cross the face of the sheer stone wall that separated him from the top of the mammoth protuberance of rock on his left. At a reckless pace, he began shimmying across the rock face, trying not to look down from the dizzying height. The few handholds and footholds available seemed achingly far apart. Kwasin was able to reach them only because of the length of his great frame, and because of the wildly desperate leaps he took to make some of them.

A lead projectile cone splintered the stone next to Kwasin's head and embedded itself in the cliff face. Warm blood mixed with sweat beaded down his cheeks where the stone fragments ricocheting from the missile's impact had penetrated his skin.

He did not stop his climb but continued bellying across the rock, his pace uninterrupted. There was nothing he could do now to stop the man except make it to the overhang quickly.

His mind emptied of all but the thought of making the next foot- or handhold. Time seemed to disappear along with self, interrupted occasionally by the chinking impact of a lead projectile on either side of him. Suddenly his trancelike state vanished as he stepped onto solid ground—but not too solid, he hoped. He sprinted across the ledge, making sure not to tread too heavily. When he found the spot he was looking for he did not stop at it but headed farther up the sloping mountainside above the overhang. Gauging he had reached a safe enough distance, he picked up the largest rock he could find and hurled it below. When nothing happened, he picked up another rock and threw it, and then another and another.

His target was a weak fissure where the great protuberance of rock joined the mountain. He had been sure he would be able to jar loose the narrow channel of rock that served to mortar the massive outcropping to the mountainside. A small landslide should be all it would take. But though he hurled rock after rock, no slide came.

As doubt began to wear away at the wisdom of his plan, the rocks below finally gave. The earth rumbled and cracked louder than any heavenly thunder Kwasin had ever heard and the mountain beneath his feet shook violently. Kwasin fell on his buttocks, thrusting his arms back in an attempt to stop his slide. By the time he finally succeeded, he found himself cradling an arm around a sharply projecting rock thirty feet below where he had been standing. The two massive projections of the mountainside were now gone and he looked through the dust-billowing air at the bottom of the gorge. When the air did not immediately clear, he struck out on the dangerous climb back up the mountain, which was now littered with debris triggered by the double avalanche. Arriving at the summit, he looked down to see a handful of tiny figures on the edge of the new mountain of gargantuan stone blocks formed by the landslide. The slinger had been too late.

He, along with the majority of his fellows, had been unable to get far enough from the overhang before Kwasin triggered its fall. Kwasin had killed a hundred or more men, but he hoped by the time the rumors of the day's events had spread far, the number would be exaggerated to into the thousands.

He did not return to the fort that day. Instead, he made for Wahesa's camp in the eastern mountains, knowing the general would want intelligence of the great blow against the enemy. Doubtless, Wahesa would want to strike the encampment while its soldiers still reeled from their losses.

Darkness had fallen in the mountains by the time Kwasin wandered into the camp. Above, fair Lahla the Moon was swinging her satisfied grin across the star-speckled firmament, but when Kwasin sought out General Wahesa, he found a scene that was anything but tranquil. Terrific shouting was erupting from within Wahesa's tent. Kwasin recognized the voices as those of the general and his wife. The two were having a lovers' spat, or perhaps they argued about war strategy. Kwasin could not tell because the two carried out their shouting match in the strange tongue of Daka's people.

Weary from his travels and the events of the day, Kwasin turned away from the general's tent and returned to the night guard, asking where he could sleep for the night. An officer on the edge of camp was awakened and ordered to give up his tent to Dythbeth's king. The man grumbled at first but quickly grew quiet, making a hasty evacuation from his tent when he saw the seven-foot-tall Kwasin looming above him in the moonlight. Kwasin fell asleep inside the tent listening to Wahesa and his woman presumably cursing one another in Wan"so.

Kwasin started awake in the dead of night. He had been dreaming about the oracle at Dythbeth. The old crone had been trying to tell him something, but when she spoke, her words came out like a garbled sob. Kwasin stretched out on his dry grass bedding and tried to shake off what seemed to him an ill omen.

Suddenly he sat upright and listened. For a moment he heard nothing.

But now there is was again.

He shuddered when he realized the sound resembled the eerie sobbing of the oracle in his dream. Had the oracle passed from the living since Kwasin had last seen her and now her ghost came to his tent to warn him of something? Unable to rid himself the notion, he silently unsheathed his dagger and slipped outside through the folds of his tent.

Lahla still swung above but she had climbed past her zenith, her grin turned to a scowl. At first Kwasin saw nothing out of the ordinary, but then he noticed a shimmering of moonlight in a cluster of bushes just outside of camp. With a quietness that belied his hulking form, Kwasin slunk toward the bushes as if a ghost himself. As he neared his destination, he made out a tall, dark form in the shadows before him. Swiftly he sprang at the figure, which he throttled roughly under a mighty biceps. His dagger's point pressed into the figure's soft abdomen, but he recoiled when he heard a feminine cry. He quickly whirled the figure around and in the moonlight looked down into Daka's frightened, tear-filled eyes.

"Forgive me, priestess!" Kwasin cried, releasing the woman. "I had thought you a trespasser in the night!"

Daka's jewel-harnessed breast rose and fell rapidly, and at first Kwasin believed her expression revealed fear. Then she was pressing her warm lips upon his in a passionate kiss and running her hands over his arms, shoulders, and chest.

For a moment, Kwasin thought of Wahesa, and also of Weth, and of the terrible complications that would arise should either learn of this infidelity. But his concern did not last long.

Kwasin seized up the woman in his arms and carried her back to his tent.

TWELVE

Kwasin brushed past the guards, trumpeters, and throoming bullroarers into the palatial throne room of Dythbeth. Something was wrong. The palace guards had given their king, arriving home after his long absence, too much trouble for his liking. Instead of being greeted as a returning champion, Kwasin had been made to wait in the throne room's antechamber while the herald announced his presence. When finally he entered the spacious hall and saw who sat upon the queen's oaken throne, he should have been joyful, but something told him his problems had just grown much worse.

"Behold, priestess of Kho and of her daughter, the moon, the king of shining Dythbeth!" a herald cried out.

Minruth's daughter Awineth slouched against the high seatback of Queen Weth's throne as if weighed down with great fatigue. The raven-haired woman smiled blandly at Kwasin, looking pale and worn, though even her gaunt form and the dark circles that hung beneath her large, dark gray eyes could not conceal her ravishing beauty. Beside the empress, though at a lower station, sat Weth, her expression unreadable. Her chair, smaller and less ornate than Awineth's, rested above another chair, this one empty. It was Kwasin's throne, lowered to its customary position beneath the highest-ranking initiates of the Goddess in the city. Knowing the convention failed to alleviate Kwasin's sense of dread at the loss of power it implied.

He approached the royal dais and knelt with head bowed and hands outstretched in obeisance.

"Rise, Kwasin, and tell me your story," Awineth said.

Kwasin stood up but he made note of the woman's lack of etiquette. By failing to address him as king, she both humiliated and lorded her authority over him. But Kwasin could do nothing. Though Awineth was a bitch, she was also the empress of Khokarsa and chief priestess of Kho.

In as few words as possible he recounted the results of the northern campaign. The enemy had suffered heavy losses, he told her. However, when Phoeken realized even his genius mind couldn't outwit an enemy so at home on the mountainous terrain, he had ultimately withdrawn his troops to the east. In fact, General Wahesa's intelligence supported the notion that Phoeken had personally abandoned the campaign much earlier and gone to Qoqada. There he had presumably taken over as direct commander of the ongoing siege against the bee city.

"Had the coward not been so eager to show me his backside," Kwasin said, "I would have brought back his ugly head for my empress."

Awineth did not look impressed, though she said, "Your wearisome bluster aside, you have done well to hold up the morale of Kho's children against my father's general." Then Awineth's expression darkened and her voice chilled. "But, as you say, you were not really fighting him these past weeks. While his army kept Dythbeth's forces occupied in the Saasamaro, he left and turned his attentions elsewhere. A soldier as cunning as Phoeken is not stupid enough to be baited if it does not somehow serve his own plans. The men he lost while you holed up his army were a calculated sacrifice. While you played soldier in the mountains and lost sight of the bigger picture, Phoeken was pulling my father's armies from the east to repress the rebellions in Awamuka, Qoqada, Minanlu, and Kaarquth. With sly promises of amnesty and forgiveness, Phoeken persuaded a number of the more craven inhabitants of those cities to lower their defenses. Now each of the cities has fallen. Only Dythbeth remains to stand against my father and his blasphemous followers."

The news left Kwasin mute. If he had been played for a fool, then so had Hahinqo and Wahesa. But as king of Dythbeth, Kwasin would take the full brunt of responsibility for any errors in strategy. He could dismiss Hahinqo and have him executed, but that would do nothing to lessen Kwasin's blame in the eyes of his people and the empress.

"What of the resistance in the mountains above Khokarsa?"

Awineth took a deep breath. "The great shrine at Kloepeth has also been taken. My father has subverted the lawful authority of the priestesses there and placed them under the rule of the priests."

The courtiers about the royal dais gasped. Minruth's actions were of the deepest sacrilege, a direct insult to Great Kho Herself.

"Don't underestimate my father's madness," Awineth continued. "While it's said that those priestesses who resisted have been exiled to the northern shore, popular rumor has it that the ships that carried them were lost in a storm, along with all crew and passengers. But my intelligence has uncovered an even darker truth: the captives were not lost at sea but rather murdered en route and their bodies weighted and dropped into the Kemu. I was lucky to escape when I did, though Kho knows, the journey I undertook for the Goddess was terrible in itself." Awineth remained silent while Kwasin and the shocked courtiers took in the disturbing news. At last, she continued. "My father has crossed a very dangerous line, one which threatens the fate of the entire empire. I have received word from the new oracle at Khokarsa, who remains in hiding in the mountains above the capital, that she has been blessed with a vision from the Goddess. Kho warns Her children that the war between the priests and the priestesses threatens to break apart the very foundations of the world. That is why the great earthquake struck the island and why the earth's upheavals become more frequent."

Seeing Kwasin grow somber at the news, Awineth laughed haughtily. "You fashioned yourself a returning hero, didn't you? But now you find you are merely a child playing a game you can barely comprehend. Alas, if I had been here I could have advised you. Strategy is a grand mosaic, *King* Kwasin—concentrate on one tile and you miss the larger work."

Kwasin's face grew hot. Awineth's words came dangerously close to openly defying his authority. Military matters fell exclusively under the domain of the king, and though Awineth, as empress, outranked him, custom held that even the high priestess of Kho only advised, not dictated, the actions of any city's army and navy. Awineth's deriding tone said otherwise, and Kwasin felt his authority dwindling with each word that passed from Awineth's lips. Were she not Kho's holy vicar, he would not have stood for it. Still, he had to say something to assert his power. But when he opened his mouth to speak, he received a cold and warning glare from Weth.

Minruth's daughter followed the gaze and said, "Your wife the queen has told me of your visit with the sacred oracle of Dythbeth. Since the oracle is reluctant to leave the old temple, I have summoned her priestess and sent back another to take her place. Qenwath has told me of Wasemquth's vision about you. Of the great serpent that divides your soul and holds your destiny . . . and the fate of all the land." Awineth leaned forward on her throne, and now keen excitement seemed to erase some of the tiredness from her gray eyes. "But Queen Weth has also told me something else, a thing that may be of great significance given the oracle's prophecy. It is said that Sahhindar, the brother of Resu himself, has appeared upon the island! And you, O Kwasin, by your very confession, have seen the Archer God in the flesh!"

When the courtiers had finished with their whisperings, Kwasin said, "It is true, O Queen, that in the hills outside the capital I encountered a man who met the description of Sahhindar. But what has that to do with the oracle's prophecy?"

"That is yet to be determined," Awineth said coldly. "Everyone knows that Sahhindar, like you, was exiled for displeasing the Mother of All, and that similarity is enough to cast doubt upon you, O Kwasin."

"Doubt!" Kwasin howled, laughing. "Do you think I conspire with the Archer God against Kho and all Her—"

Awineth cut off his words with an angry wave of her hand. "Say no more! Does the king of Dythbeth think to dispute the words of Kho's high priestess?" Awineth's eyes flashed with outrage, and for a moment Kwasin believed she would order the guards to attack him. Then her eyes softened, though the haughtiness remained in them. "I need you, Kwasin," she said. "I don't deny it. The people of Dythbeth will require much inspiration in the days ahead, and you have proven yourself a worthy warrior if not so much of a keen strategist. Don't worry, I will help you with the latter. For now, what you need to know is that my father has ordered his generals to let the mainland cities go and regroup their forces here. He wants to clean out any remaining opposition on the island before setting out to retake the mainland cities. Dythbeth has been a thorn in the empire's side for far too long, so my father seeks to aggrandize his armies by recruiting from among the wild mountain men beyond the northern coast. With promises of women and loot, he is also luring the wild Klemqaba from the southwestern mountains along the Kemu. He intends to raze your city once and for all and give the spoils to the half-men."

Kwasin felt incensed at the prospect of proud Dythbeth pillaged by the half-neanderthaloids, but even more so at Awineth's condescension. But Awineth had said she needed him . . . though he suspected that once he led Dythbeth to victory, she would find a way to absolve herself of her debt to him. The thought pushed to the surface his deepest concern, and he could no longer hold back the question that had burned within him since laying eyes upon the woman in the great hall.

"What has become of my cousin Hadon?" he asked, not sure he wanted an answer. "Has he too flown into Dythbeth's welcoming arms?" As winner of the Great Games, Hadon was betrothed to Awineth and should have been at her side. While Minruth's blasphemy had naturally removed his authority in the eyes of the priestesses, Hadon's claim to the throne remained valid. But then, perhaps Hadon had died helping Awineth and the others escape from Khokarsa. He could only hope.

Awineth's pale face reddened. "Hadon is a traitor," she spat. "He has flown to his backwater city, along with his filthy Witch-from-the-Sea and her companions. Should you run across them in your travels, you are to execute them on sight or feel the wrath of Kho!"

Awineth might have said more but suddenly a commotion arose from beyond the chamber's entryway. The great doors swung open and a herald called out in a hasty lapse of court protocol: "Holy priestess, General Wahesa of Mukha!"

The general strode so swiftly past the doors that the trumpeters and bullroarers had no time to sound their instruments. Anger stormed upon Wahesa's stern features, and behind him through the doors Kwasin could see many Mukhan soldiers standing with spears drawn at the vastly outnumbered palace guards.

Both Awineth and Weth rose halfway from their seats, clearly shocked and angered at Wahesa's ill-mannered entry, and, as Kwasin turned to face the new audient, he heard the women's startled gasps.

Wahesa, his face flushed with anger, had drawn his *tenu*. Its blade pointed directly at Kwasin.

THIRTEEN

A wineth now stood up fully from her throne and leveled a finger at Wahesa.

"General, explain this violation of the queen's court!"

Wahesa's head ticked as he apparently struggled to find words lost in the raging seas of his anger. Finally, looking up at Kwasin with an expression of intense hatred, he said, "I have just received word from the temple. The priestesses have performed the proper rituals and found my wife to be with child!"

"Then you should be celebrating, General," Awineth said, her voice heavy with indignation, "instead of violating my private council and attacking my guards."

Before Wahesa could reply, Kwasin folded his arms over his great chest and threw his head back in laughter.

"I do not deny bedding your woman!" he said. "But don't fault me because your priestess frowns upon your lack of skill in the art of lovemaking!" And with those words Kwasin reached out a mighty paw, grabbed the blunt end of Wahesa's *tenu*, and plucked the sword right out of the man's grasp as easily if he were pulling up a stem of dried grass to clean his teeth. Kwasin cast the *tenu* to the tiled floor and said, "Don't feel too badly, General—it makes you no less of a man that Daka desires me. You should be honored. Not only am I the greatest lover in the land, but I am also a king. Besides, I don't want either your woman or the child, so what is your quarrel with me?"

"Silence!"

Kwasin turned to regard Weth, who had vacated her throne and now stood at the foot of the dais. The queen's clenched fists trembled, her eyes consumed with passionate rage.

"Not only are the actions of both of you an outrage to me," Weth said icily, "but you have also both affronted the graces of Kho's high vicar." She turned to glare at Kwasin. "Your shameful behavior reminds me of Minruth and his squabbling priests. We are in the midst of a civil war!"

Wahesa placed a hand upon the hilt of his short sword. "A war which cannot be won without the armies of Mukha," he said.

The queen of Dythbeth looked at the general as if she wanted to draw the ceremonial dagger that hung on her hip and use it to flay the man alive. But instead she heaved a deep sigh and said, "How do you know, General, that my husband is the father of the child Daka carries?"

"The priestess in the Temple of Kho told me I cannot be the father," Wahesa replied. "And I have seen the way Daka looks at Kwasin. Once again the man has violated a priestess of Kho—the blasphemer should never have been allowed back from his exile!"

"A priestess cannot be violated if she takes a lover willingly," Weth said, "even if she is married to another." She narrowed her eyes at Kwasin. "I shall speak with Daka and determine—"

"And before that I will have Kwasin's head!" Wahesa cried, drawing his short sword and advancing on Kwasin.

Still smirking, Kwasin reached for his own sword. He left it sheathed, however, when many courtiers began running up the steps of the dais, inexplicably ignoring the fight about to break out between their king and the general of Mukha.

Kwasin turned to face the dais. Awineth lay in a heap on the floor beneath her throne. Many priestesses converged around her, one of them placing Awineth's head in her lap and whispering quiet words to her queen. Another priestess rushed from a side room carrying a ceramic urn and a swath of white cloth. She broke through the circle of women and knelt at Awineth's side, moistened the cloth with water from the urn, and began stroking the wet linen across Awineth's forehead. A moment later Awineth's eyes fluttered open and she regarded the faces around her as if they were strangers and she had no idea of her whereabouts.

The woman who had brought the cloth, whom Kwasin recognized as a priestess of Qawo, goddess of healing, asked for the throne room to be cleared, but Awineth sat up and lazily shook her head. With a croaking voice she insisted that the audience remain, and after the priestesses lifted her back onto her throne, she exclaimed, albeit weakly, "I have been granted a vision from the Goddess!"

Astonished gasps filled the chamber. Kwasin, though not one of the gaspers, felt an icy chill run down his spine at the thought of Kho's spirit manifesting itself in his presence. Wahesa, he noticed, had sheathed his sword and was looking worriedly toward the throne. It seemed his anger had passed with Awineth's swoon.

Awineth waited as shock of her pronouncement settled in among the chamber's occupants. After a lengthy period of silence, she said, "Kho is angry at the bickering of Her children. She warns that Her worshipers will destroy themselves if they do not forget their petty disagreements and come together for the good of the Goddess and the land. Kho decrees that it is especially important for the matter of the unborn child to be settled as She wills, or terrible strife will fall upon Her people. The child is destined to become a tremendous force in the unfolding of the future, one who will sway events of great magnitude. It is the judgment of Kho that the child will be raised by the king and queen of Dythbeth. The honor of Wahesa has not been sullied, for it was the Goddess Herself who ordained the adultery. To prove his fealty to the Goddess, however, King Kwasin must guard against future infidelities. If he fails in this regard, he and his future kin will surely tempt Great Kho's wrath."

Then the empress rose from her throne, her frame slouching with apparent fatigue. "The matter is settled," she said. "The Goddess has spoken and I will hear no more of it." Then, shooing off her attendants, Awineth descended the dais to make her way from the chamber. As she passed Kwasin, she stopped briefly and in a low, scornful tone whispered, "If you do not keep out of trouble, I will have another vision, this one decreeing your immediate execution." With one last glare at Kwasin, she exited the chamber with her attendants in tow.

FOURTEEN

K wasin staggered down the wide marble steps of his totem hall, feeling as if the Shapeless Shaper had snatched his soul and stretched its ghostly form until it oozed like a thick, specter-laden syrup from his throbbing skull. He had spent the afternoon deep in his cups among his fellow Bear people, participating in an array of wild rituals as he and his totem brothers celebrated their recent victories against Minruth and the profaners of Kho.

But that had not been Kwasin's only reason for imbibing the many great pitchers of mead and millet and sorghum beer offered him. While he held little trust in Awineth's vision and her interpretation of the oracle's vague words, deep in his heart doubt assailed him. Had he truly failed the Goddess by indulging in his loveplay with Daka? Had he thereby jeopardized not only the fate of the land, but also the outcome of Kho's great struggle against Her impudent son, Resu? Because of Kwasin's lustful indiscretion, Wahesa had almost pulled his troops from battle, an action that would have surely spelled doom for Dythbeth and all the worshipers of Kho on the island. Only Awineth's swooning vision, whether a sly ruse or a true warning from Kho, had prevented disaster.

No, he had not come to celebrate what in all likelihood was merely a fleeting victory for Dythbeth. Rather he had entered the hall of the Klakordeth to forget himself in an orgy of drinking.

By the time he departed the hall, however, he found the alcohol had only deepened his feelings of remorse.

Too drunk to successfully descend even the broad, shallow steps of the hall, Kwasin lowered his great frame to his haunches and sat halfway down the steps, head and heart beating drums of pain.

"Those who try to avoid destiny through drink often forge a worse one!"

The voice that rang out from behind clanged in Kwasin's inebriated head like many large bronze gongs. As the voice echoed against the insides of his skull, he thought it sounded vaguely familiar. Then, when he placed it, he groaned and cradled his head deeper into his chest.

"Go away, bard," Kwasin's deep voice rumbled, "or I'll call my Bear brothers to take you inside and make you perform the Dance of the Castrated Baboon!"

A moment later Bhako was sitting on the steps beside Kwasin. "I merely read aloud one of the inscriptions carved into the stone archway above the College of Awines," Bhako said, pointing to the grand structure opposite the sea of pedestrians, "surely the wisest son our city has ever spawned. And how he was treated! Exiled to Bawaku because the syllabary he invented was considered sacrilegious—but how times have changed! Now he is revered in the city that once spurned him and the syllabary is taught in every temple. Even you can read at least a little of it. No doubt you have taken notice and reflected many times upon the irony of that particular inscription. After all, the archway faces the hall of the Klakordeth, as well as the Temple of Khukhaken, both home to many great drinkers. And, according to my research as royal bard, two of your most frequent haunts before your exile."

Kwasin considered tossing the bard down the steps but even the thought of lifting a hand made his stomach lurch with sickness. Finally, when his belly settled somewhat and no longer felt as if it might erupt like holy Khowot, he managed to say, "I take no advice from a man who died trying to fly."

"It is said that Awines never drank beer or wine," Bhako said, "but was rather drunk on wisdom. If I might humbly offer some of the latter . . ."

Kwasin dragged up his head and glared darkly at the bard. The man's voice was all too cheerful, and Kwasin decided that, if he must, he would risk being sick for a chance to throttle the loudmouthed troubadour. But Bhako was already getting up to leave.

"Then I'll say nothing," the bard said in apparent surrender. He headed down the steps but upon reaching the street turned and called up quietly. "Except that it will do no good for the morale of the citizens to see their king hung over. If he must be in public, he should at least go to the temple of the Great Mother, where the congregators might think their king reels with divine rather than worldly spirits."

Bhako's white robes became lost in the sea of pedestrians thronging the busy avenue.

For a great while Kwasin sat on the steps, at first occupying his beer-sodden mind with ways he might torment the bard the next time they met. But then Kwasin cursed. Bhako, though an annoying fool, was right. Kwasin knew his indiscretions had caused enough trouble already and he did not want to further undermine the effort of the Goddess by having his people doubt his competency as king. It would do no harm to go to the temple and make an offering. Besides, he didn't feel like returning to the palace and dealing with Weth and the empress.

His mind made up, he swayed upright on wobbly legs. Immediately Kwasin's guards, who had been standing farther up the steps under the awning of the totem hall, came to their king and surrounded him. His head still throbbing from drink, Kwasin tottered off toward the temple.

When at last he stood before the garden that nestled in front of the Temple of Kho, he knew he had made the right decision. The walk along the temple road had helped invigorate his alcohol-numbed limbs and already the fog of his mind was lifting. A priestess who emerged from the garden path smiled when she saw her king but, smelling alcohol on his breath, she blanched.

Doubtless she recalled Kwasin's drunken visit to the temple nine years ago. Nevertheless, after calling back down the path for two of her initiates to accompany her, the woman bade Kwasin to follow, taking him down a narrow trail off the main pathway that ended at an artesian well. Here Kwasin was permitted to drink— which he did, deeply—after which he was asked to take off his clothes. The priestesses then blessed him with libations of the painfully frigid well water, which left Kwasin shivering despite the oppressive mugginess of the overcast summer day. He was then led back to the main path and from there to the steps of the great domed temple itself.

Kwasin climbed the steps and entered the building's nine-sided entrance, passing through the outer chamber, with its pale red-and-blue toned murals depicting the creation of the world by Kho. He tried to ignore the occasional giggle or passionate murmurings that arose from an adjoining room where the holy prostitutes entertained their patrons. His business here was not that of carnal pleasure, after all, but rather to ask forgiveness for the trouble his great lust had caused in the first place.

He left behind the outer chamber and entered the next room. Here he knelt before a broad-based altar crouched on nine ornately gilded iron legs. The lack of food offerings startled him. Prayer beads and other religious trinkets had replaced the usual offerings of fruits, berries, and bowls of cow, goat, sheep, and hare blood. Despite the trinkets, the altar's welcoming base lay mostly bare. The priestess who accompanied him, noting his concern, remarked, "Food becomes scarce even among the rich. If the king does not wish to spare his supper, a precious belonging will suffice."

Kwasin nodded. "It is wrong," he said, "to deprive Kho of Her proper offerings. Summon one of my guards to bring back a bowl of fresh bull's blood from the palace to place upon the altar." The woman raised her brows as if unaware any cattle still lived in the city, then departed on her mission.

Things were getting more desperate than he'd realized. Now he wondered forlornly if his Bear brothers would be left without drink, having squandered the last of their dwindling supply of alcohol upon their insatiable king. Phoeken's soldiers still ranged the countryside outside the city and, according to Awineth, treaties were being made that would pull troops from across the empire to once again lay siege to Dythbeth. Kwasin's patrols had found little to salvage from the burned and pillaged farmlands, and the bay had already been fished out to support the pitiful remnants of Dythbeth's navy. The arrival of Wahesa's armies only made an already grave situation much worse.

Kwasin prostrated himself and prayed. He had always been able to take care of himself, even against the worst of odds. But now he was responsible for an entire city and, by the grace of Kho, the empire itself. Though he knew how to inspire men to face their deaths, he now admitted he had little knowledge about how to govern and protect them in the long term. Perhaps Awineth had come along at just the right time. Though a manipulative she-demon, she was shrewd, and because of her experience in her father's court, she might know enough of politics to steer the unwieldy population and keep it from revolt. And as long as she felt his presence inspired the allies of the Goddess, she would put up with him. But as soon as she felt differently, then—

He started as he looked up from his prostrations. He had thought himself alone in the room, but now in a dark corner he saw a pair of eyes glimmer with the flicker of the torchlight.

"Come out of the shadows and show yourself!" Kwasin's words echoed queerly from the walls of the stone room.

Suddenly a woman emerged from the darkness. It was Nelahnes, keeper of the temple and the priestess who had presided over Kwasin and Weth's marriage ceremony. The shapeliness of the woman's nearly naked form made Kwasin's heart beat faster and he leered at the priestess, temporarily forgetting the great problems that assailed him.

"I am impressed," Nelahnes said, running a hand suggestively over the girdle of gold circlets that adorned her otherwise bare thigh. "Is the mighty King Kwasin humbler than I have been led to believe?"

"O priestess, your breathtaking beauty does indeed make me humble!"

Kwasin's heart fluttered like the wings of a bee ready to pollinate. It had been too long. His many attempts to get Weth into bed since their marriage had failed. It was no wonder he had fallen victim of Daka's passions, and could Kho really begrudge his needs? Had not the Goddess Herself imbued him with the lust of the stag?

He could not mistake the woman's longing gaze, and neither could he mistake the flames of lust that consumed him. Suddenly he found himself being led by the priestess back through the first chamber and into one of side rooms reserved for the divine whores. Once inside, Nelahnes kissed him wetly upon the lips, and then she was pushing him gently away so she could slip out of her girdle. Languidly, she stretched out upon the room's well-cushioned divan and, moaning softly, beckoned Kwasin to join her.

Kwasin did not need the invitation. Even his hangover could not take away the impulses that now possessed him, and he lay down upon the divan, nearly smothering the woman with his passionate embrace. Unlike Weth those many years ago, Nelahnes did not resist Kwasin's advances but only pulled him closer, whispering her amorous enthusiasm heavily in his ear.

Just as Kwasin began to lose himself in their lovemaking, he thought he heard something in the chamber behind him. By Adeneth's great breasts! he thought, unable to dismiss the feeble though persistently nagging voice which was all that remained of a conscience otherwise buried by lust. Though he tried, he could not shake the feeling that an angry Queen Weth stood behind him, her dagger falling toward his unfaithful back.

He turned around just in time to see a soldier running at him with his spear. Kwasin rolled out of the divan, one naked foot kicking out sidewise to deflect the oncoming spear, the other aimed at the soldier's kneecap. Though Kwasin, now on the floor, did not see what happened next, he later reconstructed it from the three sounds that followed: a sharp cracking, a man's throaty cry, and a woman's husky scream. The cracking was the soldier's knee-cap snapping under Kwasin's blow. The man then reeled forward toward the divan, crying out in pain, his spear still extended before him. The woman screaming was Nelahnes reacting to the spear that had just impaled her abdomen.

Kwasin leaped up and, pulling the soldier from the moaning woman, hurled him against a wall. The man, trying to recover, drew his iron sword as he pulled himself up on his good leg. Kwasin now recognized his opponent as Rowaku, the same sergeant who seemed suspicious of Kwasin's allegiances during the journey to the old temple in the swamps. Before the man could even hobble a single step, Kwasin pulled the spear from Nelahnes' body and ran the weapon's long, two-edged blade deep into Rowaku's chest. Blood spurted from the man's mouth as he collapsed and, in the room's dim torchlight, sprayed Kwasin's naked frame with dark crimson.

On the divan, Nelahnes was gasping and bubbling her last breaths. She had rolled onto her side. Blood streamed down one corner of her mouth, and she cradled her knees to her chest. Kwasin knelt beside her and grabbed the woman by the back of the neck, forcing her to look into his eyes.

"You lured me here to assassinate me!"

Nelahnes said nothing. Her eyes screamed with silent horror.

Kwasin drew close and whispered in the woman's ear. "You're not dead yet," he said. "A gut wound is bad enough, but I can make your last precious moments much more painful. Speak, priestess!"

Nelahnes sputtered, coughing, but a moment later she managed to talk, though with some difficulty. "Fortune brought you to me . . . or so I thought. Rowaku was to kill you before he escorted you back to the palace. Then you came to the temple and . . . knowing your reputation . . . I . . . I figured I would provide more than ample distraction for Rowaku to complete his mission." Now Nelahnes smiled, her teeth glistening with blood. "Taphiru and I were to share the throne," she continued, her voice rasping heavily. "You have spoiled my half of our plans, but my lover will still rule Dythbeth." She laughed, coughing up more blood. "Minruth has promised it to him . . . assassins . . . many . . . paid off several in high places . . . and already his arrogant daughter Awineth . . . and your wife . . ." The woman's lids fluttered for a moment and then her eyes glazed with death.

Kwasin grew cold. He rose and ran from the death-scented room, retrieving his clothes and sword from where they had been laid out for him just outside the entryway to the first chamber. As he hastily donned his kilt, the priestess came up the temple steps bearing the bowl of bull's blood he had requested for the altar. The woman looked in horror at the blood smearing Kwasin's body and gasped, her trembling hands threatening to drop her burden. She must have thought history repeated itself and he had again raped a priestess and slain the temple guards. He could have tried to explain, but he could spare no time. The lives of the queen and the empress were in danger, if the two had not been assassinated already. He leaped down the steps past the priestess, whom he heard cry out for help a few moments later. Apparently she had discovered the body of her superior, Nelahnes. He would have much to sort out later, but just now he needed to get to the palace.

His guards, minus the man he had killed, were waiting for him on the street as he bolted from the garden path. He shouted at them to follow in haste and without question if they valued the lives of their queen and empress. Still, he did not trust the men. Where one traitor could be planted, so could another, especially when someone as prestigious as the keeper of Kho's sacred temple was party to the conspiracy.

All too long seemed the temple road as Kwasin ran along it in the direction of the palace, but finally he was crossing the moat and sprinting up the palace steps. As he passed inside, he volleyed orders at the royal guards to lock down the palace and to seek out and protect Queen Weth and the empress. The guards leaped to their tasks, though Kwasin could not but wonder if one or possibly even all of the men could be in on the plot. Perhaps he should not have warned the guards at all but rather acted as if nothing out of the ordinary were underway. Too late for that. But then again, if the men were part of the coup, wouldn't they have attacked the king when he approached? He shook the questions from his mind and concentrated on finding Awineth and Weth as quickly as possible.

He entered the throne room and found it empty, then passed into the queen's antechamber, startling three priestesses who cried out at seeing Kwasin's blood-streaked countenance.

"Where is your queen?" Kwasin growled.

"She is in her chambers and not to be disturbed." The priestess who spoke moved in front of the passageway leading to the queen's quarters. "The queen has commanded it!" the woman added when Kwasin advanced toward her.

Kwasin's face must have blackened at her words, for the woman shrank before him, though she did not move from her position blocking the doorway.

"The queen is in danger! I don't care about—"

A woman screamed somewhere down the corridor. The priestess before him dropped a hand to the dagger on her hip, and now Kwasin understood why the customary guards were not stationed outside the queen's antechamber. The three priestesses were part of the conspiracy.

With a shout of rage, Kwasin shoved the woman out of his way and dashed down the corridor toward Weth's chamber. He turned at the end of the hallway and entered the room, his rage turning to anguish at the sight that met him.

Weth's unmoving form lay sprawled in the room's center, her white robe now darkened with red. An expanding puddle of blood pooled across the bright, mosaic-tiled floor. Kwasin knelt beside his wife but dread Sisisken had already taken her spirit. He kissed her dead lips, swearing to holy Kho that he would make her murderer pay.

Whoever had killed her must have done so only moments before. He scanned the room for an exit other than the corridor from which he had entered. He saw nothing until his eyes alighted on a stone block in the wall directly adjoining a large wooden wardrobe. The large wall piece, though identical to its companions, was set slightly ajar. Further, the murals painted on the plastered wall above it looked a shade brighter than those adorning the rest of the chamber, as if someone had recently moved the wardrobe from the spot.

He knelt by the block of stone and ran his fingers along its exposed edges until he found a groove that permitted a fingerhold. Kwasin pulled with his fingertips and the large rectangular stone facing swung out easily on oiled hinges, revealing the dark maw of a sharply descending tunnel. He knew of the complex maze of passageways that snaked beneath the palace, utilized by the priests and priestesses for their secretive purposes, though he had not yet had time to explore those accessible to the king. Quickly, he grabbed a torch from a wall sconce and descended into the pitch-black abyss.

After making several dizzying turns in the seemingly unending labyrinth, Kwasin began to doubt the wisdom of his actions. He cursed, realizing he had lost his way in the dark warrens when Awineth needed him most. Then, just as he determined he would try to retrace his steps back to Weth's chamber, he noticed a faint glow from a side tunnel ahead. Kwasin tossed his torch down the tunnel behind him, not wanting to alert anyone ahead of his presence, and padded forward toward the light.

The side tunnel narrowed, forcing Kwasin to turn his massive shoulders and proceed sideways. Now the floor angled sharply as the tunnel rose back toward the lower levels of the palace. At a reckless pace, Kwasin shuffled up the steep incline, once falling on his stomach, the skin on his chest scraping painfully against the rough flooring as he slid downward. But Kwasin was nothing if not a creature of stubborn determination. He thought of Weth's pale, lifeless face, picked himself up, and ascended again.

Light streamed through an opening above and ahead of him. Finally, his hands and knees bloodied, Kwasin pulled himself up to the lip of the opening and gazed into a spacious chamber. Three men, two of them bearing spears, stood with their backs to him in front of Awineth, who had drawn her long, jeweled ceremonial dagger. She was cursing the men, calling them traitors that the Goddess would wipe from the face of the earth like insignificant insects. On the other hand, she told them, if they put down their weapons and swore allegiance to her, she would make sure they were properly rewarded with *nasuhno* and positions of power in the government.

The man in the center, a mohawk-headed priest, laughed at her. "All that separates me from the kingship of Dythbeth is your death. By now my assassins have killed that loutish giant Kwasin—only Resu knows how he was allowed to ascend the throne—and I myself have just thrust my own dagger into the breast of Queen Weth."

A red haze filled Kwasin's vision as at last he recognized the man who stood before him—Taphiru, the treacherous priest and murderer of King Roteka. But how had the priest entered the city? Only the most loyal of sentries had been posted at the city's gates. One of them, however, must have betrayed his king and empress. He would interrogate the sentries later.

Rage broiling within, Kwasin leaped at the three men. He did not possess his ax, having left it under guard in his palace quarters when he had departed for his totem hall, but he still wore a short, heavy sword. He pulled the blade from its scabbard and slashed deeply into the neck of the soldier on his right, cutting clean through the man's leather neck guard.

Taphiru leaped forward toward Awineth, but the empress lunged viciously at the man with her dagger. Taphiru tried to retreat, but ran into the falling body of the second soldier, whom Kwasin had just cut down with his sword. The priest skidded to his knees, then moaned in panic as he tried to leapfrog away from Kwasin. But the man did not leap quickly enough. With the butt end of his sword's hilt, Kwasin knocked the dagger from the priest's hand and encircled his own giant hand around his victim's throat. Taphiru's eyes bulged in their sockets, but Kwasin only squeezed harder. He did not intend to kill the priest—not yet anyway. There was too much information that could be wrung from him, knowledge about who had participated in the plot to overthrow Awineth and the royalty of Dythbeth.

Then, unexpectedly, Taphiru's body jerked violently and his face underwent an abrupt metamorphosis. His lips, which had been pulled back over his teeth as he struggled for breath, went limp, and his eyes, just a moment before trying to leap from his skull, softened and became dull.

Kwasin looked down and saw the tip of a dagger disappear from where it had protruded out of the center of Taphiru's stomach. He released his grip on the priest, who toppled to the floor.

On the other side of Taphiru's corpse stood Awineth, clutching in both hands the bloodied ceremonial dagger, her dark eyes flaming with wild satisfaction.

FIFTEEN

K wasin could not blame Awineth for killing the priest. Blood-lust in the heat of battle was not a thing to be second-guessed, certainly not by him. Still, in the weeks that followed, he could not deny the problems caused that day by Taphiru's death. Not only had Awineth by her actions forever silenced the plot's chief instigator, but a short time later three bodies were found in the palace, their necks broken. The corpses were those of the priestesses who tried to prevent Kwasin from stopping Weth's murder. Someone in the palace from among the priests, priestesses, or military had silenced the three women, and that person—or persons—would be after Kwasin and his empress.

One thing did become simpler for Kwasin after the attacks: Awineth now seemed to trust him, at least more than she had before. And while she did not always include him in her decision making, she did summon him frequently to her royal offices. Once she even spoke of rebuilding the navy and sending a great fleet to plunder Hadon's outpost city after the war on the island was won. The city's great wealth, she said, would help the empire get back on its feet. And, of course, she had an old score to settle with Hadon. She would give Kwasin command of the fleet, as well as half her share of the spoils, if he would bring back Hadon's head. Kwasin grinned with approval at the idea, and was also pleased that Awineth now included him in her distant plans.

In the many meetings he attended, Kwasin fought to remain silent as Awineth voiced her decrees—for the empress of Khokarsa did not consider her ideas about Dythbeth's future open for discussion, even with the city's king. Very often, however, Kwasin's patience wore thin. Upon one such occasion he erupted in protest at Awineth's unquestioning reliance upon the network of priestesses.

"You cannot use them!" Kwasin complained. "They can no longer be trusted!"

Awineth rose from her seat, her beautiful features made harsh with anger.

"The coup could only have succeeded in killing the queen," Kwasin went on before she could speak, "because some of your faithful priestesses have forsaken their sacred vow to Kho."

"The disloyal priestesses were not under my direct supervision," Awineth snapped. "I cannot be faulted if Queen Weth failed to properly screen her attendants. But that is a minor issue compared to the larger one you raise. If the people believed that I, Kho's high vicar, had no faith in the network of priestesses, the entire resistance on the island would crumble in an instant. We are in a Time of Troubles unlike any other, Kwasin! My father seeks to establish the primacy of the male, and everywhere across the empire his irreverent priests are lifting up the sungod to the level of the Goddess. And my sources tell me this is not the worst to come, that my father not only seeks to make Kho the subordinate of Resu, but that he will ultimately throw Her from the pantheon altogether! He would have done so already but the people need time to adjust to his deceptions. While the townsfolk might go along with his blasphemy, those in the country—and they are numerous—are less willing to believe my father's lies. Already he places great strains upon their patience by recruiting the island's rural population to continue work on the Great Tower, even as he sends their fathers, brothers, and sons to fight and die in his profane war."

Kwasin shook his great mane of hair. "I've had enough!" he exclaimed. "As we sit cowering in the palace with our poison testers, Minruth the Mad will kill us in our sleep. You won't win this war until you have rid yourself of the rats your father has set among us!"

Awineth looked at him skeptically. "And how do you propose to do that?"

"I will bait them myself! Each traitor I find will wish he had never heard the name of Kwasin!"

"Or 'she,'" Awineth added mockingly.

Still smarting from Nelahnes' betrayal, Kwasin almost lost control of his anger. Then Awineth smiled.

"Do what you must," she said. "Military matters are your concern, and about that I can do nothing. There are provisions in the law, however, for those who interfere in religious matters. And until the priestesses decide the issue of Queen Weth's successor, I am the interpreter of the law."

As Kwasin turned to leave, Awineth added, "And watch yourself around Kho's daughters—they have all been ordered to steer clear of you. I know of your passions, Kwasin, but if you find a woman who seeks to entice you, she may well give you a kiss as welcoming as Nelahnes'."

Scowling, Kwasin left the room.

For the first time since he had been crowned king, the throngs of increasingly disgruntled citizens watched Kwasin leave the palace grounds unaccompanied by armed escort. General Hahinqo had blanched when Kwasin told him his plans and urged his king to reconsider. But Kwasin remained firm. The only way to fight an invisible enemy, he said, was to draw him out, to make him think one's guard had been lowered. Finally, sensing the battle over his king's notion was lost, the general had shrugged and set off to oversee the construction of new siege defenses.

Kwasin felt for Hahinqo's great burden. Minruth's forces were already reassembling in the hills beyond the great plain, in numbers that daunted even the combined might of the Dythbethan and Mukhan armies. Hahinqo was in the process of drawing back the allied forces, while simultaneously organizing the remainder of his soldiers to undertake the excavation of great trenches in the earth on the perimeter of the city's outer wall. The trenches would make the enemy's task of storming the city much harder. Further, new spears, javelins, and oil-soaked missiles that could be hurled from the walls needed to be made, and the general was organizing a civilian auxiliary army—mostly made up of women and children—to help with the weapon-making. All that, Kwasin knew, would be a wasted effort if his plan failed.

The crowds parted before their king as he strode forth through the streets. Every now and then Kwasin noticed a familiar face in the crowd, but then he would look casually past the face and continue on. For the most part, however, he failed to see the men stationed in secret among the masses of pedestrians, or those who stood looking down at him from rooftops or out of high windows. The audaciousness of his plan, he thought to himself, was not that he allowed himself to walk among the people. Rather the plan hinged on the fact that the men of his secret guard were trustworthy and not in league with Minruth's conspirators. Hahinqo, however, had personally vouched for the men, and Kwasin made sure that each of them was handpicked from among those he had led into battle himself.

The first day Kwasin had gone out thus did nothing except to enflame the curiosity of the populace. Never had King Roteka walked abroad without escort among the masses, and he had certainly never mingled with the commoners in the taverns, as Kwasin did that afternoon and in the days that followed. At first, Awineth had chided Kwasin, warning him that he set a bad example for those in high office. Kwasin pointed out that his actions in no way broke any law, and that Awineth herself came dangerously close to committing an unlawful offense by interfering with a sensitive military operation. Awineth had fumed. She soon backed off, however, when she began to understand that an unanticipated benefit sprang from the king's unorthodox mixing with the lower classes. It seemed that Kwasin's descent into the coarser strata of Dythbeth's population, far from tarnishing his public image, only served to enhance it. The city's inhabitants were quickly coming to regard their king as one of their own, a real man of the people.

This newfound enthusiasm for their king, Awineth realized, might be channeled into a potent weapon to win the citizens' hearts and minds in this dark time of war, doubt, and famine. Meanwhile, gloating at Awineth's reluctant support, Kwasin proceeded with his plan.

The days passed and nothing eventful transpired. If any of the conspirators took note of Kwasin's habitual jaunts to the shops and drinking halls about the city, they did nothing to give themselves away. And then, just as Kwasin began to believe the traitors had either fled the city or were on to his game, an assassin drew forth from the shadows and struck.

Kwasin had been drinking one evening at the Inn of the Mute Hyena, a local watering hole frequented by palace servants not far from the royal citadel. He sat at a table in a semiprivate alcove overlooking the main room in which the tavern's patrons could be seen engaging in drinking, eating, and general merrymaking. The clientele seemed especially jovial this night, despite the bad news coming in from the front. Kwasin was not greatly surprised. One reason might be that the tavern, serving the city's most wealthy, was still stocked with alcohol, a luxury that was becoming scarce in taverns that catered to the middle classes. But the real reason, he knew, was that the Dythbethan spirit soared freer than the spirits of the other cities in the empire. Dythbeth was the oldest city on the island besides the capital, and many times in its long history had its people stood up against would-be conquerors. This time, Kwasin reflected, might be different. The empire had expanded greatly since the days Dythbeth last thumbed its nose at the capital, and the forces wide and near that now assembled against the City of the Leopard God were unlike anything Kwasin's ancestors had ever faced.

And so, as he pondered the queendom's strengths and weaknesses, Kwasin failed to notice that the man who came to refill his flagon with sorghum beer was not the same who had served him earlier that evening. When he did realize it, it was almost too late.

Kwasin had just taken a deep swig of beer when shouts exploded from the kitchen. An instant later, two members of his secret guard burst out of the kitchen and into the room. Kwasin immediately spat out his mouthful of drink, believing his men had uncovered a plot to poison him. That, however, was not the danger.

As his men ran through the startled patrons to get to him, Kwasin sensed someone behind him. He grabbed hold of the table in front of him and whirled it behind. The table crashed into his server. A gleaming dagger flew into the air and clattered on the oaken floorboards. The mad lust of battle almost seized Kwasin as he leaped at his attempted assassin and throttled the fallen man. Then Kwasin remembered that the man must live or he would not be able to give up his secrets.

He released the man and thrust him at the guards who had now reached the scene. The assassin struggled, but Kwasin's men secured him in irons they had brought along for just this purpose. Before the captive was hauled off, Kwasin took a close look at the fellow. Though the man might have been mistaken for any bald-headed, middle-aged frequenter of the tavern, Kwasin noticed that his lack of hair was by design rather than natural. The man's pate, though bare, revealed a slightly darker shadow running down its center. It was obvious the man had recently shaved a narrow shock of dark hair from his head in an attempt to do away with the distinctive haircut that marked him as a priest of Resu.

That same day the traitor, a lower-echelon palace priest named Dykeko, was brought to a specially prepared cell beneath the palace citadel. Here Kwasin had arranged for a pet of the old king to be boarded and chained to a wall. This was a large and magnificent male leopard said to have been descended from the giant cat that once terrorized the inhabitants of ancient Dythbeth. Kwasin had discovered King Roteka's leopard by accident when a group of soldiers employed at the palace had carted out the proud, though half-emaciated beast. Since food was becoming scarce, the soldiers had intended to slaughter the leopard and divide the animal's meat among themselves. Kwasin, however, could not stand to see such a prideful creature killed with such disrespect, and certainly the spirit of Khukhaken would not look favorably upon Dythbeth's king if he allowed one of his leopard children to be dispatched in such a contemptuous manner. It was then that Kwasin realized he might have a way to use the animal that would at once please Khukhaken and also help root out the traitors.

Kwasin ordered the palace guard to have Dykeko chained to the wall opposite the leopard. The priest must have been frightened at the sight of the ravenous beast in the cell with him, but he managed to feign an air of indifference. Kwasin, looking through a barred window from an adjoining cell, asked the man to reveal his accomplices in the conspiracy to overthrow the rulers of Dythbeth. As he expected, despite the screams and thrashing about of the leopard, the priest refused to speak. Kwasin only smiled. Then he placed his hand upon the crank handle of the special winch he had had his people install in the cell.

Around the winch's spool wound a heavy chain that dropped into a hole in the stone floor. Beneath the floor, the chain crossed under the captive man's cell, up behind the far wall, and out through it. The end of the chain was attached to the leopard's bronze collar and was all that kept the beast from free rein of the cell.

Slowly, Kwasin turned the crank. One by one the links reeled out from the winch. When the leopard realized its chain had slackened, it leaped in a wild frenzy at the man-thing shackled against the opposite wall of the cell. Dykeko yelled out in terror, causing the furious and hunger-driven leopard to hiss, scream, and yank harder against its chained collar.

With great effort, Kwasin reeled the animal away from the sweating man and back closer to its own wall.

Again, Kwasin asked the man to reveal his accomplices. Though the terrified captive had wet his kilt, he still refused to speak.

The leopard's chain again reeled out from the hole near the base of the wall. This time Kwasin spooled out even more chain, until the leopard's claws just grazed the captive man's torso and legs, leaving them streaked with blood. Then Kwasin reeled back the chain, but only by inches.

The beast's screams became so loud now that Kwasin had to shout to be heard above them.

"Tell me the names! Or I'll reel out the full length of the chain!"

The man sobbed. "You might as well!" he cried. "Minruth's spies will find a way to kill me even if you don't. And if I speak, you'll feed me to the leopard anyway!"

Kwasin grinned at the priest through the bars that separated them.

"Too bad then!" Kwasin yelled, and began inching forward the chain.

Suddenly Dykeko's will broke and he began shouting out names. Kwasin reeled back the beast but he asked how he could know for sure that Dykeko wasn't lying to save his skin.

"You'll find secret missives hidden beneath the flooring in my sister's home!" the man shouted. "They will reveal all!"

When Kwasin again began reeling forward the leopard, the man exclaimed, "What are you doing? I've told you what you want!"

"Khukhaken's son is hungry," Kwasin said dryly, but after gauging he had scared the man enough he pulled the leopard back to its side of the cell. The Leopard God's child would have to wait for his meal until Kwasin had verified the man's information.

Kwasin wasted no time in getting to the house of Dykeko's sister, since it was conceivable that the priest's accomplices, once they found out their colleague had been captured, would know to go there and destroy any evidence the man had left behind. Kwasin waited in the house while his men pried up the floorboards and Dykeko's frightened sister and her husband looked on. Finally, one of the king's men called out that he had found something.

Before Kwasin had time to cross the room to see what the soldier had uncovered, a low and heavy rumbling belched up from deep inside the earth's bowels. Then, the entire house shook violently.

"Kho awakes!" someone shouted.

SIXTEEN

The tremor lasted for thirty seconds. The room in which Kwasin stood rattled with such violence that his vision blurred. Halfway through the quaking, part of the building's roof collapsed, piling the soldiers on the other side of the room under a jagged heap of crumbled plaster and splintered cedar beams.

Little on earth frightened Kwasin, but the earthquake shot pangs of fear through him. He cried out to the Goddess and clutched the nearby doorframe as if he were riding the ferry of the dead to the dark depths of Sisisken's underworld.

Suddenly the room ceased its terrible shaking. Kwasin ran to the pile of destruction that was the other side of the room and began heaving up beams and digging through the powdery plaster with his bare hands.

Finally he managed to reach those of his men who had been buried, only to find them all dead, crushed by Kho's wrath. But Kho, Kwasin thought, could not have been angry at him—at least not too angry. She had not only spared his life but also allowed him to pull up from the cracked and splintered flooring the evidence hidden by the priest Dykeko. After gathering up the papyrus scrolls, Kwasin and his surviving guards ran from the ruined building and out into the street.

The district's inhabitants were coming out of their houses and gaping at the destruction wrought by the Goddess. He was lucky the building he had been in had only partially collapsed. Down an adjoining street a long row of buildings had been thrown completely from their foundations. Each of these had collapsed one atop the next in an almost precise east-to-west pattern, as if Great Kho had flicked Her divine finger against a row of lined-up toy blocks. Perhaps in the east Khowot had again erupted and sent a shockwave westward across the island. Standing amid the devastation of his own city, Kwasin could only hope this was the case, and that Minruth's capital lay smothered and utterly destroyed beneath a smoldering sea of burning ash and lava.

Kwasin and his men began thrusting their way through the throngs of distraught residents. Shock had turned to bitter anger. Having seen their king emerge from the half-ruined house, many began shouting at him, accusing him of bringing down misfortune upon their neighborhood with his ill-fated presence. Some yelled at him that he must surely be cursed, since their beloved King Roteka had been killed the very night Kwasin had returned to Dythbeth. And now Queen Weth was dead at the hands of an assassin, and who knew how many had died in the earthquake?

Though they must have felt great trepidation, the guardsmen maintained a stoic demeanor and drew in closer about their king. Kwasin hoped they could reach a safer district before the mob got the notion to hurl at them the bricks, stones, and other debris that lay scattered across the street.

At last they arrived at the main road leading past the military barracks. Here a number of soldiers greeted him, giving their king a much different welcome from the one he had just received in the poverty-stricken district behind him. Instead of feeling cursed by Kwasin's presence, the soldiers seemed heartened at the unexpected appearance of the king who had fought so valiantly at their side. Several men cheered out his name, but Kwasin could waste no time on adulation. As he jogged down the road, he shouted at those who were not already busy dealing with the earthquake's mayhem, telling them that any soldier who was able should make haste and accompany him to the palace, as their empress might be in desperate need of help. The soldiers in range of his voice immediately stopped what they were doing and joined their king.

When they neared the palace, Kwasin began to fear greatly for Awineth's safety. Even from a distance he could see that a massive fissure had cracked down the face of the citadel's great dome, the dark, jagged breach looking like a lightning bolt in the negative. An enormous amount of granite must have tumbled down inside the palace's main chamber when the tremor struck. Anyone beneath the fissure—and Awineth's duties as empress brought her often to the throne room under the dome—would have been killed instantly.

By the time he was halfway across the bridge that spanned the moat, he could see a group of priestesses congregating near the base of the citadel's eastern side. He sighed heavily, surprised at the depth of his relief. Among them he spied Awineth. The queen's antechamber, which Awineth had occupied after Weth's death, was positioned along the eastern wall of the palace, and Kwasin guessed the empress and her attendants must have fled the room by means of secret tunnels of which he had no knowledge.

Kwasin's party had crossed half the distance between the bridge and the palace when without warning the earth again began to shake and rumble. The aftershock lasted for only a moment, but another mass of the royal palace's great dome tumbled inward, its crash thundering across the courtyard. Awineth and her priestesses could be seen fleeing down the rear steps of the palace, trying to get to a safe distance away from the damaged building.

Awineth's face was drawn and pale when Kwasin finally met up with her. She took Kwasin aside from the others and said, "I know you have much work to do, but the people will need to be reassured. They will need to see me as soon as possible, and I need you to arrange it. I have already instructed my priestesses to spread word that Kho is angry at the blasphemous traitors of Minruth who have infiltrated our city. If any among the citizenry know the names of the traitors, they had better surrender them immediately or they will be struck down."

"I have news on that front which will please you, O Queen." Kwasin held up the scrolls he had recovered from the house of

Dykeko's sister. "I possess here the names of those who must be routed out."

"That is good news indeed," Awineth said. "But just before the temblor I received word from the oracle in the old temple. Wasemquth has revealed a dire prophecy from the Goddess." Awineth paused, and again Kwasin felt the unfamiliar fear course through him.

"Kho warns that if the old order is not soon maintained," Awineth continued, "She will destroy all the land, including Her faithful people. It is an ominous message, of which today's devastation is a clear harbinger, but I have begun to circulate the oracle's prophecy in the hope that it will rally the people of Dythbeth to fight even harder.

"And Kwasin," she said, surprising him by laying a hand gently upon his arm and looking up at him with softened eyes. "I will need to rely on you greatly in the days and months to come. As will the people. And for that reason, and that alone, it is best we are not at odds. Hadon, who would have been my king had he not turned and fled like a coward when I needed him most, has by his actions forsaken the Goddess. But there is no time to hold Great Games to determine who is worthy of Kho's high priestess. War, however, is a game greater than any staged contest, and in war you have indeed proven yourself a champion. Make no mistake, Kwasin, I do not love you, nor do I think that I, who have seen so much corruption and distrust, shall ever know love. The marriage will be one of convenience, and if I didn't believe it was necessary to win the war, I would never consider it."

Even with her words of denial, she reached up and placed her hands about Kwasin's neck and, drawing down his head, kissed him warmly upon the lips. Kwasin, though he was later to lament the missed opportunity, was too surprised to respond.

When Awineth pushed him away a moment later, he found her eyes had returned to their usual cold gray.

"Your city is in ruins, O King," she said frostily. "Do not dally while your people are in need." And then she turned her back on him and rejoined the party of priestesses.

SEVENTEEN

In the days following the earthquake, things became much worse for the Dythbethans. A series of violent aftershocks jolted the region over the next two weeks, bringing further devastation to the already reeling city. Soldiers had to be pulled from the task of fortifying the walls, and additional troops were recalled from the front lines to help with the reconstruction and restoration of vital services.

Further, it seemed the enemy had fared much better than the city-dwellers. The Khokarsans had weathered the quakes without significant damage, their structures at best consisting of a number of transportable tents. General Phoeken, sensing an opportunity, swarmed his troops into the vacuum left by the recalled Dythbethan armies. Before long, General Hahinqo and General Wahesa were forced to cede any gains made during the past two months, allowing the Khokarsan armies to close in on the city. Within a month after the first tremor, Phoeken's men once again loomed just beyond the city walls, on the eastern boundaries of the great plain.

The Dythbethans were also running out of food. The few remaining shops in the marketplaces lacked their usual abundance of local and exotic goods. No more the delightful aroma of freshly baked millet and emmer bread wafting in the air, nor the bountiful array of baskets bearing colorful fruits and vegetables; no pigs or domesticated buffalo waiting for slaughter; no ducks, partridges, ravens, and parrots left to quack, screech, croak, and whistle at the market-goers; and, perhaps worst of all, no casks of millet beer, sorghum beer, mead, wine, or *s"okoko*. Instead, driven to desperation by the blockade, the handful of merchants still in business had resorted to peddling the scrawny carcasses of domesticated animals such as dogs and cats, most of which had been rounded up from their owners by the merchants' henchmen. A great price was charged for the meat, which only the richest in the city could afford. And to prevent rampant thievery by the desperately hungry, the merchants were required to hire guards—paid in food, of course—for their shops. Even insects, that usually ever-abundant staple of the Khokarsan diet, seemed to have become scarce and were being sold at exorbitant prices by the merchants. But mostly it was every man, woman, and child out for his or her own family.

The feeble remnants of Dythbeth's once-proud navy had also suffered significant losses during the tremors and afterward. Great waves caused by the initial quake had sunk five biremes and three uniremes with all hands aboard. Only three weeks later, Admiral Nemusaketh was forced to defend the harbor against an all-out attack by the Khokarsan fleet. While Nemusaketh managed to hold his position and drive Minruth's Admiral Poedy back out beyond the mouth of the harbor, he had little confidence he could hold the bay for long. He had lost another seven biremes to the deadly rams of Poedy's ships. Awineth, on hearing the news, flew into a rage and ordered Kwasin to assist Admiral Nemusaketh. But before he could do that, Awineth summoned a great rally and called on Kwasin to assist her.

Standing on the high steps before the crumbing palace citadel, with the starving and disconsolate masses thronging beneath her, the queen of queens announced the prediction of the oracle.

"Great Kho," Awineth's rang out, "is preparing to shatter the foundations of the world and lay waste to her people!"

The hordes of citizens gasped. Many prostrated themselves upon the ground, while others moaned and, in an expression of great distress, beat their fists against their own heads.

"But this need not be!" Awineth cried out to the crowd. "Dythbeth must remain strong! All is not yet lost! Kho is angry, yes, but she has also laid down the groundwork for our salvation. Almost ten years ago Kho ordered the oracle to exile a man to the empire's hinterlands. Kho did this not merely to punish the man for his crimes, but also because She wanted to mold him into a warrior so great he could one day lead the battle against Her son Resu. But the plans of the Goddess are often obscure in the moment, and for reasons then unknown She also sent the winner of the Great Games to the Wild Lands to locate a mighty weapon—an extraordinary ax, made of a metal forged and tempered by the raging fires of the stars themselves! A weapon of such potent strength that—in the hands of the right hero—it might smite down Resu's armies and slay the sungod himself!"

Kwasin, like many in the crowd below, stirred uncomfortably at Awineth's words. Her sentiment went against the centuries-old tradition that placed Resu second only to Kho in the holy pantheon, and on equal footing to the Goddess according to the strict liturgical interpretation, though the latter view was largely ignored by the populace. But voicing such thoughts of deicide was perilous indeed. Awineth had been as cunning as she was careful—she had not said with certainty that Resu would be slain by the ax, but rather that he *might* be slain. Still, the implication remained clear: Kho's high vicar believed the Goddess was considering overturning the old order and removing Resu permanently from the pantheon. As Kwasin looked on in disbelief, a majority of the onlookers erupted in frenzied support of their empress, shouting out wild encouragements. The faces of the priests and their followers, however, turned white.

Awineth waited for the official criers to carry her message to the farthest reaches of the crowd and then continued.

"But the heart of Hadon—the winner of the Great Games of Klakor—turned treacherous under the temptations of a woman—Resu's pawn, the evil White-Witch-from-the-Sea—and so Hadon turned his back on his queen. But Kho, Who sees all before it happens, foresaw this and caused the sky ax to fall to another, a mortal unlike any other—half-man, half-god—who might slay all Her enemies. The defender of the Goddess," she cried, "the great hero selected by Kho to wield Her mighty weapon, now stands before you! Behold, the future betrothed of Kho's high priestess, and the future king of kings over all the land! Behold, King Kwasin of Dythbeth!"

At this moment, a priestess drew back the curtain from a framed structure that had been erected to hide Kwasin while Awineth addressed the multitude. Instantly, a thunderous cheer rose up and the spectators began chanting Kwasin's name. As he had prepared in consultation with Awineth before the rally, Kwasin raised above his head the massive ax that had once belonged to the hero Wi, and then the manling Paga. Those in the audience who were not too weak from lack of food thundered out their adulations. The priests, of course, again refrained from applause.

While the ovations, smattered with the occasional jeering, reached a crescendo, the traitors named in the missives of the priest Dykeko were paraded out and made to lay their heads upon a long stone bench that had been set up at the top of the palace steps. The accused, consisting of four priests and two priestesses formerly serving in the palace, had stood no trial other than that in the mind of the high priestess of Kho. New provisions in the law permitted bypassing the usual court system in such cases during wartime. Awineth, Kwasin reflected, seemed excessively eager to consolidate any power she could.

A naked priestess, her face shrouded from view by a veil of black linen, stood beside the prisoners as guards secured them with iron chains to the stone bench. The veil represented the unknowable visage of Sisisken, goddess of the dead, and the great scythe the woman held symbolized the tool used by Sisisken to reap the spirit from the body of those she welcomed into her dark realm. Six times the scythe swung down. Then a soldier took the hair of the disembodied heads and tied them together with rope.

Later that day, by the king's order, the gruesome bundle of heads was loaded into a catapult high atop one of Dythbeth's crenellated towers and launched onto the center of the great plain. Kwasin had no doubt General Phoeken would understand the message.

EIGHTEEN

After the rally, determined to prove himself to Awineth and reverse the series of losses that had besieged the city, Kwasin sought out Admiral Nemusaketh. He asked the admiral if he could hold off Poedy's navy and maintain his occupation of the bay for another ten days. Nemusaketh replied he could make no guarantees, but if his king so ordered it, he would hold the bay or die trying.

And so it was that ten days later, on the first moonless night of the month of the goddess Khukly in the Year of the Honeybee, Kwasin rowed out with a fleet of twenty-two black-painted long-boats on the calm waters of Dythbeth's harbor. As he paddled away from the docks he murmured a prayer to Tesemines, goddess of the night, and also sight and blindness. He would need her help if his plan were to succeed. He also prayed to Piqabes and Kho. It couldn't hurt to be too careful.

The longboats cut smoothly past Admiral Nemusaketh's stately trireme and the thirty-three surviving biremes and uniremes that patrolled the mouth of the bay. Leaving the galley fleet behind and paddling forth into the Kemu's impenetrable blackness, Kwasin felt an almost overpowering sense of loneliness envelop him. The enormity of the dark sea struck him, and he wondered at the incomprehensible game that was being played out by the deities while their mortal subjects struggled and died.

They rowed for a great while before Kwasin saw the first evidence of Poedy's fleet, a faint glimmer of light in the gloom that winked into and then out of existence. Probably the door to an officer's cabin on one of the galleys had swung open and closed, briefly revealing lantern light from within.

Kwasin looked back toward the bay. Nowhere could Nemusaketh's fleet be seen in the inky night, though he knew that by now the galleys had already begun rowing forth behind him. He was hoping for a one-two blow against Poedy's ships: first his own longboats doing the unexpected, and then, out of the pitch black of the moonless night, a strike by Nemusaketh's entire navy. Small though the latter might be, and even smaller the odds of the longboats' success, it was Dythbeth's best hope to weaken the Khokarsan blockade and possibly allow some supply ships to get through. If Kwasin failed in his mission, however, there was a good chance Poedy would take the harbor. Then, Dythbeth would fall in a matter of days at most.

A charcoal-based pigment darkened Kwasin's skin and that of the other rowers in the longboats, effectively cloaking them from the enemy galleys. Kwasin himself could only barely discern the craft that cut the waters just a few yards away, though he could hear paddles slicing the water.

He whispered to the five oarsmen in his own boat and instructed them to head in the direction of the light that had briefly shone. The boat beside him followed dutifully, and Kwasin hoped it would continue to do so. It was a long swim back to the mainland.

Having emerged into the wider Kemu, Kwasin's boat loped forward on the crests and troughs of large, rolling waves. A few stars glinted through the breaks in the clouds and, as he rose up with the boat's bow, he caught the faint flicker of lightning on the southern horizon. The rainy season was about to begin again, when rapidly forming and often violent storms were known to sweep across both great inland seas over a period of one to two months. Though he hoped the cloud cover would remain, he did not want to be caught out on the Kemu in a storm. Further, if the lightning moved northward and intensified, it could easily reveal his boats to the enemy.

He bent into his oar and quietly urged the other rowers to do the same.

The wind shifted and Kwasin and his crew had a hard time keeping the boat upright and on course. As waves broke across the boat's windward side, and cold seawater splashed over them, Kwasin began worrying that the flammable oil and resin with which the vessel had been doused would be rendered ineffective. He did not worry long, however. At that moment, the boat crested high above the other waves and he saw the enemy galley not twenty-five yards to port.

By Great Kho's teats, he was fortunate! The galley was a trireme. Tesemines must be looking down at him and stretching her toothless grin. Perhaps Kho or Piqabes would reward him too and the galley would turn out to be Admiral Poedy's ship.

He could no longer hear the paddles of the other longboat, however, and would have to trust that it still managed to pace them.

After much difficulty fighting the waves, Kwasin and his crew managed to pull alongside the trireme. The oars of the large vessel were in their upward and locked position, which was fortunate. Otherwise, anchoring to the galley's side would have been impossible; the many oars, sinking down into the water from their three banks, would have gotten in the way. And of course, had they been at their banks, the oarsmen on the galley might have spotted the longboat. As it was, the lookout on the galley's deck must have been nodding off or else had failed to spot Kwasin's boat because of the rolling waves which hid it half the time.

The linen-padded bumpers on either side of the specially equipped boat thudded against the galley's side. Kwasin and his fellows scanned the murky night for their escort but saw nothing. Kwasin swallowed a curse and signaled his men to proceed. They did not hesitate, but the little he could see of their pigment-darkened faces showed worry.

Again the cloth bumpers knocked the galley. As one, three of the seamen cast their ropes upward, each of the three-pronged, iron-legged grapples successfully catching over the lip of the lowest bank of oars. Kwasin and the two men who had not cast grapples drove their foot-long iron hooks, which were attached to a short line of rope tied to the boat, into the galley's wooden side. Now for the tricky part . . .

As Kwasin stood there on the rocking boat, the waves breaking over the vessel's side, his plan no longer seemed so smart. Nemusaketh had warned Kwasin that the dampness of the open sea would make his task extremely difficult, and maybe impossible, but the idea of setting Poedy's flagship afire, escaping on a companion boat, and opening the way for Nemusaketh's pitiful fleet to attack had been a desperate one to begin with.

Kwasin unslung the wax-sealed waterproof satchel from around his shoulders and removed from it a flint, a piece of iron, and a bag of dried tinder. The boat, though semi-anchored to the larger vessel, was throwing with the waves and knocking its port bumper repeatedly against the galley. He knew it was only a matter of moments before someone would come to investigate the noise and vibration.

He signaled one of the men to start dousing the galley's side with oil from three ceramic jugs they had brought along. When they were done, he motioned for all but one man—his backup, who also bore a wax-sealed satchel with kindling materials—to jump over the side into freezing sea water. They looked out into the darkness for the other boat and then back to Kwasin, the wide whites of their eyes appearing as pale circles against their blackened faces. Kwasin glared at them, then began striking his flint against the iron. Let them all burn with the galley, he thought.

Someone cried out above. Kwasin looked up, but seeing no one, he returned to his task of furiously striking the iron. Now he could hear the sound of men running across the deck. He cursed. The moist air had dampened the iron and he could get no spark.

"It's not going to light, we should cast off!" one of the men called quietly to Kwasin.

Still striking the flint, Kwasin swung out a leg and kicked the man backward into the sea. "Cast off then!" he yelled. He did not bother looking to find out if the man managed to stay afloat or had sunk into Piqabes' cold bosom.

Realizing their king meant business, the other men in the boat jumped overboard, leaving behind only Kwasin and his backup. Then the backup cried out and fell onto the bottom of the boat. Dim light shone down on the longboat as a lantern was hung over the side of the deck above, accompanied by more shouting. The sheen of metal, reflecting in the lantern light, revealed a dagger's hilt protruding from the fallen man's neck. The man lay completely still.

Kwasin leaped belly-first across the longboat. In the dim light he had seen the dead man's iron drop on top of his bag of kindling—maybe the man's iron was drier than his own. He grabbed the iron from the bag and began striking it with his own flint, but the stone slid off the slick metal as if the latter were greased. It was no use.

He rose to get off the boat before the men above could cast another dagger at him. Looking up he saw an orange glow wisping above him in the sea breeze. It flitted first one way and then another, before a strong gust brought it quickly to the deck on the other side of the longboat.

The ember—which must have dropped from the wick of the lantern that had been hung over the galley's side—smoldered orangely for a moment, then grew steadily in intensity. Suddenly flames were streaking across the oil- and resin-saturated wood, and Kwasin leaped from the longboat into the frigid waves before he became a part of the rapidly blazing pyre.

Kwasin, full of swagger and cocksure about his abilities when on dry land, suddenly found himself at the mercy of the waves. Or rather, the mercilessness of them. The tall swells rolled over him ceaselessly, making it difficult to breaststroke without gulping down large amounts of sea water. He turned over on his back and began backstroking away from the ship. Once, lifted up high on a wave, Kwasin saw one of the men who had jumped off the longboat. Then the man was gone, hidden behind the wall of water.

Rising and falling, Kwasin also caught occasional glimpses of the trireme. Flames engulfed the galley's port side. Men were dumping buckets of water over the side in a futile attempt to extinguish the fire, but the oil- and resin-soaked longboat continued to burn, fueling the oil-doused wooden beams of the galley at the waterline. The ship was already beginning to take on water, listing heavily to port.

One down, Kwasin thought.

As if responding to his observation, first one and then another fiery glimmer appeared through the choppy waters—and then four, five, six points of flickering yellow-orange flame broke out on the horizon. At least six of the other longboats had succeeded in setting galleys afire!

A rhythmic sound came to him over the water, then disappeared. For a moment he thought he'd imagined it, but then the deep booming returned and he could not deny it. He couldn't be sure about the direction of the sound, so tossed about had he become, but it seemed to come from the east. If that were true, then it could only be the drummers on the decks of Nemusaketh's fleet, their deep, steady beat synchronizing the strokes of the rowers.

Lightning erupted on the southern horizon. For a moment a strange image formed out of the darkness and imprinted itself on his inner eye. He saw a line of galleys—Poedy's fleet—on the open sea, some of the ships flaming in the night, others with oars extended into the sea and rowing rapidly forward toward the bay. But that was not the strange thing.

Three ships, unlike anything Kwasin had ever before seen, had materialized in the lightning flash. They appeared to be sailing through the opening left by Poedy's burning galleys, heading into the bay *against the wind*! The ships were of sleek design, with long, narrow decks, perhaps spanning sixty feet from fore to aft, but what stood out most were the vessels' strange-looking triangular sails. Not square, but *triangular*.

There! The lightning flashed again. There could be no doubt: the oddly designed craft were moving at a tremendous speed past

Poedy's ships. Already they had far outpaced the blockade and were heading into the opening of the bay. He had never seen a ship move so swiftly. These would have left behind even the fastest galley, which could travel at speeds of up to fifteen knots. At first Kwasin was afraid Poedy had unleashed some new and terrible war craft against the Dythbethans, but then he saw illuminated in a lighting flash the symbol on the sails of the speeding ships: a stylized oak tree, the symbol of Karneth, daughter of Kho. The newcomers were allies of the Goddess!

Now the tempest to the south raged. Bolts of lightning split the horizon, allowing Kwasin to see some of what was happening about him. The Dythbethan galleys were rowing forward to engage the enemy. Compared to the swift, triangular-sailed ships that sped past them, the galleys seemed painfully slow and awkward. Still, the latter were effective, he thought, as a unireme rowed on a collision course with a Khokarsan trireme. The larger vessel turned its rudder and tried to veer leeward. But the ship moved slowly, oh, ever so slowly. Before the trireme could get out of the way, the Dythbethan unireme swung sharply about in an impressive maneuver and laterally raked its ram across the enemy's stern, gutting an entire bank of oars. The unireme swung around again as it neared the aft of its opponent, a striking move that fully wrecked the trireme's steering rudder. Now completely disabled, the trireme floated dead in the water. The skilled captain of the unireme, now able to take his time, swung back out to sea. When he gauged he had attained enough distance to attain full speed, he brought his vessel back for the kill and rammed his enemy's broadside. Then the oarsmen on the unireme began rowing back-ward to extricate their ship from the trireme's side. Within minutes, the trireme sank.

Kwasin shouted for the unireme, but the crewmen could not hear him. He had little choice but to begin swimming for the southern mainland. There he would have to elude the many enemy troops which occupied the area, but what other choice did he have? He could not tread water forever.

Then came the evening's final blessing, though he was unsure whether to attribute it to Tesemines, Piqabes, or Kho. Out of the rolling waters before him lifted the bow of a longboat. Moments later, hands reached out to grab his cold-numbed arms and pulled him up onto the deck.

NINETEEN

I am technically already employed by you, O Queen," the young redheaded man was saying. "Before the civil war, I had applied to the Naval Department, but that drunkard of an admiral I spoke with threw me out! He didn't believe my ships could do what I said. But the Temple of Kho had better sense and hired me to build my fore-and-aft sailing ships for the postal system of the priestesses. All under the banner of your name, so to speak."

Kwasin, Awineth, Admiral Nemusaketh, and the wiry little fisherman's son from Bhabhobes sat round a table in a small hexagonal, marble-walled room in the College of Awines. With the palace unsafe for habitation after the earthquake, the college now served as Awineth's headquarters. The acolytes in the college assured the queen that the building was the most secure structure in the city, impervious to the worst of Kho's upheavals thanks to an innovative design conceived by the genius Awines over a thousand years ago. Perhaps the acolytes' claims amounted to more than the mere bragging they seemed to be, for indeed, unlike many of the great edifices in the city, the college had suffered not so much as a cracked flooring tile during the recent quake.

"After war broke out," the young man continued, "I was sent across the Kemus on an important errand by the priestess at Kloepeth. We anchored at Rebha the very night the pile city burned, and my ship, the *Wind-Spirit*, was lost."

Awineth regarded the man askance. "The priestess at Kloepeth?" she asked, suspicion edging her voice. "Just what errand did Suguqatheth send you on, Captain Ruseth? What cargo did you bear for her, and what port was your destination?"

Ruseth's blue eyes looked coolly across the table at his queen. "The records at Kloepeth will confirm that my destination was the city of Wentisuh, and as to what secret message I carried from the priestess, only Piqabes may say. It was lost with my vessel."

Kwasin didn't believe the freckled youth; he was holding something back. Both Awineth and Hadon also had been at the temple at Kloepeth. Could it be that Awineth believed Ruseth had smuggled Hadon to the safety of his native city, only a short jaunt across the southern sea from the city of Wentisuh? Whatever the case, Kwasin took an immediate dislike to the young sailor sitting before him.

Awineth seemed unfazed by Ruseth's apparent deception, at least outwardly. She smiled and said, "It is indeed fortunate you arrived when you did, Captain." She picked up a pomegranate from a basket of fruit on the table. "The food you have brought on your ships is a blessing to the city, though it won't go far. We are beyond desperate, and if Dythbeth falls, so fall the hopes of all who love and worship Kho. Tell me, how did it come about that you found a patron to fund the construction of your new ships, and is further aid on its way?"

"After my ship was lost," Ruseth said, "I managed to make it aboard one of the giant raft-islands of the K'ud"em'o, which took me to Wethna. From there I signed up as a deckhand aboard a merchant galley headed back to Khokarsa. I had already heard you were here, O Queen, and that Dythbeth was to be the last stand on the island for the worshipers of Kho. My trials to get to you, however, were many. Pirates attacked the merchant galley aboard which I served, and I was imprisoned and brought as a slave to Mikawuru. But Suhkwaneth tipped fortune in my favor, and the man to whom I was sold was a devout supporter of your cause. He had recently come into great fortune after sinking the *Haken*, the infamous pirate ship that has long stalked the seas around the

Strait of Keth, recovering from its sunken wreckage the legendary diamond known as the Begetter of All Jewels. When this man heard my story, he realized my fore-and-aft ships might make all the difference in the war against Minruth. Immediately he granted me my freedom, commissioning the construction of three ships to aid the forces of the queen of queens and run supplies past Minruth's blockade. And now here I am at your service, Holy One."

Kwasin had heard of the legendary *Haken*, or Death Hawk, though some referred to it as the Red Death because of its crimson sail and the bloody toll it had taken in the strait over the years. That it had sunk was one fewer thing Kwasin had to worry about.

Turning from Ruseth, Awineth said, "Admiral, what is the status of your fleet?"

Though the wrinkles beneath Nemusaketh's eyes hung heavy with fatigue, the old seaman's lips stretched over a crooked-toothed smile. "We have achieved a victory I had not thought possible, O Queen. Thirty of Poedy's galleys have found their final resting place at the bottom of the bay, and though we lost five ships, we captured another seven. Two of these are supply ships bearing food and provisions meant for Phoeken's troops. We have requisitioned these for our own military, but as you say, the food won't go far. We must get a ship out of port to seek aid while Poedy still reels from our attack. But it will be dangerous even now. The enemy still holds the waters around the island."

"That's where you come in, Captain," Awineth said, turning back to Ruseth. "I need you to take your ships and, as quickly as possible, return with help and supplies. One ship will go to Towina, from where we've received word that the allies of the Goddess yet manage to hold off the forces of Resu. The others will go to Qethruth and Bawaku to seek support from the priestesses there. It will be a difficult task because of the hard times suffered by all, but you must convince our allies to build many more ships of your new design. If they don't come quickly to the aid of Kho's high priestess, the island will fall to the supporters of Resu. And if that happens, Kho will certainly destroy all the land."

"Getting away from the island won't be a problem," Ruseth said, swagger now pumping his voice. "My ships can run circles around Poedy's fleet. And once those in Towina, Qethruth, and Bawaku see how much faster glide the sails of the fore-and-aft compared to the old square sails, they'll be clamoring to make more."

Nemusaketh's watery eyes carried doubt. "It is true I saw your ships break through the blockade, but they would not have been able to do so if we hadn't cleared the way with our attack. And your narrow vessels, which by their very design can't possibly mount rams on their bows and impact enemy ships without themselves sinking, are still vulnerable to Poedy's rams and missiles."

"I can far outpace any ram-headed galley, be it trireme or unireme," Ruseth replied. "And as long as my ships aren't lying at anchor, any missiles fired at them will be left far behind to fizzle in the sea."

The admiral grunted in disbelief. But Kwasin, recalling the speed of the triangle-sailed ships, thought Ruseth might not be bluffing.

"We have no other option," Awineth said. "The situation becomes grave. The Klemqaba warriors my father recruited from the southwestern mountains along the Kemu have begun pouring into the area. Though they are an unruly lot, more often apt to fight among themselves than attack outsiders, they are eager for loot and blood. If their commanders don't order them to do so first, they'll attack the city on their own. And the wild mountain men brought in from beyond the coast of the northern mainland aren't much more patient."

"I won't fail you, O Queen," the young sailor said.

"Don't. As of now, I authorize you to head the navy's ship-building department, feeble though it now stands. If you succeed in your mission, however, I shall make you a full admiral, answerable only to myself."

The admiral glowered at Ruseth, as if daring the freckled youth to think of himself as an equal. Then he said, "O Queen, if my business here is done, I need to get back to my fleet. I must begin drafting preparations to clear the way for this boy and his clever toys."

Ruseth's cheeks turned the bright red of his hair.

Kwasin erupted in laughter, slapping the wiry youth so hard on his back that he began to cough.

"Ho!" Kwasin exclaimed. "Fleet are your ships, Captain Ruseth, but nowhere near as fleet as the tongue of an old seaman! But I wouldn't worry, Admiral. As king of Dythbeth, I control the military and you are ultimately answerable to me. Ruseth might indeed be as smart as Awines, though I doubt it, but he certainly doesn't have the experience to outrank you."

"And does your experience as a whoring drunk who defiles temple priestesses qualify you to be king?" Awineth snapped icily.

Kwasin merely rolled his eyes, while Nemusaketh and Ruseth looked uncomfortable.

"Although I will do everything in my power to maintain the old order," Awineth went on, "some things must change if we are to win this war. We must begin to reward those who bring us results, and diminish the power of those who are ineffective. I am not speaking of you, Admiral. I am impressed with what you have managed to accomplish with so little."

Nemusaketh conceded a half-smile.

"And another thing that may change in the future," Awineth added, "is that the priestesses may have more say in military matters."

The room fell silent. The notion went against laws that stretched back hundreds of years, and precedents that dated to a time when the island was still inhabited by uncivilized barbarians.

Perhaps sensing she had gone too far, Awineth rose and said, "I have much work to do myself. Admiral, if you will, please have your guards escort Captain Ruseth to his vessel. We can't risk anything happening to our naval prodigy." And then, as if to test her authority, she looked at Kwasin and said, "And you will go to the docks to see that the food is properly distributed. Half will be dispensed evenly between the Temple of Kho and the military, and the remainder will go to the people. Double the guards at the wharves. No matter how fairly we divide the food, there are certain to be riots. But I am trusting you, as king and commander of the military, to see that the protesters don't get out of control and erupt across the city."

Thus dismissed, Kwasin left the College of Awines, descending the wide, marble-hewn spiral ramp that encircled the building. Below him, the sound of shouting children broke from the darkness of the otherwise serene night. At the ramp's bottom, a group of Kwasin's guardsmen were in the process of forcibly removing from the premises a ten-year-old boy and a girl, half his age, who might have been his sister. The children cursed the soldiers with a vicious liveliness that brought a smile to Kwasin's lips, but when he heard what they were after and saw their small, pitifully emaciated bodies, his amusement faded. The two had apparently heard about the food brought from the newly docked ships and come to beg for their share. The boy hollered that his family hadn't had any food for a week, and all he wanted was a piece or two of fruit to divide among his sister, his mother, and his ailing grandmother. The guards, under orders to keep unauthorized individuals away from the college at all cost, were in the act of removing the tenacious children when Kwasin arrived at the bottom of the ramp and confronted them.

"What kind of men are you?" he barked at the surprised guards. "You would resort to violence against mere children?"

The officer in charge opened his mouth to speak but at a dark glare from his king seemed to think the better of it.

"Take the boy and his sister into the college," Kwasin said, "and instruct my servants to give them my entire share of the new rations. Then take your guard and escort the children and their food back to their home."

The soldiers stared at him dumbstruck.

"Go!" Kwasin winked at the now-smiling boy, who proceeded to strut up the ramp before the chastised soldiers as if he were the newly crowned king and his sister the queen.

Kwasin's stomach would growl tonight, but for the moment

he would feel good about his act of charity. He also knew the feeling would not last long. Soon he would begin thinking about the thousands of hunger-crazed inhabitants of the city who would starve to death unless Ruseth managed to return swiftly and successfully from his mission. He hoped the young captain knew how much was riding on him.

When Kwasin stepped into the street, the remaining guardsmen who had not gone with the children surrounded him in a defensive ring. Kwasin growled quietly to himself, then ordered the men to remain at the college and protect the queen. He tired of the constant company, and besides, the threat of an assassin's dagger had been greatly reduced. The missives left behind by the priest Dykeko had revealed the names of those involved in the conspiracy to murder the city's royalty, and the traitors had been rounded up and executed. That was not to say some citizen displeased with the new king's rule might not take the law into his or her own hands and come after Kwasin. But that was a chance he was willing to take. His spirit roamed too freely to be forever caged. He would rather risk taunting death.

The storm brooding on the horizon the previous night had passed far to the south, and a glimmering of starlight now bathed Kwasin's great shoulders as he passed through the temple district along the Avenue of the Hero-King Toenuseth. The avenue was named after a man for whom Kwasin had garnered much respect over the past year. He could not help but identify with him. Toenuseth, who had been a mere consort of Dythbeth's chief priestess, had stood up to insurmountable odds when, almost five hundred years ago, the people of Towina had united with the savage Klemqaba and invaded the island of Khokarsa. But Toenuseth had prevailed against the enemy's massive fleet, and after his lover made him king, he went on to become one of the most revered rulers in the history of the queendom of Dythbeth. Of course, gallant King Toenuseth, slain by a spear cast by the chief priestess of Khokarsa when he attempted to take the capital, had been ultimately ill-fated. In the end, Kho had passed her judgment upon the man for his overreaching arrogance. Kwasin would not make that mistake. He had sided with Awineth, Kho's legitimate regent on the earth. If Awineth indeed married him as she had promised, he—not Minruth or Hadon—would share Kho's gratitude and favor. That is, as long as he didn't overstep his bounds.

As he looked up at the stars, Kwasin momentarily wished he could slough off the mantle of kingship and once again roam free across the trackless expanses of the Wild Lands. It had been lonely there, true, and hard to find a woman whom he could sing to and woo, and for whom he could otherwise manifest the great urgings with which the Goddess had blessed him—or, as Awineth claimed, cursed him. But at the moment he felt sacrificing companionship for freedom would make more than a fair trade.

Above, an unearthly trail of orange-blue flame streaked across the night's dark canopy, and for some reason the heavenly apparition—an omen?—made Kwasin think of Sahhindar. When the god of time, bronze, and plants had made his appearance in the hills outside of Khokarsa, he had told Kwasin to make sure Lalila and the manling Paga headed south, far south. Before it was too late, the god had said. Too late? What did it mean?

Suddenly another fiery bolide lit the sky, this one so brilliant its eerie illumination cast a momentary flicker across the city. In the brief flash, Kwasin thought he saw movement along the eastern wall. It was probably just a shadow moving with the light of the falling star, but with Phoeken's troops looming outside the walls, it was best to be certain. He left the avenue and headed down a side street to investigate.

The late hour left the city deserted and mostly darkened. Fish oil and wood had been rationed since the siege, and even the great torch that normally burned high atop the temple of Piqabes had been extinguished. The moon appeared as only the barest of slivers. Moving forward toward the wall, he passed into the utter darkness behind a large, empty grain silo. Here he remained still and listened. Up over the rim of the inner wall, he could see the night sentry patrolling along the top of the higher outer wall. About twenty yards in from the inner wall another squat silo rose. From this direction Kwasin faintly heard what sounded like stone scraping upon stone. Then the noise stopped, and a moment later he heard a creaking, like the sound of a door opening.

A man crossed from behind the silo ahead, looking over his shoulder as if wary that someone might take note of his presence. The light-colored, dark-slashed robe and a stiff roach of hair revealed the man to be a priest. He was running to catch up with another man, also a priest, who had just emerged from the shadow of a storage building adjacent to the silo.

Still hidden in the darkness, Kwasin crept forward. When he reached the silo, he discovered a door in the building's side had been left ajar, presumably by the first priest. Kwasin opened the door and passed inside.

The sweet after-smell of emmer wheat hung heavy in the empty building, and Kwasin's footfalls echoed strangely against the rounded walls as he advanced in the darkness. Near the center of the silo's round, hollow storage bin, he stumbled over something that projected several inches from the floor. He reached down, his fingers tracing the edges of what appeared to be a small, circular slab of some sort.

He lifted up the stone and peered down a shoulder-width opening in the floor. Dim flickerings came from below, revealing a ladder leaning against a shaft that descended approximately ten feet beneath the surface. Off one side of the shaft began what appeared to be the opening of a crudely excavated tunnel, jutting off in an eastward direction. Kwasin unslung the ax from his back and dropped into the hole.

Whoever had tunneled beneath the silo had worked fast. Piles of loose dirt lined the narrow, three-foot-tall passageway ahead, the walls of which were buttressed at intervals by freshly cut cedar beams. A jog in the tunnel before him prevented Kwasin from seeing the source of the light. Then, as he decided to return to the surface to get help, the light grew much brighter. Someone was coming, and quickly.

With no chance to climb back up the ladder, he quickly pressed himself against a wall of the entry shaft. The cedar frame of the tunnel's opening jutted out just enough to hide him from whoever approached. He gripped his ax and waited for just a moment, estimating the time it would take for someone to pass up the length of the tunnel. Then he leaped out, his ax swinging.

The blade of the ax chopped into the helmeted head of a crouching man, a soldier. Because of the shaft's constricting space, Kwasin's blow did not carry to enough force to cleave his opponent's helmet, but even so the man heaved forward upon his face, unconscious. The man's burning torch fell on the ground before him, illuminating the tunnel.

Kwasin almost could not believe what he saw next. Two faces, drawn long with surprise, peered from behind the body of the fallen man.

One of the men was General Phoeken—the other, King Minruth himself.

TWENTY

K wasin took no time to think. Without room to make an
effective swing, he thrust the ax's head forward with all his
strength. The toe of the ax cut deeply into the center of Phoeken's
face. Blood fountained from the crushed bone and cartilage where
the general's face had been, and then his body toppled forward
onto the fallen soldier lying in front him. Kwasin jerked back the
ax as his arm was singed by the torch the soldier had dropped.
Minruth's surprised face had vanished from behind the bodies of
the two men, and Kwasin could see the movement of multiple
figures retreating hastily down the low tunnel.

Despite having killed Minruth's greatest general, Kwasin
swore. That Minruth and Phoeken both personally occupied
the tunnel could mean only one thing: a carefully timed, all-out
attack on the city was underway.

Kwasin pulled himself back into the entry shaft and with his
ax began furiously chopping at the cedar beams supporting the
tunnel. After only a few swings, the tunnel collapsed, filling the
outer shaft and nearly burying him in the process. Quickly, he
pulled himself out of the deluge of dirt and clambered up the
wooden ladder to the surface.

Bolting from the silo, he already heard the trumpeters sounding
the alarm. Dythbeth's soldiers would be waking up in the barracks
and hastening to the defense of the walls.

Kwasin began running along the inner wall, hoping he could get the soldiers at the next guard tower to lower a ladder for him to climb up. Otherwise, he would have to go out of his way and cut through several side streets in order to pass through the gate that separated the military district from the temple and palace districts.

As he ran, Kwasin heard a commotion behind him. Looking back, he cried out in anguish. About a hundred yards away, a large hole gaped in the center of the street that ran from north to south along the inner wall. Stones pried up from the street were heaped in jagged piles around the perimeter of the hole, from which a great stream of men poured forth. Minruth's soldiers had excavated a second tunnel!

Getting on top of the wall no longer mattered. He must get to Awineth before the soldiers attacked the college. The priests he had witnessed leaving the tunnel beneath the silo indicated the enemy still had spies in the city. Surely the invaders knew where the queen was quartered and would make the college their primary target. They would also want to target the gates and storm them from the inside. Once the gates had fallen, nothing could hold back the Khokarsan hordes from flooding into the city.

An embattled turret farther down the wall exploded in a horrific conflagration. Kwasin ignored it and took off down the avenue toward the inner city. He would have to trust the men on the walls to do their best in the face of Minruth's catapults.

He ran past the temple of Piqabes, its great torch now lit and flaming in defiance of the attackers. Frightened priestesses, priests, and attendants stood on the temple steps, gawking at their king as he ran past them.

Kwasin stopped. The torch of the green-eyed goddess of the sea had given him an idea. Perhaps there was something he could do to stop the men coming from the tunnel after all.

He jogged back to the temple and asked a priestesses standing on the steps to fetch him a torch. The woman entered the temple and returned a few moments later, handing him what he had requested with a puzzled look. He thanked her and gave blessing to Piqabes, then ran as fast as he could back the way he had come.

When he again neared the hole out of which poured forth the human tide, Kwasin began setting nearby buildings afire with his torch. Not all of the buildings, of course, could be lit. Some were constructed of large stone blocks, and others from sun-dried bricks. But there were enough made of wood, or adobe and wood, for his plan to work. That is, if only Piqabes—who besides being goddess of the sea also controlled the winds—kept blowing her southwesterly breeze.

It took longer than Kwasin hoped, but eventually, one after another, the fires took. Within twenty minutes a raging inferno swept across the entire block. As the fires spread from building to building and lashed out across the streets, the Khokarsan soldiers in the area quickly found themselves trapped between the flames and the old wall. Despite frantic attempts by many soldiers to reenter the tunnel to escape the fires, the unrelenting droves of men still storming from the tunnel prevented them. And by the time the men leaving the tunnel could assess the situation, it was also too late. They too tried to get back in the hole only to find the way blocked by the onslaught of new soldiers pouring forth.

Peering through the flames at the doomed men, Kwasin grinned darkly. But he knew he had no time to gloat. Not all of the men had been trapped by the fires. He must get to Awineth as quickly as possible.

That turned out to be quicker than he estimated, for by the time he again reached the temple of Piqabes, he saw the queen and a small number of her guard running down the street toward him. Not far behind them surged a mass of soldiers, and from the anxious looks Awineth and her guards cast back at the pursuing men, they did not seem to be Dythbethan.

Kwasin ran forward and joined Awineth's group.

"What are you doing here?" Awineth screamed at him, on the brink of hysteria.

Ignoring the question, Kwasin said, "We must get you back to the palace. I'm told there are tunnels which lead out of the city."

Awineth nodded her head no. "Cut off," she said. "Too many

soldiers. The bay's been taken and sailors are landing on the docks. The west gate has been breached, and the southern gate on the palace road has been closed off. We need to make it to a tower."

"There are soldiers ahead too," Kwasin said, "though many have been caught in the fires I've set. Still, we might find a way through."

They set off running back the way Kwasin had come. Behind them the enemy soldiers were coming on fast and making up ground. But soon Kwasin and his party were forced to stop. Fickle Piqabes had changed her mind and begun to blow her great breath seaward. A massive wall of flame confronted them.

"You idiot!" Awineth shrieked. "You've set the whole city on fire!"

Unable to argue with the scorching blaze that blocked their path, Kwasin said nothing. The woman was right that he had very probably made a fatal miscalculation. But the fault was not entirely his. If he survived this hellish night, he would never again put his faith in the capricious goddess of the sea.

Quickly, they ran down a slender alley behind an outbuilding that served as temporary housing for the influx of wartime refugees. If Kwasin and his party could make it to the next street over, they might be able to escape the flames.

They emerged onto the street and found the buildings on both sides of the way also on fire. Worse yet, the soldiers pursuing them had also cut across an alley and were running toward them down the thoroughfare they had just entered. Kwasin, staring ahead at the gauntlet of flames that licked angrily across the street, saw only one way out. Still holding his ax and giving no warning, he grabbed Awineth and threw her over a shoulder. The queen's guard, sensing what he was about to do, looked at him as if he were mad. Kwasin ignored them, as he did the desperate beating of Awineth's small fists against his back and her enraged screams to be put down. Without taking time to reconsider the brashness of his actions, or even to muster his courage, Kwasin charged forward into the scorching wall of fire.

Flames seared at his shoulders, arms, thighs, and legs, and the bitter tang of singed hair mixed with the sweet aroma of burning cedar almost smothered him. Awineth screamed wildly, and Kwasin himself shouted out in crazed defiance against the blistering heat of the fires raging everywhere about them. And then the flames were behind them and Kwasin was dropping Awineth to the stone-paved ground.

Kwasin and Awineth immediately began blotting out the smoldering locks of their hair, which had caught fire in the terrifying gauntlet. Awineth's once-beautiful jet-black tresses, let down from their tight knot, fell jaggedly across her burn-reddened shoulders. Kwasin, running a hand through his own singed hair, and patting gently the sweltering burns that spattered his body, thought they had been lucky. The burns, though painful now, were not serious and would heal. If they had stayed behind to face the large number of soldiers, they would certainly have been dead in short order. Or worse, captured.

For a moment, Awineth sat in the middle of the street glaring fiercely at Kwasin as she coughed and wheezed from the smoke she had inhaled. She looked as if she wanted to claw out his eyes—and she might have done so if she could ever stop hacking—but finally she looked away, utter despair sagging her features.

She would be thinking that she had lost everything, that the Goddess had abandoned her and allowed Resu and her father to have the final, ruthlessly vindictive laugh. How she must have hated Minruth! Kwasin knew well the cold heart that lay at the core of Awineth's deceptively beautiful form, but seeing her in such a pitifully despondent state made his own heart go out to her. Minruth had denied her the husband she so rightly deserved—the hero of the Great Games—in order to maintain an aging grip upon his throne. And then, while the man who should have been king was sent off upon a fool's errand, Awineth had suffered the humiliation of being deposed and imprisoned by her own father. Now, after somehow managing to miraculously escape Minruth's dungeons, to face this! To flee, screaming in terror, from her father's soldiers as she ran through the fire-swept streets. Fate, it seemed, had only toyed with Awineth and would now leave her to die.

Kwasin hefted his ax—the mighty weapon that had at one time belonged to the hero Wi before a group of yellow-haired savages from the northern wastes took his life. Perhaps the manling Paga had been right: the luck possessed by the ax lasted only a short time for the weapon's bearer. But the oracle had claimed the ax was important, that it would either provide Kwasin's succor or his undoing, and that his fate would be shared with all the land. Summoning from somewhere deep inside himself a bleak faith in the oracle's more optimistic alternative, he pulled Awineth to her feet.

"Come," Kwasin said. "We've rested long enough."

He had no more than uttered the words when three figures leaped from the fires that tongued across the street, the flames fueled by the steadily increasing winds. The figures, three survivors of Awineth's guard, rolled on the ground moaning as they tried to snuff out their smoldering hair and clothing. Kwasin and Awineth leaped to help the men, patting them down with their bare hands. When the guardsmen had extinguished the small fires on their bodies and recovered from their fits of coughing enough to stand up on shaky feet, Kwasin asked them about the others.

One of the men, the captain in charge of Awineth's guard, nodded sadly and said, "Dead. Cut down by Minruth's men." The man coughed. "Need to keep moving. Don't think—" He coughed again. "Don't think they'll come through the flames, but not sure . . . need to protect the queen."

Kwasin managed to smile at the man, though he stopped himself short before he could clap the captain on his scalded back.

They took off jogging toward the wall. Kwasin turned to Awineth and said, "It's not over. We'll get you out of the city and off the island. Perhaps Towina still holds out." Then he smirked. "Or, if all the coastal cities on the northern sea have fallen to the sun worshipers, we'll go south and forge a resistance there." Briefly, he thought of Hadon, who Awineth suspected had returned to his backwater city. The thought of throwing himself at his cousin's mercy rankled Kwasin, and he quickly dismissed the idea. He would never be able to stomach the humiliation.

As if reading his mind, Awineth appeared even more dejected, if that were possible. She also had much reason to hate Hadon. Perhaps more than he did.

The street ended and they came out on a narrow, stone walkway that skirted the old wall. To the north a swarm of soldiers could be seen crossing into the city through a yawning hole in the wall. The emperor's siege engines had been at work, knocking clear through both fortified barriers. The Khokarsans would also be wheeling forth their massive towers of wood and, propping them against the walls, hurling down upon the defenders an onslaught of burning pitch. Hahinqo, having seen the wooden towers being constructed on the battlefield, had prepared for such a contingency and issued to the soldiers on the wall many leather hides under which they could protect themselves. But even with the hides, the assault would be horrendously appalling for the soldiers.

Kwasin barked at his companions to run south along the wall. Perhaps the military district had not yet been seized by the enemy. If it hadn't, Kwasin and the three men still might manage to flag down someone to lower a ladder, a rope—anything—to hoist Kho's vicar to safety. Awineth had said the gate on the palace road was closed. He could only hope that was a good sign, that the Dythbethan commanders had ordered it shut to prevent Minruth's troops from storming out of the central section of the city. Dythbeth, partitioned off into three fortified enclosures, would be extremely hard for any enemy, no matter how vast or well prepared, to take in a single night. One or even two sections of the city could fall, while a second or third might yet hold out. The three-in-one fortifications had been a key factor for Dythbeth in repelling her would-be invaders for over a millennium.

Kwasin grabbed Awineth by the hand and headed south along the wall, two guards flanking them and one protecting their rear. Awineth struggled to keep up with Kwasin's great strides, but at least she did not slow them down by bemoaning their fate or asking to rest. The empress of Khokarsa was certainly made of stern stuff. Or perhaps she was merely too fatigued or shock-numbed to complain or think of doing anything other than follow Kwasin's lead. It made no difference as long as they were moving forward.

Out of the darkness ahead loomed another wall, this one nearly twenty feet higher than the old inner wall that traced the perimeter of the city. This was the interior cross-wall that separat-ed their section of the city from the southern fortified military district. Kwasin scanned the top of the wall, looking for any sign the Dythbethans still held the area.

Awineth screamed, and the man on her right—the captain of her guard—fell facedown on the path.

"Slingers!" she shouted, pointing to the east. About fifty yards away several shadowy figures lurked in the darkness where Awineth had indicated. Kwasin could hear the whirring of slings as the figures advanced slowly down the street toward them.

With a rough jerk, he swung Awineth away from the oncom-ing men and to his other side, placing an arm about her waist. The captain lay unmoving on the ground, and they left him behind as they ran on. Awineth's two remaining guards, their broadswords drawn from their scabbards, drew in tight on both sides. Kwasin urged Awineth to run quicker, but speeding up only caused her to stumble and skin her shins badly on the stone road. As Kwasin helped her get back to her feet, the soldier who had assumed the captain's position cried out and fell. A sling-stone had impaled itself in the man's leg. Though the man was still alive, his injury was serious. He could not go on.

Kwasin, his nerves finally breaking, yelled out in frustration. "I won't be slaughtered like a lame ox! Take care of the empress!" he shouted at the remaining guardsman. Then, thrusting Awineth behind him, Kwasin took off down the street in the direction of the slingers.

Though they still whirred their slings, the dark forms retreated as Kwasin advanced.

"By Kho, fight me, cowards!" he shouted, but the figures only continued to back away. It maddened him that the men would not face him. Clearly Minruth had issued orders that his daughter and Dythbeth's king were to be captured alive. The thought did not reassure Kwasin. Minruth would take sadistic pleasure in ensuring that their remaining days were filled with torment and humiliation. They had caused him too much trouble.

Since Kwasin could not manage to get near enough to attack his opponents, he turned back and returned to Awineth's side. Now he and Awineth, believing the enemy was likely under orders not to kill them, stood protectively in front of the remaining guard. The fellow with the injured leg now lay dead at their feet. He had crawled along the stone path in an attempt to rejoin them, but a slinger, advancing with Kwasin's retreat, had expertly cast a stone into the man's face despite his helmet's bronze nose guard. Kwasin bent down and took the man's helmet, placing it over his own head. Though the soldiers after them seemed not to be under orders to kill him, he didn't want to trust that a sling-stone would not go astray and hit him. Besides, the soldiers didn't seem to be all that careful. They had killed the injured guard while Awineth stood only a couple of paces away.

Now Kwasin, Awineth, and the remaining guard headed east along the cross-wall. As they ran, a group of about twelve Kho-karsan soldiers, some of them bearing torches to light their way, emerged from an alley. Three javelins flew out from the men and clattered forcefully on the stone path before the fleers. Awineth, frightened, tried to stop but Kwasin pulled her on even as he reached down to grab one of the iron-shanked javelins. Awineth's guard, he noted, was coolheaded enough to do the same.

The new group of pursuers now turned from the alley and ran furiously down the stone path behind their quarry. Kwasin turned to Awineth's guard and shouted, "Now!"

Simultaneously, Kwasin and the guardsman stopped and whirled on their heels. Kwasin dropped his ax to the ground. Then he planted his feet, raised the javelin, and swung back his mighty torso. Beside him, the guardsman released his missile at the same time. Kwasin cried out in delight as both javelins hit their marks, impaling two of the pursuers. But Kwasin, seeing the soldiers only a scant twenty yards away, did not pause. With furious speed he seized up his ax and charged, bellowing like a mad bull, his ax swinging above his head.

About half of the men broke upon seeing the enraged demon-giant storming at them. Five soldiers, however, stood their ground, though within moments they all lay strewn across the cobbled street, dead or mortally injured. Kwasin had cleaved down three in his initial onslaught with the ax, and while Awineth's guard—who had garnered Kwasin's respect by also launching himself at the soldiers—cut down one man with his sword, Kwasin barreled into the last standing man and tackled him to the ground. With a massive fist, Kwasin punched the man brutally in the throat, crushing his larynx.

Kwasin stood up. The enemy soldiers who had fled were hovering thirty yards back down the way, neither advancing nor retreating. But that wasn't what concerned him. Along the western wall he saw that one of the enemy's great wooden towers had been wheeled forward, and many figures now ran along the wall top. It was clear to him the battlement at the west end of the cross-wall had been taken by the Khokarsans.

No, not the Khokarsans. The figures storming over the top of the wall were short, squat, massive—Minruth's wild Klemqaba warriors were climbing up the wooden tower to assail the city. Kwasin raged when he saw a group of the savages take down a Dythbethan soldier with their bolas and then hurl the man to his death over the wall. Now many ladders and ropes swung down from above as the hordes of Klemqaba began their descent upon the city.

Bolstered by the appearance of the savage Goat People, and perhaps thinking it wouldn't matter if they killed the king and the high priestess of Kho since the Klemqaba would undoubtedly slaughter them anyway, the soldiers who had been skulking at a distance advanced, swords raised menacingly above their small, round shields. And behind them came the slingers. Kwasin was on the verge of charging the entire group when Awineth appeared at his side.

"Leave them!" she cried. "By the time you kill them the Klemqaba will be upon us! Perhaps someone along the wall will see us and let us up."

Kwasin doubted it. The western wall was eerily absent of soldiers, Dythbethan and Khokarsan alike. If the military district had fallen, no one would remain on the other side to prevent the wild Klemqaba from moving forward across the wall. Still, Awineth was right. He might kill the advancing soldiers, but he would surrender what little chance they had of escape.

Again, they ran, angling somewhat to the east so they would be able to see anyone who might be running along the crenellated wall top. Awineth seemed to have recovered her breath, sprinting along with Kwasin and the surviving guardsman with renewed strength. For a moment, Kwasin allowed himself to hope. If only he could find a way to signal the soldiers on the opposite side of the wall—if, that is, his men had not all been slaughtered or subdued.

The guardsman running with them cried out and stumbled. A shallow dent on his helmet revealed where a sling-stone had hit him. Kwasin lifted the guard to his feet, but three more stones pelted the man in his back and he fell hard on the ground. He would not be getting up again. Kwasin picked up the poor fellow's wooden shield, handed it to Awineth, and urged her to keep moving.

When Kwasin looked up and saw a figure running east along the top of the wall, he thought he might weep. The man was one of their own, he was sure. Otherwise, the soldier would not be looking fearfully over his shoulder at the advancing Klemqaba. Kwasin and Awineth shouted and screamed, attempting to attract the man's attention.

The man looked down and slowed, but kept moving ahead along the wall.

"I am your king!" Kwasin cried out. "I order you to help your queen and empress, the holy priestess of Kho!"

The soldier stopped between two embrasures, looked back at

the wild hordes, and then, as if weighing the wisdom of offering assistance, returned his uncertain gaze to Kwasin and Awineth.

"Kho will reward you if you help me," Awineth shouted above, "but She will curse you and all your kin if you abandon Her high priestess!"

Kwasin didn't believe the appeal would work, but the soldier surprised him by crouching at the foot of the embrasure as if securing something to the stone. A moment later a rope uncoiled down the wall.

"I have done my duty to the Goddess!" the soldier cried, and then he dashed northward, leaving his empress and his king to fend for themselves.

Kwasin and Awineth ran to the dangling rope. Kwasin secured his ax to the harness on his back and pulled Awineth tightly to his chest. She wrapped her arms around his neck. Kwasin swung Awineth over a thigh and kicked off against the granite wall, his powerful muscles pulling them in fast jerking motions up the rope.

They climbed over the edge of the battlement just as a series of sling-stones barraged the wall face, the impact of the bulleting projectiles shooting off splinters of stone at high velocities. Keeping low, Kwasin and Awineth ran east down the walkway.

From his new vantage, Kwasin got a bird's-eye view of the assault on Dythbeth. Fire raged across nearly a third of the inner city, fanned by the heavy seaward breeze. A great portion of the fire would have been caused by Kwasin's defensive arson, but not all of it. A somewhat smaller though still substantial fire was sweeping through the market district in the southeast. Soon it would also expand with the winds.

On the southern side of the wall, three battlements blazed and billowed black smoke into the dark night, and an orange twinkling from the military barracks told him the garrison buildings had been attacked and set afire. The massive western gate stood wide open, with throngs of soldiers streaming through it in both directions. None of the soldiers seemed to be Dythbethan, and a number were certainly of Klemqaba stock.

Suddenly Awineth screamed. Ahead, a group of half-neander-thaloids swarmed over an embrasure and onto the wall's walkway. They surged toward the two, some holding small round shields and brandishing heavy bronze axes, others shieldless and bearing goat-hide slings and flint-headed spears.

Kwasin and Awineth stopped, but turning saw more men mounting the wall behind them. These were not Klemqaba but rather a swarthy, rangy-looking lot of humanoids—the wild mountain men brought in by Minruth from the Saasares. Kwasin would have charged them, since they stood a better chance against the mountain men than the fearsome, powerfully muscled warriors of the Goat People, but the Klemqaba were already upon them.

One of the hybrids—a hideously ugly and fearfully massive brute of a fellow—grabbed Awineth away from Kwasin and, seizing her by the shoulders, began to mock-rape her, pivoting his hips obscenely and repeatedly thrusting his long, rhino-tusk codpiece between her naked thighs. Awineth, looking surprisingly calm, did not scream or otherwise panic. Instead, with what seemed a cool and deliberate motion, she drew the dagger from the sheath on her thigh. For a moment Kwasin held his breath—even as he crushed the skull of a warrior who had charged him with a bronze ax—thinking that rather than be captured Awineth meant to take her own life. But instead, she stabbed the dagger deep beneath the edge of her attacker's cuirass, withdrew the blade, and stabbed him again and again, fighting like a cornered lioness. The brute, his theatrics done with for all eternity, clutched his chest and fell dead at Awineth's feet.

Having dispatched his immediate assailant, Kwasin recovered just in time to swing up his weapon and deflect the blow of a bronze ax that hurled at his face. His own ax, its head forged from the sturdy iron of a fallen star, glittered in the flames of the burning city as it struck the oncoming weapon, breaking its bronze head from the ox-bone haft in his opponent's hand. Kwasin rammed a giant fist into the fellow's chin, whose head swung back, his jaw cracking sickly from its joints.

Then Kwasin pitched forward on his hands and knees as something smacked his helmet and knocked all sense from his mind. The whole world clanged as if it had been struck by a mighty brass gong and, a moment later, deafness enveloped him. A biconical lead projectile, glistening darkly with blood, skidded on the granite walkway until it finally stopped between his knees. With perhaps the greatest single act of will of his whole life, he forced himself to lift his head. His vision wavered between varying degrees of blurriness before finally coming into focus. What he saw filled his heart with dismay. Awineth, blood freely streaming down her face from a deep gash on her forehead, lay crumpled on the ground before him. A black, shadowy wisp flickered to Awineth's left and then shot downward like lightning and disappeared in the ground. Was it her spirit, snatched away by the all-too-eager hands of dread Sisisken? Or perhaps it had been one of his own souls, for indeed the oracle had said he had two.

Kwasin shouted out in his mind for strength from the Goddess, but his once-mighty muscles felt frail and wasted as he strained in the futile effort to will himself to his feet. Then the long, dark curtain of night fell about him and oblivion consumed him.

TWENTY-ONE

For a period that seemed devoid of time, Kwasin dreamed. Many faces and scenes—some familiar, some strange—passed before his inner eye. He saw his cousin, the tall, bronze-skinned Hadon, seated upon an ivory throne beside Lalila, the fair White-Witch-from-the-Sea. At their feet sat Abeth, Lalila's daughter with the hero Wi, looking older than he remembered her and playing on the steps of the dais with a very young girl whose long, wavy hair shone golden bronze in a slanting shaft of sunlight.

The scene faded. Colors, forms, and shapes shifted nebulously upon the blackened background of Kwasin's mind. From them congealed the form of his mother, Wimake, laughing with great merriment as she sat upon a swath of scarlet moss near the banks of a babbling mountain stream. Beside her stood Pwamkhu, the man whom Kwasin once regarded as a father figure, running his hand along the gorged body of a serpent that curled down from a branch of a withering fir tree. Then that vision too faded, replaced by a series of images, scenes, faces, and events, passing by with such nauseating speed that Kwasin momentarily lost all sense of self. Suddenly the whirling stopped and one last scene materialized before his mind's eye: an ancient, stoop-shouldered crone bathed in moonlight—the oracle Wasemquth?—shaking her gnarled fist at a winged feminine form standing balanced atop a colossal, stone-hewn sphere.

Pain searing through his entire frame, but especially his back,

Kwasin opened his eyes. At first he was unsure whether the dream still held him. What he saw and smelled certainly seemed night-marish.

He was outside the city walls. The hot, white sun beat down upon a wide mountain of corpses heaped up outside Dythbeth's eastern gate. On top of the ghastly, fly-swarming, foul-smelling, sunbaked pile of slaughter was the death-stiffened body of a lone man, propped up and tied to a wooden post driven into the grisly foundation. Even from the great distance, Kwasin recognized the man. It was General Hahinqo. He had been stripped of his armor and clothing, and his penis had been cut off and stuffed inside his mouth.

Behind the mountain stretched the exterior of the city wall, from the merlons of which dangled the disfigured remains of men, women, and children, tied to the ends of long ropes. Along the foot of the wall, human and Klemqaba soldiers heaved body after body into massive but unfinished trenches, the same great troughs Hahinqo had ordered to be excavated outside the wall in his failed attempt to thwart Minruth's siege engines. Two large clusterings of poles and spear shafts had been driven into the ground on either side of the gate's towering bronze doors, which were swung open to reveal the blackened and smoldering ruins of what had once been the city's military district.

The world was upside down for Kwasin, literally, and now his head cleared enough to understand the cause of his throbbing pain. Trussed up like a captured lion, his naked, blood-streaked body hung down by its wrists and ankles from iron manacles attached to the center beam of a makeshift wooden A-frame. He felt nothing in his hands and feet, which had become numb from a lack of circulation, and with each breath he took, torturous, jabbing pains stabbed through his neck and arched back and shoulders. Groaning, and almost choking on his parched and swollen tongue, he tried moving his fingers and toes only to find they barely responded.

A dark form moved in front of Kwasin, blocking out the harsh rays of the sun.

"I do not believe it!" a haughty male voice cawed. "This stinking lump of flesh cannot be the lauded exile-king of Dythbeth, and certainly not the wild demon who taunted my armies and caused them to piss themselves with fear. Ah, but still a hulking bull indeed! As powerfully muscled as an ox, though I understand cursed with a slowness of mind. But an ox doesn't need brains to pull a stone block up the ramparts around the Tower of Resu."

The obnoxious, swaggering voice could belong to one man alone. Kwasin had only once before seen Minruth, in the tunnel dug by the Khokarsan soldiers beneath Dythbeth's walls, but he recognized the emperor by his likeness, which had been minted into the gold coin known as the *nasuhnohehehe*, or one thousand piece.

Kwasin, his eyes having adjusted to the change in light caused by the shadow which fell upon him, stared up at his taunter. Minruth stood with hands on hips, his obese gut bulging out over the belt of his finely embroidered leather kilt. The man had his daughter's jet-black hair and dark eyes, but his otherwise regal features were marred by a large, somewhat curved nose. Though broad-shouldered, he certainly did not look like he ever had been a hero of the Great Games. Neither did he seem the valiant warrior famed for suppressing the bloody rebellion at Sakawuru, nor the powerful man who in his youth had slain the great black leopard of Siwudawa with his bare hands.

Minruth did look younger than his fifty-nine years, however. Rumors abounded that the king of kings was preoccupied to the point of obsession with maintaining his youthful appearance. Some even attributed his fanatical devotion to completing the Great Tower of Kho and Resu to a prediction supposedly made four hundred and fifty years ago by the high priestess Pwymnes. The prophecy stated that the man who sat upon the imperial throne of Khokarsa when the tower was finished would ascend to the sky and be blessed with everlasting life. Whether that blessing came from Kho or Resu, the legend did not say, though many theologians over the years had tried to settle the debate. The philosopher-priest Qohawiten claimed the blessing obviously originated from the sungod, since the sky was known colloquially as the blue palace of Resu. The priestesses, however, refuted Qohawiten's theorem by citing liturgical stone carvings dating back to antiquity in which the sky was referred to as Kho's blue bowl, still a common expression today. Kwasin thought they were all fools, as the task of completing the tower was so vast it would never be completed during the life span of the debaters—especially if a new light-weight brick was not found, as the tower's structure could not bear much more stress. So what then was the use of arguing?

But looking up into Minruth's smug face, Kwasin found himself wondering. The man had achieved what no other king had even dared to imagine. Now that the priestesses had been defeated and he controlled the purse strings of the empire, perhaps Minruth could truly succeed in his mad quest to complete the tower.

Then Kwasin had a wry thought. If the blessing of immortality were in fact Kho's gift, Minruth had very likely forfeited his claim on eternal life when he seized the throne from his daughter, demoted the Goddess in the pantheon, and removed from the base of the great ziggurat Awodon's masterpiece of sculpture, the frieze known as *Kho and Her Children*. And if that were not enough, Kho would be further angered that her name had been dropped from what was now known only as the Tower of Resu. It would be ironic if Minruth fulfilled his dream to complete the tower only to have the Goddess leave him an old man on death's door.

Kwasin tried to speak, to tell the mad emperor of Khokarsa that he could shove his Great Tower up his corpulent backside, but his voice only croaked and grated like a bullfrog too long out of water.

"Look, it tries to form words!" Minruth sneered. "To think my daughter meant to marry such an ape!" And then the king of kings squatted so that his face hovered before Kwasin like a bloated moon. "But even an ape can be of some value if properly trained," he continued in a more appeasing tone. "You know, I would have welcomed you as a brother, a common ally of the sungod, upon your return from exile—had you only forsworn your loyalty to Kho. I would have made you one of my great champions, maybe even treated you as a son, but instead you ran amok and killed my soldiers. Still, Resu is generous and forgiving. After all, even that whore-goddess Bhukla was allowed to remain in the pantheon as goddess of the sword after she waged war against Great Resu. I will make you a one-time offer, here and now. Forswear Kho and I will let you live. I will even place you in charge of an important mission, one without which the city of Khokarsa could not hope to function. Of course, sweeping out the backed-up and stinking muck from the city's sewage canals would be an unpleasant task for most, but being as you already reek of ape shit, I think you will feel right at home."

His throat too dry and swollen to speak, Kwasin mouthed the foulest curse he could think of.

The emperor of Khokarsa merely smiled. Then he stood up and said, "A pity. Then your stubborn soul will be given in sacrifice to the glory of Resu. But not just yet. First you will serve as a symbol to all those who yet oppose the sungod. Along with another who so unwisely rejected my openhanded offer."

Minruth motioned to someone behind Kwasin, and the sound of squeaking wheels and much grunting followed. A few moments later a wheeled, iron-barred cage, to the shafts of which were chained four long rows of slaves, was carted out in front of Kwasin. Seated on the floor of the cage and slumping against the bars was Awineth.

In the last moments of battle before darkness stole away his consciousness, Kwasin had thought he had seen Awineth die. Though relieved to find her among the living, her appearance distressed him. Dried blood caked one side of her face where it had streamed down from a horrible wound on her forehead. The other side of her face, though clean of blood, was badly bruised, and her naked body, streaked with dirt and blood, bore many cuts, scrapes, and bruises. What disturbed Kwasin the most, however, was the vacant look in her eyes. He could only guess that something had snapped in her soul under the cruel treatment she had endured. Perhaps his own eyes also carried the same hollow stare, but he doubted it. His entire frame coursed with as much rage as it did pain.

"Welcome to your new home," Minruth proclaimed loudly, "in which you and my daughter will be paraded across the island so that all may see what becomes of those who blaspheme against Great Resu!"

At last summoning a weak and rasping voice, Kwasin managed to croak, "You're mad . . . The people . . . won't stand for it." He truly believed they wouldn't. To place Kho at a lower station than Resu was unimaginable enough, but to enslave and publicly humiliate Kho's high vicar! Minruth pushed his game too far. If the Goddess Herself did not smite him down first, the people soon would.

Minruth merely laughed. "The people are docile cattle who desire to be herded. Your trust in them is as misguided as your devotion to the wife of Resu. But it is true there are still some supporters of Resu's estranged wife who yet hold out in the mountains and countryside. Therefore I won't execute my daughter, though she certainly deserves to die after what she has cost me. No, when my triumphal procession arrives at the capital, Awineth will have undergone a conversion of faith. There she will found a new order among the priestesses, one happy to recognize Kho's new and proper place as Resu's willing servant." Minruth leaned in closer and whispered, "Then my chief priest will announce that Resu has appeared to him and decreed that He is divorcing Kho and marrying a lesser goddess. Kho will be banished to the dark land of Sisisken, there to dwell for all eternity. It will take time, but those reluctant to accept Resu's dominance will eventually come around."

Kwasin had no doubt Minruth would do as he said, but would the people be willing to follow the new puppet religion? The more liberal city-dwellers might, if Kho's priestess ordered it, but he could not believe that Awineth, even looking as pitiful as she did now, would ever become an accomplice to such a plan. She hated her father too much to give in to him, even under duress.

As if to contest Kwasin's thoughts, Minruth approached the caged cart and said, "Isn't that right, daughter?" Awineth only continued to stare vacantly through the bars of her prison, never once focusing her eyes upon Kwasin.

"Enough!" Minruth exclaimed. "I tire of the stench of death. Put the giant king of Dythbeth in with my daughter and let us begin the journey home. We must spread the news of my—I mean Resu's—victory."

Minruth retreated to the edge of the wall near the east gate, where he looked on, surrounded by close to forty soldiers. He must have worried that Kwasin might escape while being transferred into the cage, and attempt to kill him. Minruth was not wrong that Kwasin would have liked to have done so, but even had he the strength remaining, the subsequent actions of the emperor's men would have prevented him.

A group of twenty soldiers came forward, ten with spears pointed at Kwasin, and ten to assist in the transfer of the prisoner. The cage, only five feet wide and twelve in length, was opened. Kwasin's hopes for escaping the cage at some point in the future dwindled when he saw its unique construction. The door itself was actually two doors, one directly in front of the other, each consisting of iron bars set on massive iron hinges. The bars of the cage were not merely lined in a row but staggered in rows of three, so that even if he could pry loose a bar, several more would remain in place to block his way to freedom. For his great bulk to pass through them, Kwasin estimated he would have to remove six of the iron bars. Though the chassis on which the cage rested was wooden, a thin sheet of brass lined the floor of the cage itself. Escape through the flooring would be impossible without an implement hard enough to wear away at the metal sheet. And even if such a tool were smuggled to him, where would he hide it in the bare-floored cage? If they chained him, he might use his shackles to saw at the floor or the bars, but with all the thought that had gone into the construction of the cage he was sure Minruth wouldn't fetter him with metal.

For a moment he wondered how, with the heaviness of all that iron and brass, the bearers were going to be able to haul the cart all the way to Khokarsa without dying from exhaustion. Then he realized the question was the answer. The men would in fact die and Minruth would simply replace them. Of course, Minruth would want the bearers to travel slowly anyway, so that many would come to gawk at the prisoners and then spread the word of Kho's defeat across the island, and ultimately the entire empire.

Four of the men lifted the iron bar to which Kwasin was manacled, removing it from its wooden support frame. They carried Kwasin into the cage and dropped him onto its blistering, sun-heated metal floor. When the second of the two men who had climbed with him into the cage attempted to exit, Kwasin bit the man in the calf as he was squeezing between him and the iron bars. The man screamed, then fell to his hands and knees and scrambled out of the cage as fast as he could. The other soldiers quickly yanked from the cage the iron bar they had used to carry Kwasin. He had no chance to grab it and use it against them.

Kwasin spat out a sizeable mass of flesh onto the floor. He felt a little better. The blood had wetted his mouth some.

Now the men came to release Kwasin from his fetters. He had been right. They didn't want him to be able to grate iron against brass, no matter how small a chance it would afford him of escaping. The soldiers were careful this time. They stood a distance back, tossed the keys through the bars to Kwasin, and ordered him to take off the manacles. If he refused, they said, they would spear him to death. Kwasin began to comply, but then, after some fumbling with the keys, he called out that his hands had been constricted for too long as he hung down from the manacles. He could not use his fingers effectively enough to undo the lock. There was some debate among the soldiers about what to do, until finally Minruth, his face as red as Resu himself, marched over and shouted at the officer in charge to carry out his orders or join the pile of the dead. The chastised officer hurriedly ordered a private to approach the cage and reach inside to unlock the captive.

Kwasin squirmed on his side to position his wrists and ankles up against the bars. Then the private, his face pale with fright, reached forth and retrieved the keys, first unlocking the chains around Kwasin's ankles, and then sliding the key into the manacles on the captive's wrists. Kwasin was suddenly on his feet. The private screamed as Kwasin yanked the man's left arm into the cage and levered it against the iron bars. There was a sickening crunch. The private slumped, keeling over from shock and pain as his left arm was torn from its socket.

Soldiers rushed the cage, their spears thrust before them. Kwasin withdrew against the opposite wall of bars as some of the men drove their spears between the bars to hold him back while the others dragged their fallen comrade away to safety. Their expressions a mixture of hatred and fright, the soldiers pressed their spearpoints against Kwasin's chest, pinning him against one side of the cage. Kwasin smiled at the men. He turned the key that still rested in the lock of his manacles, tossed the manacles outside through the bars. There was nothing he could do. If he resisted, he would be jabbed with the many spears until he passed out from loss of blood.

After the men had retreated, Kwasin looked down at Awineth, whose worn, reddened eyes stared dully at the floor. She had not even reacted to his attack. He squatted down beside her and began examining the wound on her forehead while she continued to gaze listlessly into space. The gash was deep, and a large lump rose beneath the broken flesh, but as far as he could tell her skull seemed unfractured.

The cart lurched and began moving, pulled along slowly by its human beasts of burden. Kwasin took one last painful look back at conquered and devastated Dythbeth, the city where he had been born and raised until the age of ten, and which he had always thought of as home. Then, after placing an arm around Awineth and leaning against the bars of his moving prison, he fell asleep to the creaking and rocking of the cart and the grunting of its bearers.

TWENTY-TWO

A lmost a week passed while Minruth's triumphal procession waited outside the city only a few miles distant on the great plain. Though Minruth must have been eager to parade his captives before the island's population, he also wanted the grandest of processions to showcase his greatest of victories. Therefore Kwasin and Awineth sat glumly within their cage beside the dirt road to Khokarsa while slaves were gathered up from the city's surviving inhabitants and the caravan was assembled and provisioned.

Meanwhile, though they were given meager sips of water from a foul-smelling flask, the two captives starved. Dythbeth had already faced famine before the invasion, but with the Sixth Army raiding what little fare remained in the city, the food crisis worsened. Looking out over the great plain, Kwasin watched the mountains of the heaped-up dead grow taller with each passing day. But Minruth could not have his prized captives die before his procession even began, and so at last food was brought to them. Kwasin cursed, however, when the undercooked meat was tossed onto the floor of their cage. The soldier who had thrown it to them laughed.

"I hope you like your bear meat rare!" the man jeered.

Kwasin swore. As a member of the Klakordeth, he was forbidden from consuming the flesh of bears. To be caught doing so, no matter the situation, would result in Kwasin being cast out of the totem. The act was also considered ritually unclean to the population at large. Penalties for breaking the prohibition varied with local custom throughout the empire, and though bears were rare south of the Saasares, some did exist on the island in the backwoods mountains. The local priestess of an area where such an offense was committed typically sentenced the transgressor to be locked in a specially prepared and nearly intolerable hothouse until the impurities of soul and body were sweated out through the pores, usually to be followed by a thirty-day period of segregation from the community, either in solitary confinement or expulsion to the wilds. Not that many went out of their way to violate the taboo. Still, there were always fetishists among the totem who got their thrills from consuming bear flesh and were willing to endure the risk of being caught.

After staring for several minutes at the revolting morsel smoldering on the sunbaked brass flooring of the cage, Kwasin shrugged. He had eaten fouler things during his trek through the Wild Lands, and they had best eat the meat now before it spoiled in the heat of the afternoon. The rainy season, which normally brought a brief reprieve from the oppressive heat, had been delayed—yet another bad omen from Kho. In any case, the meat smelled so rank that he believed it to be that of a hyena, not a bear. And if in all honesty he believed he did not eat bear, would he truly have sinned? Of course, hyena meat was also considered unclean but at least eating it would not get him thrown out of his totem.

He tore at the tough, unpalatable flesh with his teeth, ripping off small scraps which he offered to Awineth before he consumed his own portion. At first she refused to eat, though she was not of his totem. It worried him greatly that she had not yet said a word to him since their capture, and he wondered if her languid spirit would ever wake up from its trance. But after he forced the meat into her mouth, Awineth began to chew mechanically. It gave Kwasin hope. Somewhere beneath the woman's broken outer shell, something wanted to live.

He couldn't blame Awineth for feeling so miserable. She had grown up pampered by royal attendants and instilled with the belief that her sanctity placed her high above the common riffraff. And now the high vicar of Kho was a prisoner, forced to eat unpalatable food and defecate in her own cage! The guards seemed to take a perverse pleasure in their former queen's discomfort, and often a full day, sometimes two, would pass before they would come with their buckets to wash away the filth.

Kwasin resolved to watch Awineth closely, as he feared she might try to take her own life. Then he wondered if that might not be for the best, though for his part he intended to defy Minruth's humiliations until the bitter end. For good or ill, the deities had made sure that giving up just wasn't part of his character. There was always a chance, however unlikely, that he might escape someday and get his revenge. That thought more than anything kept him going.

Later that same evening a lieutenant in the Sixth Army came by to question Kwasin. Having heard of the trouble surrounding the act of imprisoning of Dythbeth's former king, the officer stood a good distance back from the bars.

"What has become of the great hatchet you carried when you returned from the Wild Lands," the man asked, "the ax formerly belonging to the dwarf Paga?"

The question took Kwasin off guard, but what surprised him even more was the reaction from Awineth. At the officer's inquiry, she suddenly sat up straight, her eyes glimmering with interest in the torchlight.

"Well, let's see," Kwasin said, eyeing the ceiling of the cage as if trying to summon a long-buried memory. "I must have stashed it in the city somewhere, but my head is heavy and my thoughts are slow from lack of good food. If I had a piece of that venison roasting over yonder I might be able to think better."

The officer folded his hands over his chest, but a moment later he walked to the soldiers' campfire and returned with a small, greasy cut of antelope thigh. He tossed it into the cage and watched while Kwasin and Awineth ravenously consumed the best meal they'd had in weeks. After they were finished eating, the soldier asked his question again.

"I must have left it somewhere," Kwasin said, scratching his head and rubbing a greasy hand upon a thigh. He stood up and began pacing the cage, inspecting each corner with what seemed a concerned diligence. Suddenly he jolted stiffly erect, as if seized by an unexpected illumination. "I remember now! Just as your cowardly slingman came up from behind and struck me on the head with his pellet, Lahhindar, the Archer Goddess, descended from the heavens on a silver string and plucked the ax from my hands for safekeeping!"

The officer frowned and then left, apparently convinced he would never get a straight answer from the wisecracking giant who was as much a trickster as Kagaga the raven. But the officer's visit intrigued Kwasin. Why did Minruth seek the ax? Did Minruth know the oracle's mysterious motives for demanding that the ax be brought back from the Wild Lands? And what about the officer's question had so struck Awineth that she temporarily awakened from her trancelike doldrums? Of course, Awineth had told the people of Dythbeth that the ax would be used in the war against Resu, but Kwasin had been led to believe that the claim was a false one. Perhaps she felt that if the ax was still missing, there was a chance it was in the hands of the network of priestesses and might be used as a symbol of the resistance. That is, if there even was a resistance any longer. He questioned Awineth about the matter when the officer was out of earshot, but she continued to be unresponsive, though she looked vaguely like she might be thinking.

The next morning the procession got underway. In addition to the twenty-four slaves manning the shafts of the prisoners' cart, a long line of courtiers, soldiers, and slaves both preceded and followed them. Near the front of the caravan rode Minruth, pulled along by human bearers in his red-painted, gaudily decorated covered wagon. Traveling with Minruth were his many young and beautiful consorts, brought from the capital to entertain the king of Khokarsa on his campaign. Like the corpulent Minruth, all were well fed.

The slaves, however, were provided barely enough sustenance to keep them going. By the time the caravan forded the Howahinkly River and passed into the bee fields southeast of Qoqada—which took over two weeks as the bearers struggled to haul their heavy loads along the often agonizingly hilly road—nearly a quarter of the slaves had perished. Minruth was not fazed. He merely collected more slaves at Qoqada, and while his men rounded up the new additions from the region's already war-decimated population, he used the excess time to parade his captives through the city streets.

The supporters of Resu ran along with the processioners, shouting praises to the emperor of Khokarsa for his great triumph and pelting the prisoners in their cage with rotting rubbish and, when they could find it, whatever dung they could scrape up from the few animals in the city that had survived Minruth's siege. They hurled no edible food, because they had none to spare.

Many stood back from the spectacle, peering from the front doors of their dwellings with looks both disapproving and de-spondent. These would be the loyalists to the Goddess, disgusted by what they saw happening but too afraid to voice their com-plaints for fear of what the soldiers would do to them and their families. Qoqada had fared better than Dythbeth, chiefly because the city had accepted Minruth's offer of amnesty in exchange for surrender. Still, many had died during the siege, either from starvation or from the skirmishes on the walls, and when the Sixth Army finally entered the city, Minruth's promises turned out to mean little. The soldiers took what they wanted, including food, women, and in the latter instance—when the Qoqadans came to the defense of their wives, daughters, and mothers—not a few lives.

Awineth made Kwasin proud as their cage rolled through the streets and they were heckled, cursed, jeered at, and barraged with refuse. She sat with regal bearing in the center of the cage, her chin held high and her eyes now haughty instead of dull, as Kwasin attempted to shield her from the rain of vile muck and often viler invectives. Certainly she was made of royal stuff, and was, as the saying went, as tough as a rhino's heel. But when the cart finally rolled away from the crowds, Awineth again slouched, and he saw in the corners of her eyes the first tears she had shed since their incarceration.

They stayed in Qoqada for three days while the caravan rested and replenished itself with slaves. Then the procession continued its journey across the island. Kwasin overheard the soldiers guarding his cage say that Minruth was anxious to get back to the capital and see how much work had been accomplished on his tower. He had somehow continued the tower's construction despite the hardships and shortages of the war, and he was rumored to have commissioned a new architect who promised to speed things up. The soldiers to whom Kwasin listened laughed quietly among themselves, saying that Minruth could dream all he wished but the Tower of Resu would never be completed in his lifetime.

Late one night, well into the third week after their departure from the bee city, an incident occurred which made Kwasin shake with rage and frustration and sank Awineth even further into depression. The caravan was camped along the southern shore of the great lake to the northeast of Qoqada, and Minruth, intent on celebrating his own glory, had decided to open up the large store of mead, wine, and beer he had levied from the subjugated Qoqadans. As the drinking and merrymaking in the vicinity of the royal cart became ever more raucous, some of the soldiers stole into the supply wagons and made off with a share of the liquor in order to indulge in their own revelry. Thus, when a raging-drunk Minruth staggered up to Kwasin and Awineth's cage, the guards had already abandoned their posts and gone to the lakeshore to carouse with their fellows. The guards were lucky. They would not be reported, at least not that night. Khokarsa's great king was far too intoxicated to care.

As he came forward, Minruth stumbled over a root and fell to one knee but still somehow managed to maintain his grip around his wine cask. After taking another swig of alcohol, he pulled himself up on shaky feet, lifted his kilt, and arched a stream of urine into the prisoners' cage.

The captives turned their backs to the warm showers and pressed themselves up against the bars on the far side of the cage.

Kwasin swore under his breath but did not want to give Minruth the satisfaction of hearing his discomfort. Beside him, Awineth trembled with rage and, when the unpleasant deluge at long last ceased, threw herself up against the bars screaming that she would kill her father yet.

Minruth laughed, his face bloated and pale in the moonlight. "When you're angry you remind me of your mother," he said, beaming. "I wouldn't have poisoned her, but she had the gall to try blackmailing me into submission! My only regret is that I didn't get her out of the way sooner!"

Awineth beat her fists against the bars of the cage until Kwasin thought she would break the bones in her hands. It had long been rumored that Queen Wimimwi had been poisoned, and now here was Minruth, openly admitting his crime. The emperor of Khokarsa had indeed become brazen.

As Awineth carried on, Minruth's eyes burned with a light that Kwasin recognized all too well. Kwasin tensed and anger made the blood in his ears pound.

"Seeing you so distraught, my daughter, titillates me. Indeed, you do remind me of Wimimwi, and I suddenly find myself enflamed with passion. Of course, I'll have to throw you in the river to clean you off, but then . . ."

Awineth stopped banging against the cage. Slowly, she backed away from her father, her expression now one of horror. Kwasin moved to position himself between her and Minruth, but stopped himself short. Awineth looked at him, as if to make a plea for protection, but Kwasin ignored her. Instead he walked to a corner of the cage, leaned against the iron bars, and folded his arms.

Keys jingled in Minruth's hands as he swayed an uneven course toward the heavily barred double doors. Now tears streamed down Awineth's eyes, and again she looked to Kwasin. "Please!" she said.

"Who am I to interfere in family matters?" Kwasin said with a shrug.

Awineth had begun to sob when suddenly the jingling of the keys stopped.

"By Kopoethken's sagging breasts!" Minruth cried, quickly

backing away from the cage. "I'm drunker than I thought. Not that I wouldn't bed you, daughter—that can wait until we reach the capital—but to think I almost tried to open the cage with no guards present! Your mad ape of a lover might have killed me!"

Awineth regarded Kwasin, and for a moment he thought he saw understanding and possibly relief in her dark eyes. Kwasin had hated to deceive her, and found he almost couldn't. But he had been betting that Awineth's genuine terror would stimulate the twisted mind of her father enough that, in his drunken state, he would open the doors of their cage without realizing the danger to which he exposed himself.

Kwasin watched Minruth, swaying and stumbling, as he wandered off into the night. Then the two prisoners settled in for another unpleasant night. Kwasin drifted off to the sound of Awineth's weeping.

The two captives were awakened in the early morning hours by a great crashing and booming of thunder. Lightning streaked the heavens with its blinding anger, and within moments a torrential downpour was unleashed upon them. The Khokarsan rainy season had begun.

At first they welcomed the showers, and they stood willingly in the rain as it washed off the unpleasant blessing left upon them by Minruth, not to mention the odorous grime remaining on their bodies from the detritus hurled at them by the Qoqadans. Within a few minutes, however, they were so cold they began to lose the feeling in their hands and feet.

Shivering violently, Awineth pressed her naked body up against Kwasin's. Then she surprised him, as she had on the day of the great earthquake, by pulling him closer and pressing her cold, wet lips against his own. And for a period that seemed timeless, as the lighting struck about them and washed away the darkness, they gave themselves to one another.

They awoke again at dawn's first light in each other's arms. The rain now drizzled miserably and Kwasin could tell from the loud sawing snores coming from the guards' tent that the hung-over men had returned.

Then he started. A scrawny-looking youth of about sixteen years was emerging from the trees surrounding the meadow in which the procession camped. Behind the youth, who now padded stealthily past the guards' tent, a motley band of peasants carrying pitchforks, scythes, and other farming implements crept forward. One among the group stood out, an attractive, raven-haired, middle-aged woman whose distinctive Psyche-knot hairstyle, gold-ringed girdle, and ceremonial dagger identified her as a priestess of Kho.

The loyalists of the Goddess were staging a rescue!

Kwasin shook Awineth from her half-slumber and indicated the approaching group. Awineth gasped, and they both stood up and pressed their faces anxiously up against the side of their cage, their hands gripping whitely the iron bars.

The sandy-haired youth approached the double doors of their cage. In his hands he carried a large bronze skeleton key, which seemed to clank all too loudly when he slid it inside the lock of the outer door. Kwasin held his breath as the boy scraped the key's teeth against the wards of the lock. After experiencing some difficulty, the key turned and the outer door swung open.

The boy inserted the key into the second door's lock just as a cry erupted from the direction of the band of loyalists. Apparently not all of the guards had returned to their tent during the night. One of them had just staggered back and discovered the rescue attempt.

Surprised by the man's cry, the youth jerked back from the lock. The key dropped from his hands, clattering off the brass rim of the cage and onto the ground.

Kwasin growled and shook the iron door. The shocked soldier shouted out an alarm call loud enough to awaken the entire camp. At the same time, the man drew his sword from its sheath and cut down one of the loyalists before he could raise his scythe. A farmer, smarter than his fellows, began jabbing his pitchfork into the guards' tent, obviously hoping to buy time for the boy to unlock the cage. One of the men in the tent screamed, and another guard ran out of the tent only to be impaled by the farmer. But a

moment later a group of soldiers armed with swords and spears—
though clearly still half-drunken—charged in among the loyalists.
Kwasin cried out in anguish as the farmer who had attacked the
tent was struck down first. The man had been a true hero.

The boy at the lock picked up his key but in his nervousness
dropped it again. Both Kwasin and Awineth groaned. Then the
boy again rose from the weeds growing around the cart, the key in
his hand and a smile on his face. A moment later the boy died, still
smiling, when a soldier thrust a bronze spearpoint into his back.

Crestfallen, the two captives sank to the cold, damp floor of
their cage and watched helplessly as the entire band of loyalists
was slaughtered.

In the days following the incident, Awineth again lost the will
to live. The procession went on, traveling over the hills and dales
of the rolling Khokarsan countryside, while Awineth resumed
her sullen and soulless staring through the bars of their cage.
And now, despite Kwasin's attempts to force-feed her, she simply
refused to eat.

On the evening of the fifth day of her fast, Awineth awoke,
the dark eyes of her gaunt face looking startled and surprisingly
lucid. "The Goddess has blessed me with a vision!" she said, loudly
enough that the guards took note and quieted their campfire talk.
"Kho appeared to me in all Her terrible glory! She says that I must
save myself, for in the end She will triumph! But She will only
succeed in her struggle against the sungod if the people stand up
and come to my aid. She has rewarded the spirits of Her followers
who attempted to free us the other night, but those who imprison
us will be cursed! When the spirits of the latter arrive in Sisisken's
dark domain, they will be doomed to endure eternal torment!"

Kwasin shuddered. Had Awineth truly seen the Goddess, or
had she merely made up the vision to frighten the camp guards?
The guards certainly did seem subdued that evening, and he didn't
think it a coincidence when the following morning he overheard
them whispering among themselves that three of their fellows had
deserted. Awineth seemed pleased with the development.

"Kho has rightly put fear into their hearts," she said. "She has sent the men running back to their families to spread the word of my vision."

That morning Awineth began eating once again the foul, ritually forbidden cuisine offered her, saying that she must remain strong for the moment when her followers would come to free her. But over the weeks that followed—weeks filled with humiliation and suffering as the two endured the cold, whipping rains and were paraded through the streets of various villages—no further attempts were made to emancipate Kho's high vicar.

At last the day came when mighty Khowot's smoldering volcanic summit rose up slowly upon the eastern horizon and the procession marched out of the rolling hills surrounding Khokarsa and past the fields and huts that marked the city's agricultural suburbs. Kwasin, but even more so Awineth, was shocked at the state of the capital since they had been there last, now almost a year and a half ago. At that time, when Kwasin had been imprisoned in a cell beneath the palace citadel and Awineth locked away by her father, the city had lain devastated in the aftermath of Minruth's revolt. Thirty thousand had died in the uprisings that followed, and much of the capital and its suburbs had burned to the ground. Then Khowot had erupted again just as Kwasin—along with Hadon, Awineth, and their companions—managed to escape from Minruth's prison. Once more the lava had descended on the city and set much of it afire. But now the charred rubble had been razed and the stinking piles of corpses disposed with, and in place of the wreckage, new stately buildings proudly lined the paved streets of Khokarsa. How Minruth had managed the city's renovation during the costly civil war baffled Kwasin, and he could only surmise the military had enforced a brutal policy of civil service, or perhaps enacted total slavery over a great portion of the population.

And by Kho, the Great Tower! When last they had seen it, the massive ziggurat stood only two-thirds completed, rising just short of five hundred feet into the heavens. But now, by some miracle of miracles, at least another fifty feet had been added to its height. Perhaps less than a quarter of the tower remained to be constructed.

Seeing the surprised looks on the captives' faces, a guard marching beside them said, "The tides have turned—Kho subsides, and Resu provides! King Minruth says the tower will be completed before the Year of Wenqath the Hero is out!" As the Year of the Honeybee was now coming to a close, that meant Minruth planned to have his tower finished in less than two years! Kwasin gaped at the impressive structure that loomed over the city, its base nearly half a mile in diameter, its slanting stepped walls surrounded by massive earthen ramparts and enveloped by great billows of orange dust hanging ominously in the air—the latter raised by the travails of the thousands of men and oxen, looking ant-sized in the distance, working to haul cyclopean stone blocks up the ramparts. Up, down, and across the broad face of the tower, teams of workers labored to install elaborate friezes on the stonework. The carved figures rivaled in craftsmanship the work of Awodon, that bygone master of sculpture, and were in the form of many varied animals, men, heroes, gods, goddesses, and demons. The cost of commissioning the impressive sculptures must have been exceedingly vast, though it would have paled in comparison to the expenditure required to make such rapid progress on the entire structure.

"It wouldn't have been possible," the talkative guard continued, "without the emperor's new architect, Wenekaru. The man carries a genius to rival Awines, they say! I do not understand the high talk of mathematics, which is wearisome to me, but it is said Wenekaru is actually building a completely new type of structure on top of the old one. And he has at last found a lightweight type of brick, long sought by King Minruth, which will ensure that the tower will not collapse from its own heaviness."

They continued on, passing into the city through the outer eastern gate and crossing a stone bridge spanning one of the many canals of the great metropolis. Scores of residents and market-goers thronged about the procession to see their king returning from his great victory, and to gawk at the misery of his two famous captives. But Kwasin noted that only a portion of the onlookers cheered the king of kings, and that Minruth was careful to surround his royal wagon with an intimidating number of armed soldiers, who with the points of their spears sought to hold back both the overeager and the potentially dangerous.

When they passed through another gated wall and were carted past the tower workers' residences, Kwasin understood that his guess about Minruth's totalitarian tactics had been correct. Expansive stone-walled pens, marked at intervals by well-manned sentry towers, enclosed a vast district set aside for the workers. While slave labor had always been used for the construction of the ziggurat, it was clear now that Minruth had indentured a tremendous portion of the city's population to finish his dream once and for all.

"Get a good look," the guard who had spoken before said to Kwasin. "Because after the trial, which is likely to be quite a show, the slave pens are sure to be your new home. Oh, no, our beloved king wouldn't waste an elephant like you by executing you or letting you rot in the pits beneath the citadel—not when he can use you to set the blocks on his road to immortality."

Then the soldier looked up at Awineth and grinned. "And as for you, my former queen, I'm told your father has other plans."

TWENTY-THREE

The procession stopped on the edge of the Inner City and the soldiers, thrusting their spears inside the cage, forced Awineth to manacle Kwasin in heavy iron chains. When satisfied their giant prisoner was properly restrained, the soldiers swung open the iron doors of the cage and with additional chains secured Kwasin's arms, crossing them so tightly behind his back he could not move them at all. Then, to the sound of trumpets blaring, drums beating, and brass gongs clanging, Kwasin and Awineth climbed down from their cart and were led forward through the clamorous throngs of spectators.

Continuing on, the procession crossed over the arching stone bridge that rose above the moat, then climbed the wide, steep steps of the acropolis before passing through the huge bronze doors into the citadel. As they marched past the many temples and government buildings, Kwasin noted that all of the statues of Kho had been removed where possible and replaced with effigies of Resu, while those figures too large to move had been defaced by Minruth's vandals. The sight both outraged and disgusted Kwasin, and beside him Awineth's eyes burned with fury.

They approached the great domed, nine-sided palace, and Kwasin thought they would be led inside when suddenly the guards yanked hard on the chain around his neck and pulled him out of the procession. Kwasin roared and drove a massive shoulder into the group of soldiers who tried to restrain him, landing a number of them on their rears. Many in the thronging street cheered and hooted their approval, but more soldiers quickly overwhelmed Kwasin and forced him to his knees, practically jumping over one another to assail the prisoner with the butts of their spears.

Kwasin caught one last glimpse of Awineth as she was led up the broad and steep steps of the palace. She looked back at him over a shoulder, but she was already too far away for him to discern whether her large, dark eyes were pleading or remained proudly defiant.

The soldiers drove Kwasin ahead of them with their spears, while at the same time retaining a firm grip on the chain about his neck. They prodded him around the palace to a rear entrance, and after passing up the steps of the building into a spacious hall, his captors unlocked an iron-grilled door and brought their prisoner down a series of winding stone staircases and narrow corridors. Kwasin already knew their destination, for Minruth had imprisoned him beneath the palace once before.

"What of the trial?" Kwasin asked one of the soldiers. "When will I be summoned to testify?"

"Trial?" The man laughed. "It's going on as we speak, but you won't be testifying. Our orders are to hold you here until you're sentenced. I don't think Minruth would have bothered with the trial at all, but he wants to give the appearance of fairness. Now get moving, you great oaf!"

The soldier jabbed his spear at Kwasin, forcing him inside a dark cell near the end of a long corridor. The iron door slammed shut, echoing against the hallway's stone walls like a sentence of doom. The turnkey bolted the door's heavy lock, removed his key, and left Kwasin to brood in the darkness of his cell.

Kwasin had just stood up to examine his prison when the turnkey returned with the guards and opened the cell door.

"What now?" Kwasin asked, scowling.

"Trial's over!" one of the guards exclaimed. "You've been convicted on seventeen counts of high treason and sentenced to death. But King Minruth will allow you to ruminate on your multitude of transgressions while you slave on the Great Tower."

"And what of the queen?"

"You mean the former queen," the guard said. "The criers have just announced to the city that she has denounced the College of Priestesses as corrupt. Because of her contrition and her father's great mercy, she will be allowed to retain her office as high priestess of Kho and will immediately begin initiating reforms among the priestesses. But there will no longer be an empress of Khokarsa. King Minruth says that Resu has decreed it."

Disgusted by the sham trial, the lies about Awineth, and the blatant sacrilege, Kwasin said nothing. If Minruth was fool enough to let him live a little longer, then so be it. Meanwhile, he would try to find a means of escape. And after that, revenge.

But when the guards escorted him to the tower workers' district, he saw what a truly daunting feat escape would be. Not only were the workers' pens double-walled and kept under the ever vigilant watch of the sentries in the towers, but he was brought to a special heavily fortified pen which had been designed and created just for him. The pen was in reality more of a pit, fully thirty-feet deep, and a hundred feet in both length and width. The only way in or out of the pit was to be lowered or hoisted up by rope. A special wooden crane, from the sheave of which dangled a wooden platform, had been set up for the purpose of ferrying passengers from the base of the pit to ground level. When the crane elevator was not in use, it could be swung back away from the pit to prevent a person below from somehow lassoing the crane and thereby escaping. To further complicate matters for the would-be escapee, a tall stone wall had been erected from the base of the pit and rose thirty feet above the pit's rim, and a barrier of thorns wrapped along the top and sides of the encircling wall to discourage potential climbing. Not that there would be any climbing, a soldier told Kwasin, for at all times he was to be fettered in chains of bronze inside a stone prison that had been constructed in the center of the pit. And even should Kwasin escape his shackles, break through the door of the prison, and attempt to scale the walls or burrow beneath them, he would be spotted immediately by the soldiers in the overlooking towers, as the pit was lit by torches throughout the night.

Five soldiers accompanied Kwasin to the floor of the pit on the swaying platform that hung down from the crane. He would have tried knocking the men from the platform, but a noose had been slipped over his neck. A man stationed on top of the wall released the slack of Kwasin's noose from a winch as the platform was lowered. The captain in charge warned Kwasin that if he caused any trouble, the man above would draw up the noose. Then Kwasin wouldn't be creating any more trouble for anyone, the man had said with a smile.

When they reached the bottom, Kwasin eyed a number of small stone-lined holes spaced at regular intervals along the pit's perimeter. These would be components of a drainage system put in place to prevent the massive slave pit from filling up with rainwater, though it would not stop it from suddenly becoming a muddy hellhole once one of the violent seasonal storms struck the region. Because of this latter fact, a raised, stone walkway ran from where the crane dropped off its passengers to the stone prison where Kwasin was to remain chained to a granite wall when he wasn't working on the tower.

The soldiers escorted Kwasin down the walkway to the prison, unlocked and swung open the great bronze door, and brought him inside where he was secured with massive bronze chains to a wall. One of the soldiers took off the chains that trussed up Kwasin's arms behind his back, though he did not remove the manacles. A bowl of cold and watery millet gruel was set on the floor before Kwasin. Then torches in the wall sconces were extinguished and the door to the long, narrow cell was shut and locked behind the departing soldiers.

Kwasin leaned forward to lap up the contents of the bowl in front of him when a voice arose in the darkness, carrying from what must have been a cell behind his own.

"Strange is the road of fate laid down by the deities," the melodious voice rang out, "but stranger still is the road from

Dythbeth to Khokarsa! Indeed, it is as if Kho has inextricably tied us together, my king!"

Kwasin groaned upon hearing the singsong voice. Would he never be rid of the loudmouthed bard?

TWENTY-FOUR

It turned out that Minruth, not fate or the Goddess, had paired up Bhako with his former king. The romantic bard, however, saw things differently.

"It is true," Bhako explained, shouting through a ventilation shaft in the ceiling that connected both of their cells, "that Minruth has placed me in your pit because he wishes me to punctuate my epic verse, the *Pwamwotkwasin*, with a record of your final and humiliating days as a slave. But it was really Kho, acting through Her high priestess, Who orchestrated the events that led me to be once more at your side. For on the very night shining Dythbeth fell, Queen Awineth ordered me to the walls to entertain with song the war-weary soldiers serving night duty. Had she not done so, I would surely have joined the pile of the dead upon the great plain. Because on the night before that great battle of battles had yet begun, I was plucking my lyre and reciting a minor cycle in your heroic epic when suddenly, drunk on song, I stumbled and hit my head. I must have done this and lost consciousness just as the invaders attacked, for when I awoke I found it was morning and that I had fallen behind the wooden supply crate on which I had been standing as I performed. I say it must have been at the moment the Khokarsans struck, for had I fallen earlier, why wouldn't the soldiers to whom I was singing have pulled me up from behind the crate and brought me to a priestess of medicine?"

"Perhaps they'd had enough of your tuneless singing!" Kwasin growled.

Bhako ignored the gibe and continued. "Only because I was hidden behind the crate had I escaped the enemy's notice. When I got up and peered from the wall, I saw my once proud and fair city smoldering in ruins and the Klemqaba busied with their looting and raping. I even saw you, O King, trussed up before Minruth's tower of dead. Oh, how I agonized that I could do nothing to help you!"

"I am sure saving my hide was your highest priority," Kwasin murmured skeptically.

"It was, O King," Bhako replied, who must have been as keen of hearing as the fabled long-eared hare in the verse of the priestess-bard Hala. Certainly the bard was as annoying as that mischievous, though widely renowned leporid. "But by the time I had donned the trappings of a fallen Khokarsan soldier," Bhako continued, "and made it outside the walls, it was too late. Minruth had already begun to transfer you to the cage in which, to my horror, Queen Awineth was also imprisoned. And yet I did not give up. I infiltrated the army and joined Minruth's great triumphal procession. Yes, my king, though you did not know it, I remained faithfully at your side all the way to the capital! Unfortunately, only a few weeks into our journey, I was found out when I attempted to filch the key to your cage from a guard. Despite my status as a sacred bard, Minruth threw me in irons. At first I thought—and hoped, so I might soothe your suffering and woe with song—that he would put me with you in your cage. But Minruth the Mad said the sharp wit of a bard's tongue revealed his devious nature and feared I would somehow help you escape.

"Yes, the emperor of Khokarsa is quite interested in you, O King! Almost to the point of obsession, for he has heard of your many feats of bravery and knows too well the great losses you have caused him. He even had me recite to him my great epic of your adventures, saying he has in store for it a most fitting conclusion."

Kwasin had no comeback to the bard's last comment. He

was sure Minruth had long contemplated how best to dispose of Dythbeth's great hero.

Feeling even more sullen after hearing Bhako's story, Kwasin pushed aside the bowl of gruel left by the guards and, leaning against the cold granite wall, fell into a restless sleep filled with nightmares that upon awakening he could not remember.

The days, weeks, and months that followed stretched on wearily for Kwasin. The Year of the Honeybee came to a close, and the Year of the Millet progressed as the once-defiant king of Dythbeth slaved away on the Great Tower, waiting anxiously for word from the outside that the forces of the Goddess had at last rallied against Minruth. But no such news ever arrived, and what little information Kwasin did garner from eavesdropping on his guards, or from rumors spread among the tower workers, was not good.

His guards' whispers confirmed that Minruth had kept true to his word and given his daughter her life but not her freedom, permitting Awineth to live out her days in a heavily barred apartment within the palace. Probably he feared the public outcry, and quite possibly all-out revolt, that would be sure to follow if he killed Kho's high vicar. But while Awineth was more or less comfortably imprisoned and otherwise well treated, rumor had it that Minruth took great pleasure in periodically entering her chambers and raping her, despite the fact that she was said to be pregnant with Kwasin's child. Kwasin could not dismiss the disturbing stories as fiction. He had seen for himself Minruth's unhealthy infatuation with his daughter.

Upon hearing the news, Kwasin became distraught. In his wanderings, he had spread his seed far and wide with little thought of consequence for either mother or potential offspring. But now Kwasin began to feel differently, and a great worry seized him at the possibility that Minruth would murder his future son or daughter, or worse yet, raise the child as his own. He was not sure what had changed in him to cause these unfamiliar pangs of conscience, but the more he thought of the danger looming over his unborn child, the deeper also seemed to grow his feelings for the child's mother. That realization shook him more than anything. Kwasin, while always a great lover, had never known love. Always had he been a free spirit, eager to share his insatiable desire with as many women as he possibly could. Why then should his heart gallop like a crazed rhino at the merest thought of Awineth? With perhaps the exception of the fair Lalila, the woman was as beautiful as any he had known—but the world was full of beautiful women! And besides, Awineth was a bitch, a she-devil like none other! Still, though the mind argued, the heart—always the strongest of beasts—won out. He could not deny that, against his better judgment, he had somehow fallen in love with the woman.

The hearsay from the palace only made Kwasin work harder to grate his bronze chains against the granite walls of his prison as he attempted to saw down his fetters. Once he had weakened them enough, he would wait for an opportune moment. Then he would strike and, even if he did not escape, at least many guards would die before he was killed or subdued.

Kwasin also learned through the grapevine that the newly ordained order of Kho, propped up in Awineth's name, had all but caused the College of Priestesses to collapse. This did not prevent the priestesses' network from going underground and operating in clandestine fashion among the common people. Vague murmurings of the network's existence came occasionally to Kwasin through his fellow slaves, though he received no direct communication from the priestesses. Then one day something happened that made him realize he had merely been too deaf to hear the priestesses' messages. It also made him reevaluate the worth of Bhako, that constantly chattering, ever bothersome bard.

Kwasin had been single-handedly pulling a massive granite block up one of the great ramparts of dirt that angled up along the walls of the Great Tower, trying to ignore the dozens of spectators who congregated on a large wooden viewing platform and often volleyed insults at him. Minruth had ordered the platform to be constructed atop the massive stone wall penning in the tower workers, desiring to broadcast to the island, and indeed the entire empire, that the once-mighty Kwasin was now his slave. The king of Khokarsa had gone so far as to issue travel vouchers to anyone who wished to come from afar and see his famous captive. That Minruth had placed a heavy tax upon the vouchers, one which served to cancel out any benefit to the travelers, was not advertised. In fact, many of those ensnared by Minruth's voucher program now resided in the capital as indentured servants, forced to become slaves themselves because they had spent too many *nasuhno* on their trip and gone into debt. In this way, Minruth increased his already great number of stonemasons, brickmakers, carpenters, foundrymen, ropemakers, surveyors, artisans, stevedores, warehouse workers, scribes, bakers, brewers, and cooks contributing to the effort to finish the tower.

But on this day, without warning, all work on the tower suddenly halted. The guards yelled up at Kwasin to leave the granite block he had been hauling where it lay. This despite the fact he had dragged his burden only halfway up its rampart and stopping now might cause the block's wooden sledge to become lodged on the dirt-and-gravel concourse. Cursing because he knew he would later be the one ordered to get the block unstuck, Kwasin slipped out of his harness—though not his heavy bronze chains—and joined the other slaves who were being herded back to their pens. Kwasin was escorted under heavy guard to his pit, where he was lowered down by the crane and shackled to the usual wall inside his cell.

"Is that your stink I smell, bard?" Kwasin yelled up at the ventilation shaft in his cell's ceiling.

"Yes, but I'm surprised you can smell me, O King, over your own spicy excretions," Bhako replied from his own cell.

Because Kwasin wanted an answer from the nosy bard, whom he had come to rely on for much of his gossip, he held back a crude retort and asked, "Why have all the slaves been given reprieve from today's labor? Surely you've heard something?"

"The word among the workers," Bhako replied, "is that a number of traitors loyal to the Goddess have been planted among the camp guards. The traitors are here, the gossipers say, not to free the slaves, but rather to transmit intelligence from the network of priestesses." Then Bhako laughed and said, "But they have it only half right."

"What do you mean?"

"Perhaps I have already said too much," Bhako said. "What if guards have been stationed outside to eavesdrop on our conversations?"

Kwasin would not normally egg on the gregarious bard, who never seemed to tire once he began talking or singing, but now Bhako's words piqued his curiosity. "I can see the crane through the iron grille in the door of my cell," Kwasin said. "The guards who brought me here all stood upon the crane's platform when it was last lifted above. There are no guards to overhear us."

When Bhako did not reply, Kwasin cried, "Now you choose to remain silent, when you might actually have something of value to say! I am your king, as you ceaselessly remind me—never mind that I reside in a slave pit, fettered and hobbled so that I must shuffle about like an old woman. And as your king, I order you to speak!"

Kwasin was about to threaten the bard with an unpleasant accident the next time they were assigned to the same work gang when suddenly Bhako spoke up.

"I only hesitate to confide in you, my king, because if we are overheard, the well-laid plans of the network of priestesses will have all been for naught. And besides, you've been receiving their messages anyway—through me! Haven't you wondered why I'm such a good gossip? It's not from listening to the rumormongers or even traitorous guards. No, the secret communications come instead from the very spectators Minruth so vainly parades before us! But King Minruth and his guards are too stupid to understand the messages, even though they are transmitted in plain sight. Or I should rather say within earshot, for the messages come to me through my chosen medium, that of song. Certainly you have heard the women who often come to hector us workers with their derogatory rhymes? But while the insults of the women are only the shallowest sort, much deeper beneath their verse lies a secret message, coded in a type of rhyme, allusion, and meter that only a bard would understand."

"You're saying the priestesses have hidden a message in the obscene limericks hurled at us by the spectators?"

"Precisely, O King! It is another legacy left by Awines, Dythbeth's favorite son, and I only know of the secret language because I was once employed by the Temple of Kho in our native city. The priestesses know this, and only today I received a new message from them, one which bears great hope."

"Out with it!"

Bhako paused, and then with joy ringing clearly in his voice proclaimed, "The priestesses say that Awineth has given birth to your child, a boy who because of the thunder of his cries she has named Deth!"

Kwasin felt as if a god had struck him. "Has it been that long?" he said, his breath suddenly short and his extremities tingling with shock.

"Indeed! In fact it has been longer than nine months since your imprisonment. Queen Awineth gave birth a full month ago, but Minruth has clamped down so hard that the network of priestesses dared not send any messages, even in code." The bard went on to relate that, on the night of the birth, Minruth had sent two women to take the newborn away from its mother. Awineth's attending priestesses, however, killed the women and attacked the guards, slaying them. Though most of the priestesses were killed in the struggle, they managed to get both mother and child out of Awineth's locked room, spiriting them from the palace through secret passageways and tunnels known only to the initiates of Kho.

"Minruth flew into a rage when he found out," Bhako continued. "He immediately threw a cordon around the city and began a house-to-house search. But now, a month later, he has still found no one, or at least not those he was looking for."

"What do you mean?" Kwasin shouted up at the shaft. His heart pounded and he had broken into a sweat, notwithstanding the fact that the edges of the great pit shielded their enclosure from the hot glare of the sun and left it relatively cool.

"You've noticed the influx of new slaves of late?" Bhako asked. "They're the most shameful lot of humanity I've ever seen, but now I understand why. The new slaves are composed of the criminal rabble Minruth rounded up during his search of the city. Slaves by nature make poor workers, which is one reason it has taken so long to build the tower—that and the efforts of the priestesses over the centuries to slow its construction. But criminals make even worse slaves than—"

"Save your philosophizing!" Kwasin bellowed. "What do you know of the queen?"

"Sadly, nothing more than I've already told you," Bhako replied. "Even the priestesses who delivered the intelligence to me know nothing. It's assumed that she is being concealed in a house, or possibly beneath one in an underground room, somewhere in the city. Minruth is still patrolling the city's residential districts and suburbs, and he has sent spies everywhere, even among the tower workers. No one can be trusted, my king, absolutely no one."

Suddenly Bhako announced he had come to a decision. Though it was forbidden to do so without authorization from the priestesses, he had no other choice than to teach his king the secret metaphorical language of Awines. When Kwasin asked why he must learn the code when Bhako could simply translate for him, the bard replied, "What if Minruth should separate us or something unforeseen happened to me? I might fall from the tower by accident or be murdered by someone in the slave gangs. While I am a sacred bard, we are among many felons who would not think twice about harming me. If I were to be killed, you would have no way of communicating with the priestesses."

And so for the remainder of their day off from working on the tower, Bhako prattled on about rhymes and riddles and secret messages. Kwasin tried his best to understand the bard's explanations and examples but, by Hala, what did the man mean when he said that the intervals between the words often meant more than the words themselves? Frustrated by the depth and sophistication of the ancient code, and also anxious because of the information he had received about Awineth, Kwasin finally gave up. He told the bard he would just have to make sure he did not get himself killed.

Four months passed while Kwasin waited for further word from the priestesses. Meanwhile Minruth redoubled his efforts to complete the Great Tower, bringing in thousands of additional workers utilizing policies that involved bribery, deception, and frequently outright blackmail. The latter consisted of threatening to shut down crucial trade routes and thus deprive both the local island queendoms and those across the two Kemus of vital supplies. During the civil war, access to the salt mines in the Saasares had been disrupted, forcing the empire's queendoms and outposts to deplete their stores of this essential dietary mineral. Shortly after the war ended, however, the salt trade had been reestablished, and now Minruth garrisoned the mines, denying salt shipments to any city that did not provide for him a certain percentage of its population to serve as laborers on the tower.

Kwasin's guards, talking among themselves but loudly enough to be overheard, said that the king's advisors feared to question Minruth the Mad, even though his obsession with the tower threatened to bankrupt the entire Khokarsan economy. Minruth had begun to propagate the idea that he, as king, was in fact Resu himself, the sungod incarnate. Therefore anyone who questioned the king's decisions was in reality expressing a lack of faith in Resu. Under the new order imposed by Minruth and his priests, doubt in the sungod itself was an unlawful and punishable offense. If prosecuted, it could lead to imprisonment, heavy fines, and even a sentence of death.

The guards also brought news from across the island that only worsened Kwasin's already black mood. It seemed that the northern mountaineers, who had been allowed to colonize Dythbeth after the Klemqaba were through with their pillaging, had proved extremely poor administrators. Inexperienced in the complexities of running a city, they had run Dythbeth's former prosperity into the ground while the local population died off by the thousands from famine and disease. One of the guards remarked that it would take another hundred years for the population to expand before the city could be rebuilt and restored to its past glory.

Kwasin's heart sank upon hearing of the catastrophic demise of his native queendom, and as he heaved load after load of bricks up the tower's great ramparts, he began to question what he could have done differently to save his city. Perhaps he should have swallowed his pride and sought help from his cousin Hadon. News had recently spread among the tower workers that Hadon was now king of his outpost city. Further, King Hadon supposedly claimed that, as winner of the Great Games, he was still rightfully the king of kings, and it was said that he was rallying the cities along the southern sea to unite against Minruth and attack the island, though the latter may have just been hearsay. But Minruth, according to Kwasin's guards, believed the rumor. Even now, as the Khokarsan treasury strained under the weight of the tower project, he was raising an army among the subjugated cities of the Kemu to face the alleged threat from the south. Minruth had also ordered Admiral Poedy and his navy to blockade the Strait of Keth, thus preventing any vessels from entering the northern sea.

But while all of the coastal cities along the Kemu had been vanquished, one of them would not be assisting Minruth in either his military operations or his mad quest to complete the tower. Mukha's entire population was said to have been slaughtered in retaliation for having secretly sided with Dythbeth during the war while at the same time outwardly claiming allegiance to Minruth. Old King Qanaketh and the entire royal family of Mukha now resided in the dungeons beneath Minruth's citadel, awaiting a fate unknown.

The months passed among the tower workers. Twice Kwasin became so frustrated with his situation that he attacked the guards overseeing his work gang, killing three soldiers. Two of the men had been hurled by Kwasin down the face of the tower, while the third soldier's skull was crushed with a well-slung brick when he made the mistake of removing his helmet in Kwasin's presence while trying to get at an itch. Normally any such display of violence would have resulted in immediate death for the offending slave, but Minruth had issued orders that Kwasin was not to be harmed.

Or at least so Kwasin assumed. While he was being escorted back to his pit after the first incident, he asked a guard why he had not been killed on the spot.

The man, grinning, looked at Kwasin and said, "From what I hear the king has something special in store for you."

When Kwasin asked what this was, the man only continued to smile and said no more.

TWENTY-FIVE

O ne day, well over a year and a half into his captivity, Kwasin looked up at the Great Tower and realized much to his surprise that the colossal structure was almost complete. Nearly half a millennium had passed since the first stone of the massive ziggurat had been laid down by King Klakor and blessed by Queen Hiindar. Since that time many thousands of men and women had died working on the monument, not a few of them over the past three years alone. The Great Tower of the Kho and Resu—now simply the Great Tower of Resu—soared majestically into the heavens, its staggered sides rising well over six hundred feet from the half-mile-wide base.

Kwasin shook his mane of hair, as angered and saddened as he was awestruck at the breathtaking testament of blood, sweat, tears, and obsession. He took no pride in the fact that he had contributed to the tower's construction. To him it represented only the intense anguish of his captivity and the longstanding suffering of the people. Because of the tower—because of Minruth's mad quest for immortality—Great Kho had been dethroned, many of Her people slaughtered, and the priestesses and their college propped up in a hollow mockery of their former glory. And yet the world went on. The oracle's prediction of doom for all the land had not come to pass. The sun and moon continued rise and set, the rains came and went, and the great flocks of birds still winged their way across the horizon.

Now that Minruth's great project neared its final stages of completion, the majority of the hired artisans and craftsmen working on the tower, as well as a good number of the skilled slaves and indentured workers, were being redeployed to other critical duties in the reconstruction of the postwar empire. Kwasin and Bhako, however, were not posted away from the tower, but rather assigned to the burdensome and backbreaking task of deconstructing the massive ramparts of earth that squared the enormous ziggurat.

The vast quantities of dirt that needed to be moved out of the city posed a significant logistical problem for the emperor and his advisors. As the Year of Wenqath the Hero rapidly approached, Minruth wanted the area around the tower cleared posthaste. There was no time to allow for the dirt to be loaded onto galleys and freighted off, especially when the number of ships needed to do that would have choked off both the Gulf of Gahete and the Gulf of Lupoeth for months, appreciably impacting the influx of supplies and foodstuffs necessary to keep the city operating. Besides, Minruth's navy had suffered greatly during the war and the majority of his remaining fleet was currently occupied patrolling the southern Kemu.

A solution was found when a priest in the royal court facetiously remarked that there was enough dirt left to build another great wall around the capital. Minruth seized upon the idea, immediately ordering his engineers to design a broad and tall earthwork barrier beyond the eastern walls of the city at the bottom of Khowot's slopes. The volcano had last erupted only three years ago, and at that time a sea of lava had washed over and destroyed the sacred oak grove and inundated the large stone-block Temple of Kho. Many yet feared that a future eruption might belch a deluge of death-dealing lava directly into the Inner City itself, killing tens of thousands. So now Minruth sent out his criers throughout the capital to proclaim the barrier to be his gift for the citizens' patience during the construction of the tower. But the building of the lava wall only added more aggravation to the citizens weary of both war and their king's vain engineering projects. For months they would have to put up with disruptions caused by the bearers as they hauled one cartload of dirt after another eastward through the heavily populated commercial and residential district on their way out of the city.

Slowly, the Great Tower of Resu began to emerge from behind the mountainous ramparts of earth that surrounded it. Now the spectators came not to jeer at the slave-king of Dythbeth but rather to peer up in awe at the successful completion of the greatest engineering feat ever undertaken by human hands. Kwasin only glowered. He knew that the tower's completion only speeded him on the way toward his impending doom. He had long ago given up on receiving help from the priestesses. Since Bhako first informed him of the secret language of Awines, they had received no further coded transmissions. He could only assume that the conspiring priestesses had been rooted out and put to death.

Then, just as he finally determined he had nothing to lose and would attack barehanded and hobbled the forty spear-, sword-, and sling-armed guardsmen who routinely escorted him to and from his pit each day, a message arrived at last.

Kwasin had been shoveling dirt into a wagon from the shallow remains of the tower's last rampart when suddenly, carried to him on the wind, a musical voice rang out.

"Sisaweth-ken-keth-qa-sin-kwa!"

He stopped what he was doing and cocked an ear toward the observation platform that rested on top of the stone wall enclosing the work area. In the distance he could see the tiny figure of a woman gesturing obscenely at him, doubtless hoping that her vulgarism would serve as a decoy to distract the guards from the secret message she imparted.

"Phekwakwo-dy-komumim-wona-namosi-wapoebi!"

Silently, Kwasin cursed. Bhako had just taken ill with the most recent plague to sweep through the slave district and had been excused from the day's labors while he recovered in the pit. Kwasin would have to hope he could memorize the priestess's message and recite it to the bard later for translation.

"Roqaqa-dy-wona-wenti-wokomku!

While Kwasin stood before his wagon intently listening, one of his keepers approached from behind. Kwasin ignored the man and concentrated on the woman's words.

Suddenly a whip cracked loudly. Blistering pain lashed across Kwasin's naked back. Raging, though not vocally because he was still trying to listen to the priestess, Kwasin reached out with lightning speed, grabbed hold of the slave driver's whip, and yanked it from his tormentor's hand.

"Kekete-ti-gati-gar-terisiwuwu!"

The driver, seeing the seven-foot-tall giant was now armed, blanched and hightailed it back to the large contingent of guards overseeing Kwasin's work gang. When Kwasin turned back to the observation deck, the priestess was gone.

He dropped the whip and resumed his shoveling, running the priestess's words over and over in his head. The guards, relieved to see their dangerous charge surrender his weapon with no struggle, retrieved the fallen whip and left Kwasin to his toiling.

Kwasin was nearly exploding with anticipation by the time the sun set and the soldiers returned him to the enclosure at the bottom of the pit. Still, he waited to make sure his guards had ascended to the surface by means of the crane elevator before calling out to the bard in the adjoining cell.

Silence met him. "Bard, do you hear me?" he shouted again. "I bear what must surely be urgent news from the priestesses, if only I could understand the message! Wake up!"

A great fear seized Kwasin. What if Bhako had died, or was so sick that he had been moved to the surface? Now Kwasin berated himself for not taking up the bard's offer to teach him the secret language of the priestesses.

A strangled moan arose from the darkness, and a moment later came a feeble cough.

Hope leaped in Kwasin's heart. "Bhako, my friend!" Kwasin cried out, using the bard's given name for the first time since they had met. "You are still alive!" But no matter how Kwasin tried to engage the ailing troubadour, Bhako would not—or could not—reply.

Finally, tired of hearing his own voice echoing hollowly from stone, Kwasin slumped against the side of his cell and once again began diligently grating his fetters against the granite wall. Only another week, he judged, and he would have weakened a single link on each of his bronze chains just enough that with great effort he might break them with his oxlike strength. He was being careful this time to keep the worn-away areas of the links as modest and unnoticeable as possible. Three times before, just as he all but sanded down his chains to the point of escape, his guards had detected his handiwork and replaced his fetters.

One line of the priestess's melodic heckling, which Kwasin ran over and over in his head as he sawed at his chains, made him wonder if his work on the fetters would all be for naught. *"That which you dread comes in seven days!"* the woman had taunted. But Bhako had said the priestesses' messages were not what they seemed on the surface, that a deeper, less obvious meaning lay within. Seven days might mean seven months, or even seven years. Or perhaps the number seven was misleading altogether, as *namosi-wapoebi*—which could mean both the seventh day of the week or a period of seven days—was originally named after the ancient priestess Wapoebi before being replaced a couple of hundred years ago with a term more commonly employed, *namosi-sahdar*, which literally translated to *gray-sky-day*, or more commonly, *cloud-day*. Why had the priestess not used the more modern idiom? Or for that matter, why had she not said *namosi-go*, a term that translated unequivocally to a period of seven days? Was the priestess merely utilizing archaic language to make her verse more poetic, or did she mean to make subtle reference to that day of the week's ancient namesake? Kwasin wracked his brain trying to remember anything he could about Wapoebi before finally surrendering to the fact that he knew nothing. He also reflected on the phrase *"Kekete-ti-gati-gar-terisiwuwu,"* which in the vernacular meant *"Gird your loins"* but literally translated to the more vulgar *"Witness thy strength in the great python."* What could it mean?

It was no use! Kho had created him to fight, rage, and make love, not dabble in a troubadour's poetry!

Five agonizingly long days passed and still Bhako uttered no word from his cell. The last mighty rampart of earth had at last been cleared away from the tower, and now Kwasin sat idle in his cell, singing aloud in appalling tones the message from the priestess, praying to Qawo, goddess of healing, that it might wake Bhako from what was in all probability his deathbed. Though Kwasin could hear the guards force water into Bhako's mouth twice each day, and once a day clink down a bowl of gruel upon the stone floor of his cell, the bard could not last much longer.

On the evening of the sixth day after the message from the priestess, the door to Kwasin's prison rattled open and a group of guards entered. They carried with them new, even heavier chains of bronze, which they placed on Kwasin's wrists and ankles, laughing as they observed the work that had been done to his old restraints. Kwasin thought the guards would leave him alone after this, but instead they unchained him from the wall of his cell and forced him to hobble at spearpoint out into the open pit.

He asked the officer in charge where they were taking him.

"Haven't you heard?" the guard replied. "Tomorrow morning at dawn, as the Flaming God rises in all His glory upon the eastern horizon, you are to be sacrificed at the consecration ceremony of the Great Tower."

TWENTY-SIX

E arly the next morning—three hours until sunrise if the water clock he observed as he passed the guard station was correct—Kwasin was awakened in his cell beneath the royal palace and brought above to an antechamber. Here, surrounded by the ever-present guards who stood ready to spear him upon the least provocation, he was ordered to bathe in a great marble tub, after which he was administered ablutions by the robed and thickly bearded priests of Resu in preparation for the morning's ceremony on top of the highest level of the Great Tower.

Kwasin considered hurling himself at the guards, even though that would mean his certain death. If he were slain now, he would thus deprive Minruth the satisfaction of seeing his great enemy die to nurture the spirit of the sungod. According to the priests attending him, Resu required for the tower's consecration the blood sacrifice of the greatest hero of the devout Goddess worshipers. The priests claimed this would return the land to prosperity after the devastating war between arrogant Kho and Her righteous son and husband.

The idea of cheating Minruth of this final symbolic victory did appeal to Kwasin. If he martyred himself, the cause of the Goddess might yet live on in the hearts of Her followers, and one day Minruth, or whatever tyrant assumed the throne after him, would have a bloody revolution on his hands.

The priests also told Kwasin that he should be honored and filled with great joy. He would bear witness to an event unparalleled in human history, the very ceremony in which the blessed king and high priest of Resu would set the final capping stone in place atop the great ziggurat. At that moment the sungod would bestow eternal life upon the reigning king of kings. Of course, Kwasin would be dead before that part of the ritual occurred—his beating heart having been cut out and laid upon the altar—but it was an honor nonetheless to be present at this most hallowed of occasions.

Perhaps Minruth truly was mad enough to believe he would become immortal upon the tower's completion. But more likely, the spectacle on top of the tower was designed to bolster Minruth's image among a population rapidly turning against him. Though subdued, the followers of Kho were still many. They must have believed that the recent bout of plagues sweeping the city, as well as the tremors which still continued to rattle the island, indicated that Kho was displeased with the people's allegiance to Minruth.

But while Kwasin had sat in his cell beneath the palace, he had discovered something which gave pause to his thoughts of martyrdom: the latest set of massive bronze chains placed upon him by the soldiers had been peculiarly fashioned. When he tapped the individual links of the chains against the stone floor of his cell, he found the link at the joining of each manacle clinked at a different pitch than the others. He could only conclude that his shackles bore hollowed-out links at the gyves! If this was true, then the network of priestesses, or someone loyal to them, might still be in a position to help him. More likely, however, the conspirators only planned for Kwasin to break free of his restraints for one last, suicidal rampage among Minruth's soldiers. There was certainly no way the priestesses could hope to spirit away Kwasin through their secret tunnels as they had Awineth, not when he was flanked by dozens of guards and the palace and the streets swarmed with soldiers on high alert for the tower's consecration ceremony.

Nevertheless, it would be pointless to throw his life away attacking the palace guards now when he could cause Minruth much more grief by breaking free during his cherished ritual on the tower. Perhaps he could actually get close enough to attack Minruth himself. But for now he would keep an eye open for the moment when he could do the most damage. He had waited two excruciatingly long years toiling in Minruth's slave pens. He could bide his time a little longer.

When the priests were done with their ablutions, Kwasin was given a loincloth of plain white linen. While he discarded his old tattered loincloth and put on the new one, Kwasin asked that, as was traditional for prisoners about to be executed, he be permitted to make a last offering to Kho in the presence of a priestess. The priests only laughed at him. Then, with their sacrificial victim now bathed and properly clothed, they turned Kwasin over to the soldiers, who escorted him through the palace, out the great bronze doors, and onto the streets, where he found the grandest of processions awaiting him.

The darkened streets had come alive with celebrators, awakened early by Minruth's criers to witness at long last the historic completion of the Great Tower, and to rejoice in their emperor's symbolic ascension to the heavens. Despite the early hour, wine and beer flowed freely among the revelers and many shouted out lewd invectives at the legendary Kwasin of Dythbeth. Others in the crowd, however, refrained from the name-calling and, with expressions that might have been sullen or even embarrassed, turned their faces away and disappeared among the other spectators. These would be the citizens still loyal to the Goddess, unwilling to show dishonor to the great hero of their movement and yet afraid to exhibit their discontent. Right now Kwasin hated them more than the king's soldiers.

The large contingent of guards, stemming off the crowd with stern looks and raised spears, quickly positioned their famous captive behind the long line of priests in the street. Without delay the procession began moving. King Minruth, Kwasin noted, was not among the entourage. Presumably he had already been escorted under heavy guard to the Great Tower and ascended the monument so he could partake in special rites with his priests.

The procession soon passed from the citadel, descending the steps of the acropolis and crossing over the moat into the Outer City. Tiny pinpoints of reddish-orange light bled through the black morning sky in the west, evidence that the priests' rituals were already underway on the tower's uppermost level. Before long Kwasin and the cavalcade of priests and soldiers began wedging their way through the vast human sea that had poured into the open area east of the Great Tower. Many in the tremendous crowd, waiting to witness the final act of the monument's completion, would be disappointed. Most would be too far back to see anything worthwhile, while those closer to the base of the tower would be unable to see up over the edge of the tower's highest step.

As they forged ahead, Kwasin looked up. The outline of the enormous monument angled down, black and ominous, against the dark morning sky. A great sense of dread now enveloped Kwasin. He knew his ultimate fate lay at the tower's apex, that he had lived his entire life—fighting and drinking and bragging and lovemaking—to arrive at this very moment. But what would any of it matter when his heart no longer thrummed with the exuberant joys and the agonizing trials of life? Perhaps Minruth was not so mad after all to seek immortality. In the face of death, did anything but life hold any meaning? Alas, in a short time Kwasin would be in the shadowy presence of Sisisken, who would perhaps be able to answer his question.

Suddenly Kwasin's great frame trembled and he shook free of the dark foreboding. In his thirty years of life he had cheated death more times than he could remember. He would not surrender to destiny just yet. Warm blood still coursed through his veins, and as long as it did, the fire raging inside him would roar with the will to live.

Eventually Kwasin and the others left the clamoring multitude behind, passing through an opening in the base of the tower and descending a staircase until they stood in a chamber walled by huge granite blocks. Many of the priests darted wide-eyed glances at Kwasin. They must have been fearful of being trapped in the enclosed space with the terrible giant, the bringer of death and woe to so many of the followers of Resu.

A number of the guards filed into a low, narrow passageway at the back of the chamber, and then one of the priests placed a black linen hood over Kwasin's head. The priests must have still held great fear that he would escape. Otherwise, they would not have been concerned about him seeing the secret tunnels that wormed throughout the enormous ziggurat. He wondered if the soldiers knew they would also be considered a risk and that their king would probably order them killed after the morning's ceremony. Kwasin himself had witnessed the execution of the slaves who had worked on the tunnels.

Sharp spearpoints jabbed at Kwasin's back as the soldiers forced him into the passageway. He swore loudly as his forehead smacked hard against the doorway's decorative epistyle. The tunnels were not built for a seven-foot-tall, extremely broad-shouldered, big-boned man.

The passage proceeded only a short distance before it jogged to the left and its previously level floor rose to an angle of twenty-five degrees. Before long, the soldiers in front of and behind Kwasin began puffing loudly. Kwasin, however, did not become short-winded, having become used to such steep ascents while hauling mammoth loads of bricks up the tower.

The higher they climbed, the quicker came the tunnel's turns and the steeper became its incline, until the shaft slanted at a frightful thirty-five degree angle. Now, in addition to his back and shoulders scraping painfully against the ceiling and sides of the constricting corridor, after every few steps he tripped over his hobbled ankles and slid two or three feet back down the shaft. The soldier following at his heels cursed each time this happened, as Kwasin's flailing feet would strike him and knock his own footing out from under him. Though the tunnel was cool, Kwasin began to sweat. He did not want to slip and accidentally be skewered by the spear of the man behind him. But soon the soldier, tired of repeatedly being kicked in the face, backed off and widened the distance between them.

Finally the hellish climb ended and Kwasin's hood was removed. Before him was a small, brightly painted, stone-walled chamber, the size and shape of which indicated that he likely stood directly beneath the tower's twenty-seventh and highest level. In one corner of the room a staircase rose to an opening in the ceiling, through which the chanting of priests could be heard. A man in his mid-fifties, a beautiful middle-aged woman, and three boys ranging in age from five to twelve years old were already in the room when Kwasin and the others entered. Standing with their hands manacled behind their backs, and adorned in nothing but plain, white linen loincloths, the five huddled together in a corner as the teary-eyed woman whispered in falsely reassuring tones to the obviously terrified children. The man's expression, however, looked proud and unyielding. His hazel eyes and long, hawk-beaked nose hinted at his Klemsaasa ancestry. Because of this, and also the man's regal bearing, Kwasin guessed this must be old King Qanaketh of Mukha. The woman would be his wife, the high priestess of Mukha, with the children being the couple's offspring.

Kwasin felt great pity for the woman and children, but not much for the man. Qanaketh's decision to feign allegiance to Minruth, while at the same time backhandedly sending his general to attack the Khokarsans, had sealed his fate. Because of his spineless double-dealing, his family would die with him on the tower, sacrificed to the ravenous hunger of the sungod.

Still, when the old king looked up and solemnly bowed his head at him, Kwasin returned the gesture of respect. He did not know if he would have acted any differently from the king under the circumstances. Kwasin had never known the joys or the worries of having a family. And now he never would.

They waited in silence for what seemed a great while. Kwasin, taking pity on the children, began imitating to comic effect the sour expressions of the priests who stood waiting at the base of the stairs for a signal from above. Finally, the corner of the youngest boy's mouth upturned and a moment later broke into a full smile. Seeing this, Kwasin guffawed loudly, and soon all three children were giggling.

The release from worry did not last long for them. Suddenly a priest descended the staircase and announced with a sickeningly cheery voice that it was time for their part in the ceremony to begin.

As the soldiers escorted the royal family of Mukha up the stairs, King Qanaketh turned and smiled grimly at Kwasin. Perhaps the man was no coward after all.

Next the soldiers took Kwasin above. He climbed the steps eagerly, feeling a rush of energy now that the long wait was over. Too long had he been caged and abused by his ruthless keepers in the emperor's slave pens. And though he might now be bound in chains, he would face death as he had always lived, as a man free in spirit.

He emerged from the tiny hole in the ceiling onto the ziggurat's highest step, the base of which measured thirty feet in diameter. Torches burned at regular intervals on all sides of the great square of brick and stone except to the east. This was the side which in a short time would welcome the brilliantly shining and blood-red face of Resu. Already the dark sky had begun to lighten with the sungod's coming.

A tall, blunt-topped, pyramidal block of carved granite rose from the center of the tower. Wooden steps had been placed before the monolith, in front of which sat a small, blue marble pyramid, bearing on each side an image of the sun in bas-relief. It was the Great Tower's capstone, which Minruth would carry up the steps and place on top of the monolith to finish the tower and thereby be blessed with immortality.

On the eastern edge of the tower's summit loomed a large rectangular altar stone. The altar's surface was concave, and a narrow channel ran down its granite face, beneath which sat a broad-lipped, artfully decorated ceramic urn intended to catch the blood of the sacrificial victim. A number of golden goblets sat upon a low block of stone beside the altar, doubtless waiting for the emperor and his priests to dip them into the urn after it filled. Human blood rites like those planned by Minruth had not been witnessed in nearly six hundred years among Kwasin's Klemsaasa and Khoklem ancestors. The practice had ended with the death of King K'opwam II at the hands of the priestesses after he murdered his wife and, like Minruth, attempted to strengthen the power of the priesthood. Ironically, it had been the priests, playing upon the emotions of a distraught populace, who had brought pressure on the priestesses to ban human sacrifice from their rituals. Now the priests had resurrected the bloodthirsty custom they once reviled.

Kwasin surveyed the others who stood before him on the tower's summit. There was Minruth, standing upon a raised platform behind the altar with a group of his priests, looking grand and triumphant in his long red-and-yellow robes and crown of gold. The effigy on the crown's face, representing one of Resu's many incarnations, bore the likeness of an eagle of the mountains. Just below the crown, on Minruth's brow, was painted in red ochre an inverted arrow on top of a horizontal bar, another symbol of the sungod. Minruth's dark eyes burned redly in the torchlight, and for a brief moment his smug expression transformed into a satisfied sneer as he condescended to acknowledge Kwasin's gaze.

Also on the tower, lined up along the king's left, were a number of richly dressed men. Kwasin learned their identities a moment later when the priest of ceremonies called out their names, blessing them in the name of Great Resu. The men were ambassadors from the cities across the Kemu: Qethruth, Wethna, Bawaku, and Miklemres. And even a king's son from as far south as Wentisuh had come to pay homage to the king of king's staggering achievement, leaving Kwasin to wonder what inroads Minruth had made among the revolting cities of the southern sea. Strangely absent was a representative from Siwudawa. Perhaps, like they had done to the population of Towina, Minruth's soldiers had committed wholesale slaughter against the worshipers of the parrot-headed androgyne god, who were known to be fiercely provincial.

Kwasin himself stood lined up with fourteen other prisoners, including the king and queen of Mukha and their children, the others having been brought up from a lower level after Kwasin's party had ascended. As soon as the chief priest finished blessing the ambassadors, he began announcing the names of the prisoners, stating that Resu would judge them fairly but harshly for their crimes. The accused included two priestesses who had served in the Temple of Kho at Khokarsa, three important figures from among the College of Priestesses in Dythbeth, Asema, and Oliwa, and General Keruphe and Captain Nowiten, both formerly of the queen's army—all of them steadfast heroines and heroes of the resistance.

Kwasin wondered what had become of the oracular priestess at Khokarsa. With the exception of Kwasin and Awineth, she had been a greater symbol of the resistance than any other. Did the oracle still lie low in the hills outside the city, hidden among the peasants and hoping for an opportunity to one day strike back at Minruth? Or had Minruth already killed her as his troops stormed across the countryside? Kwasin did not know.

Surprisingly, three priestesses not among the prisoners also stood witness with the ambassadors. All appeared to be very young and were in all probability token representatives from Minruth's fraudulent College of Priestesses.

Suddenly Kwasin reeled forward as pain exploded in the back of his head. A soldier standing behind him had brutally struck him with the butt of his spear. Momentarily stunned, Kwasin fell to his knees while the soldiers secured a bronze collar about his neck. By the time he recovered from the blow, he found himself restrained by the collar, which was secured by means of a heavy bronze chain to a metal ring embedded in the stone floor. He had waited too long to break his weakened chains.

At a signal from the chief priest, two of the soldiers seized King Qanaketh's children and pulled them roughly from their protesting and clearly heartbroken parents. Kwasin cried out in frustration and outrage while he strained futilely against the collar around his neck.

Then, much to Kwasin's surprise, Minruth raised his arms high in the air and shouted to the guards to stop.

"Let it not be said that I am not merciful!" Minruth cried. "I shall not hold these children responsible for the crimes of their parents. They are young enough that my priests should yet be able to correct any misguided notions placed in their heads by the enemies of Resu. Take the youths below!"

But when the soldiers moved to comply, Minruth shouted, "No! I've changed my mind. There's no better medicine for ill-advised youth than a good example. Let them witness what happens to those who dare oppose a living god!"

The guards held the children in place, and Kwasin and the other prisoners watched in horror as two soldiers took King Qanaketh by the arms and brought him forward to the altar. Qanaketh for his part did not flinch but went willingly, not even objecting as the soldiers made him lie outstretched upon the altar stone and held him down.

A long, jewel-hilted dagger appeared suddenly in the hand of the chief priest. The blade flashed under the burning torches. King Qanaketh cried out softly, his body jerking violently, and then went limp. Then the priest plunged dagger and hand within his victim's abdomen and, after several moments of gruesome surgery, emerged with the prize he sought—Qanaketh's glistening, blood-dripping heart. The priest, dark crimson streaking his yellow robes, held the excised organ aloft so that the crowds below might see it. A thunderous, and Kwasin believed disapproving, clamor carried up from the multitudes of onlookers below. Then the priest, holding the organ in his blood-soaked hands, carefully cut the heart into pieces, which he passed one by one to the attending priests. Lastly, he knelt before a small iron hearth burning at the base of the altar and thrust the last remaining sliver of the heart into the flame. When smoke began to wisp up from the hearth, the man removed with ceremonial tongs the now-charred bit of heart. Then he rose and proffered the grisly delicacy to Minruth, whose eyes danced with a mad light as he took the offering, put it in his mouth, and chewed with what seemed great relish. The priests then did the same with their own raw morsels.

Kwasin, growling fiercely as he strained at his collar, saw

disgust upon the faces of the visiting ambassadors. Clearly they, like the horrified crowds below, were ashamed to see a thousand years of civilization end in such a repulsive, loathsome spectacle. The priestess from Mukha and her children had shielded their eyes, but Kwasin could see and hear them wailing.

One by one, the other champions of the resistance were led to the altar by the soldiers. Slowly the urn beneath the altar filled with blood, until it finally spilled over its brim and pooled upon the stone floor. The worst death, Kwasin had to admit, was that of Qanaketh's wife. So distraught became the children at seeing their mother brought forth that Minruth relented and ordered his soldiers to take them from the tower. With great eagerness, the soldiers complied. They too seemed sickened by their king's morbid ritual, as they tried but failed to keep their eyes from straying to the grim stacks of bodies that continued to grow higher on each side of the altar.

Suddenly Resu's blindingly brilliant eye peered up over the horizon, casting its scarlet gaze upon the hideous scene. Now at last it was time for Kwasin to go the way of the others and surrender his precious life force to the sungod. The soldiers clustered thickly about him, warily unfastening the bronze collar from about his neck. But Kwasin did not attack yet. He wanted to get closer still to Minruth. Weaponless, he would have only a single moment to kill the king before he himself was killed.

As he walked with the soldiers toward the altar, he could make out upon the altar's facing the chiseled image of a monstrously fanged python eating its own tail. The words of the oracle at the old temple of Kho in Dythbeth suddenly rang through him. *"The serpent and the ax will be your undoing or your succor, and so shall it be for all the land."* Recalling the prophecy, he felt as if struck by a thunderbolt from the heavens. The curse of the ax had indeed fallen upon him, as witnessed by his capture and the fall of Dythbeth, and he could not deny the truth of the land's downfall at the hands of Minruth's profane followers. And now to see the serpent slithering across his stony deathbed! Surely it was a sign from the Goddess that death's long hunt for him was at last at an end.

Then a thing so strange, so unexpected happened that Kwasin felt as if all time had stopped. A soft and humming melody rose up behind him in a female voice. At once Kwasin recognized it, for it was the same tune that during the past week he had recited ceaselessly in his head. But now the singsong insults that the priestess had hurled at him in the slave pens jarred something in him. Missing words and implied meanings suddenly fell into place and the hidden message of the priestesses revealed its secrets.

"Phekwakwo-dy-komumim-wona-namosi-wapoebi! Roqaqa-dy-wona-wenti-wokomku!" became not *"That which you dread comes in seven days to destroy your world!"* but rather *"Kho-komumim-phekwakwo-dy-namosi-wapoebi! Roqaga-dy-lahbi-wenti-wokomku!"* That is, *"Dread Kho comes in seven days to destroy all the land!"* And now Kwasin realized that the phrase *"Kekete-ti-gati-gar-terisiwuwu!"* was to be taken literally—instead of translating to *"Gird thy loins!"* it meant, *"Witness thy strength in the great python!"* It could only refer to the snake effigy carved into the altar's facing!

The realization sparked in Kwasin's mind for but an instant and then, as if blessed with a vision from the Goddess—which surely this was—he made the creative leap that had for the past week eluded him. It had to be that the words of the priestess were so crafted that only he, not Bhako or anyone else, would understand them. He, whose mother had died under the fangs of a snake because of his own youthful carelessness. The song transmitted a threefold metaphor. By referencing a python in their message, the priestesses sought to draw his attention not only to his own ill-fated past, but also to the stone altar before him, as well as the prophecy of the oracle: *"The serpent and the ax will be your undoing or your succor."* Seeing the serpent carved upon the face of the sacrificial stone before him, and at the same time recalling the oracle's prophecy of the ax, he could come to only one star-tling conclusion: the Ax of Victory lay hidden by agents of the priestesses beneath the altar stone!

Without taking the time to second-guess himself, Kwasin barreled forward to the startled cries of his guards and the priests before him. As he leaped forth, he pulled with herculean strength at the chains restraining his arms behind his back. Though the manacles tore painfully at his wrists, the hollowed-out links broke. His mightily muscled arms, now free, swung up and knocked down the guards leaping at him from either side.

Minruth and the priests scattered in the face of Kwasin's mad charge. Kwasin leaped over the altar just as several spears flew at him. Temporarily protected by the altar, he pushed up against its upper edge and groaned. For a moment he feared he would not be able to lift the immense table of stone, but then the two years spent straining his muscles on the tower paid off and the great altar lurched up and over, crashing on its side with a tremendous boom. There, glinting in the bright morning sunlight where the altar had stood, was the ax of Wi.

Kwasin snatched up the ax and began swinging, his first blow striking down three soldiers coming around the toppled altar. As more soldiers advanced, he chopped the ax against the chains binding his ankles. Bronze gave way before meteoritic iron and the chains split. Without pause, Kwasin jumped on top of the altar's now-horizontal side, swatting out of his way with his great weapon the jabbing spears of the soldiers and splintering them as if they were mere slivers of wood. Three more soldiers went down under three powerful blows of Kwasin's ax.

In the midst of the panic on the tower, Kwasin saw blades flashing in the hands of the three priestesses of Kho. They must have had the daggers hidden beneath their robes. Now their blades lashed out viciously at the priests, the smug expressions of which had transformed into masks of terror. Kwasin had been wrong about the priestesses. They had not forsaken their vows to the Goddess but were rather agents of a well-planned conspiracy against Minruth.

More soldiers fell before Kwasin and his ax as he stormed forward. He spied Minruth, fleeing toward the hole that led into the tower.

For a moment the soldiers held back, daunted by the mad, ax-swinging giant that hulked over them. Kwasin, taking advantage of the lull, swung back the ax, then hurled it forward and released it. The ax, because of its great size and weight, did not make a good throwing weapon, but Kwasin was desperate. In another moment Minruth would escape into the tower.

The ax lobbed toward its target, spinning handle over head. Minruth was now at the opening in the floor, turning to access the staircase. Kwasin thought the ax was going to miss, but then the weapon's handle spun around, the large bone knob on its end smacking with great force into Minruth's left eye socket. Blood spurted, and Minruth collapsed into the hole.

Kwasin howled with disappointment. He had hoped to fully crush Minruth's skull. Still, the reindeer-bone ax handle might have struck with such force that his attempted regicide had succeeded. Or deicide, from Minruth's point of view. But Kwasin would have to see the body to be sure. And he needed to retrieve the ax.

He grabbed the *tenu* of a fallen soldier and made for the dark hole into which Minruth had fallen. The soldiers, who had been regrouping on the western edge of the tower, now rallied and surged forward. Kwasin laid his hand on the ax just as the soldiers closed and, bellowing like an angry god, raised his massive weapon, brandishing it at the soldiers.

The scare tactic worked. The advancing soldiers paused just long enough to give him the advantage. He barreled ahead, laying low three more soldiers.

From behind, a priestess cried out his name. Kwasin whirled. Now a stream of soldiers was rushing up from the stairs. The priestess who had warned him fell to the ground, cut down by a priest's dagger.

Kwasin sprinted to the center of the tower and stood before the tall, spiring monolith. Then he knelt down, set down his ax, and with both hands lifted up the marble pyramidal capstone that Minruth was to have set upon the monolith and thereby seal his godhood. He raised the stone above his head, took aim, and lobbed it at the opening out of which ran the soldiers. The forty-pound stone thumped into the chest of a soldier who had just come up, knocking him and those behind and beneath him down the staircase.

But it would be only a matter of moments before additional reinforcements came. Seeing the bodies of the three priestess-heroines lying before him, bloodied and unmoving, Kwasin slung the ax's leather thong over a shoulder, ran to the summit's northern edge, and slipped over the side of the Great Tower.

TWENTY-SEVEN

Scaling the many carven deities, monsters, heroes, and heroines that decorated the face of the great ziggurat, Kwasin felt as if he had passed into an ethereal world. Here the present day vanished and the myths of ancient times sprang to life. The rising sun glanced its rays across the diverse assortment of bold and sometimes craven or hideously disfigured faces on the friezes, creating an eerie combination of shadows and red-golden light that only intensified the surreal effect. Each of the twenty-three-foot-tall levels down which he climbed placed him in the midst of a new set of fabulous legends. It was said the stonework carvings depicted not only the gods of every nation on earth, but also every species of bird, beast, and creature of the waters that had ever lived. The claim, of course, was ludicrous, but climbing down them Kwasin thought the sundry collection of beings, both real and fabled, did indeed seem infinite.

Having descended three levels, he looked down to see a large number of soldiers cutting through the crowds of gawking pedestrians, swarming toward the base of the tower. If he continued descending, the soldiers would eventually be able to take him down with their slings, spears, and javelins. Though the tower was considered holy, he didn't think fear of damaging the artistry on the tower's face would stop them from hurling their weapons at him. And the soldiers above would soon do the same. That they had not yet done so could only be a result of the havoc left behind by his violent attack.

Only fifteen feet below him the decorative stonework opened around a window. This he knew led into a ceremonial chamber used by the priests. Though he had never been in the room, he had seen it practically every day while working on the tower. It might not provide access to the many tunnels snaking through the monolith's interior, but it was worth investigating. Continuing to scale the tower would only get him killed.

He climbed down and swung in through the window, startling three soldiers who stood near the back of the narrow room. One soldier charged Kwasin with a spear, while the other two followed at the man's heels with drawn swords.

Kwasin ran at his aggressor. His ax splintered the man's bronze spearhead from its shaft. Simultaneously, Kwasin struck the man in the face with his fist. The man reeled and fell. Directly behind his unmoving form stood one of the other soldiers, his sword cutting broadly at Kwasin.

Suddenly the sword flew wildly out of the oncoming soldier's hand. The man pitched forward, a surprised look on his face. Behind his fallen body stood the third soldier, his own sword dripping darkly with his companion's blood.

"My name is Tenswath," the man exclaimed in response to Kwasin's shocked look. "I am an ally of the daughters of Kho, planted among the king's guard by the Queen Mother herself. Follow me if you value your life!"

Kwasin wanted to ask Tenswath if that meant Awineth still lived, but the man had already grabbed a torch from a sconce and was bolting down a passageway located at the rear of the room. Kwasin took off after him.

When he caught up with the fellow, Kwasin said, "You are fleet of foot, ally of the daughters of Kho." Though Kwasin was both long of stride and in excellent shape, the man could doubtless beat him in a sprint.

"In my city's competitions I was second only to my brother Gobhu, who represented Dythbeth in the Great Games," Tenswath said proudly.

Kwasin clapped the man on his back. "Lo! A fellow brother of my native land. I thought I recognized the accent. Now let us show these Khokarsan straw men what it means to oppose two warriors of Dythbeth!"

"Stealth is better than strength in this case," Tenswath replied, keeping his voice down as they continued along the low-ceilinged corridor. "The king's guard is stationed throughout the tower, and if we encounter them, all will be over for us. But I know of a secret way, an underground tunnel that leads out into the city. We must hurry. The king may also try to use it to escape."

"Escape what?" Kwasin asked. "Is Minruth such a coward that among his multitude of warriors he would flee before a single man?"

Tenswath grinned. "The king of kings has more than you to worry about, O King." The man did not elaborate, but for the first time in what seemed ages, Kwasin allowed himself to hope.

Eventually the passageway opened into a bare, granite-walled room. Tenswath pushed against the ordinary-looking wall. A moment later the section of stone grated forward and revealed a hidden passageway. Tenswath disappeared within and Kwasin followed.

The tunnel descended sharply, taking many dizzying turns. When they came to a cross-tunnel, Tenswath led them to the left. A short time later they arrived at another tunnel. They continued past it, but stopped a moment later when they heard the sound of many running feet echoing through the passageway. Someone was coming.

"Go on, O King!" Tenswath cried, passing Kwasin his torch. "Take no more turns but continue on and the tunnel will lead you out into the city!"

Before Kwasin could stop him, the man was running back to where the two tunnels met. Then he disappeared around the corner of the adjoining tunnel.

Ignoring Tenswath's order, Kwasin ran back to the intersection. When he turned the corner, Tenswath was already speeding far down the passageway. At the end of the tunnel Kwasin could see a long line of torch-bearing soldiers, at the head of which ran Minruth, one eye darkened by the blow Paga's ax had dealt him.

Tenswath stopped running and pressed his hands against the

tunnel wall in a peculiar fashion. A deep rumbling shook the tunnel and then blackness cut off the scene as the entire tower seemed on the verge of shaking apart. Then the rumbling ceased.

Kwasin swore. By pressing on the wall, Tenswath had triggered a huge stone block to fall from above, thereby sealing off the tunnel and trapping himself on the other side. He had sacrificed himself for his king. Kwasin shook his head sadly, promising himself that if he ever made his way to freedom, he would have a hero's pylon erected for the courageous Tenswath.

He turned back and continued down the tunnel. When after many turns he had descended to a point that must have been near or possibly below the tower's base, a peculiar smell filled the passageway. The rank, spongy odor grew stronger as he forged ahead. He came to a side tunnel and stopped. The stench was now almost suffocating. He thought he might have stumbled onto a branch of the city's sewage system when suddenly, out of the black throat of the intersecting tunnel, a hideous shriek arose. The hair on the back of Kwasin's neck stood erect. He had heard that same trumpeting, spine-tingling scream once before, as a youth camping with his uncle in the gloomy jungles of the southern sea. Phimeth had told him the shrieking belonged to the legendary dragon of the Kemus. Though as brash a youth as the adult he would become, the adolescent Kwasin had known he never wanted to encounter the dreaded *r"ok'og'a* in the flesh. The nightmares that followed the incident had been terrifying enough for the boy.

But now, memories notwithstanding, Kwasin was unable to resist his burning curiosity. He recalled what General Hahinqo had once told him—of how at backbreaking expense Minruth had captured a great and terrifying serpent of the hinterlands, which he had then imprisoned in the tunnels beneath the Great Tower. Kwasin had not believed the rumor then, but now a chill passed through him that was not due to the dampness of the underground tunnels.

He left the main passage and trod cautiously down the side tunnel, the broken chains that dangled from his manacles scraping against the stone floor. After proceeding only a short distance, the tunnel ended at a heavily reinforced iron-barred gate. A few feet beyond this he could dimly make out what looked like bronze grillwork. He slid open the bolt that secured the door and, noting a large ratcheted winch built into the corridor's flooring, approached the grilled wall.

Kwasin peered through the spaces between the wall of crisscrossing metal but saw only blackness. Then came a rustling. A moment later he gasped when, at the back of the immense chamber beyond the grating, a scaly sheen momentarily caught in the dim light cast by his torch. He strained his eyes into the darkness. It might have been his imagination, but he thought he could just make out a nebulous shape, dark and bulky, in the far reaches of the chamber.

He pulled back from the grating. Fascinating though this distraction might be, he had no time to waste on it. But then, seeing the winch on the floor, he wondered. The winch must open something nearby, and what if . . .

Kneeling, he seized the crank handle and began turning. The sound of ratcheting chains and groaning metal came from the adjoining chamber. After turning the crank for a minute, he stopped. He hoped he had achieved what he thought he did, but he had to get going.

He headed back out through the barred doorway and into the main passageway. Now the tunnel leveled out and proceeded straight forward. He jogged onward for what must have been half a mile before the tunnel ended abruptly at a narrow flight of spiral steps. He climbed up the steps and, reaching the ceiling, pushed up with his free hand against the stone plug above him. It lurched up and he slid it to one side. Leaving his torch burning on the stone stairs, he pulled himself up through the hole and found himself in what seemed to be a musty storage cellar filled with assorted masonry tools. He didn't take time to look around but vaulted up the cellar's creaking wooden steps, emerging into an empty, one-room house.

Screams and shouting sounded through the thin walls of the

house. Kwasin threw open the dwelling's front door and ran outside to find a city in chaos.

He was in a residential district just west of the Inner City. Citizens ran wildly down the street before him. Farther up the street a small group of spear-bearing soldiers was fighting off a much larger band of residents armed with pitchforks, kitchen knives, and even brooms. To the southwest loomed the Great Tower, its lofty, stepped face aglow in the golden morning sunlight. In the east, a thick pall of gray smoke rose from the wall surrounding the acropolis. The Inner City was on fire.

Beyond the wall of the acropolis, Khowot belched its dark smoke skyward. But Kwasin did not believe the volcano was the source of the fires, especially since Minruth's new earthworks should have prevented the flow of lava into the city. Rather, the insurgent citizens must have set the blazes.

Kwasin ran south along the street, weaving his way through the bedlam of pedestrians. Many of the panicked inhabitants were running in the opposite direction, carrying in their arms their most cherished possessions. He guessed that the area's residents had decided to flee the city to avoid the possibility of additional fires being set. They had survived the holocaust that followed Minruth's revolt and didn't want to risk being burned to death in this one. They were probably leaving the city to join up with relatives in the country who might support them until the violence of the rebellion quieted.

He jogged out of the human tide onto a less densely trafficked avenue, intent on avoiding the military district that ran along the city wall. He could not afford a confrontation with soldiers. His plan was to head west until he reached the great canal that had been used to ferry supplies from the Gulf of Gahete during the construction of the Great Tower. There he would scale down the canal's stone-paved banks, jump into the waters, and swim across the gulf to the western shoreline. He already knew the land route he would take from that point, having gone that way once before, after escaping Minruth's prison with his cousin Hadon and their companions.

A terrifying shriek arose in the southwest. Kwasin froze, but grinned a moment later with the realization that the winch in the tunnels had done what he had expected. The *r"ok'og'a* had been loosed from its prison beneath the tower. Now the beast would be running amok, raising hell for Minruth's soldiers and anyone else that got in its path. At least Kwasin hoped. So far the Goddess had rewarded his morning with success. Kho only knew it had been an eternity since luck had turned in his favor. He could only hope it was time for Kho's daughter Suhkwaneth, goddess of the scales, to pay her debt.

He continued on. The farther west he traveled, the fewer citizens he saw in the streets. By the time he got close enough to smell the water, the area was completely deserted. Ahead he saw the stone foundation that edged along the canal. A few moments later he was slipping over the foundation's side and dropping fifteen feet to the bank. A barge was docked on the opposite side of the waterway. It appeared to be uninhabited.

Two ships lay at anchor to the north in the mouth of the canal. Upon seeing them, he almost shouted out with elation. Instead of the typical wide hull and square sail of a galley, the anchored vessels each sported a narrow body and a large, triangular fore-and-aft sail. Ruseth, that skinny-armed redheaded fisherman's son from Bhabhobes, had come through!

Kwasin headed north along the bank of the canal, the city's fortified wall towering on his right. As he ran, voices shouted at him from above. Soldiers stationed on top of the wall had spotted him. He increased his speed. When he reached the end of the stone walkway, he stopped and looked out across the waters. In the distance, a great battle was being waged on the Gulf of Gahete between Minruth's galleys and the priestesses' fore-and-aft ships. The nearest of the two ships hung at anchor roughly forty feet beyond the canal's entrance, its crew not yet noticing him. Over a shoulder he saw the soldiers above coming rapidly in his direction along the wall top. He would have to make a swim for it.

He unslung the ax from his shoulder—the heavy-headed weapon would slow him down in the water, but he could not bear to part with it. He spared a precious moment to gauge the distance from shore to the nearest of the priestesses' vessels. Then, using every ounce of his great strength, he swung back the ax and cast it out over the water.

Kwasin held his breath. Iron head toppled over bone-carven handle as the ax hurtled above the watery gulf toward its target. He let out a shout of joy when the ax head impaled itself with a heavy thud into the ship's portside hull.

A spear sailed past Kwasin's head as he dived into the cool embrace of the Gulf of Gahete. His thickly muscled arms cut the waters with powerful strokes and sped him forward. Soon he found himself at the ship's side. He yelled up to alert the crew to his presence but already a heavy braided rope was coiling down toward him from above. He grabbed the rope and hoisted himself up hand over hand.

When he climbed over the ship's side, he started.

"Awineth!" he cried. "Long have my eyes waited to see the brilliance of your shining face!"

But the queen, flanked by a heavy contingent of fierce-looking guards, was not smiling. Instead, her eyes a cold gray, she turned to a guard and said, "Secure the ax from the ship's side. The oracle, who has made much of its importance, will want to see it."

Kwasin stepped forward and faced Awineth. "The ax remains with me," he said. "With it, I shall lay low our enemies and liberate the people from the sullied hands of the priests. If, after that time, the oracle still wishes to see the ax, I will permit it. But the ax—"

Before he could finish, soldiers surged from behind and clamped iron fetters on Kwasin's already manacled wrists. A man screamed, bone cracking loudly and sickly as Kwasin gave him a vicious kick to the hip. Kwasin bellowed his rage, trying to pull free of the men that sought to hold him. Several soldiers fell hard on the deck as Kwasin barreled into them with his shoulder, but then a spear shaft smacked hard into his forehead. Stunned, he buckled to his knees, and before he could summon the will to regain his feet, additional irons were fastened upon his wrists and ankles.

He looked up at Awineth, whose face, though still cold, was smiling.

"Admiral Ruseth," she said, "have your men take the traitor below! I will deal with him after my forces have won the city."

"Yes, O Queen." The redheaded Ruseth, his bronze helmet now proudly fanning the plumage of his new rank and station, appeared at Kwasin's side. "Bring the prisoner to the hold!"

Kwasin got up of his own volition and was about to rail into his guards again when Ruseth said, "It's pointless to resist, as you're already in chains. You might kill some of my men even so, but in the end they'll overcome you and toss you overboard. Unless the deities miraculously release you from your shackles, you'll sink to the bottom of the gulf and drown."

Then Ruseth did a curious thing. He turned just far enough away from Awineth that she could not see his face. Then he winked one of his pale blue eyes.

"Let's move it, seadogs!" Ruseth shouted at his men.

"Wait!"

Awineth strode forward and looked up at Kwasin. For a brief moment her frozen expression softened with emotion. Then, hate twisting her features, she slapped him hard across the face.

"That is for moaning in your sleep for that witch Lalila, even as my father had us caged and you professed your love for me! Just as with your cousin Hadon, the woman has bewitched you! I was a fool to ever place my trust in you—a mistake I shall never make again. With Kho as my witness, my next strike at you will be final!" Awineth fingered the jeweled dagger that hung from the golden-ringed girdle encircling her shapely hips. Then she turned and strode off with her guards, leaving a bewildered and disbelieving Kwasin standing on the deck.

TWENTY-EIGHT

S ay nothing until we are below," Ruseth said quietly as he and
his soldiers escorted Kwasin to the hold. The young sailor
looked as if he had just swallowed a pail of sour goat's milk.

Still smarting from Awineth's bitter reception, Kwasin fought
to hold back the surging tide of his outrage. Throughout his long
imprisonment, he had many times imagined how his reunion
with Awineth might play out if he ever escaped, but never had he
considered that the woman would betray his trust and charge him
with high treason! Of course, it was indeed possible he had spoken
lustful words regarding Lalila while he slumbered, but what did it
matter? He loved Awineth as he had loved no other. And besides,
no matter how much he loved her, was she foolish enough to
think his mind would never stray to another? He cursed Adeneth,
the goddess sexual passion and madness. Truly was she a bitch
goddess.

Restrained by the chains that bound him, Kwasin shuffled
angrily down the steps to the hold. When they reached the
bottom, Ruseth ordered his men to remove Kwasin's shackles,
including those that had been put on him prior to the tower
ceremony.

"Explain!" Kwasin boomed, turning on the young admiral.
Ruseth's soldiers jumped into action, crossing their spears protectively in front of their superior.

"Keep your voice down!" Ruseth whispered. "If you draw the attention of the queen's guards, I won't be able to get you off the ship and take you to the oracle."

Kwasin knocked the soldiers' spears out of his way and throttled Ruseth in his powerful grip.

"Tell me what's going on," Kwasin said forcefully, though he lowered his voice. "If you don't, you'll never again utter another prayer to Piqabes!"

Ruseth waved off his men, who were on the verge of running Kwasin through with their swords and spears. "We don't have time," Ruseth replied with some difficulty because of Kwasin's unyielding grip, "but if you insist."

Kwasin released his hold.

Rubbing his neck, Ruseth said, "A madness has seized the queen. The priestesses tell me her mind went when her baby died of plague, only shortly after she—" Ruseth stopped, his wincing face showing that he only now realized Kwasin knew nothing of the death of his and Awineth's child. "Forgive me, O King!"

Kwasin felt as if a leopard's claws had raked out his bowels, but he told Ruseth to go on.

"Because all sense has left the queen's mind, the oracular priestess has secretly taken charge of the army my ships have carried from Siwudawa. But the oracle knows you have become quite a folk hero among those in the resistance. She wants you by her side, O King, when she announces to the people that Queen Awineth has been deposed."

Kwasin shook his head, not comprehending. "You say Awineth is mad, and truly she must be, for I have seen it with my own eyes. But the oracle must have lost her own mind to think the queen can be dethroned. Kho's followers won't stand for it! After enduring the hell Minruth has caused them, they would rather see the land torn asunder!"

"You wouldn't be wrong, O King," Ruseth replied, "except that Awineth has gone too far. She is not content with the priestesses' contention that Resu must be restored to his rightful position on an equal footing with Kho. No, she has actually declared Resu to be a false god and thrown him completely from the pantheon! And that is not all—she has called for an end to the priesthood and death to its entire clergy. The oracle—the holy voice of the Voice of Kho—was outraged when she learned of this. She says the queen's position is as unhinged as Minruth's scorning of Kho. Both positions, the oracle says, create an imbalance among the deities that threatens to give rise to a terrible calamity, one from which the land will never be able to recover."

"Will the empire never be at peace?" Kwasin cried.

"No, O King," Ruseth replied. "The priestesses tell us that war has existed since the time Kho's mortal offspring first fell from Her divine branches. I expect it always will. But then, your question is rhetorical, isn't it?"

"What is the oracle's plan?" Kwasin asked before his patience exploded.

"I am under orders to take you across the gulf to the Terisiwuketh Peninsula, where the oracular priestess awaits with her army. A brief ceremony will be held there in which Awineth's bond to the throne will be officially annulled. Thereafter, you will be wed to Awineth's young cousin, the priestess Awamethna, who is next in line to the queenship. Subsequently you will be named king of kings and lead the oracle's army to victory against the last remnants of Minruth's forces."

Kwasin's head reeled, overwhelmed by both the rapidity and the staggering gravity of the new developments.

"But what of Awineth?" he asked suddenly. Though sanity had fled the woman, he still could not shake his feelings of concern for her. He had spent too much time while imprisoned worrying about her fate. Now not only to discover that she hated him, but also that the priestesses and their followers conspired against her—it was too much.

"Leave that to me," Ruseth replied ominously. At Kwasin's threatening look he added, "She won't be harmed, O King."

Kwasin sighed heavily. "Take me to the oracle then."

"Aye, sir!" Ruseth said. "I mean, follow me, O King."

They crossed to the back of the hold and passed up another set of wooden steps to the ship's stern. Here Ruseth already had a boat manned and ready, waiting to be lowered into the waters. As Kwasin boarded the boat, Ruseth frequently looked over his shoulder. The young sailor must be keeping an eye out for any members of Awineth's guard who might come to investigate the unauthorized activity. Fortunately, no one came. They were probably all too busy coordinating the campaign to retake the capital.

"Good-bye, O King, and may Piqabes watch over you," Ruseth said. A few moments later Kwasin was watching the still, blue waters of the channel peel back before the bow as the oarsmen propelled the boat forward.

It should have been a short trip to the peninsula, but because of the battle on the waters, the officer in charge of the boat insisted on taking the long way around, passing south of Mohasi Island and up and around the coast. Even so, traffic on the gulf was high, and when one of Minruth's uniremes spotted them, the officer ordered his men to row as quickly as possible for shore. Seeing that Kwasin's boat would make it to land before it could be intercepted, the unireme turned about, heading deeper into the gulf for easier game. Still, the officer directed the seaman manning the rudder to make for shore. He told Kwasin they would have to wait until the way north had cleared, or until after the battle had been pitched in favor of the priestesses' fleet, before again setting out on the waters. Kwasin was furious but he could do nothing.

As they neared shore, the high walls of the coliseum of the Great Games, silhouetted against Khowot's smoking cone, rose upon the horizon. Kwasin wondered how things might have been different if he, and not his cousin Hadon, had been able to compete in the Lesser and Great Games. He liked to think that after winning the bloody contests, as he unquestionably could have, he would have been man enough to stand up to Minruth when he refused to step down from the imperial throne. If Kwasin had done so, then the years of misery and suffering that followed might have been avoided. And perhaps Awineth would still love him. If she ever had.

He growled and shook off the hopeless dream. Even had he

won the Great Games, the oracle would have sent him on the same quest as she had Hadon. And during his absence, Minruth still would have seized the reins of the empire.

They pulled up on shore, hid the boat and themselves in a thick copse of trees near the beach, and waited. An hour later Kwasin was about to set out north on foot when a scout returned to announce that the priestesses' navy had drawn the enemy to the eastern channel. The way was again clear. Kwasin jumped up and, single-handedly, began dragging the boat back to the beach. A short time later they were again rowing northward.

At last they rounded the southern jaw of the two-pronged Terisiwuketh Peninsula, whose name aptly meant the Python's Head. Kwasin shuddered, remembering old Wasemquth's prophecy about his fate being tied to that of a serpent and the ax. Did the oracle of Khokarsa send Kwasin a subtle message by summoning him here? He hoped not. He tired of the vague prophecies and devious pronouncements of the priestesses and priests.

When the boat rounded the southern tip of the peninsula, Kwasin saw the oracle, surrounded by her priestesses and soldiers, standing high upon a hill above the shoreline. The woman made an impressive sight, the white shrouds of her robes fluttering in the intense winds and both hands clutched around a tall golden spear. Indeed, she looked as grim and terrible as the statues Kwasin had seen of the priestess-heroine Lupoeth.

After they had landed and climbed the hill, Kwasin prostrated himself before the oracle, making his supplications to the Goddess.

"Rise, O King," the oracle cried, "and meet your wife-to-be! Behold, high priestess of Kho and of her daughter, Lahla the moon—behold, Awamethna, future queen of Khokarsa!"

Kwasin rose. Beside the Voice of Kho—who, being in her early fifties, was nowhere near as ancient as he had imagined—stood a young priestess whose face seemed as familiar to Kwasin as her name. Then he remembered. The girl, Awamethna, had been one of the initiates who had attended him in the old temple of Kho in the marshlands outside of Dythbeth.

Truly was Awamethna a radiant thing, every bit as stunning

as her cousin, though her features ran softer than Awineth's more cutting beauty. But right now, on the heels of his stinging fallout with Awineth, Kwasin was in no mood for thoughts of women or marriage.

"Tell me, O Priestess," Kwasin said, addressing the oracle, "what do you see in the future? Will the actions we take today finally bring peace to the land?"

The oracle leaned into her golden spear and fixed Kwasin with the dark pools of her inscrutable eyes. "Your frustration, O Long-Suffering King, is not without warrant. But even though the forces of Kho have today struck a terrific blow against Her enemies, word has come that Minruth—that greatest of blasphemers—has been driven out of the city and now flies with his decrepit followers toward Khowot. Clearly he hopes to escape into the wilds beyond the volcano, where he can seek to foster a resistance of his own. Great forces whirl all about us, O King, pulling us within their furious current. There is nothing we mortals may do but remain steadfast to the Goddess and follow the flow."

"There is one thing I may do, O Holy Oracle," Kwasin said. "And that is to bring you Minruth's head!"

"Kho will bring you great blessings if you do so," the oracle replied. "But first we have other matters to attend."

"Respectfully, O Priestess," Kwasin said, "you will have to wait to wed this child to me. Perform what ceremonies you must to annul Awineth's power, but do not try to stop me from going after Minruth. If I wait around for the ceremony, he'll be sure to escape. And that I can't allow."

The Voice of Kho looked grave, but she said, "Do what you will, O Impatient One, for even I would not think to stop a spirit as mighty as your own. But be warned, what you find on Khowot's fiery slopes may not be all that you have longed for."

And with those final enigmatic words, the oracle turned her back on Kwasin, departing with the soon-to-be high priestess of Kho to begin their rituals. Meanwhile, Kwasin assembled a light team consisting of fifteen men and set out to pursue Minruth and his followers.

By the time they had marched south along the peninsula, and crossed the canal and river that stood between them and the volcano, morning had worn into afternoon. As they drew nearer to their destination, the great billows of smoke rising from Khowot's cone grew darker and thicker, all but blotting out the sun. Bolts of lightning streaked against the backdrop of the swelling black clouds, and the edges of the volcano's lofty crater glowed bright orange as lava threatened to spill down the mountain's cracked and angry face.

The soldiers accompanying Kwasin paled at the terrifying sight, but he urged them on, telling them that Kho Herself had belched forth the great clouds of smoke. She did this, he said, in order to hide them from Resu's arrogant gaze and thereby allow them to sneak up on the enemy. The frightened faces of the soldiers, however, indicated they doubted his words.

As they skirted the northwestern base of the mountain, one of the soldiers cried out. "There!" Kwasin followed the direction of the man's pointing finger. To the south he saw a number of pale dots moving across a field of hardened lava, the same area where once had stood the Temple of Kho and the sacred oak grove. The tiny figures were ascending the face of the volcano, clearly intent on circling around its southern side. From what he could tell, the party consisted of only seven or eight members.

Again, Kwasin urged his team on. Now, as they climbed upward, the terrain became rougher and more dangerous. The deep furrows of the increasingly steep cone, and the ridges arching across its surface from previous lava flows, made for slow going.

They had made painfully little progress when Kwasin spied a second group ascending the volcano. He counted only five figures among the new party, which followed only a short distance to the south of the first group. At first he thought the newcomers might be more of Minruth's supporters, but eventually, as his own group drew nearer, he was not so sure. One member of the new group was clearly a woman. Further, the first group seemed to have put on speed, as if desperate to escape the followers. Surely Minruth led the first group, but who led the second?

Kwasin got his answer a short time later when a runner approached from the southeast. Kwasin recognized the puffing and perspiring man as a member of Ruseth's crew.

"Admiral Ruseth sends word that he has failed in his mission, O King!" the man exclaimed when he arrived. "The queen, aided by those most loyal to her, has escaped!"

Kwasin cursed. The second group, then, must be led by Awineth. After her own priestesses turned against her, she must have fled the city and spotted Minruth also trying to escape. Awineth was making one last attempt to wreak vengeance upon the father who had taken everything from her.

"Why hasn't your superior sent his men after her?" Kwasin growled.

"He presently has his hands tied, O King," the runner replied. "Queen Awineth's men have managed to sink Admiral Ruseth's flagship, and though it's certain the queen's loyalists will be subdued, they're still putting up a hell of a fight. The admiral received word from the oracle and knows of your plans to go after the king. He wanted to warn you to keep an eye out for the queen." The man looked to the south. "But it looks like you've already found her."

Kwasin charged up the slope, his great strides leaving the soldiers under his command far behind. The group led by Awineth was rapidly closing on Minruth and his men. Within ten minutes, the two groups clashed.

Only two hundred yards now separated Kwasin from the skirmishing factions. Awineth's soldiers, though fewer in number, seemed to have gained the upper hand. He could see the bodies of three of Minruth's men strewn across the craggy incline, dead or severely wounded. Minruth, seeing the tide of battle turning against him, now fled the melee, heading farther up the slope. Awineth broke away from the fight and began following her father, dragging something which seemed to be slowing her progress. When Kwasin got close enough to see what burdened her, his heart blackened. Awineth was towing the Ax of Victory behind her up the steep side of the volcano.

Kwasin altered his course, veering toward Awineth.

Suddenly the ground beneath Kwasin's feet trembled, and the thick stench of ash wafted over him. He looked up to see a river of red-hot lava searing down the mountainside, following a jagged channel in the volcano's deeply rutted shell. Now the smoldering current hit a gouge in the slanting terrain, forming a tributary that snaked down and cut off Minruth's path. The emperor of Kho-karsa, his hawkish face carven in a look of desperation, looked down to see both Awineth and Kwasin running toward him. But Minruth could go no farther up the mountain. Already he winced with pain at the severe heat emanating from the lava flow. Blood streamed down from his left eye socket and the wound caused that morning by the knob of Kwasin's ax.

Awineth reached her father before Kwasin. She dropped the ax and, drawing a long, slim dagger from the jeweled sheath at her waist, attacked the man who had ruined her world.

The struggle did not last long. Minruth, though unarmed and out of shape, still remembered how to fight from his old days as a champion of the Great Games and a hero of the empire. He grabbed his daughter's wrist and twisted her arm and the dagger behind her back. Awineth, shrieking with pain and anger, fell to her knees. Minruth plucked the dagger from his daughter's grip and shoved her forward on her face. Sobbing with rage, Awineth whirled about to look up at her father, who grinned down devilishly at her. In his hands, he held Kwasin's ax. He looked as if he meant to swing it down and crush his daughter's skull.

Kwasin cried out, and now both Minruth and Awineth turned to face him.

"Come no closer or I'll kill her!" Minruth cried, brandishing the great ax over Awineth's head.

"Why should I care if you do!" Kwasin roared. "The woman has betrayed me!" But despite his words, he stopped his ascent. He stood not half a dozen yards from the two. All about them, heat waves from the surrounding lava flows wavered through the air, lending an eerie, nightmarish quality to the scene. Surely some mysterious force beyond the understanding of mere mortals had led the three to this hellish showdown.

Then Awineth began to laugh, her look of amusement only adding to the uneasy feeling in the pit of Kwasin's stomach.

"Kill me, father," she said, her piercing gaze still locked on Kwasin. "Or try. The Goddess will not permit it. She will smite you both down for your offenses against Her."

Minruth shook his head sadly, but his eyes were smiling. "My daughter's wits have cracked like the golden eggs of Korudeth out of the old legends. But I know that you love her, Kwasin—I can see the passion burning in your black eyes!"

"And your own eye," Kwasin said, "the only one left to you, burns with madness!"

Minruth only smiled and fondled the knob on the ax's handle. "For the wound you have given me," he replied, "I express my gratitude, as your vicious attack this morning has not in fact blinded me but rather allowed me to see! For when the haft of your mighty weapon smote out my eye, I was blessed with a vision from Great Resu! You will remember, the ax was brought back from the Wild Lands by the explicit order of the oracle . . . a fact which I find of extreme interest. But be that as it may, in that moment, half-blinded by your blow and toppling head over heels down the stairs of the Great Tower, I saw the future! And what do you think I saw in my vision? I saw you, Kwasin! You, the mad giant who has been the bane of my elder days, and the man who, according to the secret records I uncovered from the Temple of Khukhaken in shattered Dythbeth, was fathered by none other than Sahhindar himself! Do not look so sickly, my great opponent—or should I say ally, since everyone knows Sahhindar is the loving son of Resu." Minruth's wide grin cracked his bloated, heat-reddened face. "Have you not long wondered why your wild temperament burns hotter than any other in the land? It burns so fiercely because the blood of the Flaming God sears your veins!"

Though Khowot's wrath flamed hotly about him, Kwasin felt as if a cold hand had seized his bowels and squeezed them in its icy grip.

"Your forked tongue is only less deceitful than your daughter's!" Kwasin yelled. "With such lies you tore apart the land! And what if I am Sahhindar's spawn? Many a son has turned against his father, as this last war has shown. I have been, and forever shall be, a devout supporter of holy Kho!"

Minruth laughed mockingly. "That is not what I have seen! Did not your precious oracle pronounce that you have two souls, one which struggles against the other?"

Kwasin wondered how Minruth had learned of his visit with the oracle, and the contents of their conversation. Then he shrugged off the idle speculation. Minruth must have tortured a priestess to gain the information.

"Yes, and you must have wondered why I've been so interested in you," Minruth continued. "I can say now that it was because in my heart I always sensed the truth—and now my vision has confirmed it! You, Kwasin of Dythbeth, are my heir. No, maybe not my literal blood kin, but even more poignant, you are the blood kin of Resu Himself! And because His divine blood beats in your heart, you will live longer than any man. And one day— perhaps many years from now, my vision did not reveal the exact time—the part of your divided soul which is the strongest, that which you have inherited from your divine father, will overcome your mortal half. On that day, as my vision has shown me, you will lead Resu's followers to battle against arrogant Kho herself!"

Now it was Kwasin's turn to laugh. "They don't call your father Minruth the Mad for nothing," he said to Awineth. "Then again, madness seems to run in your family.

"But enough! I will hear no more from either of you. Minruth, come at me with your weapon, if you still have the courage to wield it. But do not weary my mind with your deranged visions! I have had enough of such delusions! You are all mad—kings, queens, priestesses, priests, and maybe the very deities themselves!"

Feeling in control of his own destiny for the first time in years, a grinning Kwasin drew his broadsword and advanced on Minruth and his daughter. He would spare Awineth and bring her back to the oracle. Minruth would come back with him as well, but only his bloody head.

Suddenly, as if responding to Kwasin's blasphemous soliloquy, Khowot—the Voice of Kho—began to rumble violently beneath their feet. Sickening fumes filled the thick, sweltering air and Kwasin and the others gasped for breath. A deafening thunder bellowed up from the ground, which now rattled so brutally that Kwasin lost his footing and began skidding down the rocky scape. He let go of his sword and flailed out his arms, finally grabbing onto a large rock and stopping his fall.

He looked up. He had slid almost thirty feet down the mountainside. Awineth was still upslope of him, but where was . . .

Then he saw Minruth. Or at least part of him. His legs and feet jutted out horizontally from behind a ridge of black dirt. Awineth was rising up from the ridge. In her hands she held her bloodied ceremonial dagger. Her eyes looked wild.

Awineth looked down at Kwasin, her expression a twisted mix of disgust and demented joy. She sheathed her dagger, which she must have recovered during the volcano's tumult, and again bent down. When she rose a moment later, her back was to him. She was skirting the slope, trying to make her way around a lava flow. Behind her, by its leather thong, she dragged the ax.

Kwasin started after her but again the mountain began its violent shaking and rumbling. Once more he fell and slid several yards down the volcano's rugged flank. When he looked up, he could no longer see Awineth. Perhaps Khowot's flames had engulfed her.

Finally, with the ground rattling beneath his feet, and his tears burning from the fumes that nearly smothered him, Kwasin headed down the mountainside.

TWENTY-NINE

"M any hunts have I led for King Mahedana, O Great One, but never have I seen tracks like these."

"Do not doubt your skills, Urudu," Kwasin replied to the tall Wan"so tracker, who sat on his haunches examining the rhino-sized, talon-like prints frozen in the black mud. "You have never before laid eyes upon such a spoor because the animal that left it lives a great distance to the south of your kingdom, in a land so far away that the very fires burning in the night's dome look strange."

Kwasin thought of the odd markings he had seen long ago in the wet sand along the shores of the southern sea, footprints his uncle had said belonged to the legendary dragon that stalked the area. But how had the beast come to be here, on the northern coast of the Kemu, high in the frozen reaches of the Saasares Mountains?

There could be only one reasonable explanation—it was the same *r"ok'og'a* that Kwasin had freed from the prison beneath the Great Tower and that had later rampaged through the streets of the capital before escaping into the island's wilds. Awineth, who had somehow managed to survive Khowot's tremblings, must have ordered the ragged band of followers who had come to her aid to capture the beast. Then they had brought the *r"ok'og'a* with them when they fled the island and crossed over to the mainland coast. But why? Did she hope one day to unleash the fearsome beast against her enemies?

Kwasin shook his head at the bizarre development. Squinting into the fierce, bitterly cold winds, he pulled his thick otter-fur cloak tighter about his shoulders and beckoned Urudu to rise. It was time to resume their dangerous ascent into the mountains. The only way to find an answer to the mystery was to trudge on.

He hoped coming across the *r"ok'og'a*'s spoor meant that Urudu would once again pick up the trail left by Awineth and the men who accompanied her. Already Kwasin had spent far too long stalking his quarry across the northern coastline. Far to the south, King Hadon's impudent coalition was amassing its great fleet. Kwasin did not want to return to the island only to find that Hadon had snatched the throne of Khokarsa out from under him. He only hoped Bhako's expedition to woo the pirate king of Mikawuru into an alliance would succeed, thus granting the Khokarsans a foothold on the southern sea. Surely Kwasin's promise of complete control of Hadon's golden city and its mining operations—including the new settlement of Kartenkloe, the gateway to the southern savannas and the lucrative ivory trade—would satisfy even Mikawuru's greedy king.

Kwasin sighed. He knew he could not return to the capital and Queen Awamethna's loving embrace until after he had completed his mission. The oracle had been clear on that point. Then again, there was nothing in the oracle's words to say he must return, nothing to stop him from setting out toward the trackless expanses of the Western Lands, where he could lose himself in the wilds and roam free for the remainder of his days. He recalled the hardships he had suffered during his eight long years of exile in the wilderness, and the loneliness that had assailed him. But was any of that worse than the deceptions, manipulations, and political back-stabbing that ceaselessly plagued the life of the king of kings of Khokarsa? He did not think so. Not after all he had endured since his return from exile.

Nevertheless, he knew he would never gain peace of mind until he found and confronted Awineth. Though he had tried to bury his feelings for her in the dark pit of his soul, he could not escape the fact that he had somehow come to love her. Perhaps that was it. He loved her because her soul was made of the same darkly streaked material as his own. Awamethna, beautiful though she was, would never fill the emptiness in his heart left by Awineth's absence. But maybe, if he saw Awineth one last time, he would wake up to the madness that had seized him. Then he might be able to forget her.

Two days later, Kwasin and Urudu entered a mountain pass and came upon the carcass of the *r"ok'og'a*. It was the strangest creature Kwasin had ever seen. The beast was about the size of a large rhino, its sleek, half-frozen body covered in reddish-golden scales. A thin mane of short, bristling hair ran down its long, serpentine neck, upon which was mounted a smallish, snakelike head. From the center of the skull, between a pair of beady, lidless eyes, projected a straight, flat-sided horn, ivory in color and about two and a half feet long, which narrowed to a sharp point. In contrast with the hooflike appearance of the *r"ok'og'a*'s front feet—each of which was in reality a bundle of short toes retracted around a thickly calloused heel—the hind feet bore long, talon-like, clawed toes that were unmistakably reptilian and without doubt quite deadly when the creature had lived.

Kwasin felt pity for the beast, which lay curled up in a shallow cleft gouged out of the side of the boulder-strewn valley. It must have escaped its human handlers and crawled here, where it had died of exposure. Urudu wanted to poach the *r"ok'og'a*'s glossy, ivory-colored horn, saying it would make him a rich man, but Kwasin told him to let the dead beast be. It had not asked for the fate that had been thrust upon it, and that was a sentiment Kwasin understood only too well.

They continued on, passing higher into the mountains. Throughout much of the next day, the sky darkened overhead as great flocks of birds winged their way southward. The birds should have been flying north at this time of year, but for the past two months the migratory patterns of many species of animals had been strangely disrupted. Urudu, who had spent much of his life in the wilds, said the animals' unusual behavior was an ill omen, though he could not say exactly what it portended. Kwasin told the tracker that he wanted to hear no more of omens. He was tired of letting the deities control his destiny. If ill fortune came his way, he would meet it and deal with it head-on, but there was no sense in brooding over vague forebodings.

Early on the third morning after finding the *r"ok'og'a*, Urudu awoke Kwasin from his slumber, joyfully exclaiming that he had again picked up their quarry's trail. Kwasin eagerly packed up his belongings and set off following Urudu into the frigid morning. Later that day, they found Awineth's camp.

Kwasin's heart sank as he ran forward on top of the ice-crusted snowfield that blanketed the mountain valley before him. On the valley's western side, the tops of several deerskin tents steepled out of the blinding white snow. He knew from what Urudu had told him that the trail they had been following was at least three weeks stale. That could mean only one thing—for those three weeks Awineth and her people had been forced to hole up in this valley, probably caught in a sudden snowstorm. That nothing rose from the smoke holes of the buried tents was an ominous sign. But then, they were above the timberline. Awineth's party would have burned through any wood they carried in just a few days. And that too made Kwasin sick with worry.

He headed for the tent in the center of the cluster. Reaching it, he began digging furiously through the snow, oblivious to the searing cold that numbed his bare hands. Urudu arrived at Kwasin's side and also began digging. When they had cleared away a good portion of the snow, Kwasin used his knife to slash an opening in the tent's side. He raised the flap and looked inside.

Snow-refracted light from outside gently illuminated the tent's interior. In the center of the tent two forms, one larger than the other, lay cradled together beneath a thick pile of furs. Kwasin could not see the faces of those under the coverings, but raven-black hair, shining softly in the snow light, spilled from beneath the furs. Neither form was moving.

Urudu laid a hand on Kwasin's shoulder. Kwasin shrugged it off and entered the tent.

Kneeling beside the smaller of the two forms, Kwasin pulled

back the furs and looked down at Awineth. She could have been sleeping, but her unmoving breasts, and the bloodless cast of her fair skin, told him otherwise. Kwasin leaned forward and kissed her cold, bluish lips.

Suddenly a coldness settled over Kwasin—not a physical cold, but rather an iciness that cut deep into the soul. He sat and absorbed the feeling, letting it sear through him, and then pulled back the coverings from the form lying beside Awineth.

It was Wahesa of Mukha, a fact which did not surprise him. According to intelligence Kwasin received before leaving the capital, Wahesa had escaped the fall of Dythbeth and gone renegade in the island's mountains. After Awineth fled into the backcountry behind Khowot, Wahesa and his band of outlaws had sought her out and offered their assistance in getting her off the island.

Next to Wahesa's corpse lay the Ax of Victory. Kwasin felt tempted to leave it there. True to the dwarf Paga's prediction, the weapon had brought him nothing but trouble. Then Kwasin shrugged. He removed the great bronze-headed club from the harness on his back and replaced it with the ax. The latter had saved him more times than he could recall and it would be a pity not to take it with him after he had come all this way. Besides, he didn't believe the superstitious manling knew what he was talking about.

Outside the tent, Urudu was uttering a curse upon Wahesa's spirit. The Wan"so tracker had been sent along with Kwasin at the request of King Mahedana, who wanted to avenge the man who had so wronged his daughter. It seemed that Daka had broken with her husband after her affair with Kwasin. Kwasin did not know the details of the dispute, nor did he ever care to, but thereafter Daka had sworn to kill Wahesa.

Since Wahesa was dead, Urudu would be denied the honor of defeating King Mahedana's son-in-law in combat. He would also be unable to enhance his reputation as a warrior by adding Wahesa's hands to the others he wore about his neck. But he could still deliver Wahesa's head to Daka, and because of that Urudu began softly humming a song of joy.

The coldness in Kwasin's soul retreated. He now felt only

numb despondency. He had not known what would happen when he finally caught up with Awineth, but this was certainly not an outcome he had foreseen.

Gently, he wrapped Awineth's body in furs and carried it from the tent. He hated the thought of leaving her in the lonely, snow-swept terraces of the Saasares. But then, Kho was the Mother of All, and all the land was Hers. Even in death one could not hope to evade the earthy embrace of the Goddess. One burial place could be no worse than another.

And so Kwasin carried Awineth out of the snow and laid her down upon the mountainside, where he buried her beneath a crude pylon of rocks overlooking the sea. After he had finished, he spent some time searching for an animal he could sacrifice to Awineth's spirit. Finally, he looked down to see a white-furred mouse burrowing its way into the snow. He reached down and scooped up the mouse. The tiny thing sniffed at his fingers and looked up at him with its round, black eyes.

Kwasin exhaled gruffly and set the mouse free. Too many had died already in the costly war between Kho and Resu. Why need-lessly snuff out another life, even one this small? Awineth's spirit would not go hungry in any case. There were still those loyal to their former queen who would sacrifice to her upon learning of her death.

He waved down to Urudu, who was placing Wahesa's head in his pack. Without waiting to see if the tracker would follow, Kwasin turned and began his slow descent toward the sea.

The day wore on as Kwasin and Urudu climbed downward. By the time they reached the timberline later that afternoon, they knew something was wrong.

To the south, the shadowy outline of the island of Khokarsa floated upon the seaward horizon. From the center of the island's hazy blue form a dark plume of smoke billowed skyward, blanket-ing the entire eastern half of the island. At the source of the black plume Kwasin could just make out a faint orange glow. Moments later a thundering boom cracked through the air and the mountain shook beneath their feet.

Khowot was erupting.

Kwasin stopped his descent, watching in horror as the distant volcano jettisoned red-hot lava into the heavens. The shock of the initial explosion must have been horrendous. He wondered if anyone in the capital could have survived it.

Then all words dropped from his mind. The flames shooting from Khowot burned brighter, until the entire midsection of the island seemed to radiate with an intensity of orange and red hues. He closed his eyes and opened them again, thinking his vision deceived him. It could not be. The whole island seemed to be lifting up out of the sea!

The Saasares boomed as if a giant heart thrummed beneath them. Kwasin reached out to grab at the jagged black rocks jutting from the side of the mountain, but as he did so he found himself thrown high into the air. His arms and legs flailed in empty space. Then he smacked hard against the face of the mountain.

Freezing-cold water was pouring down from above. A mountain lake must have shaken loose from its foundations and spilled its contents down the mountainside. Kwasin floundered to grab hold of something but the force of the downward-pouring water was too much. He slid downhill, carried along in a roiling flood of water, snow, and ice.

The mountain buckled beneath him as he plummeted downward. For a moment he found himself thrown out into the air. Then he was again sliding. His entire body throbbed with pain. Rocks, both large and small, battered against his arms, legs, torso, and head. Something large and long was falling alongside him. He reached for it and encircled his arms about it. It was a mammoth-sized tree trunk, careening down the mountainside like some kind of gargantuan sled. For a moment Kwasin thought he might ride it all the way to the sea. Then the mountain hammered against the trunk and Kwasin was once again bucked into the air, only to slam into the mountain a moment later.

He screamed but he could not hear his own voice over the roaring of the flood and the deafening thrumming of the mountain. Suddenly the angle of his descent leveled off. Instead of being carried almost vertically down the face of the mountain, he now slid at a forty-five-degree angle. Though the deluge still gushed over him and propelled him downward, its flow had lessened somewhat. If only he could find something to grab hold of to stop his fall, he might survive the tremor yet. But the mountain tore past him too quickly.

His back ached, doubtless because the ax slung across his shoulders had been hammering against it.

The ax!

He whirled about so that now he was on his chest, scraping along the rocks and dirt that hurtled beneath him. Though his entire body rattled with the mountain's furious shaking, he reached behind his back and firmly gripped the handle of the ax. With the greatest effort he had ever made, he pulled the ax from its harness. Then, with an even greater effort, he swung the ax forward.

The ax bounced away from the mountainside and almost flew out of Kwasin's hand. He gripped it tighter and, crying out for Kho to give him strength, again thrust the ax at the mountain's rocky face. Twice more he repeated the motion, each time believing the ax would tear loose from his grasp. But he did not let it go. If he did, he knew he would be dead.

Then, just as he looked down and saw nothing but empty air yawning below him, he struck the ax at the black rock with such force that the weapon's iron head shattered. A large shard pierced his shoulder, while other glittering splinters of iron shot out past him into the air. And yet Kwasin no longer fell. Part of the ax must not have broken. Whatever remained of its iron head had impaled itself in the rock.

He was dangling above a precipice that dropped five hundred feet to the sea. Hanging on to the leather thong attached to the handle of the ax, he twirled about in the air as mud and water rained down upon him. Then, as suddenly as it had begun, the flood ceased, and as he swung about he saw a sight that almost made him lose his hold.

Like some mighty leviathan of the ocean, the island of

Khokarsa was rising up out of the waters of the Kemu. But the island was now two. It had split down the center, and its two halves, east and west, were now toppling to either side, sinking into the sea. All about the island the sea churned violently, whirling in a counterclockwise direction as if a Brobdingnagian sinkhole had opened up deep beneath the waters. Then the island was gone, swallowed by the raging sea.

Kwasin bellowed with terror. Kho was at last fulfilling Her promise and destroying the land! What hope did he have, a mere mortal, against such inconceivable power? Had his entire life been but a dream in the mind of the Goddess?

Now his terror turned to rage. Rage that his destiny, and that of all the land, had come to this. That Kho would smite down the whole world in Her righteous anger.

As Kwasin hung there, looking out over the edge of the broken mountainside at the end of his world, a golden-crowned fish-eagle glided directly in front of him. He watched it soar to his right—the good luck side—drawing his attention to something he had not noticed while engrossed in the horrifying events transpiring upon the sea. Fifteen feet above him and to his right, jutting out over the broad, five-hundred-foot drop to the boulder-strewn shoreline below, was a narrow, triangular-shaped wedge of rock. Beyond the overhang, he could see a broad and apparently stable tableland.

The mountain continued its violent quavering as Kwasin dangled from his precarious position. He knew that at any moment the head of the ax might shake loose from the rock and plummet him to his death.

He looked up at the narrow shelf of rock to his right. To make it to the ledge, he would have to swing twenty feet across the chasm from where he hung. But he would also have to hurl himself fifteen feet upward. It was an impossible feat, one which even a hero of the Great Games would never dare to attempt. But then Kwasin had never been one to compare himself to others. And he could not go on clinging to the ax forever. Not when the mountain thundered its rage all about him.

Kwasin began rocking back and forth above the yawning chasm, his entire being screaming out with the will to live. If he died, then all his life would be meaningless. And that was a concession he was not willing to yield even to Kho Herself. Somehow, somehow he would achieve the impossible.

Roaring, Kwasin swung out into the abyss.

EPILOGUE

Seasons passed. The great stone walls, gilt domes, and stately minarets of the outpost city lay cracked and tumbled in the midst of the encroaching jungle. The people waited, pulling together their shattered lives as best they could. Still, many thousands died from the pestilence and famine which followed the unparalleled devastation that was Kho's wrath. Some said that if things kept going the way they were, Sisisken would soon have to close her towering gates. The grim ruler of the underworld would not have enough room in her dark house to board all the dead.

But though the citizens waited, not a single ship sailed into port. No sail had been sighted upon the sea since the foundations of the world rattled with the fury of the Goddess.

And so it was that on the first moon day of the Year of the Fish-Eagle, the oracle of the city stood high upon the steps of the Temple of Kho and called forth for the greatest hero of the land to begin construction of a great galley, in which he would sail out upon the seas and seek the fate of the motherland. The oracle did not name the hero who would lead the expedition, but there could be no doubt about whom she meant.

Two months later King Hadon stood upon the docks at the port of Nangukar, kissing the fair-skinned, violet-eyed Lalila good-bye, and also Abeth and little La. He looked about for his son, but did not see him. Kohr was no doubt still angry at him because he would not be coming on the expedition. Hadon had told the boy he wanted to bring him along, but these were dangerous times. Only a short time ago, Gamori and his priests had attempted to imitate Minruth's blasphemy. Someone had to look after Kohr's mother and two sisters in the king's absence. But the boy had not wanted to hear it and had stalked off in anger.

Hadon hoped the youth would not run off and do anything rash. But he did not think he would. Like his father, Kohr was too even-tempered and duty-bound. The anger would blow off in time.

Hadon boarded the galley, which he had christened the *Taro* in memory of his long-dead friend, and watched from the deck as the priestess poured libations over the bow. He surveyed the two dozen or so spectators standing below upon the stone wharves. Among them no bullroarers or trumpeters commemorated the vessel's departure, nor did any of the onlookers clang together brass cymbals or shout out words of encouragement to their king. Since the great calamity, there had been no celebrations. Too many had died to be joyful about anything.

As the vessel pulled away to the sound of the beaters and the splashings of the rowers, Hadon returned his gaze landward. Kohr was now standing on the wharves, one arm around his mother and the other about his two sisters. Hadon stood tall upon the deck, fighting back his welling tears, until the tiny figures on the wharves dwindled out of sight. It might be a year before he saw his family again. Or it might be never.

The *Taro* followed the coastline due north while Hadon and his crew marveled at the devastation which seemed to go on with no end. Everywhere great, thick-rooted trees knotted the sandy beaches and the jungles beyond. Here, as along the wharves of Nangukar, the sea had receded several yards from shore. There could be only one explanation for the low level of the water. The banks surrounding the far-western arm of the southern sea, known as the Bay of Dythphida, must have collapsed during the earthquake, thereby allowing the sea water to drain into the Aquthkly River, and from there out into the world-ringing sea.

If Hadon's theory was correct, the two great landlocked seas could very well drain to the bottom of their basins.

"Captain Rewenkwo says we should have reached Sakawuru by now."

Hadon broke his trancelike staring at the ruined coastline and regarded the barrel-chested manling. Though powerfully muscled, the squat fellow beside him stood on legs no longer than those of an eight-year-old child. But Hadon would never make the mistake of misjudging the maturity of his friend's keen mind. Paga was as wise as the hills.

"Are you saying the whole city is gone? That all its citizens are dead?" Hadon shook his head. Though he had witnessed with his own eyes how Great Kho had thrown down many of his own city's impressive structures, he could not fathom a whole population obliterated.

"Indeed, the red-granite city is no more," Paga replied gruffly. "It has been swallowed by its black cliffs." And then he pointed to the coastline that trailed behind them.

Hadon looked out over the waters at a dark clumping of rocks along the distant shoreline. Could those really be the towering cliffs of Sakawuru, hurtled into the sea by Kho's quaking fury? He could not believe it. But then, as the days wore on with no sign of the city or its people, neither could he deny it.

The galley continued up the coast to Wentisuh. Here they found survivors of the earthquake, but Hadon and his crew were not able to stop and talk with them. Almost as soon as the *Taro* drew anchor, Wentisuh's starved and wretched inhabitants leaped into the water and began swimming for the galley. At first Hadon allowed the swimmers to board, thinking they were simply eager to get news from beyond their native port. But then, as more and more of the rawboned, wild-eyed survivors swarmed up the sides of the galley, Hadon realized their true intention. The hunger-crazed men meant to take the *Taro* and all its spoils. Hadon shouted to the coxswain to get his rowers moving and, with swords drawn, advanced with his men to clear the deck of the invaders.

After they had beat back the last of those trying to climb up the galley's sides, Hadon withdrew to his small cabin. Several hours later, unable to sleep, he got up and returned to the deck. There he remained, staring off into the waters, until Kho's blue bowl grew black with night and the heavens glittered with brilliant starlight. He felt great remorse at not being able to help the famine-stricken inhabitants of Wentisuh, but there was nothing he could have done for them. The survival of his own people lay in question in the aftermath of Kho's wrath. He knew he would face many more hard decisions in the years to come. The fact that life went on at all was itself a blessing from the Goddess.

The latter thought returned to Hadon as the galley proceeded onward and entered the Strait of Keth. Everyone but the rowers came out on deck to marvel at the awesome sight. The sheer walls and choppy waters of the once-gloomy chasm were no more. Now a serene, mile-wide channel ran between the southern and northern seas, punctuated upon occasion by rocky outcroppings protruding from the calm waters. The small islands were all that remained of the strait's formerly towering cliffs, which Kho had also smote down in Her great anger.

"Now that the strait has been widened," Paga remarked to Hadon, "the Kemu will drain even quicker into the southern sea. Within a single generation, both seas will be gone."

Hadon did not argue with his friend's breathtaking pronouncement. The destruction of the cliffs above the strait was all the evidence he needed to convince himself that their world was dramatically changing.

Leaving the broad seaway behind, Captain Rewenkwo now headed the galley north by northwest. Whereas the southern sea had been a beautiful blue-green, the waters of the Kemu quickly turned a muddy brown. Paga claimed this indicated that the earthquake had in reality been a seaquake. The fact that the waters had not yet cleared of the churned-up sediment, he said, was proof that great forces were still at work beneath the seabed.

Several times each day Captain Rewenkwo consulted his lodestone compass, and at night compared his notations to the patterns of the stars. Soon it became clear that the man was agitated about something. Hadon asked him what was wrong.

The old seaman shook his compass as if it were broken. Then he swore and said, "I took my first voyage to the capital when I was only eight years old. Since then I've made the circuit across the Kemus every year of my life, even during the war when I commanded a smuggling ship for the Temple of Kho. Next week I'll be fifty-two. Every bone in my body tells me the island should be looming off the fore. But what do I see?" He waved an arm at the brown waters stretching from horizon to horizon. Again, the gray-haired sailor swore.

Hadon told the captain to keep his voice down. There was no need to alarm the crew until they could prove, one way or another, what had or had not happened to the island.

But Hadon's concern had been needless. By the time the tall ridges of the Saasares rose upon the horizon, it became evident to everyone onboard that they had either overshot the island or that it had altogether disappeared beneath the Kemu's murky depths. Hadon ordered the captain to follow the coast eastward. Two days later the ruins of Miklemres appeared off the port bow.

Unlike the survivors of Wentisuh, the inhabitants of the northern mainland posed no danger to the crew of the *Taro*. Too few of them remained to be a threat. Eager to exchange gossip, Hadon brought aboard the half-dozen dirty and emaciated men and women who had waved from shore. Their story was as shocking as it was grim.

The entire island, they said, was gone. One of the men claimed he had seen Piqabes herself, Kho's green-eyed daughter, reach forth her great hand from the waters and pull the island down to her cold bosom. A woman, the man's wife, disagreed, saying that it was Resu who had destroyed the island. She knew this because she had witnessed his fiery breath split the island in two. The couple argued at great length over what they had seen while Hadon and his stupefied crew looked on in astonishment.

The survivors from Miklemres also told Hadon that many of their fellow citizens had survived the catastrophe, though many had also died, both during the great tremor and afterward from disease and starvation. And then, shortly after the earthquake, a wave of previously unknown foreigners stormed into the valley from the west. These were a fierce people, small in stature, but numerous and deadly, wielding forbidden bows and poison-tipped arrows. The king of Miklemres, who had survived the earth's upheaval, fell back before the attacking tribes and led those citizens who would follow him higher into the mountains. The four men and two women sitting on the deck before Hadon were all that remained of those who had stayed behind to face the fierce hordes. Hadon asked why his crew had spotted none of the encroaching warriors along the coast, but his new guests replied that the invaders, with no one remaining in the area to fight, had moved on.

"What of Queen Awineth?" Hadon asked. The last news his people had received from the island was that the College of Priestesses had annulled Awineth's authority and placed her cousin upon the throne. And Kwasin! Hadon's spies said he had been named king of kings!

Suddenly Hadon's guests looked uncomfortable.

"They are aware you are the winner of the Great Games, O King," a slim, white-robed man standing next to Hadon whispered.

Hadon looked questioningly into the large, russet-brown eyes of his bard, Kebiwabes.

"They know you were planning on invading the island," the bard said, "and they are unclear whose allegiance they should follow. Even now, with the land destroyed, they do not wish to betray the man who defeated the tyrant Minruth."

Finally understanding, Hadon assured his guests that he no longer had any interest in the crown of Khokarsa. Kho had shattered his ambition along with the world. And besides, Hadon said, he had not formed the coalition of southern cities in order to attack Kwasin, but rather to stand in defense against him.

The distrustful looks softened and eventually Hadon weaned from the survivors of Miklemres the information he desired. It seemed the oracular priestess had sent Kwasin off on a quest to find Awineth and her followers in the eastern Saasares. For all his guests knew, the two had both survived the destruction of the island.

The news did not exactly please Hadon. Kwasin and Awineth had each given him more than a fair share of trouble. Still, he could not shrug off his sense of obligation to them. If it remained possible they still lived, then he must search for them—to satisfy his own curiosity if nothing else. He ignored Paga's advice that it would be better to leave them in the wilds, though he agreed that, if found, the two would only complicate his already difficult life.

For weeks Hadon's expedition searched the coastline along the eastern Saasares without success. Then, on the very day Hadon decided it was time to turn the galley about and head home, a search party led by Paga reported in with the news of an exciting discovery. When Hadon asked what this was, Paga replied, "You had better come see for yourself."

His curiosity mounting, Hadon accompanied Paga and his men back to shore and up the treacherous face of a broken mountain. Having climbed to an altitude of five hundred feet, they mounted a broad plateau overlooking the sea. Here Paga pointed across a twenty-foot-wide chasm to the face of an adjoining mountain. At first Hadon saw nothing but rubble and debris. But then he gasped.

Across the chasm, a huge shelf of the mountain had collapsed into the sea below, leaving a narrow ledge of rock and dirt jutting out over empty air. An object, embedded into the face of the overhanging rim, glittered brightly in the sunlight.

"Your eyes are not mistaken," Paga said in response to Hadon's incredulous look. "But how did the ax of Wi come to be here, thrust into the face of a shattered mountainside?"

Hadon edged closer to the brink, trying to get a better look. Truly it seemed as if the ax had been purposefully driven into the rock. Could Kwasin have been caught on the mountain when the great catastrophe struck? Had he tried to stop his fall by impaling the ax into the mountain's stony face?

"I can tell by your expression that you are thinking the same thing as I," Paga said. "But it would be foolish to believe that even someone as strong as your cousin could have held on to the handle of the ax during the earthquake that knocked down half this mountain. And even if he had, not even a Nukaar, one of the long-armed hairy half-men of the trees, could have swung the twenty feet up and across the chasm."

Hadon scanned the distance from where the ax lay embedded in the rocky overhang to the ledge where he, Paga, Kebiwabes, and the other members of their party stood. Not only would Kwasin have had to jump across the twenty-foot gulf, but he also would have had to swing himself fifteen feet upward to the ledge. Paga was right. No man could make such a leap, not even a Great Gamester.

But then again, if anyone could have done it, it would have been Kwasin.

Looking down at the waves crashing against the rocks below, Kebiwabes exclaimed, "Alas, good-bye to Kwasin! Never again shall I know a man as strong . . . nor as mad!"

Hadon was about to lead his men back down the mountain when suddenly he turned and again looked out over the chasm. It would be a shame to leave the ax behind, he thought, especially when he had the means at hand to procure it. And besides, it would make a good souvenir for Kohr. It might even make the boy forget his anger at not being allowed to accompany the expedition.

Thankfully Hadon's training for the Great Games had made him a skilled lassoer. But even so, it took all seven men in his party to pull the ax from the black stone after he had ensnared it. When at last he hoisted up the rope and examined the ax, Hadon feared the effort had all been for nothing.

"It's ruined," he said. "The head of the ax must have splintered when it was thrust into the rock."

Paga asked if he could see the weapon, which had been crafted by his own hand many years ago in a faraway land. Hadon handed him the worthless ax.

"There is still enough iron left," Paga said, rolling the glittering weapon in his hand. "I might yet be able to rework the head, though it will never be the mighty hatchet it once was. Still, stature is not everything. If I'm lucky, I might fashion it into a kind of poleax, one better used for pecking than chopping, though still a weapon to be reckoned with."

Pleased with the manling's assessment, Hadon announced that it was time to return to the ship. They had already lingered too long on their journey and the time had come to head home.

Later that day, as Resu set in the west and Lahla the moon rose over the eastern mountains, Hadon stood alone upon the bow of the *Taro*. He looked out over the rolling waters of the Kemu, waters that one day in the not-too-distant future would disappear, replaced by exotic jungles, yawning deserts, and rolling savannas. He was anxious to get back to his city. His people would face many daunting challenges in the years ahead. The city would have to be rebuilt, new sources of food and other vital materials would have to be obtained and exploited, and defenses would have to be built up to fend off invaders seeking for their own his queendom's relative wealth and stability. The staggering enormity of the work threatened to overwhelm him.

But it was also, he knew, an exciting time to be alive. And he was not alone. He would have his friends and family to help him endure the many trials and tribulations that would assail him in this newly remade world. For what more could he ask? The world had always been made up of hardship, and it was a fool's dream to think it would ever be otherwise.

He watched a fish-eagle plummet to the surface of the water, only a moment later to soar up gracefully into the sky with its bounty.

Kho had spared his city when She had laid waste to so many others, and for that Hadon was thankful. He would return to the city of gold and little jewels and, with Lalila by his side, rule over it for the good and well-being of his people. And who could say? With the blessings of the Goddess, some luck, and a lot of hard work, his descendants might yet gaze upon the city's gilt domes and soaring towers for many thousands of years to come.

KWASIN AND THE BEAR GOD

The following novella by Philip José Farmer and Christopher Paul Carey, originally published in *The Worlds of Philip José Farmer 2: Of Dust and Soul* (Meteor House, 2011), is set between the first two chapters of *The Song of Kwasin*.

When Kwasin crawled from the tiny fishing boat and began hauling it up the sandy slope, he did not know he trod upon the City of the Snake. If he had, he thought later, he might have rowed back out to sea as quickly as his great muscles could carry him, eager to face the boatload of Minruth's sailors headlong rather than risk disturbing the demons and spirits rumored to haunt this place.

But then again, he was Kwasin, defiler of the Temple of Kho. Even the fact that the Goddess had cursed the grounds of these timeworn ruins might not have been enough to give him pause. Still, in his heart, he had never forsaken Kho, even when the oracle had cast him from civilization and doomed him to exile in the Wild Lands. And secretly he knew he could not escape the superstitions of his people. Though Kwasin was as brave and free a spirit as any that walked the land, the folktales instilled in him during childhood sometimes spoke with a voice louder than that of his adult rationality.

By the time he had hidden the boat amid the thorny flora that grew along the seaside cliffs, Kwasin was already beginning to have misgivings about his chosen landing site. Looking down the beach to his right he could make out in several places broad and flat outcroppings of granite emerging from the sand at irregular angles. Surely these were the remnants of an ancient quay. Farther up the slope shadows arched eastward from vague but towering projections vaulting slantingly in what seemed an unnatural fashion out of the uneven landscape. The shadows were darker emanations within the penumbra of the mountains that rose sharply from the site's western periphery.

The mountains were the Saasanadar. In order to get to Dyth-beth he would either have to go around them by boat along the northern coast of the island or head deeper inland and pass to their south. Both routes carried great risk. Minruth's forces were everywhere, including on the waters at the mouth of the Gulf of Gahete. Only minutes ago Kwasin had barely escaped the notice of one of the king's galleys. Or he hoped he had. The bireme had appeared just as Kwasin was rounding the narrow cape that curved into the sea just east of the beach where he had then landed.

His boat now safely hidden, Kwasin sprinted up the slope and into the shadows. Here the land leveled out, although dark, barrow-like mounds rose in places out of the grassy mud and all around him jutted the immense, shadow-spawning projections. A breeze was blowing steadily from the northwest in advance of a storm front. In the distance, lightning flashed, followed a few moments later by a deep booming.

A closer examination of the projections quickly confirmed his suspicions. The giant outcroppings were not natural formations but rather great monoliths of ancient construction, and the drawings carved upon them, though but faintly visible in twilight's shadow, only heightened his fears about the place.

The symbols on the stones did not resemble modern hiero-glyphs. Rather, they were crude, pitted images, graven by primitive hands and likely dating to an era long before Awines invented his syllabary. Some of the petroglyphs depicted Kho as the Bird-Headed Mother; that is, as a steatopygic and large-breasted woman with the head of a fish-eagle. Many of the monuments, however, bore another image: that of a long-fanged serpent coiling tightly as if its deathly embrace meant to draw blood from stone. Everywhere the serpent carvings were surrounded by swarms of spiral pictographs.

He recalled the scribe Hinokly once remarking upon the ancient spiral found in the early stonework of the Klemreskom, the Fish-Eagle People who first populated the island of Khokarsa. The scribe had said Awines had adapted the symbol into the Khokarsan syllabary to represent Kho, in correspondence to the ancient glyph's original meaning. Then Hinokly had laughed darkly and said that Awines had not wanted the glyph in the syllabary to match too closely the primitive image, so he had altered it, for it was said that he who gazed too long at the deasil spiral would become as the living dead, lost for all eternity enraptured by Great Kho's terrible beauty.

Kwasin had scoffed at the latter notion, but he told the scribe he had seen similar spiral pictographs carved into the cliffs near where he had lived along the southern sea as a youth. Hinokly had told him the images were doubtless carved there by the aborigines long before the priestess-heroine Lupoeth first explored the region, and their existence so far south was proof that the symbol was ancient indeed.

Kwasin shuddered in the cool shadow of the black stones that rose about him. Were the carvings of the Goddess and clockwise-spinning gyres warnings from Kho to avoid this place or else risk facing the snake demons said to inhabit the ruins?

He did not know, but gazing up at the whorls and slithering creatures decorating the age-old monoliths, he was sure of one thing—he indeed stood among the moldering ruins of fabled Miterisi, the City of the Snake.

Kwasin started as a parrot screeched and flew out at him from behind one of the great columns of stone. He shook his head as if awakening from a trance and forced himself to turn away from the spirals. How long had he been standing here? He could not say for sure, but the scribe's superstitious yarn about getting lost in the vortex of Kho's ancient symbol had apparently played upon his ingrained fears about the site.

He cursed. Looking back to the beach, he saw two sailors emerging from a skiff in the shallows. Now they were dragging the craft toward shore. A second skiff—empty—already lay upon the beach, its crew nowhere in sight.

Since he had begun gazing at the stones, the temperature had dropped several degrees and the breeze from the approaching storm now blew with increasing force. If it had not been for the bird, how much longer would he have stood there unknowing?

Kwasin dropped the thought from his mind and slipped behind the nearest monolith, swearing silently.

For a brief moment he had again felt drawn to stare at the whorls.

He crouched behind the enormous stone and listened. Other than the occasional parrot's chittering caw, the sea breeze, the occasional clap of thunder, and the surf lapping in the distance, he could hear nothing. He slipped the leather thong of his ax from around his shoulder and relished the comfortable feel of the weapon's half-petrified antelope-bone handle in his grip. Then he peered from behind the stone.

A sword thrust violently upward from the shadows, sheening in a flash from the heavens. If the lighting had not illuminated the blade, Kwasin might have missed it amid the rapidly diminishing twilight.

He swung his ax. Earthly iron clanked against the meteoritic iron of Kwasin's weapon. His attacker, whom Kwasin could make out only vaguely in the dimness of the gully below him, grunted at the blow. Overcome by fury, Kwasin leaped downward.

If his attacker had also held a sword in his off-hand, it might have been Kwasin's final action. But the man didn't, and instead of meeting instant death, Kwasin kneed his assailant in the abdomen with the full force of his downward leap. The man sprawled on his back in the sloping ditch, momentarily stunned, while Kwasin finished him off with a single blow of his ax.

Something whirred past Kwasin's head as he rose from the corpse. A loud crack came from the monolith above him and small bits of stone showered down upon his head and naked shoulders. Then Kwasin was running for the next monolith. Though the monument he had just jumped from behind was nearer cover, it was not in his nature to remain on the defensive, even against an opponent wielding a sling. He would face his attackers head-on.

Kwasin almost stumbled midstride. For an instant, he thought he had seen a naked female figure standing tall upon one of the stone monuments, lit up in the fleeting brilliance of another heavenly flash. The figure had held forth what looked like a crooked, snake-headed staff. Or it could have been a real snake. He could not be sure. The whole thing might have been a false apparition, conjured in his mind by the unnerving images of Kho and the coiling pythons upon the tall, black stones.

He made it to the monument but paused only briefly behind it. Then he was running again, this time toward the shore, jumping over the rocks and small boulders that littered the scape between the barrowlike mounds. If any sling-stones whirred past him, he did not notice.

Cold rain sprinkled Kwasin's face as he ran. A moment later, the darkened heavens clamored with fury, and in the next, a deluge of hail and sleet assailed him in what was surely a bad omen. The sungod Resu—who, in his rage at his mother and ex-lover Kho, had sided with King Minruth in the bloody civil war—was also the god of rain.

A javelin hurtled at Kwasin out of the dark but its deadly point missed him, thudding into the muddy ground before him. Kwasin jumped over the weapon and veered to his left toward where he judged the javelin had come.

Then he saw the thrower emerge from behind a mound not twenty strides away, winding up his sling for a throw.

Kwasin looked for cover, but seeing none, roared in competition with the heavens' din and charged the slinger. Kwasin knew it was a desperate act, but maybe the sight of the furious seven-foot-tall giant charging forward would cause the slinger to flee or to fumble his throw.

The tactic had worked for Kwasin in the past, but the slinger who now confronted him seemed frustratingly cool and level-headed. He continued to whirl his sling as Kwasin closed upon him, tightening the revolutions of the weapon's cradle to compensate for the changing proximity of his target.

Blood drained from Kwasin face. He would take the full brunt of the projectile at close range.

Suddenly, the man reeled. The sling-stone shot out of its cradle, flying off harmlessly into the night.

Kwasin ran forward and examined the man, who had pitched forward into the slick, gravelly mud, facedown and unmoving. For a moment, Kwasin saw no wound upon the man. Then, running his hand over the man's back in the freezing rain, he felt something protruding from the skin: a thistle-fletched bamboo dart, impaled deeply.

He grabbed the fallen man by his long hair, lifted up his head, and placed a hand before the man's nose and mouth. Though frigid rain pelted Kwasin's palm, he felt warm, shallow breaths upon it.

The dart was doubtless tipped with a paralytic.

Kwasin dropped the man's face into the mud and looked about. Perhaps he had not imagined the woman atop the monolith after all.

After dispatching the man, Kwasin got up and again made for the shore. This time, however, he proceeded at a cautious jog, his roving eyes seeking to penetrate the gloom of night and storm.

Kwasin arrived at the shore to find it unoccupied except for the two empty skiffs. Grinning darkly, he went to work with his ax smashing great holes in the bottoms of the boats, all the while keeping watch inland, though he could no longer see farther than a few yards in the storm-wracked night. Finished with his sabotage, he looked out to sea, wondering what had become of the bireme that had landed the party of marines on shore. Doubtless she was having a hard time of it on the storm-lashed waves, and he could only hope her captain had taken the vessel back out to sea to avoid being driven into the shallows.

A man's throaty cry turned Kwasin's attention away from the sea and back inland. Still thwarted by darkness, he took off rapidly toward the ruins and the direction of the shout, his great ax held ready in both hands.

When he came to the top of the slope he could just make out the form of a woman in the murk of the ruins ahead. Her long, dark hair whipped wildly in the wind and in her hands she held a long tube. In a crouched stance, she crept forward toward a crumpled form several paces before her on the ground. The form could have been an outcropping for all Kwasin could tell, but in context of the cry he had heard only moments earlier, the scene told it all: the woman had struck down a marine with her blowgun and she was quietly advancing to ascertain whether her dart had fully immobilized its target.

Then, to his horror, Kwasin perceived amid the shadows a dark, man-sized figure moving up just behind the woman. Kwasin bellowed a warning but it was too late. The woman screamed as the shadowy figure enveloped her. The bamboo tube of the blowgun clunked hollowly as the woman flailed it against an adjoining pillar in an attempt to repel her attacker. Then the tube clattered to the stony ground. The woman grunted as if struck and went limp.

Kwasin was already running into the ruins at the first glimpse of the woman's attacker, but by the time he arrived at the spot, he found the man had slipped into the shadows, apparently dragging the woman with him. For a moment, Kwasin bent low and looked for prints in the muddy ground, but the black night made the endeavor impossible. He got up and began running frantically from monument to monument, rapidly circling behind the stones in search of the marine and his captive.

As Kwasin stepped out of the rain beneath the protection of a half-toppled monolith, something cold and soft slithered across his ankle. He froze. Looking down he saw a grotesque and bloated wormlike form glide across the black ground, its pale skin patterned evenly with darker diamond-shaped markings. The priestess's python, free of its mistress, must have sought out the relative dryness provided by the vaulting pillar.

He shuddered, thinking of his mother's death by snake bite when he had been but ten years old. While the serpent that had struck and killed his mother had not been a python, the pictographs on the surrounding monuments unnerved him. That, and the dreams that had assailed him since his return from the Wild Lands—horrendous visions of his mother's death, played over and over until he thought he might go mad. What did they mean? Might the nightmares presage his death in the ruins of cursed Miterisi?

But adversity, rather than daunting him, more often served Kwasin as a catalyst to overcome what he considered self-weakness. And so, biting back his revulsion, the giant leaned over, lifted up the snake, and looped it over his great shoulders. Despite the cause of his mother's death, he held no deep fear of snakes. It was only Goddess-forsaken Miterisi that now unsettled him in this regard. Following his mother's death, he had frequently forced himself to handle serpents, much to his cousin Hadon's dismay, who awoke all too often to find a slithering companion in his bed.

This last thought brought a grin to Kwasin's face, and thus distracted, he almost stumbled into a narrow opening in the ground that he had overlooked in the dark. A fortuitous lightning flash, however, prevented the accident, and also revealed a distinct handprint in the mud that ringed the stone-lined, circular hole. The marine had taken his captive down into the underground chamber—perhaps an ancient storage bin for grain or some other harvest—in the hope that he could wait out the giant who sought to slay him. The man had apparently taken the woman as a fail-safe—if Kwasin cornered him, the man would threaten to kill his hostage.

For a moment, Kwasin considered his options. He could move one of the small boulders that littered the site overtop the opening and thus seal the marine in a living tomb. This would require the least risk and effort on his part, but he would also be entombing the woman who had risked her life to defend him. He could also drop down into the hole, hoping the element of surprise would aid him. The marine, however, would be waiting below to dispatch Kwasin with his sword. But it was a third option that Kwasin found the most appealing.

Slowly and carefully, he knelt down beside the hole and uncoiled the python from his shoulders. As the snake slithered down an arm, Kwasin lowered the creature toward the opening in the ground. The python paused briefly; then, finding a ledge of rough stone cropping from one side of the hole's interior, it slid down into the earth.

A fleeting guilt tinged Kwasin's conscience as he thought of the woman, a guilt he quickly cast off. To live, one often had to do unpleasant things, even if that meant risking the life of a potential ally. Besides, he had seen the woman handle the snake when she stood illuminated by lighting atop the stone pillar—the python appeared to be her familiar. Had he not also seen the oracle at Dythbeth seemingly command her sacred serpent before his very eyes upon the occasion of the pronouncement of his exile to the Wild Lands? The priestesses of Kho—and this woman was certainly one—seemed to have an affinity with their ophidian pets. Surely the woman's own snake would not harm her.

But doubt returned as Kwasin stood above the hole, the rain running in small waterfalls off the colossal column of black stone. For a long while he stood there waiting, until the fury of the storm abated to a gentle drizzle and he began to wonder if the man had indeed crawled into the pit. Then, at last, it came—a choked-off male scream of utter terror.

Kwasin grinned. His inspired decision had been the right one. After all, in cursed Miterisi, was it not best to ally with the local snake god than to fight against him?

A short time later the woman crawled slowly up out of the dark mouth in the earth, the whitish-scaled, diamond-spotted python draped over her back and coiling around a shoulder and arm. She was indeed a priestess, as evidenced by the jewel-studded ceremonial dagger sheathed upon her shapely hip. She must have recovered the blade from her captor after the snake had strangled him.

Kwasin made the sign of Kho and the priestess's strong white teeth glistened back at him in the darkness.

He had been about to speak but stopped himself abruptly. Did the woman's canines look a little too long, a little too sharp? A little too . . . snakelike?

Kwasin frowned at himself, then laughed—a trifle nervously, he thought. No, it was just these cursed ruins playing tricks on his mind once more. When he saw the woman in the bright daylight he was sure she would appear as ravishingly and humanly beautiful as the darkness of the night hinted.

"What are you looking at?" the priestess said. "We must hurry. Now that the storm's abated, the shipmates of the sailors we've killed will likely come ashore looking for their men. Let's go!"

The woman reached out for his hand, but Kwasin hesitated. When the woman had spoken, had he merely imagined that her tongue flicked out from between her luscious lips in a most unmistakably reptilian fashion?

Kwasin frowned again. Then, uttering a half facetious—and half serious—prayer to Kho, he took her cold, tiny hand in his own warm, giant one and headed out into the night.

Kwasin awoke the next day in the little temple that rose from the center of the grove of the sacred python. Through the little window beside his bed of sleeping furs, he could hear the gentle tinkling of the creek that wound around the temple and through the forest. With a heavy sigh of contentment, he flung aside the furs, sat up, and regarded the lithe form of the priestess that lay sleeping beside him.

The sight of the naked woman aroused him, but not enough for him to wake her for more lovemaking. Although the priestess was of uncommon beauty, that beauty also was of uncommon strangeness. The darkness had not deceived him about her teeth— her canines had indeed been filed to points resembling those of a serpent's fangs. He lightly touched the numerous scrapes on his shoulders and chest where she had raked him with those teeth while in the throes of passion.

A chill ran through him as he recalled his night with Madekha. Her movements during foreplay had been eerily snakelike, and though she had kissed him as lovingly as any warm-blooded woman, he could not mistake the soft hissing between kisses. But then, he should not have been surprised—what did one expect from the high priestess of the Spotted Python Totem? And he could not say he did not enjoy himself at the time.

The woman reached out to pull the furs back over herself, then groaned lightly and opened her eyes with a silent yawn. Seeing Kwasin, she smiled.

"Sinuneth welcomes you this morning, O Giant Warrior." The priestess now looked past Kwasin to the pile of furs and linens piled up at the head of the oak-framed bed.

Kwasin's skin crawled as he slowly turned his gaze to where she looked. Then he jumped up out of the bed, cursing loudly.

The priestess's diamond-spotted familiar glided out from the deep mass of coverings and coiled caressingly around its mistress's outstretched arm.

The woman laughed and said, "You did not seem to mind Sinuneth's company last night."

"You mean the snake was in our bed while we—" Kwasin bellowed another curse and began donning his lionskin kilt.

"I don't advise you to leave the temple by daylight." Madekha let the snake slither from her arm and back onto the bed, then arose and continued. "If a worshiper from the village sees you, it might get back to T'agoqo and his jealousies will be all the more enflamed. Though he and his fellow priests have thus far resisted King Minruth's blasphemies, I hold little faith they will continue to do so. T'agoqo has only maintained a thin façade of faithfulness to Kho because he desires me and I have dangled out the thread of hope. He knows he will never have me if he publicly turns against the cause of the Goddess, but if he learns I am harboring a legendary criminal and that I have invited him into my bed . . ."

Madekha arose and rang a small iron bell, and before long two young, raven-haired priestesses entered the chamber. "See to his needs," she ordered them, and then regarded Kwasin.

"We have much to discuss, O Kwasin. You are a criminal, exiled by the oracle at Dythbeth for crimes against a daughter of Kho, and we must address that fact before we speak any further. But we are also in a Time of Troubles, and even the Goddess must seek aid where she can find it." She motioned to the priestesses to escort Kwasin from the chamber, but as he passed through the doorway she called out to him.

"Behave yourself with my priestesses," she said as he turned back. "They will clean you up and take care of your desires, but if you harm them in any way, you will awake in Sisisken's dark house before you even know what has struck you."

Kwasin smiled innocently and traced the sign of Kho with his fingers, but deep inside he felt troubled at the snakewoman's words.

A little over two hours later, Kwasin met with Madekha beneath a portico behind the temple overlooking the well-tended grove to Terisikokori, the local python goddess. The storm had passed and the strong, late morning sun shone down through the trees, causing the leaves that had blown to the ground during the previous night's torrent to glisten with a golden light. Already the day's oppressive heat fought to break through the shade of the trees.

Above, Kwasin heard the cry of *datoekem*, then spied one of the large, white-winged gulls arcing overhead through the trees. It reminded him of the proximity to the shore of the temple and the adjoining village of Kaarkor. Madekha had told him the sea-girt cliffs of the Saasanadar lay not a quarter mile north of the hallowed grove.

With a nod, Madekha dismissed her attendant, who had come with news of Khowot's recent eruption and the devastation it had once again wrought upon the capital. It seemed that Minruth blamed the disaster on the prisoners who had just escaped from his prison, proclaiming their breakout had precipitated a great shouting match between Kho and Resu. But though the prisoners had made their getaway, Minruth asserted that Resu had won out in the end, for had not the god of the sun and rain quickly brought the blessed showers that saved much of the city from the fires that threatened to destroy it? Still, Resu was angry that the escapees had succeeded, and if they were not caught soon, the sungod would punish the mortals in the capital for their incompetence. Further, Minruth had sworn vengeance on any city, village, or individual that came to the aid of Kwasin and the other escapees. The priestess was taking a great risk by harboring him.

"You look refreshed," Madekha said, not unpleasantly, though her face betrayed worry at her attendant's news. "But then you will need to be, for you have much work ahead of you in the days to come, O Kwasin."

"It is not my intention to stay here, O Priestess," Kwasin said. "I can't tarry here and fight your battles. Those I have yet to face lie westward, on the road to Dythbeth, where I intend to clear my name."

Madekha smiled grimly. "There is truth in what you say, but do you think you can just walk into Dythbeth and demand forgiveness from Queen Weth?"

Kwasin said nothing. He had not truly thought out his plans for accomplishing his goal once he arrived at his birth city. Not that he had had the time to do so since his flight from the capital.

"But the oracle did pronounce that you would be permitted to return to the land when Kho so decrees," Madekha went on. "I, of course, am not in a position to speak for Kho on this matter, but that is not to say I cannot aid you. After all, you saved my life in the old city, although it is true I would have been in no danger had it not been for you. But it was my decision to enter the ruins of Miterisi all the same, prompted as I was to go there by a vision from the sacred python herself, and I don't regret slaying the followers of Minruth's new order. I owe you . . . well, if not a favor, then an opportunity."

As the priestess spoke, Kwasin had the sinking feeling he was about to be pulled into a business of which he wanted no part. What she said next convinced him of it.

"Much has changed across the land even since you returned from your exile and were imprisoned. Minruth's profane revolt has spread to the outermost corners of the empire. While it is true that Dythbeth yet holds out against the sun worshipers, the cities and towns all around her are falling fast. And though the rural areas and mountain villages remain in large part stolid against the ambitions of Minruth and his wicked priests, that is not to say they have gone untouched. One such village—profaned by the blasphemers, and very dear to me for reasons I will soon explain—lies in the path of your journey westward across the island: the village of Q"okwoqo."

Kwasin nodded in the Khokarsan negative, feeling as if one of the Nukaar, the long-armed hairy half-men of the trees, had reached down out of the jungle, taken hold of him in its viselike grip, and pulled him up into its dark abode. The woman meant to trap him with her so-called opportunity.

"I have no interest," Kwasin said, "in the age-old struggle between the priestesses of Kho and the priests of Resu. Kho helps him who helps himself! She cares nothing for the mortals who merely get in Her way or who attribute their own self-serving prattle to Her divine lips!"

"Hear me out, Kwasin!" Madekha snapped. "Do you forget I can turn you in to the priests in the village if you displease me?"

He recognized the desperation in the woman's voice as well as her conviction. She would not hesitate to execute her threat if he crossed her. Besides, he was desperate as well. If she could truly help him make amends with the Great Mother at Dythbeth, could he resist her offer, no matter the task given him?

"Go on," he said at last, but he did not hide his displeasure.

"Only two days ago," Madekha continued, "my cousin Tswethphe—an acolyte serving the village priestess—arrived from Q"okwoqo. She reports that a small band of soldiers has taken the village, and that the priestess escaped into the wilderness with only my cousin by her side as the soldiers struck. The priestess sent Tswethphe to neighboring Dythbeth to ask for succor, but King Roteka is too busy fighting off Minruth's legions to be bothered with the troubles of a small mountain village. And so my cousin left Dythbeth and crossed the island to throw herself upon my mercy."

"Why does this backwoods village concern you, priestess? Your cousin is safe in your arms, and Q"okwoqo is but an insignificant abode of mountain-dwelling yokels." Kwasin had heard of the rustic mountain village, having lived out his early years in Dythbeth at the foothills of the Saasamaro. He could think of no strategic importance the place might bear upon the struggle against the sun worshipers.

"Alas, I do not disagree with your assessment of Q"okwoqo, but my twin sister, Adythne, the priestess of the village, is as stubborn-headed and dogged as Kopoethken herself. She will not leave her village to the blasphemers and says she will singlehandedly launch a campaign of guerrilla warfare against the soldiers if no one comes to her aid. She will get herself killed!"

Madekha, her face flushed with emotion, paced the granite blocks that composed the portico's floor, but Kwasin only roared with laughter.

"I like the sound of your sister! Are you sure you want to trust me with her?"

The priestess of the sacred python glared at him, the points of her sharpened teeth whitening her otherwise sensuous crimson lips.

"What would you have me do," Kwasin offered when she said nothing, "bring her back to you, against her will?"

"No, she would have none of it. I know her too well. Even if you tied her up and carried her here, she would only fly back to her village at the earliest opportunity. You must aid her in her quest. That is the only way. It's a fool's errand, I know, but what other choice have you? If you agree to help her, I shall whisper into Queen Weth's ear of your efforts to free Q"okwoqo, as well as your act of heroism in defending a daughter of Kho in the ruins of Miterisi—both deeds which will go a long way toward forgiveness of your crimes against the Goddess. But if you refuse to help my sister, I may tell Weth another story, of how in a murderous rage you sought to slay me with your ax amid the ruins. And lest you think I carry no weight with the queen, know that I trained with Weth in the college of priestesses. She will listen to me."

The woman was clearly distraught. And as desperate as her sister if she thought Kwasin could liberate the village from a band of disciplined and entrenched soldiers with an ax as his only ally. Kwasin did not know whether to cry out in laughter or outrage at her opportunity-turned-threat.

"Why not send some of your own men from Kaarkor to help your sister?" Kwasin countered. "Surely some of the villagers remain faithful to you. The priests cannot have corrupted your entire flock."

"Yesterday I was weighing just that," Madekha said, "but concluded that to weaken my forces now, when T'agoqo is readying his own forces to strike, would be foolhardy. And then Terisikokori visited me in my sleep and told me to go to the ruins. And lo, there I found you, perhaps the greatest warrior in all the land! Next to your cousin Hadon, that is, the hero of the Great Games. Perhaps if you are too cowardly to help me, I should seek him out and ask him for help. He escaped from prison with you, did he not? Surely he is somewhere nearby and such a champion would not shirk the challenge I set before him."

Though he knew the woman was manipulating him, it was too much for Kwasin. "Good luck with my cousin!" he roared. "He flew like a frightened hare before Minruth's soldiers while I remained behind to slay a whole company! Had I not, then your beloved queen, Awineth, would have perished. Tell me who is the greatest hero of the land!"

"Then you accept the challenge?"

Before he could stop himself, Kwasin found himself shouting out his prideful assent.

Madekha smiled like a sly snake. "Good," she said. "In any case, I have a feeling you will find the village of Q"okwoqo more palatable than you have found Kaarkor and the moldering ruins of Miterisi. The villagers there worship Old Father Nakendar, a great *klakoru*[3] rumored to have made its lair in the caves near the

[3] "Cave bear" in Khokarsan, or literally, "great devourer of honey."

village for over four hundred years. Perhaps the Bear God himself led you to me so that you would journey to the village and help his children. And besides, the Q"okwoqo are of your totem—the Klakordeth—so you cannot treat my . . . request to aid them as some distasteful chore. It is your duty to help your Bear brothers and sisters!"[4]

Kwasin did not argue with her. The sooner he was on his way and far away from the snakewoman the better. By now, his pride had settled and he had no intention of undertaking her charge, though when she summoned a priestess to bring her a map showing the location of Q"okwoqo and proceeded to spread it out before them on the stone floor, he knelt beside her and nodded as if he were studying his mission in earnest. When Madekha asked him to memorize a passphrase she said would convey to her sister that Kwasin was her emissary, he did so as if it were the most important thing in the world. Observing that he seemed to be taking his newfound mission so solemnly, the woman beamed.

He smiled back at her widely. Besides being the greatest hero of the land, Kwasin was also a passable actor.

And so it was that as the sun fell behind the western mountains and Kwasin prepared for his departure, the village priest, T'agoqo, arrived at the temple to call on the high priestess of the sacred python. Madekha immediately ordered Kwasin into a back chamber in the temple. Only moments later Kwasin heard violent shouting erupt on the other side of the door. Then the temple's outer doors banged open and he heard the sound of many feet marching into the building.

Kwasin grabbed his ax and flung wide the door, which opened onto the temple's central chamber. Before him lay chaos.

---

[4] Given the reputation of the Q"okwoqo as bear worshipers, it may be no coincidence that the name of their tribe and village is strikingly reminiscent of "Ngoloko," another name for the legendary East African cryptid known as the Nandi Bear (note that the Khokarsan character transcribed as the letter "q" is pronounced roughly as the "ng" in the English "sing").

Two temple guards lay dead before the great door on the opposite side of the chamber. T'agoqo stood before Madekha, whose back was to the altar. Madekha's ceremonial dagger gleamed in the torchlight as she thrust it at the priest, who cried out, looking like a betrayed lover, as the blade sank into his scarlet-blossoming robes. Behind them came a group of twelve sailors, recognizable from the fish-eagle insignia of the Khokarsan navy painted on the faces of their small round shields. They must have been from the galley that hunted Kwasin, having provided T'agoqo and his priests with all the reason they needed to at last make their move against the followers of the Goddess.

Kwasin was about to hurl himself into the fray when a rapid succession of muted and airy thwocks sounded in the chamber. Six of the sailors reeled, then crumpled unmoving to the brightly colored mosaic floor. At seeing their comrades fall about them, and having witnessed the death of the priest, the remaining sailors fell into a disorderly retreat, practically tripping over themselves as they scrambled to get out of the temple.

Though Kwasin surveyed the room, he could see no sign to indicate who had blown the poisoned darts. The blowgun-wielding priestesses must have hidden themselves in secret chambers behind the walls, Madekha having likely outfitted the room in case of just such an attack upon the temple.

When he approached the altar, Kwasin found Madekha wiping her blade on the lifeless form of T'agoqo, something akin to satisfaction crossing her features. Then her expression turned to one of urgency.

"T'agoqo has sent his priests to the garrison at the foothills to summon more soldiers," she said, already leading him out of the altar room and through the two adjoining antechambers toward the temple steps. "He told me he did so this morning, so we have little time before they arrive. You must leave in haste if you are to avoid becoming entangled in Kaarkor's affairs." Seeing the unfulfilled battle lust smoldering in his eyes, she added, "As you told me earlier, it is not your desire to stay here and take up the local quarrels. I can take care of myself. Already my courier speeds to the village to bring aid. Much blood will be spilt, but the cause is not a lost one. Kho's faithful do marginally outnumber the followers of the sungod in the village, and they will obey the high priestess of Terisikokori without question. And many in the garrison have wives and lovers in the village—he who turns against the faithful will feel the sting of an angry python!"

Kwasin did not doubt Madekha's conviction, but a mob of untrained country folk against a hardened Khokarsan garrison seemed like long odds on a bet. Still, he had a feeling the high priestess of Terisikokori would not be easily subdued, and further, she was right: He had no interest in remaining here among the People of the Snake. His destiny lay to the west in Dythbeth.

As they stood upon the temple steps, pinpoints of fiery torch-light flickered through the trees on the forest's edge, accompanied by the yapping of approaching dogs. It was the direction from which the soldiers would come if summoned from the garrison.

"Go, Kwasin, fly!" Madekha cried. "Fulfill your charge to me and you shall be rewarded! I have made arrangements—even should I be killed—to get word to Weth that will lobby on your behalf! Now go!"

Kwasin took hold of the woman and kissed her passionately. Then, grinning with the sense of adventure that had seized him, he sped into the forest in the opposite direction to the coming soldiers, bearing only the ax he had brought with him.

He intended to head inland and pass well south of the Saasanadar on his journey to Dythbeth, perhaps stealing a boat and accomplishing a lengthy stretch of his journey floating down the river that fed the island's great lake. But the presence of the soldiers to the south meant he would not be able to take the direct route. Right now his primary concern was getting the soldiers and their dogs off his trail.

With no plan other than to open as much distance as he could between himself and the enemy, Kwasin cut a beeline north through the grove of the sacred python. His great strides carried him quickly through the knee-high grasses that grew between the dark trees, but the soldiers were closing on him. If they released the dogs from their harnesses, the unbridled canines would quickly catch up with him.

Then, abruptly, the forest ended and Kwasin found himself almost barreling headlong off the soaring granite cliffs into the sea. He reeled back, his wildly swaying arms spread behind him as he teetered on the precipice. Far below in the darkness he heard the surf crashing violently against the cliffs.

Despite the coolness of the evening sea breeze, he broke into a sweat. Without knowing it, he had almost entered Sisisken's dark queendom.

Behind him in the forest the hellacious barking of the dogs drew nearer. As far as he could see to either side, the moonlight revealed only a level span of the stark and unfaltering granite cliff top.

By the sound of the barking, he judged the dogs to be only three or four hundred yards off. And now he saw two, then six, then a dozen torches flaming in a wide arc across the forest—the soldiers had fanned out in their pursuit and were now almost upon him.

Swallowing back the sick feeling that rose from the pit of his stomach, Kwasin backed up several paces. Then, clutching his ax with all his oxlike might, he charged toward the cliff's granite rim, howling like a mad gorilla. He kicked off from the edge, and then the night air took him.

He fell for what seemed far too long. Perhaps dread Sisisken would yet entertain him in her dark house.

Just over a week later saw a very much alive Kwasin climbing the mid-reaches of the northeastern Saasamaro on the far western corner of the island. Tall though the cliffs above Kaarkor had been, the precipitous plunge had ended in what amounted to a perfect high dive as Kwasin parted the cold, dark waters with a precision that would have won him a gold crown and a standing ovation had he performed the feat in the Great Games.

The journey after that had not been easy. When Kwasin circled back inland and reached the wide river that flowed south of the Saasanadar, he had been unable to find a boat to steal and carry him on his way. So instead, with the ax given to him by the manling Paga, he had chopped down a great teak and, with a backbreaking and laborious effort he never wanted to repeat again, fashioned from it a crude dugout canoe. The craft, however, was barely riverworthy, and after many frustrating mishaps in which the boat capsized and he nearly drowned, Kwasin was forced to finally abandon his wayward creation and proceed on foot.

Not long after this, while passing south of the vast and waving emmer fields of Awamuka, Kwasin had spied a large contingent of soldiers marching out of the north. After some reconnoitering, he determined the assemblage belonged to Minruth's Sixth Army, the division representing the capital itself and the most battle hardened of them all. Despite Madekha's threat to malign him to Queen Weth if he failed to aid her sister's village, Kwasin had intended to head south as the *kagaga* flies, taking the shortest route to Dythbeth by passing along the shores of the island's great lake. But seeing that the massive body of soldiers would quickly bisect his path, he had been forced to make haste and detour far to the west. Before long, the heights of the Saasamaro, blanketed in green swaths of cedar and pine, loomed before him.

Here he had thought of Madekha's sister and shrugged. He might as well check in on her village and ascertain the situation. Perhaps the soldiers had moved on and he could beseech Adythne to speak on his behalf to Weth—the priestess was, after all, of his totem, and he had saved her sister's life. More likely, the woman had died of starvation in the wilderness or been captured by Minruth's men. If he could, he would find out, to satisfy his curiosity if nothing else.

In any case, he wanted to see if the stories about the Bear God were true. Long ago, the young Kwasin had listened as his godfather, Pwamkhu, related to him the legend of Old Father Nakendar. It was said the Bear God had lived in his cave near Q"okwoqo for over four hundred years, brought to the island by the hero Rimasweth, whose soldiers had captured the enormous cave bear in the mountains near Kethna during their historic expedition to free the poetess Kwamim from Gokasis, the legendary pirate king who once almost toppled the empire. Kwasin had believed the tale as a child, but now he knew better: the elders of his totem said bears lived no more than half the life span of the average human. But even so, there could be some shade of truth in the matter. Perhaps the original cave bear's descendants lived on in the isolated mountain area. Small, though rapidly dwindling, populations of brown bears were known to exist on the island, brought here long ago from the far northern mainland; it would not be impossible for the beast to have bred successfully with these bears, thereby producing progeny that kept the legend of Old Father Nakendar alive.

And so, recalling the maps Madekha had shown him of the region, Kwasin footed his way up the long arm of the northern Saasamaro that would, if he was not mistaken, eventually lead him to the valley of the Q"okwoqo. Passing higher and deeper into the mountains, he saw evidences of recent encroachment by soldiers: the charred remains of a cooking fire here, an ax-toppled cedar there. These could have been attributed to a band of local hunters, but the orderliness of the sites convinced him otherwise; soldiers almost always kept their camps tidier than the average backwoods hunting party.

The next afternoon, having descended into a forested valley on the eastern side of the range, Kwasin spied a group of ten soldiers bathing in a natural hot spring in a clearing overlooked by a rocky slope. With the men were six women—likely locals from the village he sought—who seemed to bear the soldiers no ill will, and, if their giggles and frolicking meant anything, were even enjoying themselves.

Kwasin watched the party from a distance for some time, taking passing note of what appeared to be a cave blocked off by a boulder slide at the top of the slope. He was on the verge of sneaking into the clearing and making off with the soldiers' kilts, harnesses, and weapons—which lay upon the edge of the steaming pool of turquoise water—when suddenly the men and women drew themselves from the spring, their bathing finished, and began donning their clothes.

Slowly, Kwasin withdrew into the woods. He had no desire to take on the soldiers without knowing if they were part of a larger force stationed nearby, which, if Madekha's intelligence was accurate, they were. That the soldiers were Khokarsan and not from Dythbeth, he had no doubt; he had listened to them long enough to determine that from their accents.

Kwasin did, however, cautiously follow the party, which took up a well-worn trail through the trees that, after about half an hour of walking, led to a little village in the forest circled by an intimidating thorn boma. The party entered the boma through its only means of ingress, a stout wooden, bronze-reinforced gate, after speaking a password to a sentry through a speak-hole in the door.

Curious about the situation in the village, Kwasin climbed a thickly leaved oak on the perimeter of the village clearing. From this vantage, he observed three clusters of huts, the longhouse where undoubtedly were held the rituals of the Klakordeth, a large mess hall likely erected after the soldiers seized the village, and a high interior cedar stockade that encompassed a quarter of the village and seemed to be the designated living area for those natives who had resisted the soldiers. But not all of the villagers were confined within the pen; some were at work, under the close watch of their guards, beginning construction on a watchtower near the gate, while others—by far the minority—moved about the village more or less freely while they carried out various chores for their new masters.

The reconnoitering told him all he wanted to know. The situation was grim for the bulk of the villagers. Madekha's hope that he could emancipate Q"okwoqo from Minruth's forces was nothing but a wishful dream.

He climbed down from the oak and faded into the woods, intent on getting away from the village as quickly as possible. He would go to Dythbeth as he had originally intended and take his chances with Queen Weth.

When Kwasin was not yet half a mile from the village, he thought he heard a woman's voice come to him upon the warm forest breeze. Yes, there it was again. He froze and listened. The words were singsong, almost as if the speaker addressed a child:

"In the beginning was a formless substance which gave birth to Kho, the Great Goddess. She fashioned the earth, the air, the sky, the stars, the moon, and the sun . . ."

Quietly, Kwasin moved through the forest in the direction of the speaker.

"After eons, being lonely," the voice continued, "she copulated with the world and had daughters. These she assigned as watchers over the air, the sky, the stars, the moon, and the sun. She created a great tree with many fruits and birds which rested on the tree. The daughters ate the fruit and copulated with the birds, and from these were born all manner of life, including Old Father Nakendar, who mated with his mother's sister, Besbesbes, the goddess of honey, and produced a great variety of bear children, which is why you, my magnificent friend, can't get enough of the nectar of your bee cousins."

A meadow opened up before Kwasin who, wide-eyed, his jaw hanging, peered through the underbrush at an incredible site. Indeed, there was a woman in the wood—a beautiful, young woman, her lustrous hair night-black, with a delicate face that was identical in every way to Madekha's, though perhaps somewhat more wholesome, and not at all serpentlike. But lo! It was not a child whom the woman addressed with all the affection of a doting mother—but rather a great brown bear, standing upright, fully ten feet tall on its hind legs, as the woman reached up and fed it honey from her dripping hand!

In the tiny hand went, into that great fanged mouth, to be licked by an enormous pink tongue, and then out again it came, miraculously unharmed. Then the woman dipped her hand into the ceramic jar she held nestled in the crook of her arm, withdrew the now-honey-covered hand, and plunged it again into that terrible maw.

To see the tiny creature before him do what he, the mighty Kwasin, would never think to do astounded him. He had heard folktales in the lodges and halls of the Klakordeth of an ancient trickster-hero of the totem who had donned bearskins and went to live among a sloth of bears, creating trouble for all the humans and mythological creatures that encountered him. But never had Kwasin believed old Klaklaku to be other than a fable. Now, his heart thrumming with envy at seeing this woman interact so intimately with his totem animal, he wondered.

But soon Kwasin's heart beat rapidly for a different reason as the bear dropped to all fours and began huffing and growling in his direction, swinging its long-snouted head wildly and baring its awful fangs. The woman quickly stepped back from her ferocious companion and swung about to face Kwasin, who, having heard from his totem brothers about what to do if one unexpectedly encountered a hostile bear in the wild, remained as still as he could. If the animal came any closer, however, he would stand up, making himself as tall and threatening as possible, and roar like a demon. There was no sense trying to run—even the fastest sprinter in the empire could not hope to outpace a charging bear.

Now the woman spoke sternly to the bear, telling it to lie down. The bear continued to huff until she repeated the command again, this time pointing assertively at the ground. To Kwasin's surprise, the bear complied, placing its chin on the carpet of grass and whining like a chided dog.

"You, in the woods!" the woman shouted. "Come out, slowly, or you'll anger Parbho and he will eat you."

Kwasin crawled out from behind the lavender where he had been hiding and stepped slowly into the meadow. The bear whined louder as Kwasin advanced, but stopped when the woman admonished it with a command of "Stay!"

"You don't look like a soldier," she said, her eyes narrowed. "But I will have Parbho kill you all the same if you don't tell me what you're doing in these woods."

Kwasin smiled disarmingly and, spreading his arms wide, made an exaggerated bow, keeping his eyes on the woman, and, of course, the bear.

"I am Kwasin," he said, "an emissary of Madekha, high priestess of the sacred python at Kaarkor and holy daughter of Kho." And then Kwasin spoke the words Madekha had said would convince her sister he spoke the truth.

The woman started upon hearing the secret phrase, and then her face, surrounded by the dark firmament of her hair, lit up like the most radiant star in the night sky, her lips parting in a gleaming smile. If not for the bear, Kwasin doubted he would have been able to resist taking her up in his arms and covering her with his hot kisses. Then he thought, if not for the bear, of course he would not resist it.

"My sister sent you?" the woman asked, hope ringing clearly in her voice. "You have brought men from Kaarkor to wage war on the soldiers who have taken my people?"

"No, O Fair Adythne," he replied, "for I can only assume that is your name. Your sister faces troubles of her own in Kaarkor, and needs all the men she has to protect her sacred office. She's sent only me, Kwasin, slayer of men and monsters, and the greatest lov—"

For a moment the woman had looked forlorn, but now she cut him off, her vision seeming to turn inward as if already she plotted a scheme and his boasting words were but bothersome spores upon the wind.

"It is just as well," she said over his words. "A large and unwieldy band would only cause the soldiers to garrison themselves in the village and threaten to execute hostages until the attackers departed. And you are indeed a giant, and one man may sometimes achieve what an army cannot. Especially if that man is made invincible."

"I don't know of what you speak, O Priestess," Kwasin said, "but let us first understand one another before we talk of—"

"Yes, yes," the woman said eagerly, "you are foreign to these parts, unfamiliar with our village, and want to know how it is that I am so friendly with Parbho here."

It was not what Kwasin was thinking. He only wanted to make clear to the priestess that she was delusional if she thought he would fight her battles for her—that the only sensible thing was to accompany him to Dythbeth, where she could give testimony to clear his name, and also ask for assistance for her village from King Roteka and his army. But the woman gave him no opportunity to make his case.

"Parbho," Adythne continued without pausing, "is one of seven bears we have trained in the village. We, the Klakordeth of Q"okwoqo, have a long tradition of intimate dealings with our sacred animal, going back almost half a millennia. Oh, how you should see them dance and jump through hoops of fire during the festival days of Kho-wu! But they are much more than just pets—they are our spirit guides, and we of the village could not go on without them. That is why, when the soldiers stormed Q"okwoqo, I set the bears free from their cages—I could not risk that they might slay the spirit guides and use their meat for stew."

Here the woman paused to coddle Parbho's glossy brown neck, and, at seeing the bear react by licking her hand like a playful pup, Kwasin's intended words vanished from his mind.

Now Adythne's beautiful features darkened. "But the soldiers have blocked up Old Father Nakendar in his cave. He would have starved by now had I not fed him what slim morsels I've been able to catch in the woods, dropping them down through the sacrificial opening at the summit above his cave."

"The Bear God is real?" Kwasin said, somewhat dubiously.

"Of course, he is," Adythne snapped. "He lairs in the cave above the northern hot springs—the sacred waters the soldiers defile with their ritually unclean bodies." Then the priestess's expression grew yet darker. "But I hold an even greater fear than for Nakendar, who, being divine, is surely just biding his time in his cave while the mortals about him bicker. I have just been to the village and exchanged messages with one of my acolytes by means of the mirror code employed by the daughters of Kho. She has told me that late one night, about a week ago, a gang of drunk soldiers slipped into the stockade without their commanding officers' permission and at sword-point marched away with a half dozen children while their mothers cried and screamed and pulled at their hair in dismay. Two men were killed, and a third gravely injured, trying to stop the soldiers. Now, a week has passed and the children have not returned.

"The days grow dark for the people of Q"okwoqo," Adythne said, looking weary, "and I, their priestess, have been unable to help them. Indeed, if not for the presence of the spirit guides, madness would have consumed me by now. But now that you have arrived, O Mighty Kwasin, we will set things right. And yes," she added, regarding him slyly, "I know who you are, and of your larger-than-life—if outright criminal—reputation. But that is something I intend to wield to our advantage."

At these last words, the beautiful Adythne beckoned Kwasin forward, took his hand in hers, and led him past the suspicious, beady red eyes of her bear to the edge of the shaded meadow. Here she knelt on the ground before a pile of dead underbrush, which she proceeded to move aside until a smooth, round stone was revealed half embedded in the reddish-brown soil. She leaned forward, dug her fingers into the earth around the stone, and, groaning, pulled aside the covering. From the deep hole beneath where the stone had been, she drew forth a large bundle sealed tight in waxed antelope hide. Then she stood up and held out the bundle with an air of reverence.

"It is the sacred pelt of a she-bear once worshiped by the Klemklakor in the lands far north of the Saasares, near the Ring-ing Sea. The she-bear killed and ate my great-great-grandfather, but then choked on his bones and died. Or at least that was the story told by my great-great-grandmother, who brought back the bear's hide when she returned to her home village of Kaarkor. The pelt was passed to me from my mother, who, while not of the Klemklakor, had inherited it from her mother and understood the sacramental nature of the pelt. And it was while I was partaking of the laurel leaf during the orgiastic rites of my former totem that the old she-bear came to me and told me I must travel to Q"okwoqo to become a sister of the Klemklakor. She also said that neither blade nor spear nor fire would touch him who wore the she-bear's pelt into battle."

Adythne untied the antelope-sinew strings that bound the bag and unfurled a magnificent black-furred bearskin, its cured head still attached and serving as a sort of coif. Sinew cords hung from the hide, allowing the wearer to secure the pelt to the arms and shoulders.

"And for that reason," she said, proffering the pelt to Kwasin, "I pass the holy mantle to you, O Great Warrior, to wear for your protection until you have freed my people from the wicked followers of the sungod. You must, of course, relinquish the pelt after you have achieved our goal, for I intend to pass it along to a daughter of my own one day."

Kwasin took the pelt—for indeed it was a splendid specimen, one he could not help but admire as a member of the Thunder Bear Totem—and swept it over his great bronzed and muscled shoulders. He smiled appreciatively at Adythne, but only briefly.

"Like your sister," he said, sloughing the cloak from his shoulders, "you make a compelling argument. But I can't take up your local burdens. I'm steadfast on a mission to see Queen Weth, and—if she still lives—the oracle Wasemquth, who exiled me from the land eight years ago. For too long have I wandered the wilds, distracting my lonely soul with whatever trouble I happened to stumble across. But our causes lead to the same place. You can't make the dangerous journey to Dythbeth without escort, but I can take you there. There you can ask the queen to urge her husband, King Roteka, to send a force into the mountains and free the good people of Q"okwoqo from the soldiers of Minruth the Mad. And it would be but little trouble for you to put in a good word for me, who saved your sister from certain death—or worse—in the ruins of cursed Miterisi."

Since Kwasin had encountered her, Adythne had paused in neither thought nor action long enough to entertain the possibility that Kwasin might not be interested in joining her single-minded quest to free her village from the soldiers. Now, upon hearing Kwasin's little speech, the woman's face flushed with anger and resentment.

"You are the mad one, O Kwasin the Ill-Fated!" Adythne snatched the sacred pelt from Kwasin's hands and shook it out with an angry flourish as if his mere touch had defiled it. "For Weth—the very priestess whose ravaging by you doomed you to exile from the land—will have you executed upon sight! And were I to be seen in your company, my loyalties too would be thrown into question, and no hope would my people have of succor from Dythbeth." Behind them the bear, roused by his mistress's anger, began growling lightly as Adythne continued. "No! We must fight the soldiers now, with as much stealth and cunning as I can design—for it is clear your dull-witted mind is not made for either. Your course would do nothing but condemn us to imprisonment in King Roteka's dungeons!"

Adythne was certainly spirited, but Kwasin had known that even before he laid eyes on her. Who else would abandon her mother's totem in favor of adoption into a foreign one? He knew, however, that such things were done in certain rare cases. Sometimes, in a remote village, an infant's or toddler's mother died leaving behind no direct living matrilineal relatives. If no member from the mother's clan stepped forward to adopt the child, the village priestess had leeway to reassign the child to another totem. There was almost always a great aunt or a distant cousin able to adopt the child, and if the child was old enough, someone from the mother's totem would adopt it, no matter the hazy nature of the relation—for were not all totem brothers and sisters of the same spiritual blood? But Adythne had not only switched totems; she had become a high priestess among her adopted people—how Kwasin would love to hear the tale behind that!

The thought of being spiritually separated from his birth totem disturbed Kwasin. Though he had not been among his Bear brothers during his eight years in exile, he could not imagine cutting himself off from the Klakordeth forever. The spirit of the bear ran too deeply within him.

He could not, however, blame the woman for her decision to switch totems. The Thunder Bear Totem was of hardy stock, the cream of the crop as far as Kwasin was concerned, even if its members did tend to indulge a bit too heavily in alcohol and, from time to time, killed one another in drunken rages, or in ritual games of strength and endurance. But they were bears at heart, his spiritual brothers and sisters—and bears liked their honey, and were also prone to outbursts of violence when the mood set upon them—so how could anyone hold it against them? Because of this, Kwasin did not begrudge the woman her stubbornness either.

And so, instead of arguing with Adythne, Kwasin merely bellowed with laughter.

"You are courageous, O Priestess, and I wish you luck," he said, "though I doubt you will find it." And with that he slung his ax over a shoulder and strode leisurely into the forest.

Through the trees he heard the priestess curse him, and then, loud enough that he knew she meant him to hear it, she said, "Come, Parbho, we shall free the village ourselves. You, at least, are no coward."

Kwasin walked on through the cedars for some time, trying to keep his thoughts on his goal of reaching Dythbeth and seeking exoneration of his crimes. Soon, however, his conscience began to prickle. He could not keep Adythne's final words from his mind.

Had he not accused Hadon of exactly the same sort of cowardice for failing to remain behind with him to fight Minruth's soldiers in the capital? Had his desire to clear his name and abrogate his exile—strengthened by the dreams of his mother's death that wracked his sleep—at last squelched his seemingly bottomless well of boldness and spontaneity? Not to mention—and here his pride truly stung—his fearlessness?

He muttered a curse. Then, he laughed.

Truly had the priestess worked a spell over him, one that had almost succeeded. No, he thought, not just Adythne, but her sister as well. Both, he mused, had shrewdly and cunningly worked their magic on him—the snakewoman had planted the seed and the bearwoman had sought to harvest it. But he would not be distracted from his mission. Maybe, if the oracle did pardon his crimes, he would return to the Saasamaro with a stalwart band of King Roteka's soldiers and rout the enemy from Q"okwoqo. But not until he again walked free within the empire.

Kwasin continued on through the woods. Soon he found his mood had lifted and again he began to feel like his old self.

Then came the tart stench of death amid the strong smell of the cedars.

When he found the bodies of the children, blackness consumed him.

Kwasin knew now that he could not go to Dythbeth. Not yet anyway. He could not let the atrocity go unpunished, no matter his previous plans.

That so-called civilized citizens of the empire had committed such a profane act against the innocent made him feel ashamed of his desire to return to civilization—he had never seen such vile barbarism in all his years among the savages in the Wild Lands. But war, Kwasin knew, sometimes made people commit atrocities they would never conceive of enacting in peacetime. Still, that did not excuse the actions of the soldiers who had done this. He would make them pay for their crimes. He had no doubt the corpses were those of the children abducted by the drunken soldiers about whom Adythne had raged.

What had set him on the path that had led here? He might have set off from the meadow on any number of paths through the forest, but he had taken this one. Had the Bear God truly guided him here, as Madekha had suggested, so that Kwasin would remain and help Old Father Nakendar's people? Or perhaps the Goddess Herself wanted him to stay and fight, for Her own unknowable reasons. He did not know, but the end result was the same. One moment, he had been on the road to Dythbeth, caring little for anything but his own self-interest; in the next, a path of blood and death lay before him.

Though a dark rage had seized him, he set about the task of burying the dead innocents. He had no tool but the sharpened head of his ax to dig the graves, but he could not turn away from the unpleasant chore, notwithstanding the furious urge to take up the war trail straightaway. What these children could not expect of life, he would assure they received in death. When he could, he would hunt down a wild boar and sacrifice it so that their spirits would not hunger and thirst. But now he had only the time to bury their mortal remains.

The early afternoon having passed at his grim labors, Kwasin set off for the meadow where he had last seen Adythne. It took him longer than he would have liked to find the place, and when he did, the priestess was not there. He did, however, find her spoor, as well as that of the bear. The two had set off in different directions, the bear toward the southwest where the forest deepened as the valley widened, and the woman, not surprisingly, in the direction of the village.

After following Adythne's trail for fifteen minutes, the spoor disappeared beneath the fresh bootprints of many men. He tracked the party a short distance before noticing a woman's footprints diverging from the group. He followed her tracks but found they made only a little loop through the woods before rejoining the prints of the main party.

Standing beneath the vaulting cedars, Kwasin reconstructed what had transpired. Adythne had set off from the meadow and quickly parted with the bear. Perhaps she had commanded the bear to head into the deep woods, where the animal would be less likely to have a confrontation with the soldiers. About half a mile from the meadow, Adythne had spied a group of soldiers in the forest, at which point she turned to the east. From the length of the woman's stride as well as the shallow impression of her heels, Kwasin could tell she was at this point running, as if the soldiers had seen her. She had gone a distance and then stopped beneath a sprawling pine amid the cedars before finally turning back in the direction of the soldiers. Then she had been caught.

But why had the woman detoured from the party of soldiers only to return to be captured by them? Unless . . .

Kwasin jogged back to the great pine and looked up into its array of widely spread limbs. He grunted approvingly when he spied what he sought, then pulled himself up among the branches and climbed high into the pine.

When he neared the top of the tree he plucked from between two joining limbs what the woman had cached there: the tightly wrapped antelope-hide bundle that contained the sacred bear pelt. Then he returned to the ground with his prize.

Kwasin removed the pelt from the waxen hide, eddied the pelt over his well-muscled shoulders, and sat down glumly beneath the great pine. His head couched in his hands, he sighed deeply. He thought of how he had abandoned Adythne in the forest against her urgings that he help her defeat the soldiers occupying her village. Now those soldiers had caught her.

That the all-too-determined priestess would have been apprehended by the soldiers sooner or later did nothing to assuage Kwasin's guilt that he had not assisted her. He was not one to live his life imprisoned by feelings of remorse—he did what his heart told him and bore the consequences. But since he had returned from the Wild Lands, something had changed in him. His actions no longer seemed as certain as they once had. Perhaps he had become unaccustomed to civilized companionship. Or possibly the feeling of uncertainty was due to the dreams that plagued his nights, or maybe the furious battle between Great Kho and Resu that shook the land. Why, he wondered, had he so desired to return to the empire that spurned him to begin with?

Of course, he knew the answer. He had suffered a terrible, soul-aching loneliness while in the wilds. But when he had returned to civilization, a stark feeling of *nothingness* had rapidly descended upon him, even more smothering than the isolation he had faced in the far-flung land of the savages. In the hope of filling that void of nothingness, he had seized upon the idea of returning to Dythbeth and obtaining a pardon for his crimes. But now, in the mountains above his homeland, the emptiness remained and he wondered if he would ever find that which would satisfy the cravings of his soul.

As Kwasin sat brooding thus, his head cradled deeply in his hands, something cold and wet nudged his forearm. He lifted his head and nearly leaped to his feet when he found himself looking into the large and terrible dark eyes of a great brown bear. It was all he could do to keep from jumping up, but he knew that if he moved suddenly, the bear would become enraged and all would be over for the mighty Kwasin—the bear's horrible fangs would devour both body and soul, and even dread Sisisken, goddess of the underworld, would be left wondering what had become of him. The nothingness that he feared most would blot him out forever.

And so Kwasin sat there, unmoving, watching the bear. That it was Parbho, the bear that had accompanied the priestess Adythne, he had no doubt. In fact, the bear had a forlorn look about it, as it sat on its haunches, snorting and nudging Kwasin gently with its cold, black nose. Almost, Kwasin thought, as if the bear understood its mistress had been captured by the soldiers—as if, finding Kwasin in the forest with the sacred pelt of the she-bear draped about his shoulders, the bear sought comfort from the man-thing. Did the bear believe, because its mistress had commanded it not to attack the man-thing, that Kwasin was consequently its mistress's friend? And by extension, the bear's friend?

Kwasin did not question his attribution of human emotions and motivations to the bear; all living things were by extension the children of Kho, the Mother of All, and even the deities felt love and hate and greed and sorrow. The bear was no different.

Of course, Parbho's playful nosing of Kwasin might simply have been due to the pelt the human wore. As a holy artifact, it was likely used in the sacred rituals of the Klakordeth, and Adythne had said the villagers thought of their trained bears as spirit guides. Doubtless Parbho had taken some role in the totem's rites and was accustomed to the scent of the pelt, which must have reassured the bear in the absence of its mistress.

Boldly, though hardly sure of the wisdom of his action, Kwasin reached out a hand and scratched Parbho behind an ear. The bear tilted its head and, if Kwasin was not mistaken, smiled at him as it whined affectionately.

Kwasin smiled back with genuine delight, but he was careful not to bare his teeth. He did not want the bear to mistake his grin for a threatening snarl.

For some time Kwasin sat with Parbho, caressing the beast as friskily as he dared. The bear even rolled onto its back in apparent jollity, and then back onto its feet to push Kwasin with a playful nudge that was at the same time forceful enough to almost send the human sprawling.

Finally, Kwasin decided he had to get to his feet and assert himself at some point or he might be trapped playing with the frolicsome bear until it grew tired of playing and turned on him. Slowly, the sacred she-bear pelt still about his shoulders, he rose. As he did so, the bear got to its feet as well and let out a deep growl that froze Kwasin where he stood.

Then inspiration struck him. He would not merely wait to see what the bear would do next. Adythne had, after all, said her people had trained the animals to dance. And so Kwasin crouched down on all fours and began to act out one of the ritual dances of the Bear people. As he danced, Kwasin also began chanting in gruff tones a primordial song of his totem. The ritual was, in fact, the Dance of Klaklaku, reputed to depict the same motions of that legendary hero of the Klakordeth, who, donning bearskins, had convinced a sloth of bears to adopt him. If the dance had worked for his ancient totem ancestor, Kwasin thought, perhaps it would work for him as well.

At first the bear just watched him. Kwasin thought that from its look the animal believed the human to be mad, that at any second the bear would leap upon him and tear him to bloody pieces with its great claws and teeth. But then, much to his surprise, Parbho jumped in behind Kwasin and began following him in his dance, acting out the same motions that had been passed from Bear brother to Bear brother down from the time of Klaklaku himself!

Kwasin was amazed. But he also understood he had been lucky. Bears, whether trained or not, were by their very nature wild and deadly animals, and he had encountered this one under just the right circumstances. The villagers must have taught Parhbo just this same ritual dance, one of the most ancient of his people. Seeing Kwasin attired in the sacred pelt, doubtless worn by Adythne or another totem member during the local rituals, and then watching the man-thing enact the familiar dance of Klaklaku, the bear was probably only doing what he had been taught to do as a cub.

Just when Kwasin felt the day could not grow stranger, he

heard a rustling from the forest. Suddenly, out walked another brown bear, just as giant as his brother Parbho. Still Kwasin did not stop his dancing and singing. He feared too much what would happen if he did.

In the same manner as Parbho had at first done, the newcomer sat on his haunches and watched Kwasin intently. Then, as if waiting for just the right timing in the ritual, the newly arrived bear rose up on all fours and swayed in behind Parbho, mimicking the exaggerated motions of the dance.

When the third bear, and then a fourth and a fifth, arrived, Kwasin did not question it. Nor did he do so after all seven of the bears mentioned by Adythne had come and joined in the ritual. By this time Kwasin had lost himself in the dance and now fully believed himself possessed by the spirit of his ancestor, Klaklaku the Man-Bear. And who could have doubted it to see Kwasin thus, leading bear after bear in that erratic dance upon the forest floor! Sometimes he stopped and rose up on two legs, hands lifted up like raking claws; at other times he fell back again upon all fours, swaying back and forth and huffing and growling no differently from the great ursines that trod so closely behind him in the circling path of the dance.

How long the impromptu ritual went on, Kwasin was unsure, but at last he—and he believed the bears as well—grew tired. He knew the dance could not go on forever, and if stopping his wild motions would cause the bears to turn violently upon him, so be it. If he had to die, then at least he would exit this world directly following one of the most supremely satisfying experiences of his life—the exalting of his ancient ancestor's soaring spirit in communion with the spirit guides of his people. If his bear cousins devoured him, Kwasin knew in the utter conviction of the moment that old Klaklaku would be there to welcome him into the afterlife.

Following the traditional means to conclude the dance, Kwasin leaped high into the air with a roar and then collapsed upon the ground and lay still. Through slitted lids he watched the bears as they attempted to imitate his closing leap—they were, of course, too heavy to jump fully off the ground as he did—and then flopped onto the forest floor in apparent exhaustion. For several minutes the ursines lay there with Kwasin. Eventually, one bear arose and sniffed one of its companions before finally swaying off at a leisurely pace into the woods. Then the other bears followed suit, one after another, until only Parbho remained lying next to Kwasin. Finally that great beast too rolled up onto his feet. He walked over to where Kwasin lay, sniffed him, and padded off toward the north upon some errand only the bear could know.

Contented in a way he had never before known, Kwasin stood up and watched the bear disappear into the woods.

The next few days were busy for Kwasin, and though he regretted leaving Adythne in the hands of the soldiers while making no attempt to free her, he knew he needed to invest some time and much patience if his plan to help the priestess and her people was to succeed. Still, if he waited too long, he would be too late.

Though he worked hard at his preparations during the day, at night he lingered outside the village walls eavesdropping on the villagers. On the first night he learned nothing of importance, but on the second he overheard two sentries discussing how their commandant, a captain named Riwaphe, intended to sacrifice Adythne to the sungod as an example to the people of Q"okwoqo. The ceremony was to occur at dawn on the morning of the second fire day of the month, in only five days.

Because of this intelligence, Kwasin was forced to speed up his preparations, working within a timeframe much shorter than he considered wise. But then, the Bear God was on his side. What other sign did he need of the god's favor than the bizarre congregation of the dancing bears of Q"okwoqo that had communed with him? Old Father Nakendar was looking after him. He hoped. He would need the Bear God's help if his daring plan was to succeed.

On the morning of the month's second cloud day—the sixth day since his arrival in the area and the day before Adythne's scheduled execution—Kwasin set out for the nearby hot spring. His experience with the bears had struck him profoundly, and he wanted to pay his respects to the Old Father before the night of trials that lay ahead and ask the god for his blessing and for strength.

Kwasin made sure to keep a watchful eye out during his journey to the spring. Over the course of the preceding days, he had observed the officers in command at Q"okwoqo make something of a daily ritual out of hiking out to the spring and soaking in the soothing hot waters. Always did the soldiers leave the village at the point when the sun had descended approximately halfway from the zenith of Kho's blue bowl, filing along the same forest path with a number of local women who, from their attitudes, seemed to be seeking the favor of the officers so that they might elevate their social status in the new order of things. Today Kwasin arrived at the spring in the late morning, well ahead of the soldiers' expected visit.

He climbed the high, rocky prominence that overlooked the spring, stopping briefly at the ledge upon which rested the great boulder that sealed off the entrance to the Bear God's cave. After examining the obstruction for a few minutes, he continued on. At the slope's summit, the land leveled out and Kwasin walked only a short distance before coming upon a scattering of branches and dead brush. He cleared these away and examined the sacrificial opening about which Adythne had told him.

The circular opening was just over five feet in diameter and rimmed with expertly fitted blocks of white, red-veined marble. A thick bear smell came up out of the hole from the black abyss of the cave, and though Kwasin strained his eyes, he could see nothing in the darkness below. Perhaps the Bear God had at last succumbed to the very mortal afflictions of starvation and thirst. It had been at least six days since the priestess had last visited the god and fed him, and for all Kwasin knew it could have been much longer.

"I am Kwasin, brother of the Klakordeth!" he shouted down the shaft. "I have come to help your people, O Nakendar!" His own words came hollowly back at him from the enormous cavern below, but other than the echo, he heard nothing.

"Hear me, Old Father!" he cried again. "I seek your blessing in destroying the enemies of the Q"okwoqo!"

Finally Kwasin grew tired of staring down into the murk. Concluding sadly that the cave bear must have really died, he rearranged the dead foliage over the opening and went off to look for lunch.

He ultimately found his meal in the form of a termite colony nested high in a tree. He would have preferred to roast the insects but he could not take the chance of building a fire, which might alert the nearby soldiers to his presence. But he needed his strength for what was to come, and so he had to make do fishing the insects out of their nest with a stick and eating them raw. This was not much of a concession; many Khokarsans ate their termites raw by choice.

His belly full, Kwasin climbed down from the tree and lay down in the shade of a great boulder on the rock-strewn slope overlooking the spring, where he thought to rest for but a few minutes. Soon, however, his meal made him sleepy and he drifted off into a deep slumber.

When the sound of laughter and splashing water below awakened him, his first impulse was to pull the sacred pelt of the she-bear over his head and continue sleeping. Then, remembering his whereabouts, he cursed groggily.

He rose to discover Resu's weltering red eye had already slipped below the western mountains, the heavens staining the forest a dim crimson. Beneath him at the foot of the slope, the band of officers, their two foot soldiers, and the women who accompanied them frolicked in the warm waters, oblivious to the giant that observed them from behind a boulder.

Kwasin cursed again. His hopes to assail the village while Captain Riwaphe and his officers were absent at the spring were now dashed. But then, as the sleep-fog cleared from his mind, he remembered that the Bear God had come to him while he slept.

Or rather, Kwasin had come to the god, for in the dream he had sat before Nakendar in the darkness of his cave. All that Kwasin had been able to see of the god was the eerie glow of his terrible red eyes; the Old Father, however, had spoken to him in a series of huffing growls that, somehow, Kwasin understood. And he had told Kwasin that the sleep that had overcome him was not due to a lapse in the mortal's determination. No, the god had cast the slumber over Kwasin that he might advise him. There was, according to the Old Father, a more effective way to keep the officers from the village, and one that would not leave the god hungering in his cave-prison.

Recalling the task with which Nakendar had charged him, Kwasin grinned widely.

There was no use in wasting time. He stepped from behind the boulder in full sight of the party below, stretched wide his arms, and let out a cavernous yawn.

Instantly, the laughter and chitchat of the frolickers ceased. The soldiers stood up in the steaming waters, their naked forms glistening redly in the fading twilight, their mouths dark circles of surprise. Then, at an order from the captain, the men scampered out of the pool and began donning their clothes and picking up their weapons.

Kwasin smiled broadly and waved down at the soldiers; then he turned about, lifted his kilt, and mooned them. He stood thus only long enough to hear the soldiers' curses, then lost no time in ascending the slope. He did not think the men carried slings, but he was uncertain.

When he reached the summit, he waited. The soldiers would have to get much closer if the Bear God's plan was to succeed.

He grinned when he saw that, as he had hoped, the captain led the charge up the rocky incline, with the four other officers and two infantrymen just behind him. Kwasin felt relieved to discover they carried only their swords.

Finally the captain, red-faced and panting heavily, pulled himself up onto the summit. As the man did so, Kwasin feigned a startled expression, then turned and sprinted across the plateau. He did not, however, sprint too quickly as he did not want to get too far ahead of the man.

Kwasin looked over a shoulder and saw the captain only a

couple of yards behind him, with the other soldiers in a tightknit group directly behind their superior. Then Kwasin leaped over the scattering of branches before him, swung around, and stopped.

There was a crash as the captain fell through the fragile lattice of brushwood that covered the stone-lined sacrificial opening, then the heavy thud of a body hitting the stone floor of the cave below. The other soldiers, directly on the heels of their captain, could not stop their forward momentum. Kwasin grinned like a demon at seeing their dumbfounded faces just before they tumbled as one into the black pit. Their bodies too thumped hollowly as they made a series of rapid impacts upon the cavern floor.

He bent over the hole and shouted down at the groaning men.

"That is your punishment for sealing up Old Father Nakendar and leaving him to die! May his spirit gnaw on your shinbones for all eternity!"

Kwasin remained at the edge of the hole, listening to the continued groaning and sobbing of the men below. He felt no remorse for dooming the men to die in the cave. After what the soldiers had done to the children and to the Old Father, he only regretted that they would not suffer more.

Suddenly, from somewhere deep in the cave came a hideous, moaning scream. The hair rose stiffly on the back of Kwasin's neck and the men below began to shout out in terror.

The bloodcurdling scream came again, now nearer to the bottom of the marble shaft. Kwasin bent over the hole, trying to penetrate the darkness, his giant frame tremoring. It was not every day that one heard the scream of a god.

The men were now shrieking in utter fright. Then came the sound of slashing claws and a gut-wrenching chomping of bone, followed a few moments later by complete silence.

No, the silence was not absolute. He thought, if he strained his hearing, he could just make out a faint rasping of breath. Then he saw, caught faintly in the evening's fading light, what appeared to be the glimmer of two large, reddish eyes looking up at him.

Kwasin backed away from the hole, his heart pounding, his body covered in a cold sweat.

Half numb with shock, he stumbled back down the slope to retrieve the sacred she-bear pelt where he had left it by the boulder. Briefly, he looked for the women who had accompanied the soldiers, but they were nowhere to be found. Doubtless they had run off into the woods after hearing the hideous cry of the Old Father.

Shaken to his core by what he had seen and heard, Kwasin could not say he blamed them.

Kwasin knew he had to move fast. The sky had already darkened and he needed to get back to his camp near the village as quickly as possible. He hoped the bears had not wandered off. If they had, his plan would fail.

As he ran through the dark woods, the preposterousness of what he hoped to do made him wonder at his sanity. But it also exhilarated him. If he was able to beat the incredible odds and succeed at his intent, then his name would forever be sung in the halls of his totem. A new ritual dance would be initiated to record his great deeds for the posterity of all Bear people. They might call it the Dance of the Imprudent Giant, and he would become as legendary as Klaklaku himself.

But more than just vanity drove Kwasin on. When the Old Father had come to him in the dream, he had told Kwasin it was time to choose sides. To stand on the side of Kho, the Mother of All, and give sustenance to the great tree from which all life sprang. Or to turn his back on the Goddess and kindle the smoldering flames that were the lies and arrogance of Resu—to stand with the sungod until his blistering gaze reduced the world tree to nothing more than a dried and blackened husk. The Bear God had told Kwasin he must either help the people of Q"okwoqo or turn against his totem brothers and sisters and slay them. According to Old Nakendar, it was because Kwasin had for so long remained a disinterested party in the conflict between Kho and Resu that his soul so greatly feared oblivion. Kwasin's own petty goals and desires were but nothing compared to the flowering of Great Kho's will or the sungod's burning desire to murder his mother and former lover, the Creator and Replenisher of all things.

And so it was that Kwasin—defiler of the temple of Kho, exile from the land by order of the Voice of Kho herself—took the side of the Great Mother in the war between the deities. He now recognized the battle for Q"okwoqo for what it was—not merely a local matter, but rather the touchstone of his destiny. Perhaps in his heart he had known this all along but his head had denied it. Was this why, since his return from the Wild Lands, his mother had plagued his dreams with visions of her death? Had she been trying to send him a message from her shadowy station in Sisisken's dark house—to urge him to stand with the Goddess against the blasphemers or risk the extinguishing of his soul as the snake that had bitten her had struck down her own life? If the nightmares now ceased, he would know.

At last he came to his camp, about half a mile from Q"okwoqo. This was his new camp, the original having been positioned far enough away from the village that the soldiers would not detect the smoke from the training fires he lit. He had relocated here only yesterday, the site's proximity to the village being crucial to his plan.

For a moment, his heart sank. Where were the bears? He began to think they had loped off into the forest as they were wont to do at night after their training sessions, knowing that if they had, Adythne was doomed to die at sunrise upon the altar of Resu. But then, as he searched the woods just beyond the camp's perimeter, he saw in the dim starlight cast down between the branches seven large, dark forms upon the forest floor. He sighed with relief. The bears had not fled after all.

Now came one of the most dangerous parts of his scheme—and there were many. When he had trained with the bears, it had always been in the light of day, as his plan was to task the animals early that afternoon when the contingent's officers were away from the village and soaking in the hot spring. He did not know how the bears would react to a disruption in their routine. Bears were for the most part diurnal. Would they follow their training in the pitch black of night? Or, when he woke them, would they revert to the untamed beasts they were at heart and attack him?

There was only one way to find out. Kwasin donned the sacred pelt of the she-bear, which he had carried with him from the spring. Quietly, at first, so as not to startle the bears, he began to sing the crude ballad he had composed to accompany the bears' training. This he had set, rather wryly, to the tune of "Bear Mother Mistakes Her Teeth for Her Anus," an ancient and bawdy folksong about a popular heroine of his totem.

At hearing Kwasin's crass singing, the bears awoke, one by one, some of them huffing as they were roused. This set Kwasin's heart racing, as he knew the sound indicated the animals felt threatened. A few moments later, however, the huffing ceased, and he felt a great hairy body brush up friendlily against his bare thigh. He continued his singing and began dancing in the same manner as he had during the bears' training, first in a wide orbit around the camp, and then, after the bears had begun to follow behind him, off into the forest in the direction of Q"okwoqo.

Every so often Kwasin looked back to make sure his outlandish company was still in tow. But he did not need to do so; he could hear well enough the sounds of their heavy bodies crashing through the forest. He hoped the sentries in the village would not hear them coming, but there was nothing Kwasin could do about it if they did. Perhaps the sentries would be so startled at seeing the giant and his ursine entourage emerge from the woods that they would be temporarily immobilized. It might even buy him enough time to launch his attack.

But Kwasin did not need to worry about being heard. Even before he reached the village, the sound of great revelry came to him through the trees. The jubilant shouting, laughter, clapping, and singing was loud enough to cover any noise made by the bears, and also of such volume that he began to worry it would disrupt the spell he had succeeded in casting over the animals with his song and the movements of the ritual dance. The soldiers must have been celebrating Adythne's coming execution upon the altar of Resu at sunrise.

By the time Kwasin and his companions arrived at the edge of the village clearing, the deep throoming of drums had erupted from inside the surrounding thorn boma. Kwasin tried to calm the bears as best he could with both song and gentle cooings, but his hairy cohorts were obviously upset by the noise and celebratory fires within the village. Knowing he had little time before the animals became so agitated that they would either turn on him or break for the woods, Kwasin went into action.

He began by removing himself a short distance from the bears and laying upon the ground a half-dozen torches saturated with the fat of an antelope he had speared a few days earlier. He had carried these from his camp in the same antelope-hide sack Adythne had used to hold the sacred she-bear pelt. Out of the same bag he removed tinder, a flint, and a piece of iron; the latter he had stolen from a farmer's hut on his journey across the island. Crouching on the ground, he struck flint against iron until the tinder caught a spark and smoldered into flame. He dipped one torch, then another, into the burning tinder. Then, having gathered up the unlit torches in an arm and holding the two burning ones in his other hand, he ran boldly into the clearing and stopped directly before the gate, in full sight of the sentry stationed atop the newly constructed watchtower.

The sentry stood up on the narrow platform on which he had been squatting and looked down at Kwasin, surprise apparent on his long face. For a moment, the man seemed too startled to act, but then he cried down at the revelers below. No one, however, seemed to be able to hear him over the drums and raucous clamor of the festivities.

Kwasin couldn't have hoped for better circumstances. While the man yelled down trying to catch the attention of the oblivious celebrants, Kwasin cast one of the burning torches at the wall of the thorn boma just to the left of the iron-reinforced gate. Thanks to a lack of rain over the past few days, the wall bloomed almost instantly with fire. He lit another torch with the one remaining in his hand and threw it onto the wall to the right of the gate, grinning wickedly as it caught fire just as quickly as his first throw.

A third torch went flaming into the village where he judged the hall of the Klakordeth was situated. Although it pained him deeply to set fire to the sacred lodge of his Bear brothers, he had earlier reconnoitered the camp and discovered the soldiers were using it as a barracks. He suspected many of these would be celebrating in the hall and hoped he might trap a great number of them in the burning building.

He lit the fourth torch and hurtled it over the gate at the watchtower just as a soldier carrying a sling mounted the narrow deck and joined the sentry at the tower's top. Though the torch disappeared from view as it fell behind the top of the fifteen-foot-tall gate, Kwasin knew it must have landed and ignited the dry wood of the tower when the two men hastily abandoned the platform and began climbing down. Before passing from sight, the slinger paused and shook his fist angrily at Kwasin.

Quickly, Kwasin ignited the remaining torch and began whirling it in wide circles in unison with the torch already burning in his hand. He did this following the same motions he had employed in his training sessions with the bears over the past few days, having gotten the idea from the priestess Adythne, who had told him the bears had been taught to jump through hoops of fire during the annual festival days of Kho-wu. As he whirled the torches, Kwasin sang with all the passionate gusto he could summon his crude, part-improvised lyrics to the tune of the ancient folksong about Bear Mother.

Parbho, who in his mistress's absence seemed to have taken a special liking to Kwasin, was the first of the bears to emerge from the woods. He bounded up to Kwasin and stood up on his hind legs, as he had been taught to do, just as the bronze-plated wooden gate swung open. Behind the open gate, two dozen panicked-looking soldiers and villagers were stampeding forward. At the sight of the growling, upright bear that confronted them, those in front screamed and tried to turn back into the unbridled exodus pouring from the gate. Then all hell let loose as Parbho's dark-furred friends gamboled out of the woods and followed their brother's example, rearing up on their hind legs directly before the mass of fleeing, panic-stricken humans. Still bellowing his bawdy song, Kwasin swung both of the burning torches simultaneously forward in the direction of the gate. This was the motion he had used to signal the bears during their training sessions to charge forward and leap between two blazing practice fires.

Again, Parbho was the first to obey. He came down on all fours and bounded toward the gate at frightening speed. The soldiers and villagers tried to break to either side of the charging bear, but many were knocked to the ground and trampled by their terrified comrades. Others went down beneath the clawed feet of the eight-hundred-pound animal.

One man, an older fellow in priestly robes, kept his cool and stood to one side of the gate, shouting at Parbho in an authoritative tone to stay. He must have been one of the bears' trainers or was mimicking commands he had witnessed other trainers use with the animals. It was a valiant effort, Kwasin thought, but too late. Already Parbho was past the man and leaping between the burning walls into the village. And behind him, one after another, came the other bears.

Two soldiers broke from the chaotic mass of screaming fleers and ran directly for Kwasin, who threw his remaining torches in their faces. The action bought Kwasin enough time to unsling his ax from his shoulder and smash both of their skulls with a single swing of his weapon. Then he ran, roaring, his ax whirling, through the throng of frightened humans, following the last bear through the flame-ringed gate.

Inside the village walls chaos met him. Tongues of reddish-orange fire licked the night sky above the watchtower and totem hall. Hysterical villagers stood outside the hall shrieking frantic prayers at the deities to save those trapped inside. Though dark smoke billowed from the windows and doorways, a few of these ran heedlessly into the burning building after loved ones they believed to be inside. The bears were in a frenzy now; if they recognized any of the villagers who had once trained and fed them, they did not show it. The spirit guides were angry, and many lay dead or horribly mauled beneath their great fangs and claws.

Suddenly, the wind gusted from the west and the flames from the hall of the Klakordeth swept out over the gulf separating the building from the village's stockaded quarter. Kwasin swore. The faithful of Kho who had resisted the invading soldiers were still penned up in the stockade. Almost instantly, the cedar poles that walled in the prisoners—baked dry from the recent hot spell—began crackling with rapidly spreading flames.

Kwasin made for the stockade but found himself confronted on all sides by panicked villagers and soldiers. He roared like a demon and swung his ax in an attempt to clear a path before him. The tactic worked to some degree, as many in the mob fell back before his mad charge. He must have made a terrible figure, he thought—a seven-foot-tall giant, cutting down his foes with his glittering ax and dressed in the sacred pelt, the snout of the dead she-bear jutting up behind his head like some dreadful cowl. Still, some of the soldiers tried to take him on, and one of these succeeded in slicing a nasty wound in Kwasin's thigh before the giant's great iron ax swept down and crushed the man's face.

The deeper into the village Kwasin passed, however, the fewer foes he found in his way, until, at last, he stood before the roaring inferno that was the stockade. Desperate shouts to unlock the gate came from the prisoners on the other side of the wall. Kwasin yelled back that he was trying to get them out, but that the stockade's gate, along with the entire the wall, was afire and he'd have to find another way. This did not stop the frantic pleading.

Great waves of sweltering heat singed the hair on Kwasin's arms and chest as he stalked up and down the fiery wall, looking for an opening in the flames. Finally, he stopped where the wall burned most furiously. There he stood for some time, peering into the blaze, trying to see how much of the wood in that section had been burned out. It was not easy to tell, but now the wind had shifted again and was sweeping the flames back into the pen where the prisoners were trapped. They would not survive much longer.

Again, he swore. Then, drawing the sacred pelt protectively over his head and torso, he barreled headlong into the hellish conflagration.

Kwasin choked on the dense, sickeningly sweet cedar smoke as he crashed heavily into half-charred timbers. The wall held, though it had buckled under the impact of his ax, which he had swung before him as he ran. He roared as the sacred pelt burned and crackled, the flames searing his back and shoulders. He fought to breathe.

Again, he swung his ax. This time, the burned-out cedar posts splintered. Screaming wrathful obscenities at Klykwo, the goddess of fire, Kwasin shouldered his way through to the other side of the wall.

For a moment, he could see nothing through the thick, black smoke that sought to smother him. Then the wind shifted yet again, blowing the scorching flames and choking smoke to the south, away from the prisoners' enclosure.

He tore off the still-burning bear pelt and threw it on the ground. Then he bent over and began coughing uncontrollably. When he looked up between coughs, a frightened-looking Adythne was standing before him. She looked distraught at seeing the remains of the sacred she-bear pelt smoldering on the ground, but then she grinned.

"It is as the old she-bear spirit told me in my dream! He who wore her pelt into battle would be invincible! Even fire would not touch him!"

The painful reddish burns all over Kwasin's body and the gruesome wound in his thigh argued against the priestess's assertion, but he could say nothing to refute her. He was still too busy coughing.

While Kwasin was recovering, a large group of prisoners came up behind Adythne, their frightened faces straining to look hopeful as they regarded the newly arrived giant.

"Quickly," Adythne said. She took Kwasin by the hand and began leading him back from the fiery wall, motioning her people to follow. "If the winds shift again," she said to Kwasin, "we'll all die beneath the flames and smoke. You, O Giant Bear Man, must use your gleaming ax and break through the stockade's outer wall!"

Though his lungs felt like they had been raked repeatedly with a rusting iron file, Kwasin accompanied the priestess to the outlying wall and began chopping at it with his ax. After a wearisome effort, and not a few glances back at the burning enclosure to motivate him, Kwasin succeeded in hewing down three cedar poles near their bases, creating a wide enough space for him and the prisoners to pass through.

Kwasin and Adythne in the lead, the group ran across the clearing and assembled in the woods a short distance from the village. Here the priestess gathered the escapees about her. These amounted, all told, to about sixty men, women, and children, though Kwasin estimated that perhaps only twenty-five of them might make able warriors.

"Though we are all tired," Adythne said to the group, "we must strike the enemy while they are routed! We cannot falter now when our victory over the sun worshipers is so near! We must reenter the village and get weapons from the armory." To Kwasin, she said, "The weapons are stored in an outbuilding in the southeast corner of the village, untouched by flames."

"What of the spirit guides?" a man asked, his worried face making it clear he had no desire to reenter the blazing village. "They have been angered and will eat us!"

Adythne scowled at the man. "It is the spirit guides who have freed us, Tethwa. They will not harm the faithful. And if Nakendar's children do devour us, our flesh will only strengthen them as they rise up to slay the enemies of Kho."

Tethwa grumbled something beneath his breath, but he shook his head in obeisance to his priestess.

Kwasin, for his part, did not relish the idea of returning to the hellhole that was Q"okwoqo any more than Tethwa. But he had come this far against staggering odds. Why not, one way or another, see it through to the end?

After a deep sigh and a silent prayer to Kho, Kwasin led the party back to the fiery main gate.

When dawn broke, few of the survivors of the previous night's devastation were happy. Q"okwoqo lay in ruins. The longhouse of the Klakordeth, many huts and outbuildings, the stockade, and a long stretch of the defensive wall had all been reduced to little more than ash and smoldering cinders. Villagers and soldiers alike stood about looking tired and dejected, their feet and hands stained gray-black with soot.

During the night, Kwasin had succeeded in reentering the village and recovering the weapons from the armory, and with these he led a guerrilla force against the soldiers who had regrouped outside the walls. Many of these men fled into the forest upon being attacked, but Kwasin and his band of twenty men and four women slingers managed to hole up a number of soldiers in the village. These had huddled in an area not beset by fire, deciding to wait it out there until morning rather than risk being killed by the guerrillas in the dark.

Now, as Kwasin and Adythne entered through the main gate in the dawn light, the soldiers looked up as if their very souls sought to flee their bodies. When Adythne began hurling holy curses at them, they bolted for the main gate and fled into the woods. Kwasin, utterly exhausted and relieved that he did not have to fight them, only laughed at the men as they ran past and shouted a number of disparaging epithets about the manhood of Minruth's soldiers.

After the soldiers and a handful of traitorous villagers had been chased into the woods, Kwasin accompanied the priestess as she poked about in the ashes searching for the remains of the sacred she-bear pelt. Finally, looking defeated, Adythne sat down on a half-burned post.

"It is no use," she said. "The sacred pelt has returned to the spirit world." Then Adythne's smoke-reddened, dark-circled eyes brightened. "But not all is lost. By a divine miracle of the Bear God himself, the spirit guides have all escaped the flames and now wander the woods. You, O Kwasin, will help me round them up, and then, with your ax, you can help my people cut down enough lumber to rebuild the totem hall. And when you have finished constructing it, you will lead a glorious dance in the new hall, after which I shall take you into my hut and show you my gratitude."

Kwasin sighed heavily. The priestess was certainly beautiful and the thought of the reward waiting for him in her hut was, without question, enticing. But he knew staying here and rebuilding the village was not in his future.

He did, however, have one last chore he felt obligated to perform before he left the valley of Q"okwoqo.

The evening before Kwasin took his leave of the priestess and her village, Kho and Resu pealed the heavens with great blinding flashes of lightning and fearsome claps of thunder as they waged war against one another. Who won the battle, Kwasin could not say, but the heavenly tumult only strengthened his resolve for the task that lay ahead.

The next morning Kwasin ascended the steep, rain-sodden slope overlooking the local hot spring. The climb was a treacherous one. The ground, powdery and brittle from the recent dry spell, had given way in many places to small mudslides. Twice, Kwasin lost his hold and slid painfully down the face of the rocky escarpment. But he was determined. He had a debt to repay.

At last, he pulled himself up over the ledge that jutted out from the slope before Old Father Nakendar's cave. Kwasin stood up and examined the boulder that blocked the entrance. The size of the great stone was daunting. He could not begin to guess its weight, but it was certainly more than even his prodigious strength might hope to move.

But he had an idea. If he could not move the boulder by himself, perhaps Great Kho, goddess of the earth, could give him a little help.

He unslung his ax and began assailing the dirt at the base of the boulder with the weapon's massive iron head. Soon, the earth began to give way.

Too late, Kwasin realized the flaw in his plan. After several swings of his ax, the ledge as a whole—already weakened from the recent downpour on dry soil—began to crumble beneath his feet.

He fell to his knees as the ground on which he stood yielded, the ax falling out of his grip and tumbling end over end down the escarpment. The great boulder groaned as it teetered forward, the soil beneath it sieving down the slope in great rivers of earth. Then, the boulder gave.

Kwasin kicked off just before the ledge completely collapsed, barreling his chest into the sharp rocks that rimmed the lower edge of the newly opened cave entrance. There he hung, his dust-covered, muscular arms thrust out over the edge, clinging with the barest of holds to the face of the escarpment. For a few moments, he could still hear the roar of the boulder as it wreaked havoc on the slope.

Now the lower edge of the cave's base began to crumble beneath his weight. He slipped down another foot before desperately flailing out and finding another hold.

He looked down. The landslide resulting from the great boulder's tumble had sloughed off a huge portion of the slope directly below him, a deep and narrow gouge that dropped fifty feet to the rock-strewn base of the escarpment.

Again, dirt crumbled and he felt his hold giving way.

He breathed a prayer to Kho. Soon he would see Sisisken's terrible face and be led down to her shadowy underworld. He only hoped the people of Q"okwoqo would from time to time sacrifice a bull or a goat to his spirit so that he would not hunger. If they did not, who would?

Something warm gripped his wrist. An overpowering, rank bear smell saturated the dusty air. Suddenly, he felt himself being pulled upward as the earth crumbled beneath him. Then, he was sitting on the firm ground inside the cave, peering through a cloud of sunlit dust and out over the rocky scape. In the distance lay the clear and steaming turquoise waters of the sacred spring.

Although it took all his will to do so, Kwasin turned and looked up at the towering dark form beside him. When he did, he gasped, his heart pounding.

The thing that met Kwasin's eyes smiled down at him. Or it might have been a grimace. It was hard to tell with those terrible teeth and the unnerving, red-rimmed, all-brown eyes. Its jaws protruded, more than a man's but less than an ape's. Still, the face was unmistakably bearlike, and when the creature spoke a single word, Kwasin gasped again, though he did not at first understand it.

Then the hairy form stepped to the rim of the cave and lowered itself gracefully over the edge. Kwasin watched, stupefied, as the creature climbed slowly but nimbly down the rock-tumbled slope to the western side of the great abyss, finding holds where Kwasin could discern none. When it reached the bottom of the escarpment, it headed southwest, toward the deep mountains. Finally, it disappeared in the dark trees.

Kwasin's heart went on beating heavily as he sat for a great while at the mouth of the cave looking out over the spring. Eventually, a wide smile stretched across his face. Though the word spoken by the Old Father had been strangely pronounced, Kwasin believed he understood it at last.

His mother had once told him, after all, that divine blood ran in his veins, though she had not elaborated on the matter.

Yes, there could be no mistaking it.

The Bear God had called him "Brother."

ADDENDUM 1
THE WORLD OF KHOKARSA

The Khokarsan Calendar

Philip José Farmer

THE NINE-YEAR GREAT CYCLE:

1. Year of the Fish-Eagle
2. Year of the Hippopotamus
3. Year of the Green Parrot
4. Year of Gahete the Hero
5. Year of the Sea Otter
6. Year of the Horned Fish
7. Year of the Honeybee
8. Year of the Millet
9. Year of Wenqath the Hero

The Khokarsan year begins on the vernal equinox (our March 21). The year is divided into twelve months of thirty days each, with five "festival" days (Kho-wu days) at the end of the year. The week is ten days long. The month is named first, then the day.

1.	Sea-day	6.	Mountain-day
2.	Earth-day	7.	Cloud-day
3.	Moon-day	8.	Fire-day
4.	Tree-day	9.	Beer-day
5.	Bird-day	10.	Sleep-day

MONTHS (after Kho's daughters and sons):

1. Piqabes (goddess of the sea)
2. Sisisken (goddess of the underworld and death)
3. Qawo (goddess of healing and birth)
4. Khukly (goddess of birds)
5. Wasu (goddess of mountains)
6. Resu (god of the sun, rain, and war)
7. Sahhindar (god of gifts, plants, bronze, and time)
8. Adeneth (goddess of sexual passion and madness)
9. Klykwo (goddess of fire)
10. Bhukla (goddess of war before usurped by Resu, patron goddess of Towina)
11. Nanumim (goddess of floods)
12. Lahla (goddess of the moon)

THE PLANTS OF KHOKARSA

PHILIP JOSÉ FARMER

A hunter or forager needs roughly twenty square kilometers to support him. Under cultivation, the same area can sustain six thousand people. If men were still dependent on hunting and food-gathering, the earth could not support more than thirty million. In the upper Old Stone Age, around 12,000 B.C., it is doubtful that there were a million people over the entire earth. Some have estimated it as closer to a hundred thousand. Not until the Agricultural Revolution (the cultivation of plants and domestication of beasts) around 8000 B.C. did the human population begin to increase.

The area around the two great seas of Central Africa had abundant fish and bird and animal life. But it was remarkably devoid of plant life edible for men. There were no plants suitable for the Agricultural Revolution. Almost all of the plants which we think of as African were brought into Central Africa in fairly recent times. Thus, from what we know today, the Khokarsan civilization could never have arisen.

This novel postulates, however, that plants suitable for agriculture did exist around the northern sea (the Kemu on the map) sometime soon after 12,000 B.C. That they were not present in 7000 B.C. can be accounted for by two reasons. One, the Great Cataclysm destroyed the civilization and started the drainage of the two seas. Two, number one would have been enough to see the extinction of those plants which depend upon man to survive. But the change in climate made the northern sea area arid, and many of the plants that would have survived without man perished in the desert climate. The southern area became covered over with jungle and rain forest and savannas, and this change exterminated plants which could not survive in this environment.

The man known as Sahhindar (later deified) seems to have brought in many plants from the southern shore of the Mediterranean and from the Near East. He taught the peoples on the northern shore of the Kemu how to develop cereal plants through hybridization of grasses and how to cultivate these hybrids.

The plants which he introduced are as follows:

Emmer, which belongs to the wheat genus *Triticum dicoccoides.*

Millet, of the tribe *Paniceae.* The Khokarsan millet was related to the present African millet, *Pennisetum spicatum.* Millet stands between wheat and rice in protein content, and unleavened bread and beer can be made from it. The Khokarsans also developed a pearl millet, related to *Pennisetum glaucum*, which was a rainy season crop.

Sorghum, *Andropogon sorghum.* Both this and the millets above are derived polyphetically from hybridization of a small number of wild African species. These species were wild, however, in a much later period and may have been descended from millet and sorghum which reverted to type after the Great Cataclysm. Whatever the truth, whether they were present in 12,000 B.C. or brought in by Sahhindar, Khokarsan religion stated that Sahhindar had brought them in. From sorghum are made bread, beer, porridge, cakes, and pastes.

Papyrus, *Cyperus papyrus.* From the head of this plant, garlands for the shrines of the gods and goddesses. The wood of the root can be used for fuel or made into various utensils. From the stem are made sails, boats, mats, cloth, cords, and writing materials. Sandals and tow for calking the seams of ships can be made from it. Its pith can be cooked or eaten raw.

Possibly, this existed on the shores and in the swamps along the northern sea when the first people entered this area. But, again, religion stated that Sahhindar brought papyrus in.

Flax, probably derived from the wild form *Linum hispanicum*, native to the Mediterranean and Near East regions. The Khokarsans made linen cloth, flax paper, and linseed oil from varieties of this plant. The oil was also prepared to make a mucilaginous cake for cattle feed.

A type of radish, used as a condiment.

Celery, related to the *Apium graveolens* which grew wild on the Mediterranean shores.

A sugarbeet, developed from an early variety like mangel-würzel.

Parsley, *Petroselinum crispum*, a biennial plant used as a garnish.

Pomegranate, *Punica granatum*, undoubtedly brought in by Sahhindar from the Mid-East, probably from the area known today as Iran. It has a fruit with a slightly acid sweet flavor, and the sweet syrup grenadine was prepared from its fruit.

Peas and garden beans also seem to have been imported by Sahhindar.

Plants indigenous to the northern sea area were:

A large tuberous root, a rhizome, distantly related to the yam and called a "yam" in this series.

Various types of pondweed. Several species had become adapted to the open waters along the coasts and provided food for ducks and other waterfowl.

Olive trees. These grew native on the lower ranges of the northern mountains (the Saasares and the Saasawuwos) and transplants were made to the highlands around the upper part of the northern sea. To bear fruit, olive trees require winter temperatures near freezing but not lower than 50° F. Raw olives can't be eaten because of a bitter glycoside, but processing gives pickled olives, and olive oil was also an important trade commodity.

Lavender and rosemary. These low evergreen shrubs were indigenous in the foothills of the two northern mountain ranges. They provided perfumes.

Pine trees. Useful for wood and resin, and its cones make bread or hog food.

The incense-tree (family Burseraceae). From this comes aromatic gums, balsams, and resins. The latter is used for salves and medicines, including vermifuges, perfumes, and incenses.

Laurel trees, *Laurus nobilis*, native to north Africa. The leaves, when chewed, made an intoxicant for the oracular priestesses and the orgiastic female totem-groups.

Mushrooms.

A species of green cabbage.

Hollyhock, *Althaea rosea*, raised in the highlands. This is a beautiful green plant, inedible but esthetic.

The oak.

Boxwood, related to *Buxus balearica*. This makes musical instruments and various decorative objects turned on wood lathes. It is also used for inlaying, for rulers and mathematical instruments, for small carvings, and makes attractive plantings.

The grape. Several species of the genus *Vitis* grew on the highlands of the northern mountain ranges. *Vitus* was, in the historical times, indigenous to the northern temperate regions, but it must be remembered that the Ahaggar and Tibesti middle heights had in this late Ice Age a temperate climate. From *Vitis vinifera* the Khokarsans made wine; other types of vine produced grapes and raisins. Because of their expense, grapes and wine were confined to use by the upper classes. Beer from millet and sorghum were the necessary preference of the lower classes.

While we're speaking of alcoholic drinks, we might as well note the *s"okoko* (water of life). The production of this was limited to a small area in the highlands of the mountains forming the back country (the present Cameroons) of the Klemqaba. The principal ingredients were emmer mash and springwaters which had seeped through red granite formations and then through peat moss. (The latter no longer exists in the warmed-up climate of today.) This made what was, in essence, a type of scotch, though modern palates would find it unendurably harsh. The Klemqaba liked it, however.

Plants imported from West Africa by the expedition under Nankar, circa 10,900 B.C.:

The red berry called *mowometh*. This is *Dioscoreophyllum cumminsi*, a juicy little red berry native to West Africa and only recently discovered. (See *Signature Magazine*, March, 1973.) This is the sweetest natural product known, three thousand times sweeter than sucrose (sugar) on a weight-for-weight basis. It is a protein, not a carbohydrate, and is the first protein to elicit a sweet taste response in man.

Hibiscus esculenta, known more familiarly as gumbo or okra. Its partially ripened fruit can be cooked like asparagus, pickled, or cut up for soups and broths. Its seeds can be cured and dried to make a sort of coffee bean. The leaves are used for poultices.

African mahogany, *Khaya senegalensis*.

Ebony, of the genus *Diospyros*. Its hardwood qualities are well known, but bees make a distinctive and delicious honey from nectar in its flowers.

Mead from bee-honey was a drink popular to all classes but it was more expensive than beer.

Note: "Banana" is an African word, but the plant seems to have originated in Asia and to have spread at an early time to the Pacific islands and West Africa. The Nankar expedition was far too early to have encountered the genus *Musa*.

A Guide to Khokarsa

Christopher Paul Carey

CAST OF CHARACTERS

Abeth Lalila's daughter by the hero Wi.

Abisila Commandant of a fort near Miklemres.

Adythne Chief priestess of the village of Q"okwoqo on the island of Khokarsa; sister of Madekha.

Awikloe Chief priestess of the Temple of Lupoeth in Opar.

Awines Genius born in Dythbeth in 11,153 B.C. (447 A.T.) who conceived for the first time algebra, the science of linguistics, knowledge of the circulation of blood, the invention of the catapult, Greek fire, wooden blocks for printing, the water clock, the magnifying glass, and a solar calendar, among many other inventions, theories, and formulations.

Awineth 1. Daughter of Minruth IV and Wimimwi, born in 10,031 B.C. (1569 A.T.), who became chief priestess of Khokarsa following the death of Wimimwi; 2. chief priestess of Khokarsa in 11,550 B.C. (50 A.T.) who established a chronology that begins with the completion of a temple to Kho in 11,600 B.C. (1 A.T.).

Bessem Exiled son of the hero Keth. Founder of Mibessem.

Bhako Kwasin's bard; a native of Dythbeth.

Bhaqeth One of the hero twins of Khokarsa; with his twin, Klaqeth, he slew the mighty *ko'bok'ul"ikadeth*, a giant, three-horned, armor-cowled rhinoceros in a valley to the east of Sakawuru. One of Minruth's great warriors.

Bhaseko Captain of the galley that brings Hadon to the Great Games of Klakor.

Bohami Major from a fort near Miklemres.

D"otipoeth General from Miklemres.

Daka Daughter of King Mahedana of the Wan"so.

Damoken Competitor in the Great Games of Klakor in 10,011 B.C. (1589 A.T.). A tall, thin youth from Minanlu and a superb swordsman.

Darbha Priestess of the Temple of Kho in Opar.

Dedar Hadon's sister; daughter of Kumin and Pheneth. Moved from Opar to the mining settlement of Kartenkloe with her husband, Naquth.

Desweth Legendary figure who, along with his brother Noqawi, was responsible for the now-obsolete custom that a younger brother should sacrifice himself for his older brother.

Dykeko Lower-echelon palace priest in Dythbeth.

Gahete First person to land on the island of Khokarsa (11,800 B.C.). Entombed on the side of the volcano, Khowot.

Gahoruphi Soldier in Rebha loyal to the forces of Kho.

Gamori King of Opar; husband of Queen Phebha. Ascended the throne after the previous king was slain by pirates in the tunnels beneath the city; overthrown by Hadon.

Gawethmi Captain in the Mukhan army.

Gobhu Competitor from Dythbeth in the Great Games of Klakor in 10,011 B.C. (1589 A.T.).

Gokasis Pirate king of Mikawuru who captured Opar in 10,448 B.C. (1152 A.T.).

Hadon Son of Kumin and Pheneth. Competitor from Opar in the Great Games of Klakor in 10,011 B.C. (1589 A.T.) and the cousin of Kwasin.

Hala 1. Legendary bardess who composed the first epic poem, *The Song of Gahete*, in 11,530 B.C. (70 A.T.).; 2. priestess of the Temple of Kho in Opar during the reign of Queen Phebha.

Hahinqo General in command of Dythbeth's army.

Heliqo Priestess-doctor who in 10,061 B.C. (1539 A.T.) discovered the connection between malaria and mosquitoes.

Hewako Wrestler from Opar and Hadon's nemesis in the Great Games of Klakor in 10,011 B.C. (1589 A.T.).

Hiindar Queen of Khokarsa circa 10,460 B.C. (1140 A.T.); daughter of Queen Pwymnes and wife of King Klakor.

Hinokly Sole survivor of an expedition sent by Minruth to explore the shores of the Ringing Sea (the Mediterranean Sea and North Atlantic) beyond the Wild Lands. Encountered Sahhindar, Paga, and Lalila while on his journey.

Hoseko Competitor in the Great Games of Klakor in 10,011 B.C. (1589 A.T.). A short, powerful man from Bawaku.

Kadyth One of Minruth's great warriors; known as Kadyth the Silent.

Kaheli Customs officer from the fort at Nangukar.

Kagaga Competitor in the Great Games of Klakor in 10,011 B.C. (1589 A.T.). His name means "Raven" in Khokarsan.

Kaminsuh General Wahesa's Lieutenant in the Mukhan army.

Karsuh Priestess of the Temple of Piqabes in the pile city of Rebha.

Kebiwabes Bard assigned to Hadon's expedition to the Wild Lands.

Kemneth Priestess of the Temple of Lupoeth in Opar. Attended the temple school with Hadon.

Keruphe General of the Ninth Army. Loyal to Awineth.

Keth Hero from Kenesu who discovered the strait leading from the Kemu into the southern sea in 11,110 B.C. (490 A.T.).

Kethna Hero who circumnavigated the Kemuwopar (then called the Kemuketh) in 10,832 B.C. (768 A.T.). Founder of the city of Kethna.

Kethsuh One of Minruth's majors.

Khonan King of Khokarsa in 11,400 B.C. (200 A.T.) who led an expeditionary fleet that founded the port of Siwudawa in the country of the Klemsuh, thus marking the beginning of a long series of campaigns against the Klemsuh of rural areas.

Khosin Competitor from Towina in the Great Games of Klakor in 10,011 B.C. (1589 A.T.).

Khukly Competitor in the Great Games of Klakor in 10,011 B.C. (1589 A.T.).

A GUIDE TO KHOKARSA

Klaqeth One of the hero twins of Khokarsa; with his twin, Bhaqeth, he slew the mighty *ko'bok'ul''ikadeth*, a giant, three-horned, armor-cowled rhinoceros in a valley to the east of Sakawuru. One of Minruth's great warriors.

Klakor King of Khokarsa and winner of the first Great Games in 10,460 B.C. (1140 A.T.), which thereafter were named the Great Games of Klakor in his honor. Began construction of the Great Tower of Kho and Resu.

Klamsweth Giant hero from Khokarsa's past.

Klyhy Head priestess at Nangukar, the port of Opar, and the mother of Hadon's son, Kohr.

Kohr Hadon's son by the priestess Klyhy.

Komseth One of Minruth's soldiers tasked with capturing Awineth on the Isle of Karneth.

Komwi Soldier in Kwasin's guard.

Kumin Hadon's father; husband of Pheneth. Once an honored *numatenu*, he was reduced to being a floorsweeper in the temple of Kho after losing an arm while attempting to defend his king against outlaws in the tunnels below Opar.

Kwamim Legendary poet who composed Khokarsa's greatest epics, including *The Song of Kethna* and *The Song of Rimasweth*. Taken prisoner by the pirate king Gokasis in 10,427 B.C. (1173 A.T.), but later rescued by the hero Rimasweth in 10,420 B.C. (1180 A.T.).

Kwasin Hadon's giant cousin; the son of Hadon's aunt, Wimake. Exiled from the land by the oracular priestess of the temple of Kho at Dythbeth for ravaging a priestess and killing some temple guards, though he will be permitted to return when Kho so decrees.

Kwobis Competitor in the Great Games of Klakor in 10,011 B.C. (1589 A.T.)

Kwona Exceptionally long-legged competitor in the Great Games of Klakor in 10,011 B.C. (1589 A.T.) who was from Qethruth and competed against Hadon in the long jump.

Lalila Woman whose people lived to the north of the Wild Lands beyond the Ringing Sea. Along with Paga, she was befriended by and placed under the protection of Sahhindar. When Hinokly returned to Khokarsa, Minruth decreed that Hadon must bring Lalila, her daughter Abeth, and Paga back to Khokarsa. She is tall, violet-eyed, and golden-haired. Also known as the Witch-from-the-Sea and the Risen-from-the-Sea; Lalila means "moon of change" in Khokarsan. See H. Rider Haggard's *Allan and the Ice-Gods* for her earlier history.

Likapoeth King Gamori's general.

Lupoeth Priestess-heroine who explored the southern sea, discovering gold-, silver-, and diamond-bearing clay at the future site of Opar in 10,810 B.C. (790 A.T.), and who later came to be regarded as a demigoddess. The Gulf of Lupoeth on the island of Khokarsa is named after her. See *Exiles of Kho* by Christopher Paul Carey (Meteor House, 2012) for the story of her adventures.

Madekha Priestess of the temple of Terisikokori at the village of Kaarkor on the island of Khokarsa; sister of Adythne.

Madymeth Former king of Opar, and Gamori's great-great-grandfather.

Mahedana King of the Wan"so.

Methsuh Hadon's brother; son of Kumin and Pheneth.

Mineqo Priestess of a fort near Miklemres.

Minruth I King of Khokarsa who in 10,866 B.C. (734 A.T.) refused to honor the age-old custom of sacrifice of the king after nine years of rule and instituted the custom of sacrificing a substitute. He proclaimed Resu to be the equal of Kho and began the long struggle between the priestesses of Kho and the priests of Resu.

Minruth IV King of Khokarsa who ascended throne in 10,049 B.C. (1551 A.T.) after winning the Great Games. Married Demakwa (first wife, d. 10,034 B.C. [1566 A.T.]) and Wimimwi (second wife, d. 10,013 B.C. [1587 A.T.]). He is a descendant of the Klemsaasa, who seized the throne and did away with the custom of sacrificing the king after he had ruled nine years. Minruth is fifty-six years old at the time Hadon competes in the Great Games in 10,011 B.C. (1589 A.T.). Also known as Minruth the Mad.

Miwanes Hero of Sakawuru. One of Minruth's great warriors.

Mokomgu Chamberlain of Awineth.

Mokwaten Tadoku's second-in-command; from Qethruth.

Moqowi Competitor from Mukha in the Great Games of Klakor in 10,011 B.C. (1589 A.T.).

Mumoma Klemqaba priestess on Hadon's expedition to the Wild Lands.

Nagota Man from Bawaku, one of Hadon's scouts and hunters on his journey to the Wild Lands.

Nanwot Chief priestess in 11,600 B.C. (1 A.T.) who controlled the mead-making industry.

Naquth Husband of Hadon's sister, Dedar. Resident of the mining settlement of Kartenkloe.

Nelahnes Priestess who served as chief keeper of the Temple of Kho in Dythbeth.

Nemusaketh Admiral in command of Dythbeth's navy.

Neqokla Priestess of the Temple of Lupoeth in Opar. Formerly the keeper of the Chamber of the Moon in the Temple of Kho in Opar.

Noqawi Legendary figure who, along with his brother Desweth, was responsible for the now-obsolete custom that a younger brother should sacrifice himself for his older brother.

Nowiten Captain of Awineth's personal bodyguard.

Onami Doctor in Hadon's company during his journey to the Wild Lands.

oracle of Khokarsa The oracular priestess of the Temple of Kho at Khokarsa; went into hiding in the mountains above the capital after Minruth IV's revolt.

Paga A one-eyed dwarf from north of the Wild Lands beyond the Ringing Sea, and protector of Lalila after the death of the hero Wi. His true name is Pag, though this is pronounced "Paga" by most native Khokarsan speakers. See H. Rider Haggard's *Allan and the Ice-Gods* for his earlier history and the story of how he came to craft his ax.

Phebha Queen of Opar; wife of King Gamori.

Phekly Priestess at a fort near Mukha.

Pheneth Hadon's mother; wife of Kumin.

Phimeth Hadon's paternal uncle. Known as "the greatest wielder of a *tenu* in Opar." The young Hadon and Kwasin lived with Phimeth in his cliff-side home in the caves near Opar.

Phoeken Minruth's genius general.

Poedy Admiral in charge of Minruth IV's navy.

Pwamkhu Kwasin's godfather; husband of Wimake's best friend.

Pwymnes Chief priestess of Khokarsa in 10,460 B.C. (1140 A.T.). She established the Law of Pwymnes, stating that the victor of the Great Games became the husband of the chief priestess (if she accepted him) and was crowned king of Khokarsa. Games occurred when the old king or the chief priestess died. However, the reigning king could keep his kingship if he could induce the dead wife's daughter to marry him, or if she lacked a daughter, the nearest relative to assume the priestess's throne. Any man was eligible to compete in the Great Games as long as he was not a slave, a neanderthaloid, or a Klemqaba.

Qabho One of Minruth's soldiers tasked with capturing Awineth on the Isle of Karneth.

Qanaketh King of Mukha.

Qasin Chief of the Red Sea Otter clan of the K'ud"em'o.

Rewenkwo Captain of the *Taro*.

Rigo Taro's beautiful lover.

Rimasweth Hero of Khokarsa who in the years between 10,423 B.C. (1177 A.T.) and 10,420 B.C. (1180 A.T.) rescued the poetess Kwamim and slew Gokasis after the pirate king captured Opar.

Riwaphe Captain in Minruth's army in command of an advance company of soldiers invading the Saasamaro on the island of Khokarsa.

Roteka King of Dythbeth; husband of Queen Weth.

Rowaku Sergeant in Kwasin's guard.

Ruseth Young sailor from Bhabhobes who invented the fore-and-aft sail; captain of the *Wind-Spirit*.

Ruwodeth King of Khokarsa who crushed a revolt in Miklemres in 11,450 B.C. (150 A.T.).

Sembes Lieutenant in the guard of the Temple of Resu in Opar. Hadon's childhood playmate and a competitor in Opar's Lesser Games in 10,012 B.C. (1588 A.T.).

Seqo Member of an outlaw band in the wilderness beyond the city of Khokarsa.

Sahhindar Also known as the Gray-Eyed God, the Archer God, and the god of plants, of bronze, and of Time. Legend has it that he stole Time from his mother Kho and that is why she exiled him from the land, dooming him to wander on the edge of the world. Sahhindar was said to have been able to travel in time before Kho took away his power. Though revered as a god, Sahhindar makes no claim to divinity, and he is undoubtedly the time traveler John Gribardsun from Philip José Farmer's novel *Time's Last Gift.*

Simari Priestess of the fleet that brought Hadon to the Great Games of Klakor in Khokarsa.

Sekoko Famed boxer from before Hadon's time. Known as "the great Sekoko."

Suguqateth Chief priestess of the Temple of Kho at Akwaphi.

Tadoku A native of Dythbeth, Tadoku is about forty years old at the time of *Hadon of Ancient Opar,* a *numatenu,* a major in the Fifth Army, and second-in-command of Hadon's galley on his mission to retrieve Lalila, Abeth, and Paga from the Wild Lands.

T'agoqo Chief priest of the village of Kaarkor on the island of Khokarsa.

Tahesa One of Minruth's soldiers tasked with capturing Awineth on the Isle of Karneth.

Taphiru High priest of Resu in Dythbeth.

Taro Hadon's friend from Opar, and a competitor in the Great Games of Klakor in 10,011 B.C. (1589 A.T.).

Tenlem Member of an outlaw band in the mountains above the city of Khokarsa.

Tenswath Loyalist to the cause of the Great Goddess planted among King Minruth's guard by Awineth; brother of Gobhu, who represented Dythbeth in the Great Games of Klakor in 10,011 B.C. (1589 A.T.).

Tethwa Citizen of the village of Q"okwoqo in the Saasamaro on the island of Khokarsa.

Toekha Husband of Wimake and a prominent merchant in Dythbeth. He died in a skirmish with bandits while Wimake was pregnant with Kwasin after serving as a divine prostitute in the Temple of Khukhaken in Dythbeth.

Toenuseth King of Dythbeth from 10,490 B.C. (1110 A.T.) to 10,478 B.C. (1122 A.T.). Set out to conquer the island of Khokarsa, but was killed by a spear thrown by the chief priestess of Khokarsa, thus discouraging the idea of kingship for many years.

Tswethphe Acolyte under Adythne at Q"okwoqo; Madekha's cousin.

Urudu Tracker under the command of King Mahedana of the Wan"so.

Wahesa General in command of Mukha's army.

Wakewa Old boxing trainer in Khokarsa who tries to enlist Hadon during the Great Games.

Wemqardo Soldier in the guard of the Temple of Kho in Opar.

Wenekaru Minruth's architect. Discovered a new type of lightweight brick to allow for the completion of the Great Tower in Khokarsa.

Wenqath Also known as the hero Wenqath. The ninth year of the Great Cycle is named after him.

Weth Queen of Dythbeth; wife of King Roteka.

Wi Deceased mate of Lalila and father of Abeth. See H. Rider Haggard's *Allan and the Ice-Gods* for his complete story.

Wiqa Competitor from Qaarquth in the Great Games of Klakor in 10,011 B.C. (1589 A.T.).

Wimake Sister of Phimeth and Kumin; mother of Kwasin. Died from snakebite.

Wimimwi Minruth's second wife (married 10,013 B.C. [1587 A.T.]), and Awineth's mother. She prophesied the destruction of Khokarsa if the priests failed to abandon their efforts to raise Resu's status to the level of supreme creator.

PEOPLES AND TRIBES

Gokako Apish slaves of Opar. The Gokako practiced group marriage and were known to be free with their wives. They were a short, squat, massively chested, and slant-browed people, i.e., Neanderthals.

K'ud"em'o People of the Sea Otter Totem who dwell on the coast below the city of Bawaku, as well as on colossal rafts that float across the Kemu.

Khoklem ("People of Kho.") A people who wandered down from the Saharan savannas to the shores of the northern inland sea sometime before 13,000 B.C. and eventually went on to settle the island of Khokarsa. Those of Khoklem stock tended to be short, snub-nosed, and thick-lipped; they had straight dark hair, and their skin was darker than that of the Klemsaasa. The Khoklem language, like the speech of the neanderthaloid tribes on the coastline northward of the Strait of Keth, utilized click-consonants.

Klemkho Alternate name for the Khoklem.

Klemklakor Descendants of the Klemsaasa left behind in the Saasares by Minruth I in 10,875 B.C. (725 A.T.).

Klemqaba ("People of the Goat.") Wild half-neanderthaloid, half-human people who lived in or near the Strait of Keth and were sub-jugated and forced to pay tribute by King Minruth IV. They were short and broad, and blue and green tattoos decorated their skins. Their standard was a carved figure of Kho as Goat-Headed Mother.

Klemreskom ("People of the Fish-Eagle.") Tribe of Khoklem who first landed on the island of Khokarsa in 11,800 B.C.

Klemsaasa ("People of the Mountains.") Tall, hazel-eyed people, often with long, beaked noses, and sometimes having red hair and freckles, who first appeared in the mountains north of Miklemres in 11,450 B.C. (150 A.T.). They seized the city of Khokarsa in 10,875 B.C. (725 A.T.), and their chief, becoming king of Kho-karsa, was the first to bear the name Minruth.

Klemsuh ("The Yellow People.") Group of people who drifted into the middle-eastern coast of the northern inland sea at about the same time as the Khoklem, sometime before 13,000 B.C. They had yellow-brown skins, straight and coarse dark hair, and slight epicanthic folds.

Nukaar Hairy half-men of the trees; paranthropoids.

numatenu "Heroes of the broad sword"; a warlike class of swords-men similar to the samurai. By custom, only the members of the *numatenu* were allowed to use the slightly curved, blunt-ended broadsword, although this was not strictly observed.

totems A sampling of the many diverse clans among the cultures inhabiting the shores of the two inland seas includes: the Ant Totem (Hadon's totem), the Bear Totem, the Beach Baboon Totem, the Crocodile Totem (Lupoeth's totem), the Fish-Eagle Totem, the Goat Totem, the Green Parrot Totem, the Leopard Totem, the Pig Totem, the Red Sea Otter Totem, and the Thunder Bear Totem (the Klakordeth, Kwasin's totem).

Wan"so Tribe from the Western Lands ruled by King Mahedana.

RELIGION AND FOLKLORE

Adeneth Goddess of sexual passion and madness.

Akwaphi Local river godling in the region around the town of Akwahpi on the island of Khokarsa.

Begetter of All Jewels Legendary diamond said to have been recovered from the wreck of the *Haken*, an infamous pirate ship that stalked the seas around the Strait of Keth. See Christopher Paul Carey's short story "A Kick in the Side" (*The Worlds of Philip José Farmer 1: Protean Dimensions*, Meteor House, 2010) for more information.

Besbesbes Goddess of bees and mead.

Bhukla Goddess of war before she was usurped by Resu. After Resu took her domain, she became goddess of the sword. Bhukla is the patron goddess of Towina.

Bikeda The ancient sun goddess, who eventually became the male god Resu.

C'ak'oguq"o Goddess of healing of the K'ud"em'o people.

Cold Snake, the Creature rumored to dwell in the thick mud of the subterranean river beneath Opar.

G'xsghaba'ghdi Goddess of the Gokako's forefathers.

Great Cycle, the Nine-year cycle of the Khokarsan calendar, represented by a fish-eagle, a hippopotamus, a green parrot, the hero Gahete, a sea otter, a horned fish, a honeybee, a millet plant, and the hero Wenqath.

holy prostitutes A Khokarsan woman who was not pregnant at the time of her first marriage, and had never before delivered, was required to serve as a prostitute in the temple of a deity for a period of one month. Conception as a result of this duty was regarded as being of divine origin, despite the fact that the latter-day Khokarsans understood the male sperm was responsible for conception.

Karneth Goddess of the oak, manifesting in the form of a half-woman, half-tree. She is the daughter of Kho.

Kasukwa Godling of the river that flows past Opar and empties into the Kemuwopar.

Kho The Great Mother goddess of the Khokarsan people. Also known as the "Creator and Replenisher of all things," "White Goddess," "Mother of All," "Goat-Headed Mother," "Bird-Headed Mother," etc. Kho is represented in the form of a steatopygic, huge-breasted woman, with the head of a fish-eagle, a parrot, a hippopotamus, or a goat.

Khukhaken The Leopard God, the divine consort of Khukha-qo.

Khukhaqo The Leopard Goddess, "Our Lady of the Leopard"; patron goddess of Dythbeth.

Khuklaqo The Shapeless Shaper.

Khukly Goddess of birds; "the heron goddess."

Klaklaku Ancient trickster-hero of the Thunder Bear Totem.

Klykwo Goddess of fire.

Konabasi Froglike demon said to lurk in the swamps near Dythbeth.

Kopoethken Presumably a goddess or a figure out of folklore. Hadon says, "Run as if Kopoethken herself was after your manhood, Kebiwabes!"

Lahhindar The Gray-Eyed Archer Goddess.

Lahla Goddess of the moon, Kho's fairest daughter; patroness of music and poetry.

M'adesin The Raven-Goddess.

M'agogobabi The mosquito demon.

Nakadeth Ancient hero who allegedly stole a pair of magical shoes from an evil spider and walked across the skies upside down so he could cross over a treacherous range of mountains.

Nakendar Great cave bear rumored to have laired in the caves near the village of Q"okwoqo in the Saasamaro on the island of Khokarsa for more than four hundred years.

Nanumim Goddess of floods.

Piqabes Goddess of the sea, green-eyed daughter of Kho. Also known as "the green-eyed Our Lady of the Kemu" and "Goddess of the Two Seas."

priestesses of Kho The clergy of the Great Goddess Kho. They often wore caps made of oval and circular gold pieces confining hair that was tied in a Psyche knot. Their high priestess was the queen of Khokarsa.

priests of Resu The clergy of the sungod Resu. They wore flowing, tassled, bright-yellow, scarlet-slashed robes and their heads were shaven except for stiff roaches of hair from the forehead to the nape of the neck, brushed and kept stiff and upright by eagle grease. After King Minruth IV's revolt, they sported mustaches and beards in defiance of ancient tradition. Their high priest was the king of Khokarsa.

Qawi Name of the first man created by Kho.

Qawo Goddess of healing and birth; "Our Lady of Healing."

Renamam'a Possibly a deity of iron or metal; upon seeing Sahhindar's steel knife, a hillman in Akwaphi exclaims, "By Renamam'a . . . !"

Resu God of the sun, rain, and war.

rosary String of prayer beads, utilized by Khokarsan priestesses and priests, as well as the common people.

Sahhindar The Gray-Eyed Archer God; the god of gifts, plants, bronze, and Time. See also the entry for Sahhindar in the Cast of Characters section above. For more on his backstory, see *Time's Last Gift* by Philip José Farmer.

sign of Kho (new) A sign of supplication to Kho signified by touching the forehead with the tips of the three longest fingers, then describing with them a circle that sweeps out and over the loins and ends on the forehead.

sign of Kho (old) A sign of supplication to Kho signified by touching the forehead with the tips of the three longest fingers, then touching them to the right breast, the genitals, the left breast, the forehead again, and ending up on the navel.

Sisisken Goddess of the underworld and death, Kho's eldest daughter; "the grim ruler of the shadow world."

Sleeper, the The god of Paga's people.

stone of C'ak'oguq"o Sacred healing stone of the K'ud"em'o, who had a prophecy that stated if the stone were ever lost, the two great inland seas would dry up.

Suhkwaneth Goddess of the scales.

Takomim Goddess of trade, thieves, and the left-handed.

Terisikokori Local python goddess worshiped in the village of Kaarkor on the island of Khokarsa.

Tesemines Goddess of the night.

W"uwos Goddess of the red-headed female eagle.

Wasu Goddess of mountains.

Wootla, the ("The Voices of the Moon.") Priestesses of the temples of the moon.

GEOGRAPHY AND LOCALITIES

Akwaphi Town in the valley of Kloepeth on the island of Khokarsa.

Asema Port city at the southern tip of the Gulf of Lupoeth on the island of Khokarsa.

Avenue of the Deities-as-Birds Broad avenue between Opar's inner gate and the Temple of Kho. So named for the rows of granite monoliths lining the walkway to the temple's entrance, the upper ends of which are carved into the shapes of deformed and exaggerated birds.

Awamuka Port city on the northwestern coast of the island of Khokarsa.

Bawaku Major port city on the western coast of the northern inland sea.

Bay of Boqawenqady Dythbeth's harbor.

Bay of Dythphida Far-western arm of the southern inland sea.

Beswakly River near Dythbeth that empties into the Bay of Boqawenqady.

Bhabhobes Seaside town on the island of Khokarsa.

Bohikly The Niger River, discovered by the expedition of Nankar in 10,915 B.C. (685 A.T.).

Boulevard of Khukly A thoroughfare in the city of Khokarsa.

Chamber of the Moon Sacred inner court of the Temple of Kho in Opar.

Door of the Nine Gigantic nonagonal door leading into the Temple of Kho in Opar.

Dythbeth Major port city on the western coast of the island of Khokarsa, and Kwasin's birth city. Known historically for its fierce independence, Dythbeth sided with the priestesses in the bloody war against King Minruth IV. Home to the Fifth Army.

Great Tower of Kho and Resu Immense ziggurat being constructed at the capital of the Khokarsan Empire, begun by Klakor in 10,460 B.C. (1140 A.T.). When Hadon witnessed it during the Great Games, its base was almost half a mile wide in diameter, with staggered stories that rose to almost five hundred feet.

Gulf of Gahete Long, narrow gulf on the island of Khokarsa stretching from the city of Khokarsa to the northern coast.

Gulf of Lupoeth Long, narrow gulf on the island of Khokarsa stretching from the city of Khokarsa to the southern coast. Named after the priestess-heroine Lupoeth.

Inn of the Red Parrot Inn at the town of Akwaphi on the island of Khokarsa.

Inner City Inner part of the city of Khokarsa, enclosed by high black granite walls.

Isle of Karneth Islet in a lake in the wilderness beyond the city of Khokarsa.

Isle of Lupoeth The landing place of the priestess-heroine Lupoeth during her exploration of the Kemuwopar (then called the Kemuketh). Later a white domed temple was erected there as a shrine to Lupoeth, and males were forbidden on the islet.

Kaarkor Village located at the foothills of the Saasanadar on the island of Khokarsa.

Kaarquth Major port city on Khokarsa's south-central coast.

Karhokokly River that runs past Dythbeth and empties into the Bay of Boqawenqady.

Karkoom Port village approximately four hundred miles up the coast from Qethruth, consisting of a population of approximately five hundred, and a cluster of huts and longhouses on stilts behind a stockade; situated at the end of a narrow harbor formed by two rocky peninsulas.

Kartenkloe New mining settlement in the time of Hadon and Kwasin, rich in copper and some gold, and heralded as the gateway to the southern savannas.

Kemu ("Great Water") Great northern inland sea of ancient Africa, located in what is now the Chad Basin.

Kemuketh ("Sea of Keth.") Old name for the Kemuwopar, the great southern inland sea of ancient Africa.

Kemuqoqano ("Ringing Sea.") See entry for Ringing Sea.

Kemuwopar Great southern inland sea of ancient Africa, originally called the Kemuketh but later renamed; located in what is now the Congo Basin.

Kethna City fifty miles east of the Strait of Keth. Kethna paid tribute to Khokarsa but required every merchant ship that passed through the Strait of Keth to pay a heavy tax for the privilege.

Khokarsa ("Tree of the Hill of Kho.") 1. Name of the empire spanning the two Central African seas at the end of the last Ice Age; 2. name of the island first discovered by the Khoklem hero Gahete of the Fish-Eagle Totem in 11,800 B.C., which later became the seat of the Khokarsan Empire; 3. name of the capital of the Khokarsan Empire on the island of Khokarsa; home to the Sixth Army.

Khosaasa Coastal mountain range northeast of the capital on the island of Khokarsa.

Khowot ("The Voice of Kho.") Great volcano on the island of Khokarsa just east of the capital city.

Kloepeth Twenty-mile-long valley in the mountains to the north of the city of Khokarsa.

Kunesu Port city on the southeastern coast of the island of Khokarsa. Home to the Ninth Army, which sided with Awineth during Minruth IV's revolt.

Mibessem Ancient city founded by Bessem, the exiled son of Keth, located in the lowlands (now marshlands) along the southern inland sea just beyond of the Strait of Keth.

Mikethna Alternate name for Kethna.

Miklemres City on the northern coast of the northern inland sea.

Minanlu City on southwestern coast of the island of Khokarsa.

Mineqo City located just east of the Gulf of Lupoeth on the island of Khokarsa.

Mikawuru Pirate city on the northwestern coast of the southern inland sea, founded in 10,757 B.C. (843 A.T.) by criminals and political refugees from across the northern inland sea. Also the name of an earlier pirate city located on the fjord coast northwest of the strait into the southern sea, founded by the hero Anesem and a group of Bawakans who escaped the occupation of Bawaku by King Madymin and his army.

Miterisi Ancient ruined city located in the foothills of the Saasanadar on the island of Khokarsa. Literally, "City of the Snake."

Mohasi Island in Khokarsa's Gulf of Gahete, with a fortress situated on its western tip.

Mukha City on the northwestern coast of the northern inland sea.

Nangukar Port of Opar.

Notamimkhu Seaport on the island of Khokarsa to the north of the valley of Kloepeth.

Oliwa Major port city on the southeastern coast of the island of Khokarsa.

Opar Hadon's home city, the region of which was first explored by the priestess-heroine Lupoeth. The name literally means "I don't understand you" in the aboriginal speech of the area.

Owalu Major Khokarsan city.

Phetapoeth Mountain village along the southern Kemu.

Poehy Naval-base island in Khokarsa's Gulf of Lupoeth.

Python's Head Two-pronged peninsula projecting from the mainland of Khokarsa island; in Khokarsan, "Terisiwuketh."

Q"okwoqo Secluded mountain village in the Saasamaro to the north of Dythbeth; its inhabitants worship Old Father Nakendar, a great cave bear rumored to have laired in the caves near the village for more than four hundred years.

Qethruth City on the eastern coast of the northern inland sea.

Qoqada City on western Khokarsa island, famed for its honey.

Rebha Pile city located on the inland sea just north of the Strait of Keth. Rebha was an important reprovisioning and refitting port, controlling the southern part of the Kemu and watching over the Strait of Keth.

Ringing Sea The Mediterranean Sea and North Atlantic; in Khokarsan, "Kemuqoqano."

Road of Kho Wide stone-block-paved highway that meanders from the wall of Khokarsa's Inner City up the steep side of the volcano, Khowot.

Saasamaro Mountain range to the northwest of Dythbeth.

Saasanadar Mountain range to the northwest of the city of Khokarsa.

Saasares Mountain range on the northern and northwestern borders of the Khokarsan Empire (known in the present day as the Tibesti Mountains). In Hadon's day, the slopes of these mountains were covered with olive trees on the lower levels, oak higher up, and then fir and pine.

Saasawabeth Mountain range on the northeastern coast of the island of Khokarsa.

Saasawuwos Mountain range on the northeastern border of the Khokarsan Empire (known in the present day as the Ahaggar Mountains).

Sakawuru Red-granite city where Hadon stopped while the *Semsin* resupplied on the way to the Great Games of Klakor in Khokarsa. The city was established by colonists from Mikawuru. Minruth IV quelled a rebellion there when he was younger.

Saqaba Major port city on Khokarsa's eastern coast.

Sigady Naval-base island in Khokarsa's Gulf of Gahete.

Siwudawa Queendom on the eastern coast of the northern inland sea. Also, the aboriginal parrot-headed androgynous deity of the people of Wentisuh.

Strait of Keth Narrow strait that connected the northern and southern inland seas.

Street of the Overturned Hives Street in the pile city of Rebha.

Temple of Kho Specifically, a temple on the side of the volcano, Khowot, on the island of Khokarsa and the abode of the oracular priestess, although generally many temples dedicated to Kho existed across the empire of Khokarsa.

Terisiwuketh See entry for Python's Head.

Tower of Diheteth Five-hundred-foot-tall cedar, stone-based lighthouse tower at the pile city of Rebha.

Towina City on the western coast of the northern inland sea. Kwasin was shipped there immediately after being sentenced to exile.

Wentisuh (From "wentis," meaning "land" or "country," and "suh" meaning "yellow" or "gold.") City where Hadon and the *Semsin* stopped on the way to the Great Games of Klakor. Wentisuh was inhabited by a brownish-yellowish-skinned people with coarse, straight black hair, long, thin, and beaked noses, and a fold of skin in the inner corners of their eyes. See H. Rider Haggard's *Allan Quatermain* for an account of the modern rediscovery of the descendants of Wentisuh, whose city was known as Zu-Vendis.

Wethna City on the southeastern coast of the northern inland sea.

Wild Lands, the Uncivilized regions beyond the borders of the Khokarsan Empire.

Western Lands, the Region to the west of the Khokarsan Empire.

ADDENDUM 2
PHILIP JOSÉ FARMER'S
NOTES AND CORRESPONDENCE

NOTES ON THE KHOKARSA SERIES

The following pages from Philip José Farmer's Khokarsa files show the development of certain ideas that, in one form or another, found their way into the final manuscript of *The Song of Kwasin* and "Kwasin and the Bear God." The great difficultly Farmer was having because of editor Donald A. Wollheim's insistence to use the word "Opar" in the third Khokarsa novel's title quickly becomes evident, with unlikely options considered such as *Near to Opar*, *Far from Opar*, and even *Far from and Near to Opar*. Intriguing titles for installments in the series beyond the third novel are also offered: *The Sea of Opar*, *The Falling of Opar*, *The Siege of Opar*, and *Heroes of Opar*.

The notes also illustrate the development of Kwasin's character, whom Farmer originally planned to name Khonan, which translates to "slave of Kho" in the Khokarsan language and was meant to be an homage to Robert E. Howard's iconic sword and sorcery hero, Conan the Cimmerian. Even so, Farmer's notes reveal that the character was from early on inspired by Kwasind from Henry Wadsworth Longfellow's *The Song of Hiawatha* (as well as Hercules and Gilgamesh, according to Farmer's correspondence).

The reference in the notes to "the freeing of the waters" alludes to a mythological and literary theme presented by Jessie L. Weston in her classic study of the origins of the Grail legend. Here Farmer assigned his two major heroes mythological challenges to overcome and thereby save the land before the goddess Kho would display Her wrath and destroy Khokarsa's two great inland seas: Hadon was "to slay the dragon," whereas Kwasin was "to defeat Minruth." While Farmer ultimately had another task in store for Hadon (to fulfill the prophecy of his daughter's birth in the city of Opar), Kwasin's task in the series remained the same.

Also in these notes we see Farmer deciding to incorporate into the Khokarsa series the legendary ax of meteoritic iron known as Inkosikaas, also called the Ax of Victory, from the works of H. Rider Haggard. The Khokarsa novels fill in the missing history of the ax, which was first crafted by Paga (named "Pag" in Haggard's novel) for the hero Wi in *Allan and the Ice-Gods*, then passed back to Paga, who in turn bequeathed it to Kwasin in *Hadon of Ancient Opar*. The ax would next go to Hadon's son, Kohr (see *Hadon, King of Opar* by Christopher Paul Carey, Meteor House, 2015). Many millennia later the ax would be won by the great Zulu warrior Umslopogaas in Haggard's *Nada the Lily*, who used it to defeat the mad giant Rezu (note the similarity of this name to that of Farmer's Khokarsan sungod, Resu) in Haggard's *She and Allan*, and who smashed its head, thus destroying the weapon, on the altar of the lost city of Zu-Vendis in Haggard's *Allan Quatermain*.

Farmer makes a reference on the same page of notes to a vase that appears in Haggard's classic novel *She: A History of Adventure*, pointing out that the depiction on the amphora of a hunter shooting an arrow from a bow indicated that either the inhabitants of the lost city of Kôr had abandoned the Khokarsan taboo of the bow and arrow or the archer was a barbarian who had no such taboo. Readers may recognize that the very same vase appears in a scene in *The Song of Kwasin* in which Kwasin is given an elixir by a priestess in the old temple of Kho at Dythbeth, and may be intrigued at the true identity of the archer illustrated on the vessel.

Also included in the following notes is a Khokarsan creation myth. This text eventually found its way into "Kwasin and the Bear God," a novella by Farmer and Carey that readers may find in this book.

Lastly among the notes reproduced here comes Farmer's complete Khokarsan syllabary and list of Khokarsan glyphs.

Readers who would like a more in-depth description of the syllabary should consult Farmer's article "The Khokarsan Language,"
included in the bonus materials of the Restored Edition of *Flight
to Opar* (Meteor House, 2015). A concise table of the Khokarsan
syllabary and glyphs may be found online on Farmer's official
website at www.pjfarmer.com.

Hadon & his friends
(Khonan — like Kwasen, the Strong
& his Orpheus — Orbeabor
friend — Kibiwabo — the Bard

Task of the Hero

from Weston's "From Ritual to
Romance"

Hadon's task — freeing of
the Waters —
    slaying a dragon —
around Opar — the creature
done in Willy Ley's book?
on the Ishtar Gate — ?

Two heroes — alternately —
Hadon & Kwasin —
Kwasin, to defeat Minruth
& save the land before the
Goddess destroyed it —
Hadon's — to slay the dragon — ?
or something else —
Next Opar Story —

HEROES of Opar
    title

(16)

She, p 223 - vase, picture of a hunter
shooting an arrow — so ancient
K8rapo ~~did~~ have arrows - we be
a picture of a ~~native~~ barbarian
shooting — this probably—

[Umbupa]
[She & Ali. - p62 - back regions of Port. S.E.
Africa [Mozambique]
[Gath houses]
⊕ [Axe of Rezu — then Umsl —'s
the original axe of W,i, made by
Pag?]   Check on this—

Seasons: rains heaviest when sun is
overhead - equinoctial months the heaviest—
so Rezu is also a rain god—

Winds make a difference
Further from the equator — the 2 maxima
merge into one — in midsummer—
July in north hemisphere—
so Khokarsa has July rainy season—
Op or two seasons—
equinox - March 21, September 23
Story starts

Creation Myth:

In the beginning was a formless substance which gave birth to a Kho- the Heat Goddess. She fashioned the earth, the air, the sky, the stars, the moon, & the sun. After eons being lonely, she copulated with the void & had Daughters, these she assigned to watch over the ~~earth~~ [   ], the sky [   ], the stars [   ], the moon [   ] & the sun [   ]. She created ~~all life on~~ a great tree with many fruits & birds which nested on the tree. Her daughters ate the fruit & copulated with the birds, & from these were born all manner of life.

KHOKARSAN SYLLABARY (check)

numbers: pe / — p'e ⋀ — 110 symbols
          110 syllables

poe // — p'o⋌ ⁊// — (all these are base
                      units also having a
          pi /// — p'i ⋀/// — general verbal sense—
                              of [illegible] motion toward,
                              through, along, into, over,
                              below,

indicates
check (5)
t' = [illegible]   te — (2) — te ⋀ — the — tet, tell, t'ell
check
c' = [illegible]   toe = — t'o⋀ = — thoe — [illegible could clearly have
check   been originally part
g' = k' etc.   ti ≡ — t'i ⋀ — [illegible]
                                                  [several lines illegible]
                      ta ≠ — t'a ⋀ ≠ — tha — [illegible] related
                                              — [illegible] the

[Mishlebl]   te ⋀ (bird genus term) ⋀⊤ t'e — Aume?
p239   de (d''e) = ⊤   [illegible]
, ''   ty ⱦ   ⋀⊤ t'y — Hot Algonquedy
                      du ⱥ (1)   ⋀⊤ t'a — [illegible]
                      do ⱨ   ⋀⊤ t'o — [illegible]

                      ke ∿   ∿ k'e — [illegible]
                      ko ≋ (3)   ∿≋ k'o — South—
                      ka ⊼ (4)   ⊼ k'a — [illegible]
                        ku ‹ k'u = ≋

② ɓɪ ɓʼɪ ɓʼɪʼ

~~ʌ̃ʊ~~ ~

ɓɪ ɤ

ɓa ʞ ~~(to) pig~~

~~ɓɒ ʞ (b) pig~~
~~s = ts~~

(t)se ɤ

(t)si ʞ (hostess, host, hospitable being welcomed/received in.

sa ʞ (8) (hill, temple, want protre(sm)
sa(c'a) ꞮꞮ
~~su ꟷ~~ so(< c'a) = · ꟷ

ga oo

go ~~oo~~ (7)

~~guoo~~ ——— go < g''u = oo

he ʌ (10) hehe (hundred) (helele) thousand

ha ʌ (hawk)

~~ho ʌ~~

(3)

me ∨ (city   mi ∨
             ma ∨
ma ⩒   ma(m'a) ⩐ (m'a) = woman
ma(m'a) ⩒   mo ⩱
mo ⩐ (9)   mu ⩲

ma ⩐

ne <

na ⪡ (stone, hard, stubborn)

no ⪦

nu ⪩ half-man, degraded, low

qa > heart

qo → (qo < q"0) = →

lu ⅂ (+)

la ⅂ (moon)

lu ⅂ (priestess)

⑤

A-we-neth
child-fire-white
Ar-te-ne-thi
child-bird-white

re B

re B

reu B

we Ɵ ~~Estom~~ (fire

waʒeƟ (baby, child)

B⁰(Ɵ)₀ B̄

W⁰(⁰)₀Ɵ̄ — great, large, grand, important

bha Ħ (green)

bho Ħ̄ (blue)

~~phe M~~
~~phoeM~~
~~phi M~~

kha C

kho Ɔ (Hasysom Ooky)

8

khu ∈

kwa ⊃ (=) ~~(syllable of [illegible]~~, urging, ~~[illegible]~~, [illegible],

kwo ∋ (syllable of address, attention getter

klwe ○

kly θ (÷)

kla Ō (eater, devourer, killer) Klably θ Ō

peth ⊤ → par ⌶ (meaningless syllable)

poeth ₸

ton ⊥ (X) (cutting, shearing, dividing) wound, decision

cutter ~~[illegible]~~ a butcher's shop

teth ±

dheth [illegible] thunder, loud,

dhyth [illegible]

dhar [illegible] (grey

family—
mahuw-gall
children = white = gull

⑥ Hunson
Eyes black

Kwa-sen
lightning black
west
shame or fire

Ton ⚌ ( ) red
sunset

Keth 4 (head first, chief) keth

Kem 4 (water) Kehm

Kem ₮ (death) Kehm

Kar 4 (tree) Kahr

Kom 4 (fresh) Kohm

Kor 4 (honey) Kohr ♯

Geo ⊢ (burn orig. originality from escape) (eskeskes?)

Beth ⊢

Ges ⊡ (ancient old, the world, aging etc.)

Seth ♀

→ sem ♀

Sen ⚢ (black)

Ses ♀ (house)

Si-sis-ken
Wallus-law-death

⑤

~~Xeroxes for Ferry~~
~~of~~
~~70 yrds~~
~~Sherburn~~
~~Father's in the Basement~~

---

sah ♀ (god, sky)

suk ⚥ (yellow, gold) *chord-nasul-god*

meth ♂

mim ♂

mun ♂ (tower)

---

mes ♂

neth ♂ (~~storm~~, white, ~~pure~~, intense, ~~pure~~)

nan ♂ (slave)

β

geth ✕

qan ✲ (5)

gath 𝕏

g ar ✕

quth ✳

lah ω (goddess

lem ♃ - finger, to slengthen - hand, or spur

hin ⬯ (eye, door, opening)

res ✳ (sun, sungod, eagle)

ruth ✳ (middle)

wem ⊤

wen ⊥

weth ⊤

wot ⊥ (voice

woo ∓

---

klem ꝙ (people, tribe, nation)

klam ꝗ

---

pwym ⲰⲰⲰ

pwam ₩

(tsweth)
sweth ≪

(tsweth)
swath ≪

~~116~~ symbols
~~116~~ syllable

116 symbols
8 singlets
108 spoken syllables

PHILIP JOSÉ FARMER'S
ORIGINAL OUTLINE

What follows is Philip José Farmer's original mid-1970s outline of "*Kwasin of Opar*," exactly as he wrote it before his requested revisions to position the story as the climax of a trilogy. Since Farmer was still as lukewarm about the original title as he had been from the beginning (Kwasin did not hail from Hadon's home city, after all, but rather from Dythbeth, a city on the island of Khokarsa), the novel was retitled *The Song of Kwasin*, which fittingly hearkens back to Longfellow's *The Song of Hiawatha* and the original inspiration for Kwasin's character in Hiawatha's strongman friend Kwasind. While the outline gives a detailed overview of the novel up through its climax, it ends abruptly just before the conclusion and closes with two alternate courses of action for Kwasin which Phil no longer wished to pursue now that the story was to be resurrected. Further, certain names and details in the outline that did not correspond with those established in *Flight to Opar* had to be revised, as did some "placeholder" names that Phil had intended to sync up later with the linguistic rules of his Khokarsan syllabary. About what he ultimately had in mind for the novel's new ending, Phil made his wishes quite clear.

outline of

Kwasin of Opar

1st scene, brief ~~past~~ recap of the situation
by some soldiers sent to kill Kwasin before he can get to
Dythbeth
//theyre brave but overpowered by his legend first and the
physical power second--all killed except one man--
//--second chapter--more recap--this being filtered thru in
small doe doses--Kwasin appears at Dythbeth, his birth place--
desc. of Dythbeth--cyclopean city in a harbor--mts surrounding it--
passes thru it--thru which storm Minrtuh's army--at great cost--
Kwasin and the chief priestess-- interim name, check on
Khokarsa syllabary--Tuku--Kwasin takes over--king of Dythbeth
is disgruntled by being displaced--later, treachery?--
assassination or king(interim) Thapun--goes to Minruth after
getting word that he'll be reinstated if he swears loyalty
and makes the sungod the chief deity--subordinate the priestesses
of the Great Mother--
//--//--make this a Burroughsian alternate chapter thing?only
if Hadon and Kwasin finally meet--not likely--
--Kwasin goes to a pass to help fight, but his forces defeated,
and he has to retreat to city,
a siege by land and sea--but if ~~the~~ Minruth's navy can be swept
away or seriously weakened, then supplies shipped in and the
land siege held off--
--Iliadic single fighting between heroes--Minruth's greatest
warriors on the plain against Kwasin--
//slingmen and bola men--wardogs--leopards--
//--barbaric splendor--artifacts briefly described--en passant--
all giving picture of Kho. civilization--
//-- Minrtuh's forces sacrifice captives to the Sungod--restoring
ancient custom, much to horror of the Dythbethans--torture--
//--
//Kwasin decides that the M. navy has to go--leads a force at
night--moonless--takes a ship, burns it--while the remainder
of D navy sweeps out to battle--
//--rams on galleys and sailing ships--
M navy ten to D's one--
//an eatthquake during the battle--and a tsunami--destroying
all of Ms navy and most of D's--kwasin barely escapes with
a very small force--but goes up into the mts with loggers and
gets more wood--or around the cape and up into the mts--
Minruths men disheartened--the Great Goddess has sent the sewave
to desory Minrtuhs men--desertion is large from Ms army--
according to spies--

//<u>Imp</u>.-- Kwasin's character is arrogant, impulsive, lecherous,
gets him into trouble with the priestesses and the leading men
of Dythbeth--theyre afraid of him--causes conflict when
total unity needed--

//--news from other places re revolt--Minrtuh has to let the
shore cities go while he concentrates on cleaning out all
significant opposition on island--then will consolidate and
start pice-by-piece, city by city conquest of rebelling cities--

is building a vast navy, people groaning under the burden--
at the same time the madman is rebuilding the great tower
and cleaning up the mess made by the eruption of the volcano
(Khowot?)--

//--asks help from a revolting state(?O on northern shore--
because of Kwasin's reputation, they send a navy and soldiers--
conflict vs K and its admiral and general--Kwasin æduces
the wife of the general--and he challenges Kwasin, but
Kwasin knows that if he kills him, then the army will pull
out--and navy with it--really needs them--

//--meanwhile, whioe siege is going on, recruits strengthening
the siergers--Minruth has recruited wild mountain men from
the mojtnains north of north shore with promise of the loot
and women to be had and also with a contingent of the wild
half-Neandethal peoples of the southwestern mts
along the Khokarsan Sea--

//--and is rebuilding a navy like mad acc. to spies to bottle
up Dyt.beth again--with very littel trade, Dythbethans in
bad economic way--

//-then four revolting cities in Dythbeth taken by Minrtuh--
led by his/general/geniud--interim name: Phaken--now the armies--
after having massacred half of pop. of each taken city and
made the rest slaves--as a object lesson, shrewdly offers amnesty,
forgiveness to the others, inc;.Dythbeth--all cities except
Dythbeth surrender and he keeps his promise, knowing what the
effect on the rest ofmisland will be--the guerrillas and
peasants offer obeisance--and the mt city and great shrine
where Haon took refuge is takne--but Minrtuh doesnt slaughter
the priestesses, instead places them under rule of the priests--
many resist and are presumably exiled instead of being killed-
sent to northern shore, but rumor has it that a storm sank
the ships carrying them, another that they were killed en route
and their bodies dropped weighted into the sea--

//almost forgot: Minrtuh's daughter also flees to Dythbeth--
the interaction between them--shes mad at Hadon, who shld be
the king because of his prefernce for Lalilah--

//she comes in not too long after Kwasin did--he wld like to
marry her, sees himself as being king after Minrtuh is defeated--
and she finally gives in, tho pissed-off at his affair with
the chief priestess of Dythbeth and the king s daughter--
but politically a good move--

//--helps in the war--very shrewd woman--a military genius--
her presence along with Kawsins inspires the Dytybethans--

Mvn = Nvm) Cit (awr =
nvith = rod) Tovr(Culyln

Minrtuh establishes primacy of man in the family--takes
away age-old rights of women--everyhwere the goddess is
made an equal to the sungod, and M plans eventually to make
her subordinate--doesnt want to push against the solidly
establ shed worship of the goddess too fast--but institutes
 charges of malfeasance against various high priestesses--
charges of blasphemy, etc to discredit them--

//imports workers from all over the northern part of empire--
a babel of tonguesp-the semi-Mongolians of (?) send workers
are sympathetic with M in his desire to make the male pantheon
the chief--

--M's daughter pregnant by Kwasin--she declares that she and
Kwasin will rule after M defeated, word gets abroad thruout the
island and to the city-states--these want to keep the old
customs and religion, but the rulers like being independent--
however, theyre influenced strongly by the priestesses and
the people, and she shrewdly offers them a cut in taxes tribute
after she's on the throne--

--she and Kwasin plan to launch a navy and troop vessels
against Opar after island won--its great wealth will help
empire get back on its feet, besides, both she and Kwasin
hate Hadon--

--Minruth sends more besiegers-- a new navy shows up--
straining Ms resources, but he knows he has to conquer
Dythbeth, get Kwasin and his daughter, and cut off the head
of the revolt--on the plain a vast army of motley makeup--
hard to keep discipline, fighting amongst themselves--

//the D8s gird their loins for the final struggle--but Minruth--
showing up to leadthe armies--doesnt know whether to starve
them out--a long procedure--or make a massive assault, which
will be costly--or perhaps try more assassins--

decides to try the assassins first--twenty promised great
monetary rewards--high positions in government-- they go out,
one by one, and fail--

//first, tho, what happens when the general challenges
Kwasin?--problem solved when Ms daughter forbids them to fight--
a vision sent by the Goddess or the patron female deity of
Dythbeth (which, by the way is so named because a hero neamed
Dythbeth founded it later after clearing the land of the leopards
that infested it--inc the giant leopard thatd ravaged the land--
acc. to legend)

the goddess ordered her to tell K and Tuku (Kukolda?) to settle
their argument for the greater good of the goddess and her
people--the general is to let his wifes child by Kwasin--
tho acutally no one knows who the father is--to be raised
by the high priestess and Kwasin as their onw--generals honor
is saved because the adultery was ordered by the goddess herself--
the child will be a tremendous force in the future, a great
person(she shrewdly doesnt say whether it will bea girl or a
boy)--

//--general accepts this decision, his face saved--but tells his
wife that after they get back to home-city, hell divorce her--

//--another slight tremor, and recap of the sayings of the oracle of Khowot about the land being forever destroyed if the old religion not maintained in pristine form--this heartens the Dythbethans--

//Kwasin's speech at the rally--

//the armies of Minruth advance after the last assassin is killed and his head thrown down--or hand-delivred by Kwasin to a sentry at dead of night--

//--the Minruthian navy comes in at same time--Dythbethans been hard put to get enough to eat--all domestic animals, cattle, sheep, pigs, goats eaten though the pigs are tabu(check this)--hares also sacred but eaten, then dogs, cats, mice, rats, insects--these form part of Khokarsan diet anyway--for the first time, the city rid of mice and rats and cockroaches--

//but then three ships come in with new supplies-rationed out to the warriors and children--

//--Kwasin, about to go into battle, gives most of his food to two starving children, tho a bastard in many ways does have a soft heart in some respects--

//-- the assault--towers of wood on wheels pushed forward--burning pitch but hides of leather help prevent warriors from getting burned--
and two tunnels which were started at beginning of siege have been completed-- during story Kwasin finds one, makes raid in which he kills the general and almost gets Minruth--this is blocked up, but the other he doesnt know about, and when the assault starts, troops pour out from several blocks from the wall, at last moment, break up the stones of street above--

//--no way out,have to win or die--several points under massive attack--including two gates--the navy comes in,overwhelming galint but small D fleet--then sailors assault the main gate of the harborside--

//--Kwasin, learning of the troops from the tunnel-sets fire to the houses around the neighborhood in which they are, burns up most of them but fire cant be controlled--heat is terrific--Ms dtr denounces him for being so dumb--the gates are finally taken except where Kwasin is--the stampede of the people from the fire makes fighting difficult-they overwhelm the soldiers in one gate, pour out but are killed or taken captive-- a sad day for Dytbeth--
//--Kwasin and Ms daughter--Awineth-- go along the wall, pressed by soldiers coming after them--Minruth has charged that both be taken alive, which handicaps the soldiers--they just pus them along, hoping they'll run into another force on wall, be trapped--
//--one by one K's men are killed, until only the two left--
//surender or leap off wall?--slingmen come up, Kwasin charges roaring, and a stone hitting his head helmet stuns him--

//he wakes, bound hand and foot, trussed up as if he were a lion--outside the wall, while the city burns--the heads and penises of the dead D8s stuck on p poles--the penises in their mouths--those taken captive not slain but to be sent to the work on the tower--worked to death--

Minruth exultant despite great losses--decides to take the two
back in a cage drawn by the slaves, a triumphal procession--
and sends couriers out to spread the good news(bad for many).
This'll take the heart out of the last few cities, and he promises
amnesty to them--

//--the procession takes a long time--Awineth and Awasin
naked, subject to winds and rain--food thrown into cages as
they're wild animals--have to defecate in cages--but they are
cleaned up with buckets of water thrown in--

//at night, sometimes, Kwasin, always horny whatever the
circumstances, screws Awineth--until theyre discovered one night--
then torches on them all the time--

//during procession, a raid by loyals to rescue them, but it
fails--

//Kwasin works at his bonds, chews them, strains, hoping to
weaken them--given ritually unclean food but they eat it--

//Awineth decides to starve herself rather than do tta but she
weakens--finally says that a vision told her to save herself,
the goddess will triumph in the end--if the people come to her
rescue--this news istransmitted via grapevine thruout the
island--

//they come into a restored Khokarsa, the capital, a great
parade--where a trill is held and they're doomed. Awineth is
put ina heavily barred apartment where she is otherwise
well-treated, Minruth rapes her tho she bears Kwasin s child--
he plans to kill the baby at birth--but secretly--still afraid
of people's wrath if he shld kill the high priestess's baby--

Kwasin is put to work on the tower, heavily guarded, in
chains of bronze--does herculean feats in lifting--parties
from the city and other places allowed to come in and see him--
at a distance--so they can witness and broadcast that the hero Kwasin
is indeed now a slave--

//--to punish the city of Mukha for having aided Dythbeth--
Minruth sends a fleet and troop ships to attack it--
//--if it falls, maybe the others will surrender--Minruth gives
the city ultimatum, surrender or everybody in it slain--

//--at night, put in the slave pen but in separate fenced
enclosure and always heavily guarded--torches burning, eyes
on him--Awineth bears a girl baby, but the priestesses attending
her kill the two women sent by Minruth and attack the guards,
slaying them. they get the baby out, spirited out through
secret passageways and tunnels only they know--most of them
killed in struggle, or do they poison the food of the guards--
and is A. also rescued--word comes that she has fled the
island, probably going to Opar, tho no one really knows--
Minruth is enraged, crazed, but puts out word denying the tale,
saying that both Awineth and baby died during childbirth--
//does K believe this? does at first, then slave grapevine tells
him the truth--

//--20th level built--Kwasin decides to sacrifice the greatest
hero of the devout Goddess worshipper to the sungod on top
of 20th level--

X--<u>change</u>: Minruth has thrown a cordon around the city--

word is that Awineth is concealed with baby in a house or perhaps an underground room somewhere in the city--Minruth makes a house-to-house search, resulting in many criminals being discovered--enslaves them for work force**<u>comment about how bad slaves are as workers</u>**

no find. M also sends out undercover agents, spies, ect to find her. no find.

//people around Minruth know what a strain building the tower is but are afraid to say so.

//-Minruth has resettled Dythbeth with the northern mountaineers, who dont know Khokarsan civilization, make bad traders, workers, artisans; the colonization is a failure--mighty Dythbeth awaits rebuilding, a ruined partially inhabited city--will be a hundred years before expanding population allows its rebuilding and repopulating--

//--salt trade has been reestablished--salt mines in the mts. the main supply--

//--northern cities submit--southern states still resistant--but no conquest of them now, have to strengthen the island--then, some day, the reconquest starts--but Minruth, like Kwasin and Awineth, plans to bypass the rebel cities and launch a great epxedition against Opar--word finally comes of Hadon's triumph, now king of Opar, and rumors that hes planning to unite the southern cities and attack the island--still claims hes rightfully the king of kings--but this may rumor, no foundation, Minruth believes it--

--then word comes to Kwasin--Awineth sends it--thru the many faithful--look under the sacrificial stone, or is it in a <u>riddle</u> to deceive the spies, informants, which he has to figure out?--which he does just before he arrives at the top--meanwhile, while wrking, has been wearing out the bronze chains, but theyre regularly checked, and on day of sacrifice, new chains to be put on--

//with great pomp and ceremony, kind and entourage ascend the tower to the top, accompanied by the high priest of the sungod-- then the carefully chosen guests, incl. those from shore-cities, Qethruth, Mukha (Mukha s king and family slain and new king instated, other cities, incl. ambassadors and king's son from Wentisuh? represented)-- a great festival proceeding this, ceremonies honoring the sungod--with crumbs thrown to the Goddess--some traitor priestesses here--neophytes

4545 given high rank bribed or threatened if didn't cooperate--//--word also sent to Kwasin that hed be helped--populace is somehwat sullen or at least restrained--

//--new chains put on him--but he discovers that its cleverly wrought--hollow links at gyves--strong enough to resist the strength of an ordinary man, but not Kwasin--

//--

Philip José Farmer

//--change: king of Mukha and family not slain, kept as
sacrifices to the sungod, they go first--pitiful, little
children sacrificed--or about tobe, but Minruth, to appear
merciful, spares them, ~~but5tfei4t4~~ at last minute, but their
~~fother~~ father has his heart cut out and the priests eat
the raw heart after cutting it into bits and burning part--
the sungod eats the burned flesh--part of corwd pleased
at this bloody spectacle--rest is horified and ashamed--
a thousand years of civilization have made this custom
repulsive, loathsome, to the ᴸhokarsans--

//--some heroes and heroines of the rsistance also slain--
eleven in all, ᴸwasin to be the last--he finally sees what
the riddle means--his great axe, once Wina's? now Kwasin s--
is hidden under the altar, temporary--
he breaks the chains, pulls out the stone and starts to
lay about him--confusion as the priestesses, some of them,
pull out knives fɾom their robes and stab the priests and
some soldiers before being slain--

//Minruth takes off yelling for help. ~~But~~ But Kwasin cuts way
thru crowd after him, then, aided by some of the slaves and
by inspired people still faithful, who know theyre going to
die but willing to do so, slay guards and courtiers--

//--below, two stories filled with soldiers--Minruth is knocked
down when Kwasin throws the axe but the handle hits him and
he isn't killed-- Kwasin gets handle back, Minruth fallen down
stairs and knocking soldiers on steps down--and with axe
tied to his back climbs down the tower on the many carven
deities, mosnters, and heroes--

//--   some soldiers go after him, others throw spears,
swords, shɪelds, slingstones--all miss tho some get close--
below, a riot breaks out, slaves overwhelm guards--but other
soldiers attack, then citiens attack-- in midst of melee
Kwasin arrives, axs his way out, leads the ~~a5145454545454545~~
mob to victory;
(note; the soldiers would8ve inspected the tower for hidden
assassins the night before, but it was an offcier faithful
secretly to the Goddess who planted the axe--

//--then the tables are turned; the king and his soldiers
trapped in the tower--   bathing
after resting, eating, and drinking, and taking willing
priestess into a house for some love-making, Kwasin decides
not to starve the king and force out--take them by force--
Awineth appears, and she declares herself as the ruler,
and Kwasin as her king--ignoring Hadon's claim-- fighting
still going on in various parts of theᴖcity--navy engaged
in civil warrIF THE KING CAN BE KILLED, will put an end, for
time being anyway, to the war.

//--must be done fast before kings loyal forces somehow get
the upper hand--

//-Kwasin puts on some armor, a helmet, thick leather leggings--
then leads the attack but it s uphill, up the stairs, floor
to floor--when he gets winded, lets others go ahead--
finally, the last stand on the tenth floor--ᴸwasin breaks
thru--and while his men mop up in the vast floor, he chases

//--the king can stand, and fight, jump, or try to escape.
but below is a crowd, and so he stands and fights, though now
(what?) 58?) out of condition and never the man Kwasin is--
(has had special soldiers, sworn to silence, build at night
a secret route of passageways) and when Kwasin bursts onto
the top, sure of triumph, the king is gone?--

//--searches, then finds the plafe after he batters at the
stone panels and breaks some--goes down after the king,
through passageway after passageway--until deep below the
tower: a complex of tunnels such as beneath the great palace--
some blocked off by the earthquake of two years ago, some
by more ancient ones--(what about light?)--takes torch from
group that was burning during the ~~ceremony~~ ceremony--
~~finally seeking to sadangreduse hdfagand musthknherthr~~ route--

cautious, king knows the route, like a dangerous rat--finally
comes to a tunnel leading upward to the harbor, but the king
releases a floodgate, and water almost drowns K. he survives,
swims upwardd, sees king in a boat, paddling out to get the
wind for the sails. takes a small boat and paddles after him.
⌐but king is pikced up by loyal ship and Kwasin has to run
for his life--

is this OK? or change it?

alternates: ALTERNATE: going down on outside K swings in thru
a window where no one is at moment, goes thru rooms, runs into
three soldiers, the third kills the other two from behind as
they advance on Kwasin; turnes out to be a goddess-worshipper,
agent planted in kings force, takes K into secret passageways,
knows them since he was on the night shift which built them--
leads him down and out--and ꜰ꜠꜠꜡ kings force are puzzled,
some wondering the Goddess snatched him away--but M knows
and leads a small force into th passageway, though ~~vo ng~~ vowing
to kill the soldiers afterwards to preserve the secret--
almost gets K and does kill the soldier but Kwasin emerges
inside a small house--and takes off, then is piꜰced up by
A's people and gotten out of city.

hears later that a revolt in city when rumor flies that the
Goddess had preserved him, plucked him from the midst of
his enemies--but K afraid to lie and validate it;or does he decide
that, in a sense, She did, and tell a tale in ambiguous terms??
//meets Awineth in remote forest, baby has died--they decide
they'll go to Opar, throw themselves on Hadon s mercy--
he doesnt know what they planned to do with him--and with Opar
as base of operations, start war again--

//but is this feasible?wldnt they stay on island and ꜰ renew
guerrilla warfare, hoping eventually to geta force to face
Ms'.? or go to the city of -----, still holding out, and organize
a⌐ base there while at same time organziing underground in
on the island. do this. but eventually will conquer Opar,
(but do they have the slightest idea whats happened in Opar?
a ship wldve had to come with the news--thisll make a scene
early in the book--

//-- for the ending, to be fairly conclusive and satisfactory:

(NOte: method building the tower and its construction, shape,
etc.** if made of cyclopean blocks of stone--pyramidal in shape--
earth piled up on which blocks pulled up--or ramps--of wood--)

blocks — *[illegible]* high —
10 feet ~~square cube~~
[illegible] cubes

[illegible] mound as *[illegible]* —
cover previous levels with more earth?
then when completed — remove dirt —
or a mound to begin with —
or bricks — solid — forming the
core — around which *[illegible]* —
[illegible] blocks placed —
like 7 *[illegible]* of Babylon or
ziggurats —
but bricks have shafts —
passageways in them —
blocks have carved figures — heads —
animals, men, gods, goddesses, serpents,
heads, *[illegible]* living being on earth —
birds, reptiles, turtles — *[illegible]* nations —
vast cost —

base — one side — 230 meters long
M's co 410 meters but round
diameter — 300 meters

200 meters
600 ft. dia
300 ft high

plan height
150 meters
450 feet high

$\oplus$

PHILIP JOSÉ FARMER'S
ALTERNATE OUTLINE

The following alternate and incomplete outline of *The Song of Kwasin* was discovered among Farmer's papers in January 2009, a month before his passing. That it was written at a date much later than the outline in the preceding section of this book is evident from its more modern typeface and the fact that several important details in it do not align with the names and situations of the prior novels, as if Farmer had forgotten them in the intervening lapse of time and had not yet taken the time to consult the continuity. For instance, Farmer had already established in *Flight to Opar* that the queen and king of Dythbeth were named Weth and Roteka, whereas this alternate outline gives their respective names as Nelahnes and T'agoqo (alternatively spelled as T'aguq'o).

While the last two pages of the outline were unusable for such reasons, it quickly became apparent that the first two pages detailed an unwritten "lost" adventure of Kwasin set between the first two chapters of *The Song of Kwasin*. The events chronicled on these two pages later served as the basis for "Kwasin and the Bear God" by Philip José Farmer and Christopher Paul Carey, a 20,000-word novella first published in *The Worlds of Philip José Farmer 2: Of Dust and Soul* (Meteor House, 2011), and which has been reprinted in this book so readers may enjoy having access to both of Kwasin's adventures in a single volume.

KWASIN OF OPAR

(Outline)

Kwasin flees Khokarsa after end of HADON OF ANCIENT
OPAR. His adventures during this. Goes along coast in a fsfishing
boat for a while. A naval galley chases him; he gets to the beach,
sailors and marines take off after him. He kills them one by one
or in groups in the ruins of a small city whowhich legend says
was cursed by a priestess. aqrove sacred to a python nearby.
takes refuge in a small village, where the pytoness is worshipped.
beds the priestess and two others.

But offends the priest, who goes to a garrison ad and brings
back soldiers. he runs, gets away from them. dives off a high
cliff into the sea. slowly makes his way overland. trace the
route according to the map. towards Dthbeth, the city of his birth,
htho he's more often called K of Opar because of the time he
spen tethere. (recap this, his relationship with Hadon and the
uncle, genealogy of family.) hears rumors. H and Awineth fled.
Minruth is beseiging a city but has sworn vengeance on anybdody or
any city which befriends Kwasin. high priest cursed him. Dythbeth
is loyal to the Goddess. so far, Minruth not taken any action against
Dythbeth. lacks enough navy and armies to fight all loyalsts
at same time. also, K hears that shore cities have revolted,
most of thm them, and that Minruth is recruiting the wild
mountaineers of the northern shore. promising them loot, rape,
and settlement.

and recruiting the half-Neanderthal peoples of the
shoreline southwestern mts.

at same time, rebuilding the earthquake-and-volcano eruption torn
city of Khokarsa.

plans on continuing the building of the great tower (ziggurat).

in the mots northeast of Dythbeth, comes to a village where
they worship a bear. the priestess there takes him to bed and
also tells him that Awineth has fled to Dythbeth, too. ievitable
that Minruth will hear of this and attack Dythbeth soon.

she gives him the sacred pelt of a she-bear, telling him that
he will be inevitable as long as he wears it

he takes it and goes with a contingent of Bearmen towards
Dythbeth. but coming to a fort held by loyal Minruthians, decides to
enter D. with some immediate glory. and give the D's some heart.
a hundred and twenty soldiers here. e he has twenty warriors,
including four women slingers. (get SC AM. article on slingers.)
a village nearby. and a small river running by it. watches the
soldiers, catches the commandant and ten soldiers while taking
a bath and sporting with some of the village women. kills them,
demoralizing the others. sets fire to the village and thrws flaming
toctrtorches over the walls, setting fire to the huts and the
mess hall. retreats, though killing some sentries and some wo
run out with sling-stons and spears and kills five with his club.

Next day, as soldiers and villagers stand around in ashes.
appears and announces his identity and intentions. urges villagers
to attack the soldiers. some throw spears at the s's and then run off
to join K. gets villagers to deset desert, using the curses of
the young priestess accompanying him. the soldiers still have
walls of fort but will have to forage for food. the soldiesr dei
decide to abandon fort, match go dow river, then cut toards coast
before nearing Dythbeth. make dugouts, K having set adrift or
burned the boats. also set fire to the fields, burning up crops
and released goats and cattle and fowl.

river has crocodiles. he swims out, upsets two boats,
swims away laughing. crocs tear into the soldiers but don't
boulder
touch him. next, drops a bulde on the lead boat from a branch
above. calls on them to surrender, join the Goddess' worshipper.
one officer urges his men to fight. a soldier stabs him, and
ss' surrender. and so enters the great plain on landward side of D.
as a conquering hero, having sent a messenger ahead with news of
his coming and triumph. but shrewd enough to take a different
route in case messenger captured or betrayal.

Note: takes six seven bears with him and lets them loose
during the fire. these bears raised by the villagers, fgfight
with them, trained to do so. ???

greeted by the king, queen-priestess, and diginatraies and
whole populace--already a legend, a superhero, everybody wild
about him, apparently. also, Awineth (recap). but discord, the
king, his name, T'agulqp, wishes to put to deathe the soldiers
of Minruth whom K has recruited. a confrontation, deided in favor
of K but R T' is pissed-off. K marks him as an enemy. and he
makes advances to Awineth who puts him off, for the time being, anyway.

The queen-priestess is Nelahnes.

     K considers the military situation. the defenses, supply
lines, ships, morale, food stores, water supply, etc. the intelligence corps. etc. M will send a navy which will transport an
army. It wont sail into the Dythbeth Bay, too dangerous. will
land at southern shore of peninsula and march over. at the same
time, no doubt, another army will march or perhaps boat down
various rivers and join the other army. the navy will try to
bottle up the mouth of the bay, no easy feat, since it's
about 3½ miles wide. may besiege and try to starve the Dythbethans
out or attack at once.

     K not one to just wait. finding out from spies and info from
loyal peasants and villagers, waits on south shore near the
village of --------. Minanlu, however, must be taken. if taken, then
the army can sail row up the river to the plain of Dythbeth.
as the navy of M comes around a headland, Ks navy attacks it.
a pitched battle. K's is beaten but not without inflicting
staggering losses. the surviving M ships take refuge in a
sheltering bay and camp at base of mts. meanwhile, other part of
Ms navy tries to bottle up the bay mouth at same time the seond
army comes down on the _____ river and then marches
across the plain of _____. Minanlu besieged, then
stormed. and army comes up the _____ river and on road alongside
to join the army.

     siege begins with a direct attack after Minruth's general
_____ demands surrender of Awineth and Kwasin and the rulers
of D. offers mercy to rest, if they declare Resu the supreme
monarch. offer rejected.

     but M can't cut off all supplies. Kwasin challenges the
champions of M in individual duels. kills the first three, and
from then on ofers declined. catapults brot up, cf. Sc Amer. article
on catapults.

meanwhile, in D. K woos Awineth. at same time, beds the queen,
Nelahnes. is caught by the king, who, in rage, orders K. slain.
palace guards attack half-heartedly. Awineth restores peace but
king is sullen. food supplies short but adequate at this stage.
then Ms navy bulls its way into the bay. Ks navy defeated but
not without inflicting heavy losses. K has beefed up the ram-
galleys of Dythbeth, uses Greek fire here, too. nevertheless,
a second attack burns up the wharfs and all naval ships of K
destroyed or scattered. another army joins Ms forces--after
its successful storming of the rebel city of Qaarquth. and its
razing.

the whole island is in a mess, tho. agriculture disturbed.
taxes heavy. but the king, Minruth, transports another army of
wl wild mountaneers. these challenge K, who kills their champions.

another attack is beaten off. Ms men tunnel under, three
of them. K locates and kills the miners but mining started again.
food starts to get shorter. a Minruth spy gets into contact with
Dythbeth king, offers him kingship if he'll kill Kwasin and
surrender the city. Minruth has so many troubels hes willing to
temporize. mae make concessions. besides, a priestess has declared
that Kwasin will be Ms death.

Awineth says that unless theres a drastic change in situation,
Dythbeth is doomed. Kwasin tries to assassinate the Minruth, who's
come to the scene to direct the soldiers himself. it fails, but
K manages to get away, dives into the river.

the last attack. D king T'agoqo, gets a gate opened at same
time men come from a tunnel. Kwasin sets the city afire or its
set afire by Greek fire cast by Ms forces. and he and Awineth
are captured. but not before Kwasin kills T'agoqo.

they're taken in cages on triumhal march back to capial,
Khokarsa. where Minruth says he will sacrifice them on the
top of the half-built tower. some tremors during this.

Minruths chief priest _____announces that Resu has
appeared to him and announced hes divorcing Kho, taking
a lesser goddess _____ as his wife. Kho is to be banished
to the land of her sister, Sisisken, to dwell there frforever.
this is a mistake, since faithful refuse to belive this, think
the priest is lying. other revolts trouble Minruth, who
then hurries up execution, thinking that if Awineth is slain,
tethen heart will go out of Kho-worshippers.

CORRESPONDENCE ON THE KHOKARSA SERIES

Philip José Farmer first came up with the idea of writing the Khokarsa series in 1971. By this time, he had begun corresponding with John Harwood, an active member of Edgar Rice Burroughs fandom with an extensive knowledge of popular literature, who had provided important feedback to Farmer on his seminal work of creative mythography, *Tarzan Alive: A Definitive Biography of Lord Greystoke* (Doubleday, 1972). For a number of years, Harwood had been collaborating with another Burroughs fan and scholar, Frank J. Brueckel, whom Farmer acknowledged in *Tarzan Alive* as "the foremost scientific apologist of the Burroughs world," and anyone who has read Brueckel's articles on Burroughsiana will recognize that this epithet is by no means an exaggeration. It was the intersection of these three learned and imaginative individuals—Brueckel, Harwood, and Farmer—that would soon lead to the creation of the Khokarsa series.

Since as far back as 1935, Brueckel had been speculating on the idea of the motherland civilization of the lost city of Opar from Edgar Rice Burroughs' Tarzan novels. But it was only many years later, after reading John Harwood's article "The City of Unseen Eyes" (*The Burroughs Bulletin* #13, 1962), that Brueckel felt a renewed interest in the concept of Opar's motherland. Soon Brueckel and Harwood joined forces and began a lengthy period of research into the ancient history of Opar, the culmination of which was a monumental article titled "Heritage of the Flaming God, an Essay on the History of Opar and Its Relationship to Other Ancient Cultures." According to Brueckel and Harwood, Opar's motherland, which they called "Atlantis," was not located in the Atlantic Ocean, but rather on an island in one of the two great inland seas of ancient Africa, which had long since drained and dried up, leaving little evidence of their existence beyond the presence of Lake Chad.

In the summer of 1971, Vern Coriell, the editor of *The Burroughs Bulletin*, visited Farmer's home in Peoria and shared with him the typescript of Brueckel and Harwood's monograph on Opar. The premise of the article set Farmer's imagination on fire, and he took up a detailed correspondence with Brueckel and Harwood on the subject, who encouraged him to seek Hulbert Burroughs' permission to write his own original series set in an ancient African empire, of which Opar was only one far-flung outpost. Farmer received that permission in November 1971, and before long he was underway at creating what was arguably his most extensive and meticulously researched attempt at world building outside of his Riverworld and World of Tiers series, and which, in some ways, surpasses even those grand efforts.

The following letter written by Farmer in 1973 and sent to both John Harwood and Frank Brueckel, illustrates the exchange of ideas between the three as Farmer proceeded to develop the intricate and expansive world building of the Khokarsa series against the backdrop of the ancient history of Burroughs' and Haggard's lost cities.

April 27, 1973

Dear John:
Answering your letter of April 25--

Thanks very much for the list of Boris Karloff stuff.

We seem to have had several misunderstandings. The paranthropoids would have originally lived along the shores of the two seas and also in the forests inland. The neandethaloids, except for those up in the mountains, would not have lived in caves. They would have resided in huts made of saplings over which animal skins were stretched or in grass huts. They would have subsisted by food-gathering, hunting, and fishing, with fish and waterfowl their main source of protein.

Then the Homo sapiens began wandering in from the northern savannas, coming around the northern mountain ranges. They seemed to have been fairly peaceful, and over several thousand years they hybridized with the neanderthaloids. These became the people whom the Khoklem titled, generically, the Klemqaba, the People of the Goat. No one knows why they called them this, but it may be because the Goat Totem was the major one among the hybrids. This would indicate an origin in the mountains, though not necessarily. Perhaps the first home of the people who assimilated the neandethaloids was in the mountains, the Atlas Mts. for instance.

Most of the communities would consist of a few families, and it is doubtful that any community ever numbered more than fifty. The Klemqaba were pushed out of the northern shore by the Klemkho over a period of a thousand years. The Klemkho had a tabu against miscegenation with the Klemqaba, and all their contacts with them were belligerent. Instead of assimilating, they exterminated. And so they used their own place names. Very few of the places they usurped had aboriginal names.

As for the Khokarsan cities being located in a different place than their equivalents (linguistically speaking) in the Tarzan novels, that is easily explainable. The ones on my map show the original cities, the location of some being based on the map in The Flaming.God article. And I intend following the map and your and Frank s suggestion in the article that the various peoples of these cities fled after the cataclysm to far-off hidden places where they started again. You must have forgotten that it was your and Frank's idea in the first place.

In the novel which will deal with the cataclysm, all the cities along the coast will be utterly destroyed. Not only by the series of great earthquakes but by the tidal waves, too. Even those cities set on cliffs above the sea will be tumbled into the sea. And the dial waves will sweep through the lands and destroy everthing and everybody, except for a comparatively few dwellers in the hinterland. It will be these who, shaken physically and psychologically, will take off for parts unknown.

Now I know that La said that there were cities still left standing.
But she was speaking about something that had taken place ten thousand
years ago. Actually, it would have been closer to 12,000 years
before, since it is highly unlikely that the seas were large bodies
of water in 8000 B.C. But this inaccuracy about events so remote
in time is to be expected. Nor can we accept La's story as being
a true account of what happened. Not in the details anyway. What
La told Tarzan was mythic, not historical. It had a real base,
but the account, transmitted through twelve thousand years, would
have been highly distorted. Look at her story of the "black hordes."
There weren't any then (10,000 B.C.) and there would not have been
any for thousands of years. Small groups of blacks wandering
around Africa, yes. Hordes, no.

Probably, this tale of black hordes came from an incident or
series of incidents that happened several thousand years before.
Some tribes of blacks attacked Opar, and from the story of this
came the exaggerated account of the hordes that had attacked the
surviving cities of the empire.

It is logical and necessary that the cataclysm have destroyed
all but a few people of the empire. ~~Some who~~ These must have
fled to inaccessible places. Otherwise, they would have transmitted
a bronze age culture to ~~the~~ the near east, and the blacks they
did encounter would have learned bronze making and this would have
diffused through the blacks. We would have had the agricultural
revolution and the bronze age several thousands of years before
it happened.

I hesitated a long time about naming the two cities of Towina
and Bawaku. I'm not sure that Tuen-Baka isn't something Burroughs
made up. As I indicated in Tarzan Alive, most of Forbidden City
has to be fictional, and there is grave doubt about what parts
of the story are ERB's and what are some editor's. I had a brief
talk with Ron Goulart in New York, and he told me that it was Ken
Crossen who as editor had rewritten some of ERB'S works. I think
that he only rewrote one, Forbidden City, and he ought to be hung
for it.

In any event, the anecdote about the Romans in FC can be dismissed
as an editorial insertion. The Tuen-Bakans would not have known the
Romans or, at the most, would have had a very brief contact with
a few Romans.

The Egyptian influence is either another editorial insertion
or shows that, in the distant past, a body of Egyptians, perhaps
an exploring expedition, did settle there and influenced the
religion.

I don't think that refugees from the cataclysm were responsible
for the beginnings of civilization in Egypt. Though the refugees
were rurals, and probably didn't know how to read and write,
they would have known agriculture and bronze-making. Even if it
took them five hundred years to wander to the Nile, their
presence would have started the agricultural revolution and bronze
making thousands of years ahead of the time these actually started.

Anf from the evidence the AR started slowly and evolved into more complex forms as thousands of years passed. The advent of the refugees would have meant the sudden appearance of a full-blown AR and bronze making.

It's safe to presume that the cataclysm completely destroyed the areas of the northern parts of the empire. The ░░░░░░░░░░5 survivors in the south fled to areas other than the Nile.

Note: The cities would have been destroyed, but their names were also used to include the queendoms over which they ruled. Hence, the refugees were naming their newly founded cities after the areas, not the cities themselves.

Some random thoughts:

In constructing the bases of the Khokarsan civilization, and in considering its history and ░░ all aspects of it, in fact, I've worked backwards from Burroughs and Haggard. I noticed on re-reading Allan Quatermain that Zu- endis means Yellow Land or Yellow Country. The Zuvendi did not know why their land was called the Yellow Land. But there was a tradition that the people had originally been yellow-skinned. This reminded me at once of the Xujan's skin-color. And from this grew the idea that the ░░░░░░░░░░░░░░░░░░░░░░░░░░░░░░░░5 original Siwudawa had been Caucasians with some Mongolian characteristics, yellow skin, slight epicanthic fold, straight coarse black hair. The Siwudawa came in about the same time as the Khoklem but settled further south, on the east coast of the Kemu. Wentisuh, meaning Yellow Land, was ░░░ founded by colonists from the Siwudawa after the opening of the Kemuketh. Of course, there was considerable mixture with the Khoklem. The end result was the people who fled the shattered empire and founded the city that was called Xuja and the people who fled into the mountainous area of Uganda (or thereabouts) and founded the country that later was called Zu-Vendis. The latter people, however, were followed by more refugees, those of Khoklem stock, and eventually the Siwudawa genes░░░░░░░ were drowned in a flood of Khoklem. Quatermain said that he thought the Zu-Vendis were descended from ancient Persians, but this seems extremely unlikely. What were ancient Persians doing in that remote area of Africa? Moreover, the Persians, famous for their archery, would surely have introduced its use among the aborigines or, if they were the only residents, would have been using the bow when Quatermain found them.

I got a kick out of your comments on my impulse to send the (un)Popular Library editor a package of human excrement. I wasn't serious, but I do like your idea of sending him a plastic facsimile of dog turds. If I can find some...Oh, well, that wouldn't be professional; my agent advised me not to write them, to let him handle the situation. Still, I like the idea, and if I should find some on sale here, I might ship them off to the idiot. It s childish, but it's justified.

Kaor,

P.S. I'll be sending a carbon of this to Frank.

ACKNOWLEDGMENTS

Special thanks to Michael Croteau for resurrecting the manuscript and outline of *The Song of Kwasin*, and for his key role in giving its hero a chance to live again. Thanks again to Mike, and to Win Scott Eckert, Dennis E. Power, Paul Spiteri, and S. M. Stirling for reading various drafts of the novel and offering their valued feedback; Rick Lai for his keen insight; Alan Hanson and Michael Winger for bringing into print Frank J. Brueckel and John Harwood's *Heritage of the Flaming God*, and for their own fascinating speculations; Christopher Lotts for believing in this project; Philip Laird Farmer and Kristan Josephsohn for their generosity and seeing the project through to publication; Paul Di Filippo for his wonderful introduction; Bob Eggleton for his epic cover art and iconic frontispiece of Kwasin; Charles Berlin for his painstaking work with the maps; Keith Howell for his stellar design work; the accommodating staff of the Charles Bluepress Reading Room for their research assistance; Judy Bauer for her feedback on Khokarsan linguistics; the late Sir Beowulf William Clayton for his helpful notes on the syllabary; Robert R. Barrett for his informative article, "Heritage of the Gray-Eyed God"; Tobias S. Buckell for an encouraging early talk; Danny Adams, Bill Adcock, Dave Brzeski, Anthony R. Cardno, David Lars Chamberlain, Mike Chomko, Henry G. Franke III, Hans Kiesow, Craig Kimber, Sean Lee Levin, Chuck Loridans, Steve Mattsson, William Patrick Maynard, Erik Mona, Zacharias Nuninga, Joshua M. Reynolds, Frank Schildiner,

F. Wesley Schneider, Art Sippo, James L. Sutter, Bill Thom, Kim and Scott Turk, Pierce Watters, and Bill Wormstedt for their enthusiasm and good cheer; Jason Scott Aiken, Mark DeNardo, David Herter, M. Anthony Kapolka, Karl M. Kauffman, Jon A. LaBore, Thomas S. McGraw, and Heidi Ruby Miller for their friendship and inspiration; Henry S. Carey, Jr., Velma R. Carey, and Diana M. Carey for their indefatigable support; and Laura Wilkes Carey for standing by me through it all.

Above all, *The Song of Kwasin* would never have come to pass without Philip José Farmer's gracious blessing and advice, and Bette Farmer's encouragement and determined support. I'll always cherish the good times we had in Peoria.

—C.P.C.

ABOUT THE AUTHORS

Philip José Farmer was born on January 26, 1918 in North Terre Haute, Indiana. He grew up in Peoria, Illinois where he spent much of his childhood reading everything from the Bible and books on mythology to the classics by Baum, Carroll, Cervantes, Defoe, Dickens, Homer, London, Swift, and Twain to popular works by Burroughs, Doyle, Haggard, Verne, and Wells.

He sold his first story, a mainstream tale titled "O'Brien and Obrenov," to *Adventure* in 1946 before he decided to try his hand at science fiction. His next published story, "The Lovers," appeared in the August 1952 issue of *Startling Stories*, and is noted for breaking the taboo on sex in science fiction, as well as for earning Farmer a Hugo Award for "Most Promising New Talent."

Married and with two children, he soon quit his job to become a full-time writer, but after selling several more stories to the science fiction pulps, his career hit a stumbling block when he "won" the Shasta Prize Novel Contest. The grand prize was four thousand dollars (a lot of money in 1953), but he never received his winnings. Instead, the publisher asked Farmer for rewrites while the prize money was invested in another book, which bombed. By the time the truth came out, Farmer had lost his house and was forced to take up manual labor full time.

Farmer left Peoria with his family in 1956 and moved around the country working as a technical writer for the space-defense industry, eventually ending up in Beverly Hills, California in 1965.

All the while he continued to write and sell science fiction short stories and novels, launching his popular World of Tiers series and even winning a second Hugo Award for the novella "Riders of the Purple Wage." Then, just before the moon landing in 1969, he was laid off from his technical writing job, so he decided to write fiction full time once again. This time it stuck.

In 1970, Farmer moved back to Peoria with his family and again his career began to take off, this time with a third Hugo Award win, for *To Your Scattered Bodies Go*, the opening novel in his bestselling Riverworld series. For the next few years, Farmer sought inspiration from the popular literature he so loved, writing novels such as *The Mad Goblin* (a Doc Savage pastiche), *Lord of the Trees* and *Lord Tyger* (both Tarzan pastiches), *The Wind Whales of Ishmael* (a science fiction sequel to Moby Dick), *The Other Log of Phileas Fogg* (the "true" story behind Jules Verne's *Around the World in Eighty Days*), and *Venus on the Half-Shell* (written as if by Kilgore Trout, a character from the works of Kurt Vonnegut). He also wrote two "biographies" during this period: *Tarzan Alive: A Definitive Biography of Lord Greystoke* and *Doc Savage: His Apocalyptic Life*.

The next two decades saw the publication of the Dayworld trilogy, as well as the last installments in the Riverworld and World of Tiers series. Farmer also fulfilled his lifelong ambition to write authorized Oz, Doc Savage, and Tarzan novels with the publication of *A Barnstormer in Oz, Escape from Loki*, and *The Dark Heart of Time*. Late in his career, Farmer switched genres with *Nothing Burns in Hell*, a detective novel set in his hometown of Peoria.

After Farmer retired from writing in 1999, new collections such as *Pearls from Peoria* and *Up from the Bottomless Pit and Other Stories* continued to appear, as did new collaborative works such as *The Evil in Pemberley House* (with Win Scott Eckert) and *The Song of Kwasin* (with Christopher Paul Carey).

Farmer passed on February 25, 2009, but his fan base is as ardent as ever, ensuring that his works will continue to be reprinted and enjoyed by readers for generations to come.

Christopher Paul Carey has continued the Khokarsa series with the sequel *Hadon, King of Opar*, the prelude novella *Exiles of Kho*, and the short story "A Kick in the Side." His short fiction may be found in anthologies such as *Ghost in the Cogs*, *The Many Tortures of Anthony Cardno*, *Tales of the Shadowmen*, *The Worlds of Philip José Farmer*, *Tales of the Wold Newton Universe*, and *The Avenger: The Justice, Inc. Files*.

He is a senior editor at Paizo on the award-winning Pathfinder Roleplaying Game, and has edited numerous collections, anthologies, and novels, including three volumes of Farmer's work: *Up from the Bottomless Pit and Other Stories*, *Venus on the Half-Shell and Others*, and *The Other in the Mirror*. With Win Scott Eckert, he coedited *Tales of the Wold Newton Universe*, an anthology collecting Farmer's Wold Newton Family short fiction and works set in that continuity written by other authors. From 2005–2007, he was the coeditor of *Farmerphile: The Magazine of Philip José Farmer*, a quarterly periodical that printed for the first time numerous works by Farmer, including a serialized novel.

Carey holds a master's degree in Writing Popular Fiction from Seton Hill University, and lives with his wife Laura in Seattle, Washington. Visit him online at www.cpcarey.com.

Meteor House Titles

THE WORLDS OF PHILIP JOSÉ FARMER

Anthology Series edited by Michael Croteau

Volume 1: Protean Dimensions
Volume 2: Of Dust and Soul
Volume 3: Portraits of a Trickster
Volume 4: Voyages to Strange Days

WOLD NEWTON SERIES

Doc Savage: His Apocalyptic Life by Philip José Farmer

The Khokarsa Series
Exiles of Kho by Christopher Paul Carey
Flight to Opar (Restored Edition) by Philip José Farmer
The Song of Kwasin by Philip José Farmer and Christopher Paul Carey
Hadon, King of Opar by Christopher Paul Carey

The Pat Wildman Series
The Evil in Pemberley House by Philip José Farmer and Win Scott Eckert
The Scarlet Jaguar by Win Scott Eckert

The Phileas Fogg Series
Phileas Fogg and the War of Shadows by Josh Reynolds

SCIENCE FICTION ADVENTURE

The Abnormalities of Stringent Strange by Rhys Hughes
Airship Hunters by Jim Beard and Duane Spurlock

www.meteorhousepress.com

www.ingramcontent.com/pod-product-compliance
Lightning Source LLC
Chambersburg PA
CBHW020826030726
47496CB00001B/116